The Drowning of Chittenden

Rebecca Williamson

D. M. Kreg Publishing
dmkregpublishing.com

In loving memory of my mother, Gladys Williamson.

PROLOGUE

Autumn arrived early that year the river disappeared from the Chittenden Hills. The current ebbed. Katydids hushed their song. Stagnant air smothered the valley, and tobacco fields lay useless, gone to kudzu. Timber stood girdled and looked like twisted, old men, waiting for death.

One old man squatted beside his dog and his homemade dinghy, beached for the last time. He watched a water moccasin lift its head from the muddy waters, stare at him, then dart away under water, fleeing like the others.

Tobias Mullen plucked at the gray bristles of his unshaven chin. He knew he shouldn't be here. The TVA boys had warned him, but the old man couldn't leave his river without one last glimpse of her. She'd been like a good woman, this river, sustaining him over half a century.

Janie would be a grown woman by now.

Rising slowly, as much as his old bones would straighten, he reached into the deep side pocket of his overalls to pull out a pipe and leather pouch, worn soft with age, like himself. His callused fingers shook as he tamped the dried, pungent leaves of the tobacco he'd raised from seeds into the smooth bowl of the pipe.

For Janie. It was all for Janie.

He swiped at his eyes, misting with memories of the last time he'd seen her. That summer she'd brought the fool dog home. A puppy then, just like she was with those blonde pigtails and freckled nose. Never did come back after that, but he reckoned she had her reasons.

She was gone, as surely as the rich bottomland he'd worked most of his life was also gone. Any day, the dam would begin operation, and a flood of water would fill the valley of the deadening and destroy all that had ever mattered.

His house had been among the last ones hauled up to higher ground, up there in the woods on top of limestone cliffs. The entire valley was supposed to be evacuated by now. He glanced over his shoulder at the hole in the ground where his white frame farmhouse had stood for sixty years. Kudzu vines were already sneaking into it, no matter the growing nip in the air.

But he'd tricked those government boys after all, he thought, wheezing on a chuckle.

He shoved the pouch back into his pocket, the pipe into his mouth, then lifted the first of the empty barrels from the boat. Pausing to glance up at the white face of the cliff towering behind him, he wondered how in the name of the Almighty he'd ever get them up there. Never mind, he'd find a way. This was the only work he had left now. He wished he'd thought of it sooner.

A twig snapped.

Dropping the barrel, he jerked to attention, sending a shot of pain through his joints. *Fool!* he told himself. *Reckon it's only a coon, come to take a drink. He don't know it'll be his last one.*

He glanced down at the dog dreaming and twitching at his feet. *You never was no count. Only kept you because of Janie.*

Heavier rustling sounds made the old man step behind the barrel, closer to the side of his boat.

That ain't no coon. Reckon I'm in a peck of trouble now. Clenching the pipe between his gums, he anticipated yet another battle with the TVA boys. Slowly, he turned around.

The dog lifted his chin from his paws and opened bloodshot eyes. A low growl rumbled in his throat.

"Oh, it's only you," Tobias said. "You like to give me a start." Then the old man saw the shotgun pointed at him, and understanding spread through his gut.

The explosion echoed around him as Tobias ducked into the protective hull of his boat. The memory of blonde pigtails ebbed from his mind.

No... Janie...

First Family Tree

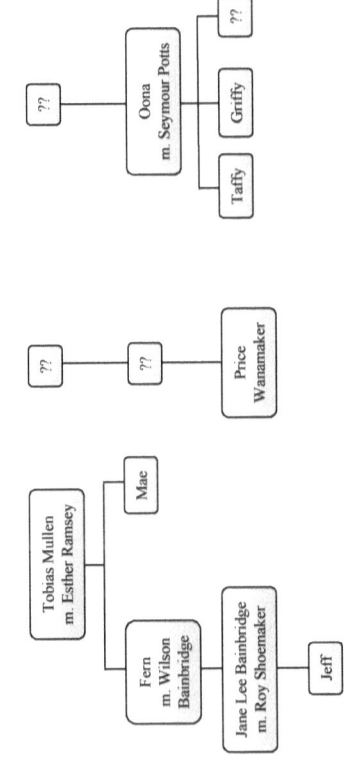

?? — Oona m. Seymour Potts

Taffy — Griffy — ??

?? — ?? — Price Wanamaker

Tobias Mullen m. Esther Ramsey

Mae

Fern m. Wilson Bainbridge

Jane Lee Bainbridge m. Roy Shoemaker

Jeff

m. = married

ONE

The road looked like a ribbon of dust. It twisted ahead, disappearing into the tangled woods that blanketed the Chittenden Hills. Janie Bainbridge shivered, despite the unseasonable heat. The road was a link from her past to her future, from the real world of numbered, paved highways to the uncharted territory that lay ahead.

She swallowed hard and steered her Volkswagen Bug a little too fast over the jarring rattles. She didn't care. She'd never felt so alone in her life as now. Not two years ago when her husband had left her, nor last winter when her mother had died, nor six weeks ago when she'd received the pink slip.

"Mom!" Eight-year-old Jeff straightened from his slump and shouted as they rounded another bend. "Look out!"

She stomped on the brakes, and they lurched forward in the sticky interior of the Bug. The woods opened in a clearing, and she blinked from the unexpected light. No more than three feet beyond her bumper, the road ended suddenly in a giant bite of erosion. A snake slipped from the crumbling drop-off, strewn with chunks of red soil and a few remnants of gravel, and slithered into the mucky water of the newborn lake that had swallowed the road.

"Looks like we took a wrong turn somewhere, Jeff," she said, laughing off her surprise. "So this is Chittenden Lake. We could've driven right into it. I wonder why there was no road block?"

Of course there would be none. They were in the boondocks. About twenty miles back, they'd driven into a blank quadrant on her map. No pavement. No road signs.

Jeff whistled softly and watched the snake through the toy binoculars his dad had given him the Christmas before he'd walked out on them. "Gosh, Mom, you didn't tell me it was going to be like *this*." He scrambled out of the car and ran to the edge of the water. "It looks more like an ocean than a lake!"

Janie opened her door and stood up to stretch. "It *is* a big lake, isn't it?" she said, careful not to contradict him. The sullen tone that had grown ever worse these last few months had suddenly disappeared. Maybe this move was the right thing to do after all.

She lifted the blonde frizz from her neck and peeled the straps of her sundress away from sticky skin. After an unusually long winter, the heat seemed too oppressive, too early this first week of June. The air smelled deliciously sweet with honeysuckle, and she inhaled deeply, hopeful about this homecoming.

He lowered the binoculars and turned to squint at her. "How could a *river* make this?"

"When they built the dam, the river flooded the entire valley."

"That's when your grandpa drowned, right?"

Searching for the words to explain, she rubbed her neck and twisted the chain holding her pendant. The family heirloom of sapphire was all she had left of her mother's family. Still, words didn't come. Silence hung in the air between them, but it was never really silent out here in the hills. That gentle breeze whispering through blackgum leaves could be Grandpa's wheezing laughter.

Was he — or his spirit — out there in the woods, watching her?

"Last year, right?" Jeff asked.

The drop-off crumbled slightly under his squirming toes. Pieces splashed into the muddy lake water below. Where they stood had once been a hilltop with a road winding down into the valley. All that was gone now. Drowned, like Grandpa.

"Mom?"

"It was last September," she said, her fingers tightening on the sapphire pendant.

The chain broke. She clutched the pieces, feeling as if she'd broken as well. "They never found his body, but they think he probably drowned."

"Gosh, is he at the bottom of the lake?"

"I doubt it."

"Maybe we'll find him."

"No, Jeff." But she wished she knew more. Mother had rejected her own father even in death.

Why?

And Janie, torn between her warm memories of Grandpa and respect for her mother's irrational fear of this place, had done nothing. Hadn't even returned for his memorial service. Now Mother was gone, too, and it was time for Janie and her son to make a fresh start in life. Grandpa had left her his property. It was a new beginning.

"Then, can we at least go swimming? Mom?"

"Swimming? You want to swim with snakes? The water looks awfully mucky. Oona wrote that it may take a year or so for the water to clear. I bet you could fish, instead."

"I guess so."

"Why the long face?"

"Nothing."

"Come on, tell me." She pocketed the pieces of the broken necklace and lifted his chin to stare into his deep blue eyes. Smiling eyes, she called them, but they hadn't smiled for a long time.

"It's just that I don't have no one to fish with."

"You mean *any* one, Jeff, but that's not so. You've got me."

"Shucks, Mom, you don't even like worms. It's not the same as — " He broke off, and his cheeks flushed.

"You mean as with Dad, is that right?"

"I guess so." He turned away abruptly, and a thick wave of hair, too long on his neck, caught a sunbeam and dazzled her with blue-black sparkles.

He had his father's hair. He even had the same dimple on his chin that Roy used for beguiling and betraying women. She scowled. Her own child didn't appear to have any of *her* blood in him.

"Lookit that stuff," Jeff cried, his attention flitting from one backwoods novelty to another.

She followed his aim to the open hillside, covered with a blanket of green. "Kudzu," she whispered.

"I bet if you shimmied through that kuuuudzu no one would ever find you."

"Grandpa always claimed that the vines grew so fast they could chase an old dog. He said they'd take over the whole valley if people didn't watch out. He never let the vines get a start on his property."

"I bet that stuff could strangle you." Jeff went through the motions of choking, and he fell to his knees. "Maybe that's what made him drown," he finally said.

She couldn't help giggling at his theatrics. Then she remembered to scold him. "You're silly. You've spent too much time in the car today." Six hours, with plenty of stops along the backroads from Indiana. Now they were almost to Grandpa's house. Here in the Chittenden Hills. Auntie Mae had called them the foothills of Appalachian foothills.

"Maybe the kuuuudzu caught him in the flood, and he couldn't get away, and the river flooded the valley, and maybe that's why they never found his body, 'cause it's still trapped down there under the kudzu vines at the bottom of the lake."

"I sincerely doubt it." She pulled him to his feet and hugged him to her. He was all she had left of her immediate family.

"Well, it *could've* happened that way," he said, squirming away and squinting up at her. "I know, Mom, let's go out on the lake and look for him."

"And how are we going to do that?"

"In a boat, of course."

"But we don't have a boat, and besides..." She didn't know the first thing about operating one. Roy had always handled anything mechanical.

"Yeah," he mumbled, his chin sagging. "The boat was only a dream."

She sighed. She had to be both mother and father to him now, and somehow she'd do it. If they were going to live on a lake, then she'd learn how to operate a boat. "Maybe we could spend a little of our savings and rent a boat."

"Huh?" His eyes opened wide, and he stared up at her from under the cover of a stray lock of hair. "But Mom, we'll run out of money."

"You let me worry about the money, young man. We came here to have a grand time this summer, so let's do it." She held out her hand. Maybe being laid off would turn out to be a good thing, after all. "Come on, let's go back to that last fork in the road and see if we can't find Grandpa's house from there."

~

"LOR-R-R-RDY, IT'S MULE KILL'N weather, and I reckon Janie's bringing it with her. Nossir, it don't set well in my bones." Oona Potts reached for the only piece of paper in her kitchen and waggled the limp program from yesterday's church service directly over her bosom, drooping from the weight of duty of raising five young'uns.

She paused for Dexter's response, but her half-brother never was one to waste words, especially when food was around. With his red cap pulled down low over his eye patch, he propped bony elbows on the kitchen table and stuffed leftover Sunday chicken into his mouth as if he'd never eaten a meal in his life. Certainly it never stayed on him the way it did with her. Oona's body had the same shape as the broad backside of a hog's hind leg. Dexter, on the other hand, stayed as skinny as a sassafras sapling. But what else could anyone expect when a man didn't have a woman to do for him for nigh onto thirty years?

"Humph!" She grunted and snapped the program at one of several flies buzzing just out of reach, a constant reminder of the curse she'd bear to her grave. That no-good husband of hers. She'd been after Seymour since planting time to fix the screens, but it seemed he always had something better to do than chores.

"That patch of corn Seymour planted is already burning up, and it ain't even knee high to a grasshopper yet." Oona clucked her tongue, thinking on her husband's foolishness. A woman's duty to her menfolk would never stop her from faulting him. "Now, you tell me just how come he wants to grow all that corn instead of tobacco like everyone else in these here parts?"

"Hogs don't eat no tobacco." His chin shining with grease, Dexter paused over his drumstick to grin at her with that all-knowing deacon's grin of his. "And Seymour's hog farming."

"You ask me, he's whiskey farming. That's why he needs corn." Oona thrust one arm across her ample bosom. Despite her determined anchor, the extra skin that dripped down from her arm jiggled with each jerk of her fanning arm.

"Naw. He's too honest."

"Being honest ain't got nothing to do with it. I thought you knowed that. Plenty of honest folks has been whiskey farming in these here parts since the days of the first settlers, but you mark my words: every last one of them will burn in hell."

"It's their God-given right."

"No good will ever come of tempting the devil."

"Oh, yes there will, woman. It's called money. Folks got to make a living. Ain't no money in hogs and tobacco. But Seymour ain't smart enough when he's sober to know how to make hisself that kind of money. That's how come you're stuck in this rut."

Just because he was a deacon of the church, Dexter thought he knew everything. "Don't be so all-fired sure of yourself. Seymour cain't keep money in his pocket any more'n you can keep fat on your bones. Nossir, I got half a notion to turn him in myself."

Dexter slammed his fist against the table. "Confound it, woman! You bring them revenuers in here and you gonna have half the county wanting a piece of your hide!"

"Well, slap my bones, but that don't scare me none. Only thing that keeps me from trotting myself down to that there revenuer's office this very minute is that he's a fureigner, and no fureigner's got the right to poke his nose into our business."

Dexter mopped his brow with the crook of his arm. The eye patch slipped away from his dead eye. He pulled it into place, then pushed his cap back from his forehead. Only time he ever took off that red cap was in church. "You keep poking your own nose where it don't belong, and you ain't no better than the revenuer hisself trying to tell us decent folks how we can make a living and how we cain't. Woman, you're going to end up with more trouble than you can shake a stick at!"

"Humph!" He was right about that, so she did what she always did when she had to concede a point — she put it out of her mind and changed the subject to suit her.

"Nossir, but this early heat don't set well in my bones," she said. "Ain't no good will come of it. I reckon Janie is plumb bringing it with her, 'cause her mama done took it away that other time. It was the same mule kill'n weather then as it is now. 'Course it was only April then." A shiver rippled through her layers of fat, in spite of the heat. The memory of Fern, God rest her soul, still produced shivers because Fern came close to taking away with her a whole lot more than just the heat. "That time when Fern up and run off. You remember?"

She should've known better than to bring it up. He went all funny-eyed on her, like a hound dog in heat, every time the subject came up. Why, she remembered a time when Daisy, Seymour's best coon dog, went into heat and ran off with a pack of wild dogs. They got into Crockett's chicken coop and killed three of his finest bantams before the old man shot Daisy.

Not that Dexter was going to run off with a pack of dogs and get himself shot up, of course. But still, she didn't like it when his one good eye glazed over with that wild look. "Settle down, honey. Let me fetch you some biscuits and gravy to go with that there chicken."

She bustled over to the humming refrigerator, so short that she had to stoop to poke inside. "'Course, you better shake a leg before Seymour gets home. He ain't gonna be none too happy iffen he catches you here on his property then sees all his Sunday chicken et up." She pulled out several parcels covered with rumpled plastic and turned to scowl at him.

Dexter snorted, and a piece of meat flew from his mouth across the table. "I ain't scared of him." A nervous tick tugged at one of his bushy eyebrows.

She knew better, but instead she said, "I reckon not, but Seymour ain't never forgot. He's got a bone to pick with you." Inside, Oona glowed with pleasure. It made her proud to have her menfolks feuding because of her, even if Seymour was clearly in the wrong going against a deacon of the church. 'Course, the church didn't mean a hill of beans to Seymour, and that was part of his problem. But he was her old man, and she'd have to put up with his faults all the way to her grave.

Dexter licked his fingers with a loud smack.

She carried the bundles of leftovers to her shiny white stove and began warming them. "Yep, I reckon Janie's bringing this heat with her."

Dexter's chair creaked with his shifting weight. "What's she want with you after all these years?"

"Why, she's family. I ain't got no choice but to take her in, whether I like it or not. It's my duty as an upright Christian woman, you see. And Janie's got herself into a passel of trouble. Left her husband, she did." The very idea!

"That so?"

Oona planted one hand on her hip, and with the other, she shook the saucepan with vigor. "I tell you, it just ain't right. I reckon Fern never done taught Janie about a woman's job. Lord knows, a man needs a woman to do for him, 'cause he cain't do for hisself."

Dexter grunted.

"Now I reckon it's up to me to teach her what's what," Oona said. "What else is family for? She ain't got no one else now that they all passed on, bless their souls." She shook her head. "You just never know. Only last summer they was all with us, and now they're all gone. First Uncle Tobias, then Mae, and now Fern. Makes you sorta' wonder who's next, don't it? Of course Janie would come here. Where else would she go? A woman all alone? With a boy of her own and no husband. Last she wrote, she didn't have no job, neither. Say, you reckon you could find something for her to do like you done for Griffy?"

"Woman, are you tetched or something? Go ask that boy over yonder at the yarb doctor's. He's got money. I ain't."

"Junior Wanamaker, you mean?" She snorted. "Uh-uh. My Bonnibelle's got eyes for him."

"She's got eyes for everyone."

"That makes no never mind. She's got her sights set on that one, and what she wants, she winds up getting, or there'll be heck fire to pay. You mark my words. Uh-uh. I ain't fixing to throw him and Janie together. 'Sides, she's a married woman, whether she likes it or not. Someone's got to teach her that, so I reckon it's got to be me."

He grunted. "You ain't got room for no more folks here."

Oona scooped the warm leftovers onto a plate and set it before Dexter. "Oh, she ain't fixing to stay with us. Wrote that she and her boy are gonna stay over yonder at Uncle Tobias's place."

Dexter coughed, then coughed some more. He scraped his chair backwards.

"Take a drink, honey." She pounded on his bony spine. "I declare. It's a danged fool thing to do. Why, that place has been closed up all winter, and I reckon it smells to high heaven."

Dexter made a choking noise and hung his head between his knees.

"It was Taffy's job to check up on things over yonder all winter, but you can bet she ain't doing it. She never does anything lessen you sit on her, and I ain't sat on her like I should ought've." She stopped to cluck her tongue and shake her head. "That girl ain't been the same since Uncle Tobias passed on. And now I reckon it's up to me to go over yonder and air out the place because Janie aims to stay there and nowhere else. Soon as her boy gets out of school. She just don't know the sight of trouble I have to go to. But that Janie won't pay no mind to no one. She's just like her mama. Has to find out everything for herself. Hey! Where you off to in such a all-fired rush?"

But Dexter didn't answer. He jumped spang out of his chair like one of Seymour's flies bit him right through his overalls. He lit out through the screened-in back porch, and then she realized that it must be all that food passing lickety-split through him. Food never did stay on him long. He hurried through the chicken yard, but when he reached the outhouse, he kept on going.

"Wait, honey!" Oona waddled after him as fast as her extra pounds would allow. "Your vittles!"

By the time she made it to the barbed-wire fence surrounding her garden, he'd disappeared into the woods. "Well, I never! There's a fine how-do-you-do. Try to feed a man that ain't got no other womenfolk to do it for him, and he don't even give a body the time of day."

∾

JANIE'S GAZE DROPPED to the sinking needle on the gas gauge. "There's that rickety bridge again. Are we driving in circles?"

"This bridge is different, Mom. Lookit, there's a house by the river."

"Looks more like a creek to me," she said, steering carefully onto the twin planks that served as a bridge. One wrong turn of the wheel, and they'd plunge into the gully. It wouldn't take much rain to wash out a bridge like this.

"Cool! They've got a dock. I wonder if they've got a boat we could borrow?"

She grinned. Her son was just as stubborn as she was. "I can't approach a stranger and ask to borrow — "

"Mo-o-om!"

The car rolled off the planks and back onto the dirt road. Only then did she look in the direction of Jeff's pointing finger, and she saw the man at once. He rose on lanky legs from the sprung coils of a vinyl chair camouflaged in the clutter of junk on the porch. In a blink, Janie saw a refrigerator, broken chairs, stacks of tires, rusted tools and assorted pieces she couldn't identify.

She might as well ask for directions. They hadn't seen another soul since the pavement ended, and they weren't likely to find anyone else soon. She stopped the car, and the man hitched up his overalls and sauntered to the roadside. A dog emerged from the brush and joined him.

The man's body odor invaded her space first, and then his grimy fingers smudged the rim of the open car window. He stooped to peer at her. A string of graying black hair fell out from under his red baseball cap and hung over the patch covering one eye. His good eye shifted its focus from her face to her loose bodice. Recoiling, she wished she'd worn a bra.

"Well, don't this beat all?" he said, shaking his head and letting out a low whistle.

"Hey, mister, you've got a cool dock!"

The man blinked and looked up to consider Jeff.

"We're trying to find Tobias Mullen's place," Janie said, "but we got lost."

His attention shifted back to her. Bushy eyebrows twitched, and deep creases lined his brow. "Ain't no one living there no more."

"I realize that, but I'm his granddaughter, and I've come to live in my grandfather's house — "

"Ain't got no call doing a fool thing like that."

"I inherited his house," she said, tensing. She shouldn't have to explain herself to a total stranger, but if she was going to live down here, then she should get off to the right start with her new neighbors. "My mother was his other daughter, you know. The younger one, who — "

"I know." The man snapped the words and stiffened. He pulled away from the car and turned to watch his dog pawing at the underbrush alongside the road.

"If you could just tell me if I'm on the right road..."

He glared at them. The muscles in his jaw tightened, and he crammed his fists into his pockets. His eye narrowed to a black slit, and he jerked his head to one side. His gesture might have indicated the direction of Grandpa's house, or a warning to leave. Maybe he was just flicking a fly from his sweaty neck. She started up the car, and they drove away in silence. Jeff twisted in his seat to watch the man until he and his house disappeared from view.

"Wow!" he whispered.

Janie frowned at her son. He must be starved for male attention.

A sliver of lake shimmered through thinning trees and filled her with renewed anticipation. Jeff lifted his binoculars to his face and aimed them at the lake, and Janie hurried the car along as fast as she dared over the ruts.

"Mom, how come you don't know where we are? You said you came to your grandpa's house before."

"Only once, and that was a long time ago, honey. Everything has changed. Grandpa's house used to be down there in the valley, by the river. They had to move his house up here to the top of the cliffs, or else it would be at the bottom of the lake by now."

He whistled. "Is there still other stuff down there?"

"I doubt it. Whatever used to be in the valley is gone by now."

"Where'd all the people go?"

She shrugged. "There weren't very many in the first place, but those who lived down there sold out to the government when they decided to build a dam. Most of those folks moved away. But Grandpa was lucky because he already owned some property up here on the cliffs. So the government moved his house for him."

Jeff fell silent until about a mile past the man with the eye patch and red cap. "Lookit, Mom, a sign!"

The car crunched to a stop, and she waited for the dust to clear before reading the hand-lettered sign tacked onto a tree. "The Resort, another development of the Wanamaker Corporation." An arrow pointed down the road.

"Wanamaker," she said. "That name is familiar."

Jeff leaned against his seatbelt and pointed in the direction of the arrow. "Lookit! There's a mailbox!"

Lopsided on its post, it was nearly hidden by a stand of gnarled cedar. Faded black letters "M...ll..." were barely legible across one battered side of the rusted aluminum.

"This must be the place," she whispered, gripping the steering wheel until her knuckles ached. Letting out on the clutch, she guided the car down the gentle incline to the driveway. Her foot slipped, the car lurched, and the engine sputtered to silence.

Locusts rattled as she sat there, staring. Twin tire tracks needled through weeds toward the house. A driveway, of sorts.

Perched on a bluff overlooking the lake, the house reminded her of the discarded shell of a locust. Abandoned. How could this drooping, weathered gray house possibly be the same cozy white frame farmhouse from her childhood? Where were the vining morning glories, and the smells of Auntie Mae's cookies, and the sounds of laundry flapping on the line?

Janie's spirits sagged.

"Cool! What're you waiting for, Mom? Let's go."

She started up the car and turned onto the tire tracks. They swished through the weeds toward the porch where Grandpa used to rock, smoking his pipe. "I didn't recognize it," she said.

Braking to a stop, she reached for the ignition, but her fingers hesitated. Uprooting herself and Jeff to come here and find family and some indefinable *something* more out of life had seemed like a good idea, but now she wondered if coming here was really putting her life together or simply avoiding reality.

"It doesn't look right up here on the cliffs."

"But no one can kick us out," Jeff said. "Maybe now we won't have to move again."

He was right. Impatiently, she flicked off the ignition switch and pulled out the keys. She'd never get ahead in life, never move beyond her series of dead-end clerical jobs if she didn't take a risk.

Jeff pushed open the car door and scampered immediately for the cliff.

"Hey!" she yelled after him. "Don't go so close to the edge."

He slowed long enough to turn and roll his eyes at her. "Aw, Mom, I'm not a baby."

"Humor me, anyway. It must be twenty or thirty feet straight down. Can't you find another attraction in all of these great outdoors?"

He paused and looked around. "Well, there's some kudzu over there. Come with me, Mom."

She shook her head. "I want to have a look at the house. And you've got five minutes before I need you back here to help unload." She climbed out of the car and watched him skip away before she could change her mind. Trying to remember when was the last time she'd seen him skip, she thought that yes, she'd made the right decision in coming here, despite his protests at leaving behind his friends.

It would be a great summer. With rent-free living and care with her savings, she wouldn't have to look for another job all summer. Maybe not even for as long as a year. She could take up a hobby. Or finally write the screenplay she'd been wanting to write ever since Jeff was born. And if things got desperate... She wouldn't think about that now. The property must be worth something.

From her purse she pulled out the skeleton key the lawyer had mailed her. Gooseflesh suddenly tickled the back of her neck, as if someone were breathing softly on her bare shoulders. She whirled around, but of course no one was there. The buzzing locusts must've disoriented her.

Sweat beaded out on her upper lip. Humidity, that's all. In the distance sounded the forlorn baying of a dog.

A piece of gravel crunched behind her.

"Jeff?" Again, she glanced over her shoulder.

He wasn't there, but a creak answered her. It had only been a faint sound. She was sure it had come from *inside* the house.

Strange.

Sweat ran down her sides as she stumbled through the weeds toward the front porch. But she didn't feel hot, not with the breeze off the lake. A small brown lump next to the first step caught her eye. She bent down to touch it, and it crackled under her fingers like dried onion skin. A locust shell. She threw it down.

Creak.

She looked up. The front door stood ajar. The door stirred slightly behind the screen as the breeze pushed against it.

Her breath caught in her throat, and her fingers tightened on the useless key. She hurried onto the porch and reached for the screen, but it slipped. The door slammed, and she reached for it again to push her way inside.

"Omigod!"

Velvet chairs, overturned.

Litter sprinkled across the linoleum floor. Broken pieces of glass lamps. Framed photos. Earthen flowerpots.

Wind blowing through an unlocked door.

Not the wind... More than wind had done this.

TWO

*J*anie hesitated, then stepped inside. Linoleum crinkled under her feet as if she'd stepped on a bed of discarded locust shells. She paused in the gloom of the front room — that's what Auntie Mae had called it. Murky light filtered through cataracts of grime coating the windows. The house felt empty around her. Neglected, without Auntie Mae and her bucket of sudsy water.

Janie bent down to pick up a velvet cushion crushed smooth with age, and dust billowed into the shadows. The house had stood empty all winter, making it an easy target for vagrants. It was a miracle that any furnishings were left.

She stepped around litter, moving closer to the overturned couch. Slash marks ripped the velvet fabric. The cushion slipped from her fingers, leaving bits of dusty nap under her nails. This was more than neglect, then. More than trash left behind by vagrants.

Someone had broken in. With a knife. She felt her spine go rigid.

Was that someone still here, hiding somewhere?

She edged backwards, toward the front door. She and Jeff should get out of here.

Where would they go?

"No one can kick us out," Jeff had said. "We won't have to move again."

Maybe not, but they couldn't *stay* here, not until she knew it was safe. She had to get help. Someone had to check out every corner of the house and make sure no one was hiding here, waiting with a knife. Who could she find to help her? That creepy man back up the road?

No. She took in a slow, deep breath to steady her nerves. She reminded herself that the house felt empty. Whoever had been here was long gone by now.

She remembered the square floorplan of four rooms. There were no connecting halls between rooms. Each room contained two doors into two other rooms. As a child, she used to run circles through the house.

Now she tiptoed across the squeaking linoleum to the front bedroom, where Auntie Mae had slept. Her four poster bed still dominated the room, but now, downy feathers spread everywhere. They'd drifted onto quilts lying in a heap at the foot of the bed. Boxes of newspaper clippings poked out from underneath, catching more feathers. Feathers spread across the room to the upright piano with its yellowed keys. Taffy, her cousin and best friend, used to play tunes there on warm summer evenings. Feathers even nestled among the empty perfume bottles cluttering the dresser's doily.

No one hid here, waiting for her. If she had interrupted the vandal, he would've heard her car's arrival and fled. No one would stick around to get caught.

Feeling more confident, she stepped into the room and crossed to the closed door that led to Grandpa's back bedroom. Its china doorknob rattled under her fingers. *Relax*, she told herself. She was just tired from the long trip and nervous from all the months of uncertainty about her future. No one would lie in wait for her with a knife.

Vandals had done this damage. That's all. Just vandals.

She tried the knob again. The door opened with a creak, and she stepped into Grandpa's Spartan room. This bed had also been attacked. A layer of down looked like a cloud covering the hook rug. Feathery tufts stuck to the oval, gilt frame of her grandparents' wedding picture. Beneath the frame, dresser drawers stood open and empty.

Oh, Grandpa, she thought. *You really are gone.*

Grandpa's room was special because it had three doors. The extra door led up to the attic, where she had slept that summer she'd come to Grandpa's against her mother's wishes. Now she crept up the narrow, wooden steps to the attic, with its sloping ceilings and trunks of keepsakes smelling like must. It seemed smaller than she remembered. More cluttered, with lower ceilings. The lace curtains that Auntie Mae had tacked up to the dormer windows still hung there, yellowed and limp with passing time.

No one up here. The hammering of her heart settled down to a steadier pace, and she clattered back down the steps, mindless now of the noise she made.

In the kitchen, broken pieces of dishes scattered across the floor. Fiesta dishes, Auntie Mae had called the rainbow-colored plates. She'd crammed them into cupboard shelves that now stood bare.

Janie's stomach turned over.

The woodburning cookstove remained intact under a thick layer of dust. In the center of the room were two wooden tables knocked onto their sides. Cast-iron pots, cereal boxes, bread, bananas, and cans of food had spilled into the debris...

The screen door squeaked and small footsteps pattered across the front room. "Mom?" Jeff called. "Wow! What happened?"

"Vandals," Janie said, her voice catching.

Jeff darted to her side, and his eyes grew wide. "You mean someone tore up the place? On purpose?"

Surveying the broken shards of her inheritance, she would see the culprit caught and punished. "We'll have to find the nearest town and file a police report. Where will we stay in the meanwhile? We can't stay here. And we can't afford a motel."

Jeff picked up the box of cereal from the floor and spied something underneath. "Hey, Mom, what's this?" He set the box down and pulled at an iron ring, but it was attached to the floor.

"The trap door," she said with a shiver, remembering the dark, dungeon-like cellar where Auntie Mae used to keep her canned goods. "I doubt it leads anywhere now that the house has been moved. It was probably too rocky up here on the cliffs to dig a cellar."

Jeff shoved debris out of the way and tugged at the ring. A few inches of darkness showed beneath the door, and Janie felt the old tightness in her throat. She pulled his fingers from the ring, and the door banged shut. "Oh, Jeff, no."

"But Mom, if it doesn't go anywhere, what's the difference?"

"Exactly. You're not missing anything." She stepped on the pull ring and crossed her arms over her chest in an attempt to still the pounding that was making her feel rubbery inside.

He stuck out his lower lip. "You're afraid of everything."

Under crossed arms, her fingernails dug into her palms. "Would we be here if that were true?" It was partly true, but she couldn't let him know that.

He glared at her, then turned away. He scooped up the cereal box and dug around inside it. "I'm hungry, Mom. When are we going to eat?"

"How can you think of food when — " Food? Grandpa had been gone for nine months, and yet the bread and fruit were fresh. She grabbed the box away from him. "Jeff, this food belongs to someone. Someone has been living here."

~

"SHOO, THERE!" OONA waved her apron at a rabbit sitting under the okra. "Iffen my boy was here, you'd end up a right fine supper," she yelled as it skittered off into the brush beyond her vegetable garden. She stepped over the barbed wire and trudged down the rows.

"Tsk, tsk." Pausing, she stooped over to pull a handful of weeds. It was Taffy's job to weed the garden, but it looked like that girl, once again, wasn't doing her chores. She shook her head. Girls were nothing but trouble, not like her boys.

Straightening, as much as her extra pounds could straighten, she tossed the weeds into the brush and glared up at the house. Couldn't count on that no-good husband of hers, either. Seymour, home no more than two shakes past Dexter's hasty exit, sprawled up there on the glider out on the back porch. His afternoon nap was always more important than providing for his family.

She continued down the rows, pausing here and there to pinch off a leaf, forcing it to grow as she saw fit. Seemed that her teaching work never would be done. At forty-nine, she deserved a rest. She was a worn-out woman, old before her time.

The brush rustled, and she looked up, putting a hand on her back to massage her aches.

"Hey there, Mama."

Pride swelled in her heart. Her son had grown into such a handsome man with his broad shoulders and strong back and thick crop of black whiskers. He'd make some lucky girl a fine catch. "Griffy! You ain't got no call sneaking up on a body like that."

"Don't call me that no more, Mama. My name's Griffin. You give it to me."

"Now, son, don't you sass me."

He shrugged and shifted his squirrel gun from one hand to the other, then pulled a handkerchief from his pocket to wipe his neck. "Whee-o, it's hotter'n blazes."

She eyed the weapon. "Ain't it awful early for you to be out hunting?"

"Maybe. But I got to hunt when I can. Game is hard to find these days, Mama, what with all them gawl-danged tourists coming here."

"Harumph. It's the deadening, that's what. It done chased all the animals further up into the hills."

"No'm. It's that big shot Wanamaker and his rich daddy aiming to bring the city here so's they can get even richer."

"Hogwash! City folks don't come here."

"What about that cousin of yours from the city?"

"Fern's little girl? That's different."

"She ain't so little no more, Mama." He set down his gun and traced a curvy outline in the air with thick, workingman's hands. His eyebrows wagged up and down.

Oona scowled. "You sound like you done seen her, but she and that little boy of hers ain't coming till the end of the week."

"They're already here."

"What?"

"I seen 'em, plain as day, drive up in one of them fancy foreign cars."

Oona felt her jaw tighten with fury. She hated to be the last one to find out something, hated to be left out. "Well, don't just stand there like the cat got your tongue. What'd she say?" Oona bit off each word.

"Didn't say nothing, 'cause she didn't know I was there."

She slammed one foot into the soft earth. "Then what was you doing down yonder?"

"Settle down, Mama. I was, ah, fishing. That's all. Then I heard this here car, so I snuck up through the hollow to take a look, and there she was."

Oona shook her head and stared absently at the pasture rolling away to a border of woods. "Well, I never... I go to a sight o' trouble for that girl, and that's the thanks I get..." Then she remembered Griffy standing at her side, and she looked up into his deep, brown eyes. "How's come you didn't go up and talk to her?"

Griffy shrugged, bringing his massive shoulders up to swallow his thick neck. "She looked powerful skittish. I figgered if I come up out of them breshes, she'd like to keel over." He scratched his whiskery neck. "Then she did a right funny thing."

"What's that, son?"

"Well, it was like she was aiming to move her stuff inside old Uncle Tobias's house, but Mama, she got this here tent thing and rigged it up."

"You mean to tell me she and that boy are aiming to sleep in a tent instead of the house?"

"Yes'm."

"Well, I declare."

"It's like I done said, Mama. Who can figger out fureigners?"

She stared off at Bossy, grazing on a far hill. There never was any rest for her. "Well, son, I hope you done kotched plenty of fish, 'cause it looks like we're gonna have us some company."

"Uh, the fish wasn't biting," he said, picking up his gun.

"Well, then, you'd best go after that there rabbit that was in my garden, you hear?" She waddled down the rows of vegetables and stepped quickly over the barbed wire. "Seymour," she yelled. "Sey-MOUR! Git yourself up, daddy."

THREE

*J*anie pounded in the last of the tent stakes and wondered if coming here had been a mistake. She was *not* going to sleep in a vandalized house. There wasn't enough gas in the car nor light left in the day for her to find her way out of the Chittenden Hills. It was too late for running away, and besides, she wasn't going to react like her mother.

She stood up and admired her handiwork. Not bad for someone who'd never put up a tent before. It wasn't her first choice for shelter for the night, but it should show Jeff that *she* could take him camping as well as Roy could. She only hoped that it would hold together long enough to get them through the night. Tomorrow she and Jeff would have the entire day to find the nearest town where she could file a report about the break-in, then clean up the house. Tomorrow night they'd sleep secure in their beds.

She stepped away from the stand of cedars protecting the tent and glanced up at the sky. The sun had disappeared behind clouds billowing up from the west, across the lake. It would set in a couple more hours, but already a premature gloom had settled into the woods. Rain was on its way, and possibly wind. She wondered if the tent would withstand the storm.

A rattling sound rose above the background buzzing of locusts, pulling her out of her thoughts. It sounded like a truck. They hadn't passed another vehicle since turning off the pavement twenty miles up the road. The only other person they'd seen in that stretch had been the man with the eye patch.

A rusty pick-up bounced into view and slowed as it approached Grandpa's place. Its two occupants stuck elbows on the rims of their rolled-down windows and peered at her. The truck sputtered, then turned into the driveway and coasted through weeds to the Bug's bumper. The passenger's door opened and a large-framed woman swung down from the cab. Staring at Janie, she marched across the gravel with certainty in each firm step of the orange thongs on her feet.

"Lands sakes!" she exclaimed, extending her arms in Janie's direction.

This woman had to be Mother's cousin Oona. She'd worn odd things like this woman's dress, hand-sewn together from two different fabrics. The sleeveless bodice of large, red flowers looked like a sling catching her drooping breasts, while the ample skirt of purple paisleys flounced over wide hips.

She looked like a sturdy machine lumbering toward Janie. Her streaky, gray hair hung in lifeless clumps a little longer than her double chin, but her face shone with a zest for life and cleanliness. Her cheeks were round and rosy and well scrubbed, and her deep blue eyes twinkled. Pearly white flesh jiggled from Oona's arms as she reached out to enfold Janie in a mushy squeeze.

"I declare," Oona said with a gasp, cutting off Janie's breath with the strength of her embrace. Finally she released her to arm's length, shook her head and clucked her tongue as she looked Janie up and down. "If it ain't Fern's little girl, all growed up. We wasn't looking for you to come till later in the week, but we heard you was here already. Daddy, come on out here!"

The driver of the truck didn't budge.

"That good-for-nothing old man! Sey-MOUR!" Her voice rose to a shrill pitch. "Get on out here!"

Her entire body dipped to one side with each determined step. She bustled back to the truck and yanked open the driver's door. After a grumble of protest, the man stumbled out of his truck. He was big, too, but most of his size concentrated in his belly, which poured out the sides of his farmer's overalls and pushed the tails of his red plaid shirt along with it.

"Daddy, this here's Fern's little girl all growed up. Janie! Never could remember that fancy last name Fern decided on. Woodrow, or something like that?"

"Bainbridge." *Odd.* Mother hadn't chosen the name. She'd married it. Fern Mullen had married Wilson Bainbridge, another absent man from Janie's life. All she knew about her father was the frayed photo of a man in military uniform that she carried in her wallet.

Seymour gave her a curt nod and half of a smile. He looked as if he was going to be sick. She returned the smile, and he escaped back to his truck.

Oona took the broad backside of her working hands and smeared tears across her cheeks. "That man! Got hisself some ball game on the ra-di-o. Don't know for the life of me what's so all-fired important about it, anyhows. You 'member Seymour, don't you?"

She remembered, indeed. He was the big, quiet cousin who'd met her and Auntie Mae at the bus station that summer. Auntie Mae had taken matters into her own hands and traveled to Indianapolis to tell her younger sister that it was time the child became acquainted with her family. Fern wasn't strong enough to resist her spinster sister, and so she relinquished Janie for the summer to Mae's care. Janie adored her aunt immediately, for she showed all the vitality and motherly instincts that Fern had always lacked. When their bus arrived in the Chittenden Hills, the big, silent husband of Mother's cousin met them in his beat-up truck. "Half Way to Heaven" was painted on the side of the truck, and the child thought that was exactly where she must have arrived.

Of course *this* wasn't the same truck. Seventeen years had passed since that summer. Still, Janie stepped to the side, into the weeds that tickled her ankles, to see if any letters appeared beneath the rust. None did.

"What in tarnation is that?" Oona said, gaping at the lopsided tent. A sprinkling of gold flashed among her teeth. "And where's your young'un?"

"Playing in the woods." She suspected he was watching them from the safety of some hiding place nearby while he evaluated the newcomers.

Oona turned on her with a wagging finger. "Don't you let him go wandering too far, you hear? Don't you smell that smoke?"

"No — "

"That's fahr."

Fire, she meant. Janie felt her pulse quicken.

Oona shook her head. Fury creased her brow and underscored her darkening eyes. "That there Wanamaker boy can't keep his britches on long enough to do a deadening proper-like. He's gotta go around and burn down the whole gawl-durned woods."

"You mean there's a forest fire?" There was that name again. Wanamaker.

"He's up to no good, honey, you mark my words." Oona rubbed her bare arms. "It's fixing to rain, and I reckon that'll bring a city boy back in two shakes. There's mountain lion out there, you know, and other things not fit for a young'un. The fahr'll flush 'em out..."

Oona continued her stream of monologue, but Janie wasn't listening anymore. She didn't smell smoke, but Oona must know something she didn't. It was time to find Jeff.

~

LORD, IT WAS THE MOUTH! When that girl opened her mouth to smile, Oona liked to drop her teeth. She'd seen that smile before. Not often, of course. Seymour wasn't given to smiling much these days. Maybe...if she was lucky...no one else would notice and figure it out like she had. Meanwhile, she had her duty to think of, as always.

"Jeff!" the girl called with anxiety creasing Seymour's mouth.

Oona hung back and eyeballed her. Griffy was right. She was powerful skittish. Such a wisp of a thing she was, too. Well, Oona reckoned, it must run in the family, 'cause her half-brother Dexter was just the same. Then Oona frowned, remembering that Dexter wasn't related to Seymour except through Annalee, which made him not related to Janie at all.

"Humph!" Oona did what she always did when things didn't add up. She put it out of her mind. No use fretting over something she couldn't figure out.

Thank the good Lord that Griffy had gone right out with his squirrel gun to find more supper. She could always count on her boy. Now she could begin her task of putting some meat on Janie's bones.

"Don't you fret about him none, child," she said softly, draping a motherly arm around Janie's shoulders. "I reckon that fahr's about out by now. Besides, it's a goodly ways off, and there's men watching it so's it don't spread none. They're trying to clear the land, see. They think they're making another deadening, only they're going about it all wrong."

Janie turned a worried look on her as if she didn't see at all.

Oona sighed and tried again. "See, you got to cut a ring out of each tree and let them all die slow-like. Once the trees are dead, then you got yourself a deadening. But the Wanamaker boy ain't got the patience for that. He ain't clearing no tobacco field, neither."

She still didn't see. "What if the wind picks up before the fire is out?"

"It'd serve 'em right to kotch a little trouble. Now I ain't got time to stand out here jawing all day." She turned away from the girl and marched across the driveway toward the house. "Seeing as how you aim to move into this place, I reckon I got to check and make sure my girl's been doing her job. Taffy's supposed to keep an eye out over here, but you know what they say: if you want a job done right, you got to do it yourself. I don't trust her any farther than I can throw her."

She heaved herself up the steps and paused on the porch to catch her breath. "And then I got to get supper on — " Oona bit off the rest when she realized Janie hadn't followed her. She squinted at the girl, who'd gone all funny-eyed on her. "What's the matter, child? You look like you done seen the devil hisself." She reached for the screen door and pulled it open with a creak. "Lands sakes!" She let the door go with a slam. What she saw before her very eyes in Uncle Tobias's front room was the devil's work, all right. "Sey-MOUR!"

At least that worthless man was smart enough to recognize her calling-the-hogs voice was urgent. He scrambled to her side with as much vigor as he'd used back in their courting days. "What's wrong, Mama?"

From the cocky sound of his voice, she knew right away that he plumb knew what he was going to find inside. Then it all added up. Oona had an uncanny ability to figure things out.

"What in tarnation got into that Taffy?" she said, spitting out her words like accusing bullets at her husband. "How's come she didn't say nothing about this mess the other day when she was here to check up on things?"

But she already knew the answer. Dim-witted as Taffy was, even she must've guessed about her daddy. Guessed that this was her daddy's love nest. Something went haywire, and Seymour tore up the place in one of his fits of temper. Tore up the place, and Taffy guessed it. That's why she didn't say nothing, and that's why Seymour's standing there like the cat got the mouse but don't want no one to know it. *Why, iffen I ever kotch that man at it, I'll kill 'im. With the good Lord's blessing.*

"Taffy's been taking care of the place?" Janie said, interrupting Oona's thought. "I didn't realize that. So, she's still in Chittenden? She didn't move away from home?"

Oona turned on her with confused fury. "Lord, no." What in tarnation did she care so much about that useless girl?

And here was another useless one. Miss Janie Fancy Pants was living proof of Seymour's first fling. Nothing had been right again after that business with Fern, Oona's very own cousin. Not a day went by that Oona didn't think about her grudge, even though it'd been thirty years. And now this girl, this living *mistake*, had got up the gumption to creep up the porch steps and was standing within reach of Oona's arm. Why, she bet she could squeeze her arm around that scrawny neck and break it in two.

But Oona was an upright, Christian woman, and she knew what she had to do. She may not like it much, but if the girl was Seymour's daughter, then that made her Oona's daughter, too. Bygones were bygones, and she had to do right by her. "You're a'moving into my house," she declared.

The girl shook her head. She was as stubborn as her daddy. "I can't turn my back on this. First, I'll have to report this to the police. Grandpa didn't have a phone, so do you — "

Oona snorted. "Ain't no one got the telephone around here, but it wouldn't do you no good, anyhow. You can talk to the sheriff till you're blue in the face. Don't be so pig-headed, and come on with us. Honey, you want whoever done this to come back in the dead of night?"

"Oh, Mama, it was just a prank," said Seymour. "You know how a gang of boys is this time o' year. Sheriff's boy hisself was probably in on it."

Oona wanted to wipe that smirking half smile off his thick lips. Those lips had covered Fern, back when she was not only Oona's cousin but her best friend as well. She pushed her aggravation from her mind instead and rolled her eyes around in thought. That man was trying to cover his tracks, and it was her duty to help him. She didn't have to like it none, but at least she knew her duty.

"All right," she finally said, sizing up Fern's girl. "Sleep in that contraption if you want to, but first you're a'coming to my place for supper." She crossed her arms against her bosom and wouldn't take no for an answer. A plan was already forming in her head.

～

Janie clattered down the porch steps and hurried across the clearing to the edge of the woods where a patch of kudzu was spreading. "Jeff!" she called, trying to keep the urgency out of her voice. She peered into the gloom. Late afternoon and gathering clouds brought an early twilight to the woods despite these longer hours of summer daylight.

"Time to come home," she said, sniffing the air. Honeysuckle wafted on the breeze, not smoke. Oona must have made a mistake.

The kudzu rustled no more than six feet away. Jeff shook off the broad leaves and stood up. "You didn't see me, did you, Mom?"

She startled. "Why, no!"

"I told ya it was a neat hiding place." He grinned in triumph. "Bet you didn't know I was spying on you."

What else could hide in there, she wondered, holding out her hand to him. "Come on out of there. My cousin Oona has invited us to supper."

"That fat lady is your *cousin*?"

"Jeff! That's not nice."

"I thought you didn't have any family left."

"No one *close* is left, at least not that I know about. Oona is actually my second cousin, and she'll probably know more about the family than anyone."

The truck rumbled to life, pulling their attention to the driveway behind them. Oona closed the front door of the house then lumbered down the porch steps. "All right, Daddy, I'm a'coming. We cain't leave without the young'un." Reaching the bottom step, she looked up and saw them watching her. "There you be. Come on. You can ride in back, honey child," she said, nodding first at Jeff then at the bed of the truck.

"Oh boy!" Jeff scampered out of the kudzu and bounded over to the truck.

Janie followed more slowly. Glancing up at the sky, she decided to dig their raincoats out of the Volkswagen. She pulled out the yellow slickers and locked up the car, then turned to the truck. Oona stood by the open door and motioned her into the cab. She climbed in next to Seymour, who rolled a toothpick around in his mouth and watched Jeff in the rear-view mirror. The truck dipped as Oona squeezed in beside Janie, and then it lurched backwards up the driveway.

"Seymour, what did you mean about gangs of boys this time of year?" Janie asked, watching him negotiate the truck in reverse.

Oona poked her in the ribs and answered for him. "Oh, honey, don't you worry your little head about that none. I reckon you'll find out soon enough seeing as how you got a boy yourself."

"But — "

Seymour's attention shifted with the crunch of gears from the rear-view mirror to the one-lane gravel road rolling ahead. Oona continued to speak for him. "Honey, I reckon Seymour's just guessing about that. Sometimes boys, 'specially 'round about this time of year when school lets out every spring, like to stir theirselves up some trouble. They don't mean nothing by it. Boys is boys, and I oughta know — I got me three of 'em."

"What sort of trouble?"

"Oh, like the time some boys let loose Crockett's hogs." Oona chuckled. "Served that family right, it did. They thought they was so high and mighty. Took them near a week to round 'em all up."

"Do you think whoever tore up Grandpa's house was trying to give me some sort of message?"

Oona cocked her head. "Oh, honey, I don't reckon them boys knowed you."

"Then why would they do it?"

"Boys is jest boys, that's all. Who can say why? I reckon they don't know theirselves, neither."

Seymour snickered softly, then added, "They won't bother you again now that they blowed off some steam."

Janie turned to watch him, but he didn't return her glance. His eyes remained fixed on the road ahead, winding through hills. Oona lapsed into a rambling monologue full of names she apparently expected Janie to know. Suddenly the darkness of woods opened onto tobacco fields. Before her eyes adjusted to the glare, they crested a ridge overlooking a kudzu-draped gully. She was already lost.

The first drops of rain hit as they turned onto a narrow lane climbing uphill beside a corn field. Oona's monologue finally captured Janie's attention. "Up yonder is my acre of land," she said, waving her arm in front of Janie's nose. "Uncle Tobias done give it to us for a wedding present. It ain't much, but it's been home ever since. The old man never would give us no more, even though he had so much land he didn't know what to do with it. I reckon we couldn't help but think that once he passed on it'd all be ours."

"What do you think happened to Grandpa?"

But Oona plunged on with her tale. "He let us farm as much of his land 'round here as we wanted, 'cause he didn't figger none of it would amount to much, being so far away from the river and all. Fur as you can see, all this land belonged to Uncle Tobias. All, that is, except for a little piece down the hill yonder that belongs to my brother, Dexter."

Seymour grunted, and Janie turned to look at him. His cheeks puffed out, and a flush spread across them.

Oona nudged Janie, reclaiming her attention. "Seymour is the one that done cleared all this land and planted it and turned this place around. Don't know how we'd've made ends meet otherwise."

It suddenly occurred to Janie that she was Oona's and Seymour's new landlord.

Oona sighed and continued. "I reckon we done all right with what we got. After all, I bore seven young'uns. Lost two of 'em. My two oldest boys got theirselves good jobs working the barges out of Nashv'lle. Seymour had his hogs and corn. He's all but give it up these days." She leaned forward to glare at him. "Tobacco would've brung us a prettier penny." Then she fell back against her seat and grabbed Janie's arm. "You ain't gonna...sell the place, are ya?"

Her question sounded like an accusation, and Janie stiffened. "I haven't made any plans."

Oona grunted, released Janie's arm, and fell silent as they crested the hill. The tin roof of a shed came into view. When Janie saw the collection of broken-down cars and rusted automobile pieces surrounding it, she realized it wasn't a shed but a house. The house perched on four short stilts atop a mound of bare earth, and chickens scuttled about in the shelter beneath. A cement block served as a step to the front door, and next to it lay a big hound dog who lifted its head at the truck's arrival.

Oona pushed open the passenger door, dropped heavily to the ground, then turned to Jeff. "You run on along to the hollow and see if you can't find that there tree house my Griffy built hisself back when he was your age."

Jeff gave a yelp of delight, leapt from the back of the truck and scampered off toward the woods in the direction Oona indicated.

"Wait!" Janie called, jumping down beside Oona. "Your raincoat, Jeff! It's starting to rain."

He chose not to hear her, however, and he disappeared into brambles.

"Oh, honey, he ain't gonna melt from a little rain."

She was right, Janie thought. She had to stop worrying about him so much. As soon as she closed the truck's door, it started to roll back onto the road.

Oona chased after the truck a few feet and wagged a threatening finger at her husband. "Where you fixing to go, Daddy? We'll be having supper before too long." He didn't answer, and the truck rumbled away. Oona shook her head and muttered to herself, then marched to the house. The chickens underneath it squawked louder, lifted their wings, and ran in crazy circles, scooting out of her way.

Janie dodged the army of chickens and hurried after Oona. This house was much smaller than Grandpa's, with only two rooms. In the center of the front room stood a black stove with pipes bending across the ceiling. The pipes reminded Janie of a giant bug about to fall on her head.

"Taf-FY!" Oona shouted, crackling across the barren linoleum, past couches with springs poking through the vinyl. A ladder led up the wall to a hole in the ceiling. Oona slowed long enough to peer up into the hole, then she muttered to herself and lumbered through the doorway into the back of the house.

Janie followed her across the room and remembered Taffy — Oona's daughter and Janie's best friend from that summer so long ago. She wondered if they'd have anything in common today. Motherhood, maybe. An empty crib stood behind one of the couches.

The second room across the back of the house served as kitchen, dining room and bedroom. A curtain drew across one corner, offering privacy to the lumpy mattress pushed up against the bare wall.

Oona caressed the gleaming white edge of the largest electric stove Janie had ever seen. "My boy Griffy give me this. Don't know where he come up with that much money, but he always was one to remember his mama. Such a good boy, he is. You 'member him, don't ya? I ain't never seen nothing like this here stove. Bonni-BELLE! I declare, where is everybody? Don't know where them girls gone off to. Always disappear at supper time, they do. I reckon you're all I got." She scowled at Janie as if she didn't think much of her potential help, then she turned to a plate piled high with meat oozing blood. "Well, what're you waiting for, honey? Looks like Griffy brung me enough squirrel for supper."

Janie's stomach roiled. She gave the table a wide berth and staggered to a chair in the corner where she dropped the raincoats. "Uh, what do you want me to do?"

Oona squinted at her and sighed. "I reckon you best go out yonder to my garden and pick the last of the peas. You know what a pea pod looks like?"

She nodded, grabbed her raincoat and escaped, following the direction of Oona's pointing finger. She stumbled out onto the screened-in back porch, jammed with a chest freezer, a wringer-style washing machine, a tractor tire, two wooden rockers and a rusted glider.

Oona bustled after her. "Here, you forgot this." She thrust an empty cardboard beer flat into her hands. "Don't take all day, you hear?" She turned back to the kitchen and her plate of squirrel.

Janie slung the yellow hood over her head and pushed open the screen door. No cement block served as a step here, and she tumbled off the porch. The ground wasn't muddy yet, only soft from the steady drizzle.

The beer flat warped from rainy mist, and she clutched it to her chest as she set off along a path of stepping stones. The path sloped down a slight hill and disappeared at the chimney shape of an outhouse. Behind that was the garden, an area outlined with barbed wire and large enough to contain her two-bedroom apartment back in Bloomington. The garden nestled against the backdrop of woods, dark from the descending gloom of misty rain.

She stepped over the barbed wire, then disentangled the hem of her coat. Breathing deeply of the fresh and earthy air, she surveyed the rows of plants before her and wondered which were the peas. She recognized tomatoes from the patio variety she'd raised on her apartment balcony. Corn was obvious. However, she'd never seen pea pods outside of the grocery store, and she wasn't sure what kind of a plant they grew on. She started down the rows, peering intently at feathery leaves, wet with rain. They clung to the yellow vinyl of her raincoat like fingers trying to hold her back.

She didn't know how much time had passed searching for the peas when the feeling came to her that she was not alone. Droplets of sweat tickled her spine and underarms. She straightened from her hunch and glanced over at the backdrop of woods. Something red flashed behind a bush.

"Hello?" she called, dropping the beer flat.

Gravel crunched just then, announcing the arrival of a car, and she looked away for only a few seconds. The hill blocked her view of the road. When she turned back to the woods, all that she saw was a waving branch. The red was gone.

FOUR

*S*low as molasses that city girl was. Oona poked at the sizzling meat and scowled through the open door of the porch at Janie. What in tarnation was she doing wandering through the mustard? Oona hated having other people trample through her garden. They couldn't appreciate it if they hadn't stuck the seeds in the ground themselves. But she had to let others do some of the chores. After all, a body couldn't do everything herself.

The car driving up must be one of Bonnibelle's friends bringing her home from Lord knows where. She would give that featherhead girl a piece of her mind. Then a light tap sounded on the door frame out front.

Mercy! Anyone who knocked had to be a caller. She laid down the bent fork carefully so as not to scratch her stove top, then swiped her hands on her skirt. Halfway into the front room she saw Junior Wanamaker's head peering at her through the screen. She felt her hackles rise.

"Well, lookee what the cat drug in," she said in her friendliest voice. It wouldn't do to let him know what she really thought, not until after her Bonnibelle hooked him for sure. "You going to stand out there all day in the rain? Come on in."

She bustled back to the kitchen and began pulling dishes from the cupboards. She reckoned Bonnibelle would learn her lesson good for not being here when Junior Wanamaker come calling. "Did you get that there fahr put out?"

"What fire?" He sounded concerned, but he didn't fool her. "I don't know anything about a fire."

"I hear tell you're planning on burning down the woods to clear land — "

"Dad's idea, not mine."

"To clear land," she continued, perturbed, "for that there golf you city folks like to play in the country." She shook her head at their foolishness.

He laughed. "No one would give permission to burn acreage to clear land for *that*, and even if they did, I would never do it that way."

"Humph." She wasn't buying his story. She knew smoke when she smelled it. He was trying to contradict her, and that riled her. "Well, Bonnibelle ain't here."

"Actually, I came to see you. I need information about Janie Bainbridge, and I thought you'd be the best person to ask."

Now he wanted to butter her up, but Oona was too crafty. "I reckon if you sit a spell and wait, she'll be here in two shakes."

He scratched his head and frowned. "Janie?"

"Bonnibelle!" Was the entire world, but her, daft? "That girl ain't got no business gallivanting around the hills when there's chores to be done, and I reckon she knows it. So she'll be here right quick, and iffen you wait — "

"Allow me to give you a hand." Junior took the stack of dishes from Oona's arms and began placing them around the table.

A feather could have knocked her over. This was woman's work. Must be that there yarb doctor's witchery blood in his veins that made him pay no never mind to what was right and what was not. Oona shivered till she felt her bones rattle.

"Is it true that Janie is planning to move into the Mullen place?"

"That's a tom fool notion."

He raised his eyebrows at her. "Do you think she might be interested in selling?"

"She ain't got no right to sell something that ain't hers!" Oona moved back to the stove and yanked the fork from its grease-splattered surface.

"The courthouse has the deed with her name on it."

"I don't care. That girl ain't got no rightful claim to a place she ain't put hard work into. You mark my words."

He stroked his chin, which was naked, unlike a real man's. "Apparently Tobias put everything in her name before he took his boat out on the river that last time."

Needles of pain shot through her as if a red-hot poker jabbed at her. She could lose all that she'd worked for all her life, on account of the deadening. She wanted to scream, but she swallowed it.

"I need her piece of land," Junior continued. "And I'm on a tight schedule. Construction of the lodge begins next week, and Dad is coming for the groundbreaking ceremony."

"Humph." Her bones rattled again at the reminder of the senior Wanamaker. J.P. they called him. Short for John Price. She'd learned a hard lesson from him back when she was a girl. She'd never forgotten, and now it'd serve J.P. right if her Bonnibelle hooked his only son.

"As soon as the lodge is under way, we'll need to begin work on the first nine holes. But without the Mullen land, there will never be enough space for a full golf course. If I can't get that land, then it will change the entire focus of The Resort. It would be helpful to know now, before groundbreaking, if I'm going to get it or not." He set down the last of the plates and came to stand beside Oona at the stove. "I don't remember much about her from that time when she stayed with Tobias. We were only kids then. I don't know how I should approach her. That's where I thought you could help."

Steam rose from the skillet, matching Oona's. She shook the fork at him and bit off her words. "She's a married woman."

He thought about that for a minute or two and frowned. "When did you say she was coming?"

"I didn't." He thought he could fool her, did he? "She's already here. Out yonder picking peas." She motioned to the back door.

His face went funny, and he clumped across the floor in his cowboy boots.

"Now just a gawl-durned minute! I don't need everyone out there tramping around in my garden. She'll be back in two shakes."

He pushed his hair out of his eyes and winked at her. "I'll be careful." Then he was gone.

Just like that.

Oona's fork stabbed at the meat in the skillet. Where was that fool Bonnibelle? She'd seen the look on Junior's face. Men were all alike whether they had money or not. Whether they were from the city or not. Whether they had witchery blood in them or not. She wasn't about to stand by and watch Bonnibelle lose her chance at all that money.

～

JANIE REMEMBERED THE MAN with one eye. He'd worn a red cap. Was he the one who'd been spying on her just now? He was only curious about her, she decided, turning her attention back to the garden.

The sound of clinking dishes drifted to her from the house, and she wondered if the car she'd heard arriving had brought Taffy home. A glow of excitement warmed her at the idea of seeing her old friend again. They'd spent every day of that summer together in their childhood, roaming through the woods, spying on the grownups and sharing thoughts about their world of make-believe. She'd never had a friend since then who'd been as close to her as Taffy had been, and now she couldn't wait to see her again. She wondered if they would still be friends.

The screen door slammed, and she looked up to see, not a grown-up Taffy, but a man. He stood there, leaning against the doorframe, watching her. She stared back. Even from a distance, she could tell that he wasn't one of Oona's sons. His crown of sun-bleached hair gave him away. He wore a burgundy golf shirt and khaki trousers that screamed professional grooming. She forced her attention back to the rows of plants in the garden.

A scraping sound made her look up again. He sprang over the barbed wire in his leather boots.

"Janie Bainbridge?" he asked, extending his hand as he hurried toward her.

He was ruggedly handsome, and it irritated her that she felt like a stammering schoolgirl. His handshake lingered a moment too long. All she could do was nod. His eyes, the same shade as her mother's sapphire pendant, held her captive. There was something vaguely familiar about his face.

Finally, he released her hand and pulled out his wallet. He riffled through it, found a business card, and offered it to her. "I can tell by the look on your face that you don't remember me. Price Wanamaker."

"I see." She cleared her throat and looked away from his eyes to the card that identified him as Executive Vice President of The Resort at Chittenden Bay, a division of The Wanamaker Corporation.

"We're cousins, several times removed," he continued, as if that would prompt some lost piece of memory. "Our grandmothers were sisters."

She took a shaky step backwards. Everyone seemed related here in the backwoods.

"I guess I can't expect you to remember," he said. "We were just kids when we knew each other."

She searched his face and her memory and imagined him without the crow's feet. That summer long ago at Grandpa's, she and Taffy had explored the woods and streams and spied on... "Junior?" she whispered.

He grinned. His teeth were a dazzling contrast to his tan. "I go by 'Price' these days."

A couple of years older than her, he'd been just old enough to ride his high horse of adolescence. Too old for "kid stuff," he'd lured girls to the swimming hole that summer, providing Janie and Taffy with a perfect target for their spying.

"I'm working for Dad now," he added, nodding at the card she held in her hand.

"I don't remember your father."

"That's because he never came down to Chittenden. It was *beneath* him." He said that word as if he were sucking on a sour candy.

The air between them felt thick, and she tensed. Inside the raincoat was like a sauna.

"I believe it's stopped raining," he said, as if reading her discomfort.

She shrugged and tightened her grasp on the beer flat.

"You haven't picked any peas." He nodded at the empty flat.

"I haven't found them yet."

"They're right over there." He pointed at a tent-like construction of poles covered with vining plants. "Come on. I'll help you." He led the way and searched through the leaves for a handful of pods. "Not many left."

She pocketed his card, and they went to work. The only sound between them was the plunk of pods as they dropped onto the cardboard.

He grinned. "How do you find your grandfather's place?"

"Why do you ask?" She wondered why he'd worded his question that way.

He shrugged. "No reason. Just hope you're comfortable."

Did he, really? Maybe he knew about the vandalism over there. Whoever had torn up the place had made it unlivable for her, perhaps intentionally. Someone didn't want her to stay there, and now this man wanted to know if she was *comfortable*. Of course she wasn't. Who was he? She didn't know anything about him, other than his adolescent habits with girls.

"The place is just fine," she said. "We're very comfortable, thank you. We're very happy to be in Grandpa's house."

He squinted, looking puzzled by her outburst. He pushed his fingers through his hair, but one lock popped back onto his forehead. "I'm glad you're so happy. I expect you'll be even happier to know that you're sitting on a gold mine."

"Excuse me?"

"According to the appraiser, that is."

She didn't know anything about appraisers. "I can't afford — "

He waved her worry aside. "Dad's taking care of it."

She stood there, speechless, staring at him.

He continued pawing through the leaves, searching for more pods. "You ever thought about living in a big house?"

"No," she lied. There was a pink stucco mansion overlooking the California coast, but it existed in her fantasies. That's where she'd live when she became a famous screenwriter.

"Maybe you should start thinking about it. Your grandfather owned a sizable amount of property."

"He had a few tobacco fields, but the government confiscated his property for the dam."

He turned to look at her with a puzzled frown. "He had more than a few tobacco fields. Don't you know about the rest of it?"

She met his gaze evenly, refusing to admit that he was right, that she didn't really know anything at all about her family, that Grandpa had needed her, but she hadn't come. She'd failed him, all on account of her mother... No. She couldn't go on blaming Fern. She had to accept responsibility for that failure, and all the others, as well.

He studied her, as if her thoughts lay open to him. "Over the years, Tobias Mullen acquired a few hundred acres of wooded land up in the hills. Nobody else wanted it then." After a pause, his voice lowered with emphasis. "Today, that property is mostly lake-front, which makes some people consider it valuable."

Her heart hammered, and her palms sweat. The business card in her pocket announced something about a resort on a bay of the lake, born from Grandpa's river. This man had an agenda, something at stake, something to be gained from someone else's death, from someone's pain. A reason to make other people's business his own. She reached in her pocket, pulled out the card and handed it back to him. "Here. I won't need this."

He wouldn't take it. "I'm prepared to make you a fair offer. It'll be enough for a bigger house somewhere else."

Her jaw muscles clamped, and she stuck out her chin. She fought the urge to ask "how much?" "We've only just arrived," she said instead. Her voice came out shakier than she wanted.

A desperate look filled his face, and he pushed the stubborn lock off his forehead again. "I'm an idiot. Of course you need more time. Have you toured the property yet?"

She shook her head.

He grinned again. "In that case, I'll show you around. How about — "

"Hey!" yelled a girl's shrill voice from the direction of the house. "Mama ain't none too happy with you for taking so long."

A young woman, no more than nineteen or twenty, sashayed up behind Price. She grabbed his elbow with an air of possession, gave it a shake, then looked Janie up and down. She chomped on her gum. "Mama wants to know how's come you ain't got the peas picked yet?"

"You must be Bonnibelle," was all that Janie could manage to sputter. She'd been a baby that summer Janie was here.

"Little ol' me, in the flesh." A string of artificially blonde hair with dark roots fell into her hazel eyes. Although their exact shade was unclear, the fire simmering within them was very clear. The fire subsided to a warm glow of adoration, however, when she turned her gaze upon Price. "I wanna talk to you," she said in a sing-song voice as she stroked his arm. "Let's go yonder to our special place."

A flush spread to the tips of his ears, and his grin evaporated. He cleared his throat and said, "I'm in the middle of something."

"Oh, she can pick the peas, darlin'." Bonnibelle draped her arm on Price's shoulder and tugged at him. "Anyhow, that ain't a job for a man like you."

"Don't let me stop you," Janie said before he could answer. She flung another handful of peas into the flat. "I don't think there's anything more to be accomplished here."

Price shrugged, and Bonnibelle pulled him away. She shot a sly smile over his shoulder and cocked her finger at Janie in shotgun fashion.

Smiling and waving in return, she was torn between laughing and the desire to pelt Bonnibelle with pea pods. That girl must think Janie was *interested* in Price. She watched them move off through the pasture, then she carried the flat of peas back across the chicken yard to the house. She slammed the porch door behind her.

"Taffy? That you?" Oona called from the kitchen.

Janie took several deep breaths. "No, it's me." She peeled off her rain-coat, sighed with relief, and threw it across the glider. Then she kicked off her muddy shoes and padded into the kitchen. "Does this look like enough peas?"

From Oona's station at the stove, she frowned at the beer flat. "Looks like you got yourself a fine mess. There's a pail of water in the sink yonder to warsh them in."

Janie turned toward the sink.

"No, no, child. Don't you know nothing? You gotta hull 'em first. Makes no sense to warsh what's just gotta be took off."

Her cheeks flamed from the scolding. She'd never lived up to her mother's expectations, either. With a long sigh, she moved aside one of the plates on the table and sank down into a creaking chair to begin her task. Her fingers took on the earthy smell of crisp peas as she peeled apart their seams. "How were you and Grandpa related?" she asked in a soft let's-change-the-subject voice.

Oona planted one hand firmly on her broad hip, which jiggled as she stirred something on the stove. At first Janie didn't think she was going to answer, then Oona sniffled and spoke. "My mama and your grandmama was sisters. So your grandpa was my Uncle Tobias."

Excitement fired in her, learning about people she'd never known existed, people who were her family. She paused her work over the peas and remem-bered what Price had told her. "Then there were three sisters? My grand-mother, Price's grandmother, and your mother? Is she still alive?"

Oona nodded. "Iffen you can call it that. She's a bitter old woman and cain't remember us no more. Cain't say as I blame her, though, as we had to find her a home over yonder in Stony Lonesome. She gets care real good over there. Lord knows I cain't give it to her here, thanks to that no-good husband of mine." She stopped stirring long enough to dab at the corner of her eye with a broad finger. "You seen Bonnibelle?"

Janie nodded. "Would it be okay for me to visit your mother?"

"Where in tarnation did that girl go off to now? Was she with the Wana-maker boy?"

Janie shrugged, not wanting to talk about Bonnibelle. "Where can I find her home?"

"I reckon she thinks she'll get out of her chores that way." Oona wiped her hands on the purple paisleys of her skirt and marched over to the porch door. "Bonnie-BELLE!" She shook her head, and the gray strands of her chin-length hair fell apart into clumps. "My Bonnibelle's fixing to catch herself a man."

Oona turned away from the door with a flush on her cheeks and gold glittering in her mouth. Then she spied Janie, and her excitement faded. "Tsk, tsk. Ain't your mama never showed you how to do that?" She sat down next to her and grabbed the peas from Janie's hands. "You gotta find the rhythm. Like so."

With lightning-fast fingers, Oona demonstrated the rhythm of her strokes as she plucked pods from the box, snapped them open and sorted the pieces into appropriate piles. "Fern never could do nothing right."

"She tried," Janie said in her mother's defense. "It's not easy to raise a child alone." After the last two years, she knew exactly how tough that was.

Dinner sizzled on the stove, providing a feeling of hominess that had always been missing from Janie's childhood. She'd been raised on take-out food from the diners where Fern had worked, and home was a succession of rented apartments. Fern had kept moving, as if she was looking for something. Looking, or maybe running away.

"Oona, did you ever meet my father? What was he like?" Fern had refused to talk about him. Janie had always wondered if he was the one her mother had been running from.

The rhythm of Oona's strokes died. She dropped the remainder of her peas and stood up. "I...I..." She smoothed her hands across her hips and hurried back to the simmering skillets. "I don't recollect that Fern ever brought him round to meet any of us," she said, aiming her back at Janie.

"Why wouldn't Mother bring him home to meet the family? Was there something wrong with him?"

"Oh, honey, I reckon she thought she was too good for the likes of us folks."

"I tried contacting the military once a long time ago, but they had no record of a Wilson Bainbridge. Or else they weren't telling me." She thought of the picture in her wallet of her handsome father in his uniform. Dark, wavy hair. Wisp of a smile. Distant thoughts flickered behind dream-filled eyes. Averted. Forever averted to her.

"I declare," Oona said, her entire body shaking from her stirring motion. "It's just like Junior, ain't it? He thinks he's too good for the likes of us. He wants to be called 'Price' now that he thinks he's a big shot. His poor grandma must be heartbroke over that boy, seeing her own kin go against her. He was always such a good boy, even if his daddy did carry him off to Lou'v'lle. We all knowed Junior would find a way back here, but we never dreamed it'd be like this. Cain't figger what went wrong. Must've been that there city what done it. There ain't no stopping him once he got his sights set on something."

Janie stared at Oona. What did this have to do with her father? Oona had an amazing ability to carry on a conversation with herself, oblivious to others. Maybe she just never listened.

Before Janie could guide Oona back to the topic of her father, a creak sounded from the front room. Someone was opening and shutting the front door, apparently trying to sneak inside. Crackling linoleum betrayed the soft steps in the other room.

Oona stopped stirring. "Taffy? That you?"

"Yes, Mama." Hers was a tiny, quavering voice.

Janie dropped her peas and suddenly felt nervous about meeting her childhood friend again. Silently, she rehearsed various greetings, but none seemed to recapture the magic they'd once shared.

"Don't know why you always go tippy-toeing about like that," Oona said. "Where in tarnation you been, girl?"

"Out."

"You knowed it's suppertime."

"Yes, Mama."

"You knowed you got chores to do." Oona resumed her stirring and jiggling. "Just ain't right, a girl your age still living at home — no husband, no job, no nothing. You got two brothers that both gone off down the river and got theirselves good jobs on them barges."

Silence answered from the other room. Janie did a quick calculation. Taffy was three years younger than her, which would make her twenty-six. How could she listen to that? Janie didn't have much, but at least her life was her own, especially now that Roy was out of it.

Taffy poked her head into the kitchen, but when she caught sight of Janie, working over the flat of peas, she paled and shrank back. This couldn't be the same bold friend from childhood. This grown-up Taffy acted like a frightened doe about to bolt, and she even looked like one. Her limp brown hair was combed out of her eyes and clasped by a barrette. A clean white blouse and straight brown skirt showed off her slim figure and tidy appearance but did nothing to enliven her sallow coloring. No light sparkled from her doe-brown eyes, but they widened at the sight of Janie.

"Git yourself busy, girl," Oona said. "Iffen you don't help hull them peas, we'll have to wait for 'em for tomorrow's supper."

Without a word or glance in Janie's direction, Taffy sat down across the table, shoved aside a place setting, then reached for a handful of peas.

"It's good to see you again," Janie said, forgetting every greeting she'd rehearsed.

Taffy shrugged.

"It's been a long time."

No response.

"I've thought of you often."

Still nothing.

"You were the best friend I ever had."

Taffy's fingers paused over the peas, as if she considered a reply. But the pause was only momentary before she shred apart a pod and threw the peas, pinging into the pot.

"We all reckoned you'd come back after that summer you was here with Uncle Tobias," Oona said, filling in for Taffy's silence.

"I wanted to, but Mother wouldn't allow it. She always developed a migraine every time I mentioned the idea. I learned not to ask about Chittenden, but I never understood why she refused to talk about it. She seemed afraid of something."

"I reckon she was, bless her soul. Tsk, tsk." Oona's broad rump shook as she worked at the stove.

"But what on earth *could* she have been afraid of? Grandpa was just about the kindest person I ever met. He must've made a wonderful father."

"There's some folks that don't see things the way others do," Oona said. "Besides, Fern was always the uppity sort. Probably thought she was too good for the likes of us poor folk."

No, Mother wasn't like that. Janie choked thinking of her in the past tense. But it was true that she'd rejected her own family, for whatever reason. Now that she was gone, Janie was free to search for the answers to her questions without the fear of hurting her mother.

"Why did she reject the family?" Janie asked, deciding to be blunt.

"Some folks don't think family's so important."

"Grandpa didn't teach her that."

"Maybe it's just in their blood. Folks cain't help the way they are."

"I don't believe that. People can take control of their own lives and be the way they want to be."

For the first time, Taffy looked up at her, and Janie detected a faint glimmer of hope about her otherwise empty eyes. She smiled, but Taffy lowered her gaze back to the diminishing pile of peas.

A baby crying from the other room interrupted them. Oona backed away from the stove and lumbered to the screen door. "Bonni-BELLE!" Then, looking over her shoulder, she added, "Taffy, go and find your sister and tell her that baby of hers is like to split her britches."

"Yes, Mama." Taffy threw the rest of her unhulled peas back in the pile, then stood and turned, heading for the back door.

"Wait! I'll go with you!" Janie said, springing from her chair.

"Now wait a gawl-durned minute! Y'all ain't leaving me alone with that baby *and* supper to get on!"

But Janie was already on the back porch, slipping into her shoes. "I'll finish the peas when I come back," she said, jumping off the porch, sending chickens squawking in a flutter of wings. She saw Taffy leaning against the barn, and she felt a surge of relief. Her old friend was waiting for her.

Tufts of grass looked like green islands in the red dirt of the chicken yard, and she hopped across them to catch up with Taffy. When she reached her side, she made a move to hug her, but Taffy pulled back and lowered her voice to a whisper.

"Why'd you have to go and do that? Now Mama will skin me alive."

Janie jerked back as if she'd been slapped. "We're not children anymore."

"You think she's noticed?" Taffy's face paled as she reached to unlatch a gate in the barbed wire fence enclosing the pasture.

Janie followed her through the gate and skirted a fly-speckled cow pie. "How do you know where to begin looking for Bonnibelle?"

Taffy pointed down the sloping hill toward another stand of woods. "She likes to go to the smokehouse down yonder in the holler with anyone in pants."

"What about her husband?" Janie pictured Seymour holding a shotgun to some boy's head. In this family, though, it would've been Oona aiming the shotgun. Yes, she imagined Oona was capable of that. Where was the boy-husband?

Taffy snorted, and Janie realized there was no husband. "Mama thinks women was born to get married and wait on men. She calls it a woman's duty."

"Of course you don't believe that."

"I don't know what I believe no more. It don't matter, anyhow."

"Of course it matters. Remember that time when we followed Junior — er, Price — and some girl to the swimming hole and you jumped out of hiding and shouted 'I'm going to tell!' You got paddled for it. Where's that old spirit?"

"Maybe I finally learned to keep my mouth shut. I reckon you never did."

Janie shivered. Taffy's spirit must have been paddled out of her. She tried again. "We'll never learn anything if we always keep our mouths shut."

Taffy came to a dead stop on the side of the hill and turned to face Janie, nose to nose. "Whyn't you go on back where you come from? No one wants you here." Then she sprinted toward the smokehouse, looking like the doe that had finally bolted.

FIVE

Oona carefully heaved herself off the back porch and planted her reddened knuckles on her hips. Supper was ready, but no one cared that she'd gone to a sight of trouble for them. Janie's boy whooped and slid across the mud, chasing chickens around and under the house. Feathers flew into the air, stirring up their dusty chicken smell along with the squawking ruckus.

She pulled on the rope hanging down from the dinner bell attached to the eaves, and its clang echoed through to her bones. At least it got the boy's attention. The others had better show up right quick if they knew what was good for them. She hurried back inside, followed by the boy.

As if on cue, the old familiar rattle of the truck arrived. She'd give that no-good man a piece of her mind, taking off the way he did. The front door banged, finally, and two sets of boots clumped erratically through the front room.

"Well, lookee who's here!" She beamed at her boy Griffy, who supported his daddy's weight.

"Mama, is the bucket ready?"

"Pass (hiccup) the bucket!" Seymour sang.

"Daddy, that ain't rightly what I was fixing to do." Griffy pulled him to the sink and pushed his head into the bucket of water.

Oona wagged her finger at her husband's back. "You ain't got no call. Just 'cause *she* shows up. Well, old man, we all got things we'd just as soon forget, but that don't give you the right to go drown — "

The sound of voices suddenly penetrating the back porch stopped her. It wouldn't do for Janie to hear. *Let her think Seymour takes a fancy to the jug, long as she don't figger out why.*

She fetched the first platter of food and watched them file into her kitchen. Bonnibelle was always at the front of the line when it came to food. Junior followed at a distance, like her girl had leprosy or something. *Nossir, that will never do.* He hovered near Janie. *Uh-oh. Trouble.*

"Where's Jeff?" she asked in that city-girl voice of suuuu-periority.

"He lit off for the attic. Honey, I reckon he's just exploring." She handed the platter to Janie, then grabbed the yardstick with "Earl's Pool Hall" written all over it and poked the ceiling twice with it. "Git on down here!"

Griffy pulled his daddy out of the bucket and threw a towel over his head while the girl stood there gawking at the plate of squirrel in her hands. Seymour shook the towel off and sprayed drops of water on Oona's clean floor. He gurgled loudly then hiccuped again.

"C'mon, Daddy." Griffy led Seymour to his place at the head of the table.

Janie's young'un scrambled down the ladder and raced past Oona.

"Here, now, boy! Your pants on fahr?" Oona retrieved the towel from the floor, then flashed him a broad smile. He peered up at the gold in her mouth, and she had to chuckle. "Old Uncle Tobias, who was your great-granddaddy, bless his soul, give me these teeth, 'cause I ain't had me none before the gov'ment come to these parts."

"Weren't you born with teeth like everyone else?"

Cackling with laughter, she didn't know what was funnier — the boy, or the look of horror on Janie's face. Oona didn't mind. Not at all. She was right proud of her gold teeth. She flashed a golden grin at Janie. "Well, honey? You gonna stand there holding that plate all day?"

Bonnibelle arranged the seating to suit her fancy. She put herself in the middle with Junior to her left, next to Seymour's end of the table, and Janie to her right, next to Oona's end. Oona understood what she was doing, putting Janie at a safe distance from Junior, all the while keeping an eye on the both of them.

On Seymour's other side, Griffy sat opposite Junior. Oona knew that look. Griffy folded his arms around his plate, like someone wanted to steal it, and pointed his face at it. But his eyes looked up under the cover of his thick eyebrows to watch Junior. Griffy didn't like him any more than Oona did, but he lacked her know-how. She'd have to stop him before he spoiled things for Bonnibelle.

Taffy slinked inside then, and Griffy's head shot up. "Where you been?" he asked.

"Why do you care?"

"That ain't no way to talk to Griffy," Oona exclaimed.

"Sorry, Mama," she said, taking a bowl of steaming potatoes and setting them on the table.

"I told you, Mama," Griffy said. "My name's Griffin. Call me Griffin." Then he turned to Taffy and whispered, "I'll deal with you later."

"I heard that," Oona said, following behind Taffy with her arms loaded down with bowls of gravy, peas, and homemade cottage cheese. "I declare. I don't know why you two go on so. See iffen you cain't mind your manners. We got ourselves company." She threw a knowing look at Janie, who was staring at the rest of the bowls lined up beside the stove.

"You want all this on the table?" she asked.

"I reckon that's why I got it all out, honey." There was only some biscuits, a few carrots, some of Mae's corn relish, last year's tomato relish, and a little dab of this and a dab of that.

"Do you eat like this every day?" She set the bowls, one by one, on the table.

Oona took her seat at the real head of the table. "Lands, no. Only when one of my boys goes out hunting. Cain't count on Seymour to do it no more."

"I tol' you, Mama, I got me..." He hiccuped and heaped food onto his plate as the bowls passed round the table. "...things to do more import'n tha' woman's work."

The way he chewed, moving his mouth sideways, was like Bossie chewing on her cud. A spot of grease glistened on his prickly chin, and Oona looked away in disgust. Whatever happened to that young farm hand she and Fern squabbled over all those years ago?

He was gone, that's what, just like Oona's own corner of the world was disappearing before her very eyes. Well, she reckoned she'd have to fix that, and she may as well start tonight. "Janie, sit down and tell us when that husband of yourn is gonna show up."

Lands, what did I say, anyhows? The girl's face turned beet red, her boy shot bolt upright in his seat, Junior leaned forward a little too eagerly, and her own girl, Taffy, came to life with a bit of the old spark in her eyes.

"Not everyone's got to be married," Taffy said, daring to talk back to her own mama.

"What would you know about that?" Oona was quick to fire back her retort. "A woman's place is with her husband. Reckon you ain't learned that yet."

"Not all husbands are right for a woman, Mama."

Well, that's a fine how-do-you-do. Raise a child, and she up and turns on you. Before Oona could collect her thoughts into appropriate words, Janie's young'un interrupted.

"Mo-om," he said, like to split his britches. "Is *Dad* coming to live with us?"

"No, honey. Your dad is the one who left you and me, remember? He has no place in our future here in Chittenden or anywhere."

Oona gasped. "Well, I never! That sounds like the devil's talk, if I ever did hear it. You hush that kind of talk, hear? Now that Fern's passed on, bless her soul, I reckon it's up to me to learn you good."

But Janie wasn't paying her no never mind. The girl couldn't even look her in the eyes.

"Daddy?" Griffy said. "Daddy, what's wrong?"

Oona scowled at her husband. She'd have to be more careful and re-member not to mention that name in front of him. It irked her that he still mourned Fern, but it irked her even more that there was nothing she could do to stop it.

~

SILENCE DESCENDED OVER the table as the mound of food on Janie's plate grew. Even Oona must have regretted her inappropriate question. Overcome by a mixture of embarrassment and outrage, Janie turned her at-tention to the baby crawling on the floor with a bottle hanging between her first teeth. She paused long enough to bat at her mother's skirt, however, Bonnibelle ignored her. She was too busy fluttering her eyelids at Price. She was too young to be a mother, Janie decided, but then, hadn't she been guilty of the same thing when she'd had Jeff?

Jeff threw his fork down. "I'm not hungry no more."

She fought the urge to correct his grammar. "It's been a long day, honey. Try to eat some more, and then we'd better go crawl into that tent." Carefully avoiding the small portion of squirrel she'd accepted, she tackled the mound of food on her plate. Several bites later, she realized everyone at the table was watching her.

Price spoke for the others. "I thought you were staying in your grandfather's house."

"Tsk, tsk," Oona said before Janie could swallow and reply. "The place is a mess. Been closed up all winter, you know."

"Mama, you always get things upside down," Taffy said, sticking out her chin in the defiant way that Janie remembered. "I been taking care of it, and the place is as tidy as a pin."

Oona glared at Taffy. "Then *someone* warn't keeping as good an eye out over there as she should ought've."

Taffy lowered her face over her plate, but that didn't hide her scarlet flush.

"When can we go over the appraiser's report?" Price asked, leaning past Bonnibelle to capture Janie's attention away from Taffy.

"Ain't you got nothing better to do than stick your nose in other folks' business?" said Oona's grown son. Janie tried to find a resemblance between this hairy bull of a man and the young boy she'd known, the boy who'd put frogs under the papers in the outhouse. Now, Griffin's gaze darted between Price and his plate of food, as if he waited for some surprise to show itself. What would it be this time, a garter snake in the peas?

He looked capable of more serious mischief today, however. He was a younger version of Seymour, and he bristled as he faced Price. His bushy eyebrows knit together in a disheveled blend with the unruly black curls frizzing down to his shoulders. Thick lips curled into a sneer, and crooked teeth gleamed through the untrimmed blackness of his shaggy beard. Venom emanated from him.

Janie shivered. She would hate to come across this cousin of hers alone at night in the woods. Ignoring him, she turned to Price. "You can show me the report, if you like, but I'm really not interested in selling."

"Hah!" shouted Griffin.

But Price wouldn't leave it alone. "Three hundred acres is a lot of land for a young woman to manage alone."

"Is that how much there is?" Janie couldn't hide the surprise in her voice.

"What're you getting at, Wanamaker?" Griffin shot spittle across the table.

Price's voice remained level. "What does anyone need with so much land if it's not being used?"

"That there Mullen land is some of the finest hunting land left around here. Ain't that so, Daddy?"

Seymour's face was a pasty white, and his eyes rolled downward. He didn't appear to be listening to the conversation.

Griffin shrugged and continued on his own. "Decent folk got to hunt just to put food on the table." He glanced at Janie's plate with the untouched squirrel. "You city folks ain't got much of a appetite, do you?"

She swallowed hard and picked off a bite of squirrel. *Fried chicken*, she told herself.

Smirking, Griffin turned back to Price. "It ain't a game for us like it is for your tourists with them fancy rifles."

Price laughed heartily. "*My* tourists? Really, Potts, you give me more credit than I deserve, but I'll graciously accept it. 'My tourists,' however, will be toting golf clubs and fishing poles. If you're after good hunting, I suggest you trade in your rifle on a rod and reel. The waterfowl management program has plans to stock this lake with bluegill, catfish, crappie, bass. In fact, fishing will attract most of the tourists, and they'll bring their skills that can only benefit the communities here. They'll bring their money, more importantly, and that will mean prosperity: paved roads, city water, sewer lines, telephone service, gas heating, better schools — "

"Price done give me a job, ain't that right, honey?" Bonnibelle interrupted.

"Oh, lordy," Griffin said, burying his shaggy head in his upturned palms.

"Oh?" Oona straightened with interest. "How much money you gonna make? He already got a secretary, don't he?"

"Now hold on," Price raised his hands, and a flush deepened his tan. "It's not exactly what you think."

Oona wagged her finger at Taffy. "Looks like you could learn a thing or two from your little sister, girl."

"But it's only temporary," Price said. "It's only one project, and we need... uh...her special talents."

"Lordy, lordy," Griffin repeated, breaking into a guffaw.

"Now you hush your mouth — "

"Well, Mama, it's true, ain't it? We all know what 'special talents' Bonnibelle has."

"You big, stupid oaf! You..." Taffy sprang to her feet, glared at her brother as if she wanted to add something else, then turned and ran out the back door.

Janie scraped her chair back, making a move to follow her.

"Leave her be," Oona said. "That girl's just gotta go off and sulk. Finish your supper."

"See what you gone and done now?" Bonnibelle said, sticking her tongue out at Griffin.

"Me? What did I do?"

"Now don't you pick on your brother. It ain't his fault about Taffy."

"What's wrong with Taffy?" Jeff asked.

"Nothing's wrong with her that a husband wouldn't fix good," said Oona, her cheeks jiggling with determination.

"As I was saying about your piece of property," Price said, clearing his throat.

That's all it was to him — a piece of property. "If Grandpa deeded the property to me," Janie said quickly to cut him off, "then he must have trusted me to make the decisions regarding its fate. But I can assure all of you that I won't make any hasty decisions. There are too many questions that I need answers to first."

Seymour lifted his head and stared at her with bleary, red eyes. "Wha'd'ya mean? What kind of questions?"

"For instance, what happened to Grandpa?"

"Oh, pee-shaw," Oona said. "It's like I done told you. He was a fool old man and got caught with his pants down."

"Don't you know?" Bonnibelle smirked. "He drowned."

"I found his boat." Griffin stabbed a thumb at his own chest, swelling with pride. "It warshed up over yonder in Crockett's hollow."

"No one was supposed to be out on the river at the time," Price said. "I guess the rush of water was too strong for his boat and it capsized. His body was never found, but there are still a lot of trees at the bottom of the lake that things can get tangled in. It might still surface."

Janie fought back the tears that threatened her eyes. "But *why* would he have been on the river when he wasn't supposed to be?"

"'Cause he was too ornery." Admiration beamed from behind Griffin's whiskers. "Warn't nobody going to tell him what to do."

"Maybe," Janie said. "But if the river was flooding, Grandpa would've understood the danger of being out on it. I can't believe he would've risked his life just because he was stubborn."

Jeff perked up to the conversation. "Maybe he *wanted* to die."

A chill coursed through Janie. She didn't believe that, either, which left only one option. If he hadn't gone to the river willingly, then someone had coerced him to go. The same someone who tore up his house later? It was time to change the subject. "Then, there's the question of my mother. What made her run away from home, and why didn't she ever come back?"

"Who wants more gravy?" Oona said, suddenly heaving herself to her feet and heading for the stove.

Seymour's fist dropped onto the table, and dishes jumped. A flush spread through his pasty white skin, and he fixed his black eyes on Janie.

"Daddy?" Griffin sat poised to spring to his father's aid.

But Seymour ignored him and continued to stare at Janie. She thought he was having a stroke, and then he spoke softly. "Girl, I reckon you got too many questions."

Janie stared back, speechless. The big, gentle cousin wasn't as gentle, nor as drunk, as she'd thought. If he was expecting an apology from her, then he wasn't going to get it. She had a right to ask her questions. More than that, she had a right to the answers.

Oona, holding a pot, lumbered back to the table. "You ask me, I think Janie's making a mountain out of a mole hill. Iffen she wants to know how's come her mama run off like she done, well, lots of folks run off like that and never come home again. So what? Fern always was a little tetched in the head." Her cheeks flushed and suddenly she devoted her attention to the pot, stirring it so hard that gravy spilled.

Janie felt herself bristle as she watched Oona pour a ladle full of gravy onto Jeff's plate. Until she understood the reasons for her mother's behavior, she had no words of defense for her, either.

"Now, honey child," Oona continued, waving the dripping ladle in Jeff's direction, "whyn't you tell us what you was up to? Did you find that there tree house of Griffy's?"

Jeff's face immediately shone, and he chattered about the fort in the oak tree and the creek he'd had to wade through to get there. He pulled acorns out of his pockets and lined them up on the table as proof he'd been there. "I used my binoculars up there and spied a pirate!"

"What would a pirate be doing — "

"Mo-om, it's just pretend. His eye patch sure makes him look like a pirate."

Seymour came to attention. "Son-of-a-bitch. It's only June. He ain't got no call stepping foot on my property, not till the corn's ready."

"Daddy!" Oona's anger matched her husband's. "You hush your mouth with talk like that at my supper table. We got company. Besides, them woods ain't your property. Ain't it enough that you was the one that done took Dexter's eye? Ain't you got over that fight yet?" Then she banged the pot onto the stove and turned around to wag her finger at Jeff. "And you stay clean away from that man, you hear?"

"Mama, how's come you say a thing like that 'bout your own brother?" asked Griffin.

"*Half*-brother, 'tis all. Anyhow, nigh everyone's kin 'round here, but that don't stop some of 'em from being crazy in the head. You mark my words." Oona directed her last comment at Price as she dropped back into her chair, shaking the floor and rattling the dishes. Then, as an afterthought, she added, "I reckon Dexter ain't got no call to blame no one but hisself for his problems."

Bonnibelle yawned and jumped into the conversation. "Dexter, Dexter, Dexter. What's so bad about Dexter? He got hisself a fancy boat, so he cain't be all bad. I seen him zipping around the lake in it."

"Girl, you ain't supposed to be down there," Oona said, biting her words again.

"Mom!" Jeff, unable to contain his enthusiasm, bounced in his seat. "Maybe he'll take us to that island in his boat. You promised!"

"Island?" asked Oona with a frown. "What island, child?"

"Boat?" Griffin echoed. "What boat?"

Jeff wiggled with impatience. "You know. The island in the *lake*."

"You ain't gonna ride in no boat," Griffin said, his voice snapping.

Jeff bounced again in his seat, and a whine edged into his voice. "Mom, you promised."

"I haven't forgotten. But it may take a while."

Griffin sucked in air, reminding Janie of a bull, gathering steam before the charge. "There ain't no island out there," he said.

"Sure there is. I saw it real good in my binoculars."

"Boy, somebody ought to bust them things for you."

"Hey — " Janie started to protest, but Oona cut her off.

"Griffy's right," Oona said. "What you must've seen was a clump of trees that ain't dead yet, poking up out of the water. Sometimes it takes a while, when there's a deadening, for all the trees to die."

"But there aren't any trees on *that* island."

Oona frowned. "Well, I reckon I don't know about that. But it sure is a pity to see all that fine land under water."

"Can't we ask him?" Jeff said. "Let's ask Dexter to take us out on the lake in his boat!"

Oona snarled. "You ever git near that man, and I'll take a *hickory* to your BEE-hind."

Jeff shrank back. His eyes grew wide.

"Now just a minute — " Janie said, feeling her protective hormones kick in.

Bonnibelle laughed. "Mama, you're always mixed up. How's come you don't mind Griffy working over yonder at Dexter's?"

The ugly splotches of purple on Seymour's cheeks faded as he studied Griffin. "Son," he finally said, "a man got to do...what a man got to do." Scraping his chair back, signaling an end to the meal, he rose and disappeared behind the curtain hiding the bed in the corner of the room. Springs squeaked.

It wasn't only a man, Janie thought, who had to do what she had to do.

Griffin, ignoring them all, leaned across the table and aimed his venomous glare at Janie. "No one wants you snooping around out there on the lake *or* at Tobias Mullen's house, so whyn't you go on back to the city where you belong?"

Janie, tired of this sentiment, took a deep breath as another moment of silence descended on the table. "I'm not going anywhere until I know where my grandfather is."

Oona cackled. "I reckon that fool old man is at the bottom of that there deadening. Where else would he be?"

"No matter where he is," Janie said, "I won't leave until I find out. No matter how long it takes. Grandpa would've wanted that. I won't disappoint him." *Again*, she added silently.

"You talk like he's still alive," Griffin said.

Maybe he is, she thought, remembering the fresh food she'd found in the kitchen. Could something so horrible have happened to cause her grandfather to go into hiding?

No, she wasn't going to leave. Not yet. And no one was going to frighten her away before she was ready to go. She stuck out her chin and matched Griffin's glare, and that's when she realized all eyes had turned on her. In the corner of the room, the curtains were pulled back, and Seymour watched her, too. For once this family seemed at a loss of words.

SIX

When Janie opened Oona's front door and stepped out into dusk, the locusts rattled like a buzz saw in her head. She stumbled off the cement block. Price steadied her, took her by the arm and led the way to a silver Cadillac, looking out of place amidst the collection of junk cars.

"You must be rich, or something," Jeff said, scampering into the back seat.

Price laughed. "This isn't my idea of the best car for these back roads, but Dad insisted that if I want to be successful then I have to look successful."

"But you don't believe that?" Janie asked, noting the hint of impatience in his voice.

He shrugged. "It's his money. He's financing this venture, which gives him the right to tell me how to run the business. He's good at it, too, running businesses, that is, so I listen to his advice, whether I like it or not. But the day this car breaks down on these roads, I'll trade it in on a Jeep."

Nevertheless, the car he disliked rode smoothly over the rutted roads, through the darker areas of woods at dusk, illumined by sprinkles of fireflies. "Anyway, it's good of you to take us home." She said that word so easily. Home. Is that what it would become?

Janie wished she didn't have to face the night ahead in a tent. It wasn't the dark itself that frightened her, but the feeling of being smothered by dark. The fact that someone had been in Grandpa's house, destroying things, didn't help her discomfort. What if he returned, like Oona suggested?

"When will you be ready to take a tour of your place?" Price asked. "Tomorrow?"

Even in the deep shadows of the car's interior, she could see the anxious tilt of his head. She could almost hear him holding his breath.

She told him, then, about the state of the house, that it was more than just a "mess" from being closed up for the winter as Oona had described. She told him about Seymour's idea that a gang of mischievous boys had vandalized the place. Reporting it to the sheriff, then setting it straight would require all her attention for a while. A tour would have to wait. A decision to sell would have to wait even longer.

He didn't like it, she could tell. He hunched over the steering wheel and gripped it as if he might lose it.

"We'll change the locks," he said finally.

She laughed, but it sounded nervous even to her. "I didn't think people had to lock their doors in the country."

"Times are changing."

"Then Griffin is right to be unhappy about it."

Jeff leaned forward from the back seat and spoke to Price. "Boy, Griffin sure was mad at you! Is he always that mad at you?"

Price tried to laugh it off. "He holds me personally responsible for all his problems."

"Like, what are his problems?"

Janie waved him off the back of the leather seat and reminded him of his seatbelt. "Isn't it enough that these people have lost their river to a resort lake? That's going to change their whole way of life. It doesn't necessarily mean that anyone has a 'problem.' Try to be more understanding."

"Jeff is right, though," said Price. "Griffin's taking it harder than most. He's not going to adapt without a fight."

"Do you think that's what Grandpa was doing when he disappeared? Fighting the changes?"

Price shrugged and remained silent while he turned into a swarm of fireflies hovering above Grandpa's driveway. When the car stopped, Jeff jumped out and chased the dancing sparkles of light. Price hurried around the car's fender to meet Janie as she stepped out without his help. Against the shadows of dusk, she saw the white flash of his grin. Then he shrugged and headed for the porch. When he tried the door, he said, "It's locked."

"Because I locked it." She smiled with a trace of irritation at his forward manner. It would take a lot to stop this man once he was determined to do something. "Did you want to see the destruction?"

"Please." He stepped back and thrust his hands into his pockets, as if impatient at the delay.

He always seemed to be in a hurry, Janie thought, moving past Jeff, who was clapping his hands at the elusive fireflies. She caught up with Price on the porch and dug into her purse for the skeleton key. "Do you think whoever tore up Grandpa's house was expressing his anger at all the changes going on around here?"

He chuckled and leaned against the splintery frame of the house. "Folks around here aren't that romantic. I think Seymour's idea is closer to the truth."

"Since when is expressing anger a romantic notion?"

Studying her silently, he was a shadowy outline against a background of pink and mauve streaks, which was all that remained from the sunset on the opposite side of the lake. Finally, he said, "I might be able to help you find out what happened to him."

The sudden change in conversation startled Janie enough that her grip slipped from her bag. Catching it against her knees, she wondered if he was keeping quiet about something he already knew. "What do you mean?"

"I mean, I know people. We can ask around. I'll start with Granny Rose."

"Who's Granny Rose?"

"My grandmother. She knows a little bit about herbs and roots and that sort of thing, so around here, people call her the 'yarb doctor.' They go to her with their ailments because she can usually give them the right herb. Consequently, she knows everyone. If anyone knows anything about your grandpa, Granny Rose will know."

Her fingers found the heavy key under her wallet. "If she knows something, why hasn't she already spoken up?"

"She practices patient confidentiality."

"But surely she wouldn't keep quiet if...if there'd been..." Unable to say it, she inserted the key and rattled it around, feeling the lock tumble.

"If there'd been foul play?" He hovered close to her side as she opened the door. "Perhaps she'll talk to us if we ask the right questions."

She didn't like the "we" idea, but one way or another, she would have to meet this Granny Rose. Groping on the wall for the light switch, she found it and flicked it on. "What...?"

Price followed her into the front room. "It doesn't look torn up to me."

She surveyed the righted furniture, the pictures back on the walls, the swept-up floor. "But it *was*! Oona and Seymour saw it, too. Someone has been here cleaning up."

"Guess you have nothing to report to the sheriff now."

"No... I mean... I don't know." Had whoever cleaned this up wanted to prevent her from going to the sheriff, or simply destroy her credibility? Either way, it worked.

"Well, then, how about that tour tomorrow?"

He was too persistent, she thought. "Give me a day or two to get settled."

"All right, then. Day after tomorrow."

She had no response as she stood there, transfixed in the restored room.

∾

THE AIR WAS DEAD STILL. A body could see it hanging there in a haze over Seymour's cornfields. Nossir, it wasn't moving a lick, not even out here on the porch where Oona had come for an evening of ruminating now that the supper dishes were done, along with the day.

But she'd have to tell her stories to the chickens squabbling in the yard. Her kin all had other fish to fry. She lowered her chin into the folds of her neck and pushed her rocker into angry motion.

Humph, she thought, rubbing her palm. *What good is family for if they up and leave you?*

Soon as the last supper dish was washed, Janie said she had to get her boy to bed, and Oona said then put him down up in the attic, but Janie said no they weren't going to "impose" any longer, they had a tent rigged up which would do right nice, so Price jumped in, sniffing an opportunity same as any coon dog after table scraps, and said he'd drive them home. And they left, just like that.

She rubbed her palm across her chin.

'Course, Bonnibelle was fit to be tied. You could still hear her taking it out on Griffy, up there in the attic, which was where all five of her children had slept. Only three of them still lived at home. The curtain she'd tacked up to separate the girls' half from the boys' half wasn't enough to keep them from fighting. Griffy was such a good boy. It irked Oona that Bonnibelle had to pick on him all the time.

Dang it, but her hand itched!

No sooner had Janie left than Seymour come out from the bedroom corner, hitching up his britches and saying he had to go check on his hogs. Next thing Oona knew, she heard his truck. He was off to Earl's Pool Hall, no doubt, but she figured her husband wasn't fixing to shoot no pool.

She worked her palm furiously against the wooden armrest of her mama's rocker.

Then there was Taffy. Oona didn't rightly know what was wrong with her oldest girl. Lately, she couldn't stand to be around her kin no more. She never did come back after that tiff at supper tonight, and Oona reckoned she was still off sulking in the woods. Taffy was nervous as a treed coon these days.

Girls never was nothing but trouble, Oona thought, scratching with ragged nails. Not like her boys.

Every last one of the young'uns was too busy to keep Oona company. Every last one of them thought they didn't need her no more 'cause they were too big for their britches. They thought they could grow up and leave her all alone. Oona stomped harder against the porch floor.

And then she remembered. She stared, wide-eyed, at her itching palm. Money! Her mama had always said that an itching palm meant you was to come into money. Lord knew, Mama had been right before. Nigh on thirty years ago, she remembered now, her palm couldn't quit itching, and the next thing she knew, Uncle Tobias was giving her and Seymour an acre of land for a wedding present. Her palm itched then like it itched now, and she stared long and hard at her calluses. The more she rubbed, the more it itched.

Money! Could it be that she'd get the rest of Uncle Tobias's place, now that he was gone? Lord knew, she deserved it, not Fern's girl. All the hard work she and Seymour put in over there...

"Mama, what ya doing out here all by your lonesome?"

She nearly jumped out of her skin. "Griffy! You ain't got no call sneaking up on a body like that."

He shrugged and ducked back into the kitchen. The sound of his heavy boots like to shook the walls of the house. Pride swelled in her heart as she listened to his movements, scrounging for more vittles. Her son had growed up into such a handsome man. He had such broad shoulders and such a strong back. He'd make some lucky girl a good husband. Unlike Seymour.

"Son, what was you and Bonnibelle squawking about tonight?"

He grunted and stomped even harder.

"You still hot under the collar about that Wanamaker boy?"

Swinging a rifle in one hand and holding a piece of left-over squirrel in the other, Griffy stomped out onto the porch. "I don't like him, Mama."

"No, son, I reckon you don't. But you cain't argue with his money, and Bonnibelle's aiming to get her hands on it."

"We don't need his kind of money 'round here. And Bonnibelle don't need the likes of him."

"Maybe not, but he's got more money than you'll ever see slopping hogs for Dexter. Your daddy's already fit to be tied over that. You know he and Dexter don't get along."

A slow grin split through Griffy's fine crop of coal black whiskers. "Don't you worry none about Daddy. He don't hate Dexter near as much as you think. And as for Bonnibelle, what she needs is a husband, but not that one."

"Don't you sass your mama. You men don't know nothing, do you?" She glared at his rifle, which he was swinging like a toy. "You fixing to leave me, too?"

"We-e-e-ell, I got to do a little job, see, for Dexter."

"Tonight?"

"Yes'm. Some varmint's been stirring up the hogs and getting into his feed bin."

"And you're going to stand guard?" She broke into a cackling laughter. "Why, I never heard no sech!"

"Don't laugh, Mama, it might be more important than you think. You want a mountain lion to come 'round here and get your chickens?"

She sobered instantly. "No, son, I reckon I don't. You take care, you hear?"

"I hear ya, Mama. Don't wait up."

"Don't be gone all night, neither." She watched his hulk fade into the shadows.

Yessir, he's gonna do all right for hisself, thanks to Dexter. Long as Fern's girl don't get in the way.

It was funny how things kept repeating themselves. Her cousin Fern had come close to spoiling things for Oona back in their school days. Well, slap her bones, she wasn't about to let Janie spoil a lick for *her* boy. Nor for Bonnibelle, neither. Not one lick. She didn't care who Janie thought she was.

Oona scratched her palm and leaned heavily into her furious rocking, rocking but getting nowhere.

A train whistle moaned in the distance. Its rumble amplified over the miles, making it sound like it was just over yonder. But she knew the tracks skirted Stony Lonesome, the nearest town some ten miles away.

"A good rain is on its way, sure as the rooster crows," she said with a sigh and no one to hear her.

Surrounded by kin but all alone in the world, Oona leaned her head back and thought on the promise of a real rain, not like the sprinkles that had teased them this afternoon, only making things steamier. She hoped the promised rain would be one of those long, slow drizzles that soaked into the soil and put an end to this mule kill'n weather. Not one of the angry kinds that washed out bridges and washed away her precious topsoil.

SEVEN

Against the palette of a fading sunset, the trees blended together into a mass of blackness. Fireflies floated and hovered around the tent, flicked on their lights for a few seconds, then flitted away.

From the confines of her sleeping bag, Janie watched the descending darkness as if it were an inky ceiling crushing down on her. The familiar feelings of suffocation were mounting. She was glad that Price had left quickly, so that she and Jeff could zip themselves into the tent before it got too dark. With the house hastily restored, they could've slept inside after all; however, she couldn't disappoint Jeff by backing out of her promise to camp out.

At least Jeff didn't suffer from claustrophobia like she did. The tent crinkled and swayed as he shifted next to her. One arm wrapped around Beads, the matted lion her mother had given him years ago. Although it was losing its stuffing, it hadn't lost any of its charm.

Even unzipped, the sleeping bag made her sweat. The steamy air felt heavy and binding around her, and the two sloping sides of the tent seemed closer than they had a few minutes ago. She wiggled nearer to Jeff. The hard ground jabbed through her bag in uneven bumps. She wanted to cling to him the way he snuggled with Beads.

"Mom?"

"Hmmm?"

"What's that thing flashing out there in the lake? It looks like a lighthouse."

"It does, rather, but it's a channel marker, which is just a big buoy with a light on it. Larger boats need to stay in the channel because it's deeper there, but at night they don't know where the channel is unless it's marked with a light."

"Lookit, Mom! You can still see the island." He dropped Beads and stabbed at the screened flap.

She propped herself up on elbows and peered intently through the flap. "Is that the island you were talking about tonight? The one that got everyone so upset at Oona's?"

"Uh-huh. Boy, they sure got sore, didn't they?"

"You're right, Jeff. There's definitely an island, although it's pretty hard to see. It's so far away. Maybe a mile or so."

"But see how it looks like it's just behind that lighthouse thing? It sorta' looks like that dragon on Dad's arm, don't it?"

Janie stiffened at the mention of Roy and his tattoo. "I don't see how that's possible."

"The flashing red light on that lighthouse marker thing looks like its eye."

"Oh. You're right. I can see your dragon now." It took a child's eyes to stir her imagination. "Grandpa used to tell me a story about a dragon. I haven't thought of it in years."

"Tell it!"

"I can't remember it exactly. It was something about a dragon that lived in a cave on the other side of the river."

"Wow!"

His enthusiasm fueled her story. She could almost hear Grandpa's throaty chuckle and the creak of his rocker as he used to spin yarns to his captivated audience before Auntie Mae would come out and scold him for putting notions in the young'uns' heads. She could almost smell the rich tobacco as he puffed on his pipe.

"There were wild hills over there, on the other side of the river, and no one lived there." She couldn't remember the dragon story exactly, but that didn't matter. It was her story now. "No one ever saw the dragon, because it lived in a large cave in one of the hills. But plenty of folks had seen the smoke from its breath, and every once in a while some folks even heard it roar. Auntie Mae didn't believe there really was a dragon, but she told us kids never to go over there, anyway. And then one day Grandpa took me."

"Did you find the dragon?"

She laughed. "No, but I thought the dragon had found me. I didn't stay in the cave long enough to see if it was him or not."

"What happened?"

"It was so dark in there. The walls got narrower and narrower, and all of a sudden I felt like the dragon himself was sitting on my chest, choking me." That was the first time she'd discovered that she was claustrophobic. It was the same way she felt now, inside the tent, as the last traces of pink from twilight faded into the absolute blackness of a rural night. Grandpa had comforted her then, taking her on his lap, smoothing her pony tail against her back, whispering "there, there's" to her. She didn't have anyone to comfort her now.

"But it wasn't really a dragon, huh?" Jeff sounded disappointed.

"*Something* was in that cave. Auntie Mae thought it was probably a mountain lion, but I don't know..."

"Maybe my island is your hill with the dragon's cave. Will you take me there like Grandpa took you?"

"First, we'd have to get a boat."

"Oh, yeah, I forgot. It's just a dream. It's okay, Mom."

"There might be a way."

He yawned. "Tell me another story, Mom. Where else weren't you allowed to go?"

"Right here. We weren't allowed to come up here. These cliffs were 'mountains' to us down there in the valley. We had to stay down there. Auntie Mae warned us never to come up here."

"How come?"

"I don't suppose it would have anything to do with worry that we might fall over the edge of that cliff?"

"Is that all?"

Janie laughed. Having his attention, she enjoyed keeping him in suspense. "No, there's more. Every so often, Auntie Mae would dig up one of her favorite flowers from the garden and disappear off into the woods. Taffy and I followed her once, and she climbed up here to the top of these cliffs where she sat down and stared out over the valley. For a while we were afraid she might jump over the edge. Auntie Mae sometimes seemed a bit queer to us. People called her a 'spinster', as if that made her different. We didn't know better."

"Go on," Jeff said. "What happened? Did she jump?"

Janie laughed softly. "No, of course not. Nothing happened. She just sat there. We finally got bored and ran back to the house before we were caught.

Then forgot all about it. Until now. Strange. I wonder why she brought flowers?"

"It must have been a grave!" The whites of his eyes shone in the darkness.

"Maybe. Although, there was no cemetery."

"Oh boy, a mystery! We'll have to find that grave!"

She smiled at her son's imagination. "And then what, Inspector? Exhume the body? If anything, it was just a beloved pet. Auntie Mae had a way of loving everything that crossed her threshold."

"Why would she bury a cat or a dog up here?"

A disturbing thought, indeed. Janie shifted closer to him, but the ground still seemed as hard. "I don't know. Auntie Mae did a lot of things I never understood."

"Like what?"

"For instance, her collections. She kept everything — postcards, matchbooks, buttons, newspaper clippings."

"Maybe she buried some treasure up here!"

"Then why the flowers?"

"I dunno. They mark the spot, maybe. But just think, Mom, if it's a grave, our tent could be on top of it!"

"I'd rather not think about that."

"Maybe there's a ghost around here."

"Maybe."

Silence. "Do you believe in ghosts, Mom?"

"No. Go to sleep."

"Well, I hope I find him."

Crickets hummed steadily as the locusts' ratchety noise rose and fell. A hoot owl called, and a dog bayed somewhere in the distance. Next to her, Jeff's breathing deepened as sleep finally overcame him.

Janie watched the darkness deepen and felt her panic rise to match it. Her breath came in shallow spurts. Crickets and frogs and snakes and owls and mountain lions. All of them were out there, talking to her in their different voices. Each and every one of them warned her to go away. Like the enraged person who'd torn up Grandpa's house... A person who could move through locked doors and clean up the evidence of that rage...

Gasping, she wiggled far enough out of her sleeping bag so that she could press her nose against the screen of the tent's flap. The pattern of two red flashes from the channel marker gave her something to focus on from under the black blanket of smothering, blinding night. The dragon's eye, Jeff had called it. How could he sleep with the insects' racket?

Would this night never end? Her chin dropped onto clasped hands, and her eyes burned with fatigue.

She thought about the promise she'd made at supper tonight. Without having to pay rent, she and Jeff could live off her savings maybe for as long as a year. Eventually, though, she'd slip back into her clerical rut. Unless she could sell a screenplay... Fat chance.

Blink. Blink. Focusing on the red light of the channel marker soothed her with its hypnotic message of sleep. She counted the ripples that its beam reached across and thought about the dragon on Roy's arm.

Roy. He was one of the biggest mistakes of her life. Was coming here another mistake? She'd promised Jeff they'd stay at least for the summer.

Eighty-six, eighty-seven...

Then there were the lost dreams...

～

JANIE AWOKE WITH A START sometime later. Her back stiffened, and she lifted her cheek from the bumpy ground to peer through the tent flap. Something was out of place.

The clouds had parted, but there was no moon. Barely visible, the front porch appeared quiet. Although the red light continued to flash, something made the channel marker seem more distant now. The darkness wasn't as dark as it had been.

She blinked, but she couldn't clear the fuzzy film covering her vision. She slithered out of the sleeping bag and slowly unzipped the tent flap. As if slowness would make less noise. The rustling of the tent and grating of the zipper seemed to take forever, and still Jeff slept through the noise. Outside, she stretched her aching limbs and drank deeply the damp air of the early morning hours.

Stopping in mid-gulp, she saw what must have awakened her. It was a narrow beam of light slicing through the woods in the distance, a spotlight searching for something. The light floated through the woods, drifting slowly toward the lake. When it reached the shoreline, the light didn't stop. It stretched across the water until it disappeared somewhere on the other side of the lake. What kind of light could reach that far?

The beam of light reappeared and began its return sweep, back across the water, heading toward Janie and the tent. Something rumbled in the distance, intruding into the insects' world of noise. The approaching beam sliced through swirls and puffs... Smoke? The air was damp, not smoky.

The sound grew in intensity. The sound seemed to come from the source of light. Then, through the woods in the foreground, she saw the colored running lights of a barge, and relief washed over her.

How could she have forgotten about the barges? They'd been like passing royalty on the old river. Grandpa had stopped his work in the fields to watch them pass. Auntie Mae, with dripping hands, had always come running out onto the porch to wave at them.

Now Janie moved, also, through the small clearing that was the new setting for Grandpa's house. She stumbled over the uneven ground, toward the edge of the cliff to get a better view of this night-time procession. The channel marker twinkled through swirls of — smoke? No. A thick blanket of fog hovered over the lake. Slicing through it, a single green light floated low over the water while fog and darkness swathed the actual barge itself.

Where was the rest of it? Janie remembered the game of counting the links the tug pushed. This one seemed much shorter, as if it had no links at all. It wasn't pushing a heavy load. Suddenly, a second beam of light switched on from the bridge, pierced the fog and swept toward shore, toward the spot where she stood on the cliff.

The vessel droned closer, under its cover of darkness. A nearby movement startled her, then, and her attention switched from the lake to the cliff beneath her. Leaves rustled somewhere below, and a shadow darted out onto the rocks jutting into the lake. Two tiny flashes of light winked from the shadow, as if the person crouching directly below her had signaled with a flashlight. Janie clasped her hand over her mouth to stifle a gasp. She shrank away from the edge of the cliff, hiding herself from view in case whoever was down there happened to glance up.

The barge sputtered and died, and finally it came to a complete stop. Lake water splashed against its hull where it sat, dead in the water, next to the channel marker. Distant voices called to each other over the bumping of metal. The breeze carried snatches of words her way.

"...kotch the rope..."

"...if Earl don't get this..."

She pressed herself against the twisted trunk of a nearby cedar and strained to hear more. The murmur of voices became grunts accompanied by dull thuds. Water dripped from the thing being hauled out of the lake and onto the barge's deck.

"Hack-in-chooooooey!"

Muffled grunts and punches of protest responded to the sneeze.

"...Wen, you danged fool..."

"...penitentiary we'uns..."

"...get rid of her, or come next week..."

The darkness of night faded into the fuzzy gray of predawn. Janie sucked in her breath, filling her lungs with the cedar's pungency, hoping her outline blended into her cover. If someone glanced up at the top of the cliff...

Then a single bird startled her with a piercing chirp from a branch over-head, and she jumped away from her protection for just an instant. Lake water stirred restlessly against the rocks of the cliff. The breeze carried impatient voices. Had they seen her movement? She held her breath and waited. A rooster crowed in the distance. Finally, the barge's engines rumbled to life again. Slowly, it started off down the river channel, and she let out a long sigh.

But her relief was short-lived when she heard something bump against the rocks below. Puzzled by the barge's activities, she'd forgotten momentarily about the shadowy person on the rocks who had signaled the barge with two flashes. Someone on the barge must have read the message and stopped in front of Grandpa's house. Had it something to do with the vandalism? Perhaps whatever it was that they'd hauled out of the water had come from Grandpa's house. And now, she realized with horror, she was alone in these woods with that messenger. Maybe he'd been the one who'd vandalized the house. The one who could pass through locked doors.

Janie backed away, holding her breath with each step. She had to get back to her son. Not caring anymore whether or not she made noise, she stumbled back across the clearing and thrashed through the brush. Branches lashed at her in the grayness of predawn, holding her back. They had to make it to the safety of their car before the shadow found them, but then where would they go?

She yanked open the tent flap and reached to shake Jeff awake, but a new noise stopped her. From the foot of Grandpa's cliffs came the sound of an outboard motor, sputtering and turning over. Some small boat roared away.

Then he was gone. She slumped to the ground. No use to run now, she thought. In fact, she *wouldn't* run. She wasn't the trespasser — *he* was. And if he knew anything about Grandpa, then she'd stay and face him, if he returned, and get that information out of him. She'd look for "Earl," too, and she'd better find him fast. Next week might be too late for her.

EIGHT

*T*he fog burned off early, leaving behind the promise of another sultry day. Birds sang a medley of morning songs over the background rhythm of locusts. Criss-crossing ripples glittered on the lake, dispelling the memory of last night's sinister activities. It almost seemed like a dream. But not quite.

Sitting on a flat rock jutting out into the lake, Janie cleaned up the remains of their picnic breakfast of stale doughnuts. She watched Jeff scamper across the rocky shoreline and thought about all that she had to do. Mundane tasks, like finding a filling station, a grocery store, and a Laundromat.

And she had to find the sheriff. Mounting questions needed answering, besides the vandalism here. Earl. The barge...

Something rustled in the brush behind her, where the rocky cliff gave way to a wooded hill. Bonnibelle stood there, balancing the baby on her hip. The baby batted at the blonde ends of her mother's hair, but Bonnibelle ignored her. She stared at the lake through raccoon circles painted around her eyes, and her mouth worked hard on its wad of gum.

"Hoo, boy! Ain't it going to be another scorcher today?"

"Did you walk all the way here? Isn't it awfully far?"

"Not if you follow the crik." She nodded at the cove behind her, where a creek trickled into the lake.

"Man oh man! Don't it feel good here! Lord, that breeze!" Bonnibelle adjusted her tank top and fanned her throat. "We don't get that breeze up home. Must be the lake, you reckon? Too bad Mama and Daddy don't have theirselves a place down here."

"What brings you here?" Janie glanced at her watch. She didn't need visitors with all that she had to do.

"Mama says you got to take me and Prissy up town right quick."

"Quick? Is everything okay?"

"When Mama wants something, you don't want to stop and ask questions."

"Well, as it happens, I was getting ready to leave for town anyway. Now it looks like you can show me the way." The prospect of Bonnibelle's company was only slightly better than the other possibility of getting lost and running out of gas.

Within a half hour, they'd all piled into the VW and bounced over the same maze of roads Janie and her son had followed yesterday afternoon to Oona's house. Where they'd forked left to go up the last hill to the Potts' acre, they now forked right around a bend hidden by a bank of kudzu spilling out to the road's edge. As fast as those vines grew, Janie wondered how soon the kudzu would cut them off from town and civilization. Before the end of summer? Next week? Tomorrow?

Bonnibelle hummed with apparent contentment from the passenger seat. Resting an elbow in the open window, she angled her head to catch the full force of the air. Her other arm rested lightly around the baby, and other than that, she seemed to have forgotten that the child teetered there, reaching for things for her budding teeth to sample.

Janie kept one eye on the baby and one eye on the road, filled with ruts. She only heard half of what Jeff was saying from the back seat about the cliffs he'd already explored. When he finally finished relating his adventures, she decided to tell them about the barge that had awakened her last night and about the shadowy figure that had signaled it.

"I plumb knew it!" Bonnibelle said, tightening her hold on the baby. "You didn't see no shadow. You saw Uncle Tobias's ghost. I heard tell it come back. Ain't that just like that old geezer? Never will give up that place. Now he's got to haunt it. He always swore that when the river died, he'd up and die right along with it. No one was supposed to go down into the valley a'tall, but old Uncle Tobias, he up and disappeared one day with his boat, and we figgered he must've meant what he said."

"You mean...he committed suicide?"

"Me and Mama reckon so."

"I can't believe that. He was always so full of life. He would never take his — "

"How would you know? You wasn't ever here!"

"Yes, I was. You were just a baby then."

"Well, I mean closer to the end."

She flinched. Bonnibelle didn't have to remind her of the guilt that had finally driven Janie here.

"Wow! Mom, did you really see a ghost? A real, honest-to-gosh ghost? You gotta wake me up next time. I'd give anything to see a real ghost. I'd even give Beads. Well, maybe not Beads, but almost anything."

"First of all, Jeff, there's no such thing as — "

"My great-grandpa's a ghost!"

"No, he's *not*. For all we know, Grandpa wandered off someplace — "

"No way," said Bonnibelle. "Only way you'd ever get that old man to up and leave this place was to shoot him."

"That's an awful thing to say."

Jeff bounced in the back seat. "Did someone shoot him?"

Bonnibelle laughed, but it wasn't a happy sound. "I never said that, and you shut your mouth about it, you hear?"

An awkward silence filled the VW as they approached another fork in the road. Janie stopped the car, a habit, yielding to oncoming traffic. Of course the lane was empty.

"Lookit, Mom." Jeff leaned forward from the back seat and pointed straight ahead.

Two planks served as a bridge over a creek, meandering down the hill from the direction of the Potts's pasture. Janie wondered if this was the same creek that eventually emptied into the lake by Grandpa's house.

"Who's that?" Jeff asked.

"Oh no." Bonnibelle groaned. "Listen, can we just go on?"

Janie looked again, and then she saw her. In the heavy shade of the woods by the creek, a woman bent over her shovel. She straightened from her work and turned to look at the stopped car. She was a small woman, dressed all in black, right down to her sturdy, laced-up shoes. Her pant skirt was straight and simple, but her blouse ruffled at the high collar around her throat. A wide-brimmed hat shaded her brow. A silver bun coiled at the nape of her neck.

After only a moment of hesitation, she threw down her shovel and laid a gloved finger on her cheek. Her pale white arm fluttered a greeting at Janie as she picked her way carefully out of the woods toward the car.

"Let's go," Bonnibelle muttered, placing both arms around the baby on her lap.

Janie glanced at Bonnibelle, then back at the woman, who was pulling off her black gloves, revealing withered skin. Clutching her chest with one hand, she used her other hand to wave her gloves at them. "Yoo-hoo!"

"Let's *go*," Bonnibelle said.

"But she wants to talk to us."

Out of breath, the old woman hurried through the underbrush and crossed the road. When she approached the car, she offered a handshake through the open window. Purple ridges stood out on the backs of her bony hands. They were working hands.

"Why, if it isn't that nice, young Janie Bainbridge, all grown up!" she said, drilling her with the intense blue of her eyes. With gloves tucked under one arm, she clasped Janie's hand with both of hers. "Welcome home, dear! And this must be your son? What a fine looking young man you are! You must come and sample my molasses cookies. Is Bonnibelle showing you around? Such a dear! I hope baby Prissy is over the colic by now. Did my little remedy help?"

"Who are you?" Jeff said.

"Jeff!"

The woman tilted back her head and laughed with a sound like tinkling bells. "No, no, my dear, you mustn't scold him for being direct. It is a quality to admire. I declare, but sometimes I can prattle on, can't I? Of course you wouldn't remember me. You was just a little thing, no bigger than Prissy here. I'm Rose Bender, dear. Your great-aunt."

Janie's eyes widened with surprise. "Great-aunt Rose," she repeated.

"But you must simply call me Rose. I'm your grandmother Esther's little sister, you know."

"Then, you, that is..." Janie stammered, feeling breathless. "You're the third sister? You, my grandmother, and Oona's mother?"

Rose's smile faded, and she hesitated, as if unsure of her response. "That's right, dear," she finally said, and then brightened. "You must stop in to see me any time, and we'll get reacquainted over a pot of tea."

"Thank you. How very kind."

"I live over yonder in Chittenden Bay. Alas, I don't often walk as far as I used to, and that's why I haven't come to welcome you. I must rely on Price for my transportation, but his work keeps him so busy. You must come to me, instead, dear."

"I would be happy to." So her great-aunt was Price's Granny Rose, the yarb doctor. "Could I give you a ride home now? You can't be all that close to your home."

"Thank you, dear, but I've found a lovely little clump of goldenseal, and I need more of its root. Which reminds me..." Rose bent down to smile at Bonnibelle. "Would you remind your sister to take only the smallest pinch? Too much, and it can work like a poison."

Bonnibelle shrugged, and Rose straightened. Janie glanced back and forth between them.

"Can we go now?" Bonnibelle asked.

"Of course, my dears, you must be off." Rose waved gaily then turned her back on them and headed for the creek where she'd left her shovel.

"Well!" Janie steered the car onto the bridge. "So that was the 'yarb doctor.' Tell me, Bonnibelle, what's that goldenseal — "

"That old woman don't know what she's talking about, and you can just forget about it, you hear?"

Bonnibelle's words hit her with the force of a slap. Janie concentrated on the road ahead and vowed that she wouldn't forget. In spite of the silence hanging heavy in the car, her spirits lifted. Rose Bender, her great-aunt, might know something about Grandpa.

The road leveled out, and a broad river with a muddy expanse of stagnant water came into view. The road and the river followed a parallel course as they closed the gap to the nearest town.

"That there's called the Red Dew River," Bonnibelle finally said, breaking the silence. "Stony Lonesome's up yonder."

They rounded a bend and saw the first buildings of town. A white clapboard church sat on a knoll overlooking the river. Farther along was a cluster of squat buildings in desperate need of fresh paint. A neon sign in front of the central building read "The Lazy Dew Motel." At least, that's what Janie assumed it would read if half its lightbulbs weren't broken. In a dirt field in front of the motel, several parked cars turned askew to each other. Nothing was moving.

"There's Griffin's car," Bonnibelle said. "I got to go fetch him for Mama. Just let me out there."

Janie had scarcely stopped the car before Bonnibelle sprang out of it, then pushed the baby back into her empty seat. "I'll only be a minute," she said, slamming the door behind her.

The baby stuck out her bottom lip and screwed up her eyes. She turned to Janie and bawled.

"Oh, goodness, don't cry! Your mother will be right back." She pulled the ring of keys from the ignition and offered them to the baby. She hoped she was right.

It was an old motel, consisting of separate cottages that strung along the riverbank. Tall sycamores spread their canopy of leaves above the roofs and out over the river where several aluminum fishing boats were tied up to a dock. Down the road, past the cottages, was a similar building with a sign that simply read "Pool Hall." Nothing stirred along the row of shacks as the minutes ticked by.

"I think I'll go in and find out what's keeping her," she said after ten more minutes had passed. "Come on, Prissy. Let's go find your mother. Jeff, you can stay outside if you want, but keep off the dock. It looks as if it'll fall in, any minute."

A fog of cigar smoke hung in the dim lobby. Two wrinkled men lounged in vinyl chairs in the corner. Their conversation instantly stifled upon her entry, and the ends of their cigars glowed at her with expectancy.

After Janie failed to speak right away, the short, pudgy man poked the lanky man and said, "Well, Gus, I reckon I best go see what she wants."

He rose slowly, hitched his pants up to his paunch and limped around to the opposite side of a counter. "Well, howdy do. You must be the Potts cousin. What can I do you for?"

"I, uh, was looking for Bonnibelle." She wondered if there was anyone in town who didn't know yet about her arrival.

His potbelly shook, but the only sound that came out of his throat was a wheeze. Grandpa used to laugh like that, Janie remembered.

"She done skedaddled out the back door. She stick you with that?" He waved his stubby fingers and cigar in the direction of the baby.

"She left?" A mixture of anger and panic welled within her like the drop of baby drool that landed on her forearm.

His belly shook again, and he pushed the cigar into his broad grin, clamping his teeth around it.

"She was looking for her brother," Janie explained, as if that might summon Bonnibelle. "His car is out front."

"That what she told ya?" he said.

"She means Griffin," Gus said from the corner. "All tother boys are working the barges."

"The barges?" She turned to look at the man in the corner, his long limbs folded into assorted angles.

The short man behind the counter pulled the cigar from his mouth and frowned at Janie. "That's what he done said, girlie."

"Where do they go? The barges, I mean."

"Up and down the river."

Gus coughed and slapped his knee. "They run out of Nashv'lle and go as far as the river lets them. Mostly haul coal 'round these here parts."

"Mostly but not always?"

"Gus, I reckon I can handle this," the man behind the counter said, stabbing his cigar in an ashtray, then facing Janie again. "I thought you said you was looking for Bonnibelle."

"I am. I'm just interested in the barges, that's all."

A wheeze came from the corner. "Now, don't that beat all? Ain't nothing special about them barges, but this here girl's the second fureigner in two days asking about them."

"Gus, you talk too much. She don't care nothing about that. She wants to find her cousins, that's all."

"Bonnibelle couldn't have gone far, could she?" Janie asked, shifting the whimpering baby in her arms. "When will she be back?"

A wheeze slipped through the short man's grin. "I reckon she'll be back when she's good and ready."

She stared at him. Her mind blanked with disbelief. "What about Griffin? Where's he?"

Gus stretched and stood up slowly, towering in the corner, almost to the ceiling. If he weren't stooped over, he would've been a foot taller. "He ain't here, neither. He likes to leave his car out yonder, make it look like he's here, you know? But he ain't, not really."

"Gus — " It sounded like a warning.

"So Bonnibelle went out looking for him?"

"Oh, she didn't leave with *him* — "

"Everything all right over at Tobias's place?" The man behind the counter asked quickly. He wagged shaggy eyebrows at Gus, then turned a smile on Janie.

"As a matter of fact, no. I'm looking for the sheriff, too."

"The sheriff?" Gus said. "Dadgum it, girlie, now you're gonna have to sit yourself down and tell us all about it. Here, you can have Zeb's chair."

"There's not much to tell," she said, staying where she was, standing by the counter. "When I arrived yesterday, I found the house broken into and vandalized. I need to report it, that's all."

Gus puffed thoughtfully on his cigar, then said, "I reckon it was on account of that there trouble Tobias had with Dexter."

Janie came to attention.

"Aw, Gus, there weren't no trouble. That's all in your dotey head."

"Now, Zeb, who're you calling dotey? I ain't the one that bought his white mule."

"Grandpa had a white mule?"

"Naw, Gus here is pulling your leg, that's all. Ain't that so, Gus?"

"Humph." Gus stuck his cigar in his mouth and retreated to his corner where he folded himself back into his chair.

"Well, what about this trouble you mentioned? Did Grandpa have a fight with Dexter?"

Zeb rested plump fingers on the counter and narrowed his eyes at her. "It's like I said. There weren't no trouble. Ain't that right, Gus?"

Gus grunted.

The men knew something more about Grandpa, Janie was certain, but Zeb wasn't going to let Gus talk about it. It had something to do with a white mule. She decided to change her approach. "Well, I'm also looking for a man named Earl. Do either of you know him?"

Zeb's fingers twitched on the counter, then he reached for his cigar resting in the ashtray. He pushed it into his mouth and blew smoke at her. "Can't say as I do." He scratched his head. "Gus, you don't know no Earl, do you?"

But not even Gus was talking. The sound that he made from his corner was a cross between a grunt and a laugh.

Janie changed tactics again. "Well, what about my mother? Did you know Fern Mullen?"

Zeb searched the ceiling for his memory. "She was the little one, warn't she?"

Janie nodded. "Mother was practically raised by her older sister, Mae, because their mother died when my mother was born."

"Dadgum! Now I recollect! Fern sure was a pretty little thing. She turned all the boys' heads, and purt near caught old Gus here. I reckon he warn't so old in them days."

"Naw, Zeb. It was Seymour, not me. Seymour was a'courting her right good, then what do you know? She up and run spang off."

"Seymour *Potts*?" Had she heard them correctly? Seymour was Oona's husband. "Do you know why Mother left like that?"

Zeb rubbed the gray stubbles on his chin. "I reckon I wouldn't rightly know about that."

"Did you ever meet the man she married? Wilson Bainbridge?"

"Ain't never heard of the likes of him. You sure ask a lot of questions, don't you?"

Gus spoke up from the corner. "It like to broke old Tobias's heart when that girl of his up and run off. Not even his lady friend could — "

"Aw, Gus, shash yourself up. See what you gone and done? Naw, girlie, old Gus is just bedeviling you. Don't you pay him no never mind."

From the stony look that Zeb flashed at Gus, Janie didn't think she'd get any more information out of them. What she had to do was talk to Gus alone. And perhaps gain his trust to loosen his tongue.

"Well, thanks very much for your help," she said reluctantly and turned to go. "If Bonnibelle shows up, tell her I left."

She stepped out into the wilting heat with the baby on her hip. They were hiding something. She'd bet on it. She wondered if Grandpa's disappearance had something to do with that. Or with his lady friend.

NINE

*I*t was dang hot. Even in the shade of the woods a body couldn't cool off, Oona thought, trudging along the creek path. A jay swept down from a sassafras and scolded her. Must be a nest nearby. She paused for a moment to catch her breath and wave her arms at the cheeky bird.

"Go on, now, shoo!"

The water gurgled and babbled at her, reminding her of the noise that durned baby made. It had been one of Oona's better ideas to give Bonnibelle the task of getting Janie away from Uncle Tobias's house. That way, she'd gotten all three of them — Bonnibelle, the baby, and Janie — out from under foot. Oona needed to inspect the house and make sure Taffy had cleaned up every trace of her daddy's temper. What Oona hadn't counted on was finding that treasure poking out of Mae's sewing basket, which always sat atop the old piano. She patted the folds of her skirt and felt the outline of the envelope she'd hidden in her pocket.

She chuckled, thinking on her cleverness, and stepped carefully, thongs and all, into the cool waters of the creek. Pulling her skirt up, she splashed water on her bare legs and felt like a young girl again. Lordy, where had her life gone to? Whatever had she done to deserve her lot in life? A husband who drank to forget another woman, a brother she had to take care of because his wife had gone and killed herself, and Lord, her duties to her own young'uns. And now this double dose. Another daughter that she needed like a hole in the head, and if that wasn't enough grief, now she was about to lose the very land she'd worked all her life to get.

She was plumb worn out. She sank down onto a rock sticking out into the crik's edge, covered with a cushion of moss, and tucked her skirt around her knees. The woods weren't thick enough to keep all the sunlight out, and she liked the way it sparkled here and there. The rocks in the creek looked like diamonds, and the leaves overhead spread a pattern of light and shadows. Yessir, this was her land. She was born on it and she aimed to die on it, too.

The fact that Uncle Tobias had put Janie's name on the deed was a problem, but not one that she couldn't fix. It was always up to her to fix everything, or so it seemed.

She pulled the treasure out of her pocket. That sewing basket was an odd place for Mae to keep her mail. Maybe she'd just been forgetful.

Oona paused and reconsidered. No. Mae had always been a little tetched. After all, she'd always liked writing letters to far-off places and reading newspapers and such.

Maybe she'd been hiding this. Stretching her arm out as far as it would go, Oona squinted at the envelope and thought she saw a return address from Indiana. *Janie come from there.* But this wasn't Janie's handwriting. Someone in a hurry, taking little care, had written this.

A man.

The more she thought on it, the more she realized she hadn't hardly known Fern's older sister. After all, Mae had dipped into her daddy's white lightning, passed out, thrown up and never knew what happened when she choked to death.

From her other pocket, Oona pulled the wire-rimmed spectacles her oldest boy had brought her once from Nashv'lle. He'd promised they would help her read the church programs, and she reckoned he was right. They made her feel right proud, so it didn't matter that the little pieces of glass actually made the words run together in a blur. She settled them on the end of her nose and pulled the letter out of the envelope. Never much good at reading anyway, she tilted it this way and that until the scrawled words finally separated. Best as she could tell, this was a letter from one Roy Shoemaker asking Mae for the whereabouts of his wife, Janie Bainbridge.

~

JANIE SLAMMED THE DOOR to the sheriff's office behind her and felt the baby's small fingers dig into her throat. "It's okay, Prissy," she lied, stomping down the three steps to where she'd left Jeff playing hopscotch. She marched across the street to the grocery store parking lot, but as she approached the Bug at the edge of the lot, her anger fizzled. With her one free arm, she slapped the side of her jeans in dismay and stared at the listing car. The right rear tire had gone flat.

"That road isn't fit for cars," she grumbled, remembering the ten-mile rutted lane to town.

"Don't worry, Mom. We can change the tire."

"I've never changed a tire in my life." She didn't like the whining sound of her voice, but it came out before she could stop it. This was just another problem that single mothers had to deal with on a daily basis. Hadn't she learned by now how to handle problems?

She considered the small, brick building that housed the sheriff's office across the street, *if you could call it a street*, then turned her back on it. No, she'd solve this new problem without that deputy's condescending help, thank you. There was a filling station a few blocks away, where she'd stopped earlier for gas. The mechanic didn't have to believe anything. The flat and her money would speak for her.

She started walking, Jeff at her side and Prissy on one hip. It would've been a pleasant walk if not for the mugginess and the way her mind replayed the irritating manner of the sheriff's deputy. He'd listened to her story, but he hadn't taken any notes. What was the point, if the scene of the crime had already been cleaned up? The way he lifted one eyebrow suggested that he thought she'd imagined the whole thing. And as for her questions about Earl, the deputy leaned back in his swivel chair, crossed his arms and studied her for the longest moment before coming to a decision. "Nope," he'd said, standing up and escorting her to the door. "Don't know no Earl."

Jeff skipped over the crumbling sections of cement sidewalk, uplifted by the roots of massive oaks. Behind their gnarled trunks stood houses — rambling shells of their former glory as southern mansions. Balustrades and columns, gray from worn-off paint, stood like ghostly sentinels. Boarded-up windows protected the secrets of more splendid days. Today the mansions stood hollow. They were as empty of life as Grandpa's house.

All but one, that is. Hanging askew from the wrought-iron fence against which Jeff rattled a stick, a sign identified this former mansion as a nursing home. On its front porch sat a row of chairs, all rocking at different speeds. The white-haired heads of their occupants pointed Janie's way. Silently, these elderly patients watched her while their rockers creaked slowly back and forth. Withered and wizened, with blankets tucked on their laps, they too were shells of their former glory. What tales they could tell...

And then hope stirred in her. Oona had said that her mother lived in a retirement home in Stony Lonesome. She waved at the row of silent rockers and promised herself that she'd return.

The mechanic, who wore a patch on his gray shirt that identified him as Melvin, claimed to be busy. Janie didn't see any other customers in his cluttered office, and through the open doorway to the garage behind, she saw an empty work area. No cars raised up to the ceiling. Lots of tires sitting around. Melvin asked her to repeat her story a couple of times. From the droop of his eyes, Janie feared he would fall asleep in the middle of her story. Perhaps his mind was already asleep. He yawned wide, displaying yellowed teeth and hairy nostrils, declared he would tend to her tire "directly," then disappeared among his own tires in the otherwise empty garage.

Janie sighed. The baby hung like a dead weight, asleep now on her aching shoulder. There was nothing for her to do but wait. She dared not buy the groceries yet, as she had no idea of Melvin's definition of "directly." Nor had Bonnibelle reappeared.

A few minutes later, she stood at the gate of the retirement home.

"I'm not going in there with all those old people," Jeff said with an exaggerated shiver. "They give me the willies. Their faces are all crumpled."

"Then stay outside, but don't wander off."

He picked up a stick and started scratching in the exposed dirt where the sidewalk had broken apart. She watched him a minute, then gently shifted the sleeping baby to a more comfortable position, and opened the gate. As she walked up to the porch, the rockers stopped. Their occupants watched her intently.

"Good morning," she said to the crumpled faces all turned up toward her. The way they watched her silently reminded her of sunflowers. "Fine weather we're having, isn't it?"

The first of the rockers started up again.

"I'm looking for Oona Potts' mother. I'm afraid I don't know her name — "

"Oona?"

"What's that she said?"

"No, not Oona — "

Just then the screen door opened and a middle-aged nurse stepped outside. "May I help you, miss?" She tipped her head to one side and smiled in a friendly way.

Janie returned the smile. "I was hoping to find my cousin's mother, but I don't know her name."

"Why, that would be Mrs. Dexter. She's been napping off and on in the parlor. Why don't you come on in, Mrs. Bainbridge, and we'll see if she's awake?" She held the screen open for her and motioned her inside.

At first Janie didn't move. Everywhere she went, she was recognized. "How'd you know my name?"

"Why, it's not every day that Fern's girl come to town. News like that travels fast around here where folks don't have much else to talk about."

"Did you know my mother?" Janie stepped inside the dim hallway and followed the nurse along the threadbare carpet runner.

"Oh, my, yes. Fern was a couple years ahead of me in school, but everyone knows everyone around here. 'Course, Oona knew her the best. They were best friends."

"Oona and Mother?" Neither one of them had ever mentioned their friendship. Had it ended with a fight over Seymour?

The nurse stopped before French doors and laid her hand softly on the brass knob. "Mrs. Dexter don't get many visitors. She'll be tickled pink. Why, it'll give the old lady something to talk about for weeks."

She held her finger to her lips and winked as she cracked open the door. After a quick glance, she pushed it open farther and motioned for Janie to follow. Stiff chairs that had seen more festive days were now pushed into the corners to allow room for the wheelchairs. The air smelled of medicine and felt heavy with the solemn tick tock of the grandfather clock, which measured the monotony of passing time.

She followed the nurse to one of the wheelchairs. The old woman in it appeared asleep. Her eyes were closed, and her yellow-gray hair matted against a pillow. A stream of drool ran across her cheek.

Janie whispered over Prissy's head, hanging heavy on her shoulder. "I can come back another — "

"Nonsense," said the nurse, shaking Mrs. Dexter's arm. "Elta Mae! Look who's come to visit you."

The old woman's eyelids fluttered. She coughed and pushed a trembling hand up to her mouth. Her head rolled off the pillow, and she struggled to right herself. Her eyes were as yellow-gray as her hair, and they sagged with weariness as she tried to focus on Janie.

"Lawd a'mercy!" Her voice shook. Her fingers, speckled with age spots, trembled at her throat. "Annalee...you got the baby!" She stared transfixed at Janie. Then she moaned and slumped, unconscious, against her pillow.

"Mrs. Dexter?" The nurse pushed past Janie to bend over her patient and feel for a pulse.

Janie backed away. "I'll get the doctor."

"That's not necessary, dear. She's asleep, that's all."

"Are you sure she's all right?"

"Of course, dear." Her voice sounded unconcerned, as if this happened all the time. "The old lady just needs to rest, that's all. Maybe you should come back another time."

"She called me 'Annalee.'"

"Didn't no one warn you about poor Elta Mae's mind?"

"She must've mistaken me for someone else. Someone named 'Annalee.'"

The nurse laughed. "Oh, there's no one around here by that name. It's all in the old lady's mind. It'd be best for you to leave, dear."

"Perhaps the doctor should take a look at her."

"No. You can leave, now."

Her heart racing, Janie stumbled out of the room.

TEN

"You say you drove over a nail?" Melvin scratched his forehead, rubbing black smudge marks across his receding hairline.

"No, I — "

"Nail wouldn't leave no gash like that." His eyes opened wide as he studied her with interest. "Purt near three inches long."

"What are you saying, then? The tire was slashed?" A chill crept down Janie's spine despite the stickiness between herself and the sleeping baby on her shoulder.

A drop of sweat slid down his face, and he frowned. "I didn't say that. Warn't no nail, though."

It was a knife. Like the knife that had ripped into Grandpa's furniture. She felt the erratic hammer of her heart, and she took a deep breath to still it. "Can the tire be fixed?"

He shrugged. "You come back the day after tomorrow and I'll let you know. Meanwhile, the spare's on and in good enough shape."

By the time she returned to the parking lot where Melvin had tended to the car, she was completely soaked with sweat. Prissy was stirring, and Jeff lagged behind, struggling with the second-hand car seat she'd found. He was prattling on about having found someone to play with, but all that Janie could think of was that someone had deliberately slashed her tire. She stared at the spare, now in place, as if it would tell her who and why. Somehow she knew that this was the act of the same person who had slashed Grandpa's furniture, and she shivered again. That made the attack directed against *her*, not against a changing world. It hadn't been a vagrant who'd found an empty house to live in.

"Come on, Jeff, let's install this car seat, then go get our groceries. Maybe Bonnibelle will be back by then." She wasn't used to carrying a baby around anymore, and her arm ached as she shifted Prissy to her other hip.

"Mo-om, you can still get your money back. This car seat was way too expensive." He heaved it reluctantly into the car.

She sighed. "Why are you so worried? You know the rules about being strapped in properly. Besides, we'll consider this a baby gift."

Jeff pouted and Prissy wailed, but Janie managed to secure the car seat and lead the children to the grocery. Mechanically, she went through the actions of settling the baby into the cart with her key ring. She shook her arm and felt the circulation return, then wheeled the cart down the narrow, cluttered aisles. Jeff slipped a few boxes and bags of junk food into the cart, but she didn't care. All she could think of was *why?* Why had someone slashed her tire? It couldn't have been a mischievous prank, as Seymour had suggested. No, this was intentional. Malicious. But she had no enemies that she knew of. She didn't even know the people of this community. Oona's family had made it clear, however, that her presence was not wanted anymore than Price's land development was wanted. Was the slashing, then, a tactic meant to frighten her away? To leave behind Grandpa's land to more deserving people? Like Oona? Or Price?

It wouldn't work.

"Mom, wait up. Don't you want any of *that*?" Jeff pointed at the produce.

She paused and considered the mounds of lettuce. The slashed tire had been nothing more than a nuisance. Not a frightening thing. No. She *wouldn't* allow anyone or anything to frighten her away. She wouldn't react as her mother had. She would have her answers, and then if she wanted to, she'd leave these Chittenden Hills under her own free will. She tossed a head of lettuce into the cart and moved toward the check-out lane.

A few minutes later, Janie slowed the VW as they approached the Lazy Dew on the outskirts of town. Griffin's car was still parked in front of the motel, and next to it was a truck. A man and woman blended into one outline in the truck's cab. When Janie pulled up alongside the truck, she saw that the woman was her cousin.

Bonnibelle broke away from her grappling partner, leaned out the truck's window and hollered, "Go 'way! Cain't you see I'm busy?" Then she and the man sank out of sight.

Janie sat stunned for a moment. The baby, fully awake now in her new seat, puckered up her face and cried as she flailed at the straps. Janie's fist tightened on the gear shift, and then gravel spewed as the car lurched away. Let Griffin give his sister a ride home!

With a crying baby, it was difficult to think straight on these crooked roads. Each time a fork appeared, she made an instinctive choice, hoping it was the right one. The woods thickened around them, swallowing up the tobacco fields that had surrounded Stony Lonesome, swallowing some of her outrage. Learning her way through this maze of roads was a triumph for her. Next time, she wouldn't need Bonnibelle to show her the way.

~

MERCIFUL HEAVENS, OONA thought, yanking off her spectacles and stuffing the letter back into her pocket. Fern's girl didn't even have her own husband's last name. *Why, I never heard of no sech! It ain't right. That's all there is to it.*

Oona shook her head and wondered what would become of the world with young'uns running things. They couldn't even run their own lives right. Well, she would have to fix it, whether they liked it or not. *She ain't got no call to act so high and mighty like she done at the supper table, getting herself all huffy just because someone else knows what's best.*

Carefully, she tucked the spectacles into her other pocket, then blinked at the stream in which her feet dangled. Those dang lenses distorted her world, and she had to wait for her vision to clear, same as she had to wait for her blood to stop boiling in her veins. She hoped she wouldn't have to go to the yarb doctor for one of them there concoctions.

There was a peacefulness here in the woods, and that would work just as well to settle her. It was a peacefulness she didn't get up home. But before its magic had a chance to work, her vision kicked in, and she sat bolt upright on her rock.

What was that blue thing over yonder, creek water spilling all around it? The woods were filled with light and shadow, greens of this year and browns from years past. Every once in a while there was a touch of color from wild-flowers. But not blue. And certainly not *in* the creek. That was no wildflower.

She hauled herself up slowly and took a cautious step forward in the slippery creek bed. The blue thing sat still, while water tumbled around it. Her ankles tensed, and her toes dug into the thongs for added support as she moved, one step at a time. If she took one wrong step, she knew her ankle would twist beneath all her weight and send her head first into the water. Probably break a leg, too. So she moved slowly, carefully, and it took her a good while to reach the blue thing.

"Well, I declare!" she said, bending over to haul a jug out of the water. It was a milk jug with a blue lid, like the kind you could buy uptown at the market, but the clear liquid this jug contained wasn't like any milk that she'd ever seen.

She dropped the evil thing back into the water, then hurried toward the bank, moving too fast over the slippery, uneven creek bottom. Her right thong must've wedged itself under a rock, because all of a sudden it wouldn't move. Her body kept moving forward, and before she knew it, she was falling.

Arms flailing, she landed heavily on her knees. Pain wrenched through her body. She twisted her foot free and rolled over in the water. Soaked up to the line where her waist used to be, back when she was still a girl, she allowed herself the pleasure of tears.

She went to church every Sunday morning and the revival meeting every Friday evening — whatever had she done to deserve these hardships of her life? She bawled until she had no tears left, and it was then that she heard the rustling in the brush. And the nervous cough.

"Ma'am, are you all right?" a man's small voice asked.

She could've died right then and there! She lifted her head from her arms and saw the face peering at her from behind the brush alongside the bank of the creek. "Who said that? Come on out here where I can get a look at you."

He was a man, but he was as small-boned as a girl. Oona could tell he wasn't a boy, either, on account of that thick mustache that half hid the look on his face. She prided herself in being a good judge of character, and she knew that this man didn't want to step out of his hiding place in the brush. And since he was a fureigner, that could only mean more trouble for Oona.

∾

BY THE TIME JANIE GUIDED the VW into a spot between the junk cars surrounding Oona's house, she'd regained a sense of control over her anger. Someone here was about to relieve her of the burden of Bonnibelle's baby and her relentless wails. However, the only signs of life were chickens scuttling under the house and the dog lifting his drooping jaw from his paws. Seymour's truck was gone, and the front door was closed. Alarm replaced some of her initial anger.

"Looks like no one's home, Jeff."

"I'll go look in the treehouse. Maybe someone's there," he said, reaching for the door handle.

"Not likely." And then she couldn't help smiling at him. "Oh, go ahead. Who knows? Maybe you'll find someone out back."

She watched him scurry out of the car and bound away, out of sight into the woods. Her smile faded. She wished Jeff had met Grandpa. Both of them were souls at home in these Chittenden Hills. Despite the condition of Grandpa's house and Oona's unwelcoming family and Price's pushy sales effort, she'd have to make it work for them here. And the list of obstacles was growing, as her trip to town had proved. For Jeff's sake as well as her own need for a sense of identity, they *would* have a successful summer here.

"Well, Prissy, shall we see if anyone's home who can give you lunch?" She unstrapped the baby and backed out of the car.

Silence answered the hollow-sounding knock on the door. Maybe she could push open the door and help herself to diapers and bottles. Prissy could nap in Grandpa's recliner while Janie unpacked a few things. Surely someone would claim the baby after an hour or two, then —

The door opened a crack, and a slice of face peered at her.

"Taffy, am I ever glad to see you! We've been to that town of yours, Stony Lonesome — "

"Ain't mine. My town was Chittenden, and it's down yonder at the bottom of the lake. Drowned." Her chin quivered and dipped low, and a wispy string of pale hair swung across her face.

"May I come in?"

She stood away from the door without opening it further, which Janie interpreted as an invitation.

"Where's your mom?" Janie asked, pushing her way inside. She put the baby down in her crib, then hurried into the kitchen to find a bottle.

When she finally supplied it, the baby whimpered in gratitude. Janie returned to Taffy's side. "I went to visit your grandmother. Something happened to her."

Taffy turned her back on her, and one shoulder shrugged with indifference.

"She's very ill."

That didn't get a response, either.

Something very strange was happening here, Janie thought, and it made her feel uneasy. "Don't you care?"

"Why should I?"

"She's your grandmother!"

"So what?"

"Look, I don't know what's happened to you, but you can't convince me that you don't care, not even a tiny bit. You're the one who used to give Auntie Mae a hug for every cookie she gave you. Remember?"

"Times was different back then."

"What about the way you stood up for me last night, the way you defied your own mother?"

"What about it?"

"That's a woman who cares. Look, can you turn around and face me?"

Taffy put her hands to her face, and the curve in her back shook. Janie took a step closer and reached out to touch Taffy's shoulder. Taffy pulled away.

"Go ahead and cry," Janie whispered, following her across the room. "Then tell me about it when you're ready."

"Ain't n-nothing to tell. Reckon I don't feel so good is all."

"I thought you looked pale. Have you always been this thin? When we were kids — "

Taffy whirled around and struck at Janie's reaching arm. "What do you know? You come sashaying down here to Chittenden like you own the place, but all you care about is the money you can get now that the woods are crawling with developers. You don't care nothing about us."

"You've got it all wrong."

"Mama said if you really cared anything about us that you would've come back here a long time ago."

Janie backed away and crumpled onto the couch. It was true that she should've come back, but her absence was for other reasons — for her mother

— not because she didn't care about Grandpa. "Tell me, Taffy, what do you do when your loyalties are divided?"

Taffy frowned. "What would you know about that?"

"Plenty. Oh, I wanted to come back here, but my mother wouldn't hear of it."

"And you let that stop you?"

"I didn't want to hurt her. Then I got married and had Jeff. It was a struggle just to keep going every day. Roy, my husband, was no help. He was the biggest mistake of my life. I guess we all make them. And now I'm just trying to pick up the pieces and go on. I know it's too late for some things. Like Grandpa... But Taffy, it doesn't have to be too late for us."

"I don't know. I just plumb don't know no more."

"Your grandmother called me 'Annalee.'"

Taffy lifted her chin. Her eyes widened, and fear shone through them. "Mama ain't going to like to hear that."

"Why? What did she mean? Who's Annalee?"

"No one. Grandma is crazy in the head, that's all. What else did she say?"

"Well, she mentioned the baby, but she didn't have a chance to say anything else. I guess the sight of Prissy and me made her pass out. Or else she had a stroke. The nurse didn't seem concerned, though." For all Janie knew, the old woman was dead by now.

"Listen," Taffy said, pacing like a nervous animal. "We won't tell her. We *can't* tell Mama. It'll be our secret, you hear?"

"What do you mean? I have to tell Oona. What if her mother is dying?"

"She ain't. It's like I said. Grandma's crazy in the head. She does this all the time. Thinks she sees things that aren't real. Mama's just like her, so I reckon I'm next. The craziness runs in the family. Maybe you got it, too."

Janie suppressed a shiver. "Your mother will want to visit her, won't she?"

"No! She'll want to *kill* Grandma if she hears about..." Taffy put her hand to her mouth. Maybe she thought she'd said too much.

Janie finished the sentence for her. "If she hears about Annalee? Surely you're exaggerating?"

"Why don't you just go away and leave me alone?"

"Fine. It's your turn to take care of the baby." Janie stood and strode to the door.

"I don't want it! You've got to take it!"

Hands on the door knob, Janie stopped. She turned and smiled. "You want me to take the baby with me? Okay, I'll do it. On one condition. Tell me who Annalee is."

"I hate you, Janie Bainbridge!" Taffy stormed toward the kitchen.

The burden of remorse weighing on her, Janie stood there several minutes, watching the doorway where Taffy had disappeared. She'd gambled and lost a friend in the process. She'd also lost the opportunity to ask her other questions, like the ones about Earl and his connection to the barge. Slowly, she moved toward the crib and lifted Prissy with her bottle into her arms. Then she turned back to the front door. She'd meet Jeff outside.

"Wait!"

A small voice stopped her, and Janie turned to see Taffy leaning against the door to the kitchen. Her cheeks were stained with tears.

"I...I need a favor."

Janie's heart soared with hope. "All you have to do is ask."

Taffy sniffled and pulled away from the doorframe, as if she'd reconsidered.

"Please, Taffy, ask whatever you like."

"Well... You got to swear on a stack of Bibles seven foot tall never to tell a soul."

"I don't have that many Bibles, but you can count on me. What's the favor?"

"You got to swear."

"Okay, I swear."

"You can't tell Jeff neither."

"I won't. What's the favor?"

"Can you drive me to Stony Lonesome?"

Janie swallowed hard. It wasn't her favorite place, not after her adventures there this morning, but she knew she had to return. There was the matter of her tire, after all. And this business of Annalee and her own family history. If she couldn't get anyone's cooperation, she'd have to investigate on her own. The courthouse would have records. "You want to go now?"

Taffy's eyes flew open wide with panic, and she stared down at her faded skirt. "'Course not now. But soon."

"I have to go back to town day after tomorrow." Janie didn't see any point in telling her cousin about the tire.

"Good enough." Taffy sagged as if a weight had been removed from her shoulders.

"And?" Janie asked.

"And what?"

"What about the favor?"

"Ain't nothing else. That's all."

"You mean *that's* the favor?"

Taffy looked as if she would burst into a fresh torrent of sobs. "You swore you wouldn't tell! Not even Jeff!"

"And I won't. I promise. But I can't leave him alone."

"Then bring him here. At ten, but don't tell Mama why. Make up something. She'll put him to work. I'll meet you out in the road on the way to town."

"I guess I can do that. But why is this a big secret? Don't you go into town all the time?"

From the back porch came the squeak and bang of the screen door, interrupting them. "Mom? I couldn't find anyone."

"Remember," Taffy warned in a low hiss, "not a word of this to him!" She reached for the iron ladder and climbed the side of the wall to the attic bedroom.

Janie watched her disappear through the hole in the ceiling. When she felt a tug on her arm, she looked down at her son.

"Mom? You okay?"

She nodded slowly. "Looks like we're in the baby-sitting business a while longer. Let's gather up a few things for Prissy and then go home."

Home. She'd said it so easily, even though she didn't have a home, not yet. And then a thought struck her. Was the reason for Taffy's secrecy because she intended to run away from hers day after next?

ELEVEN

"Mom, how come Dad doesn't want to live with us anymore?"

Jeff's question caught Janie by surprise, and her hold slipped from the steering wheel. The car bounced into a rut, and its sudden movement matched the lurch of her heart. "People change, honey, and your dad changed his mind about where he wanted to live."

"I bet he'd want to live *here* if he only knew about this neat place." Jeff turned away to stare out the window at the woods. The tangled mass of branches and leaves appeared to bounce up and down from the motion of the car over the rut-filled road between Oona's place and Grandpa's.

"He *did* know about Chittenden, but he refused ever to come here. I guess he wasn't very interested in family." *There's an understatement*, she thought, swearing under her breath at Oona for bringing up the matter of Roy last night at supper.

"You know, Mom, the people here aren't so different. They talk kind of funny, but they're just the same on the inside as anyone else. I bet Dad would like it here better now that there's a lake and all the tourists Aunt Oona doesn't like."

Janie sighed. "First of all, Oona isn't your aunt. She's my mother's cousin, which makes her my second cousin and your third cousin. And second of all...Jeff...please remember that it was your dad who walked out on us without any word of where he was going."

"But Mom, what if he changed his mind? How would he ever find us?" Jeff's lower lip protruded further and further. "We moved."

"We *had* to, honey. I couldn't afford the house on my salary alone." She frowned and felt her patience slip away. "Besides, I tried to find your dad through his mother in Indianapolis, but she didn't even know where he was. I left Auntie Mae's address with her as a way to contact us." *Which was more than I should've done*, she thought, clutching the steering wheel until her knuckles ached. She swallowed hard, and then continued. "Even if your dad wanted to come back to us again, I wouldn't want him to. Not anymore. Not after the way he treated us."

Jeff turned away as if she'd slapped him.

Damn! It wasn't fair that Roy had left her alone to deal with this. Maybe she should explain about his long absences. The women. She'd already taken Roy back more than once, and she wasn't about to do so again. But she couldn't bear to hurt Jeff even more by making him understand about his father. Not yet. Not until he was a little older. She had to give her son a sense of stability first.

"People change, honey. It's part of life." She reached over to squeeze his shoulder, but he shrugged away from her. "Jeff, I promise we'll talk more about this when you're older. I won't do what my own mother did to me and keep it all to myself."

Finally he turned to stare at her. "What if you die first?"

"I'm not going to die, not for a long, long time."

"Grandma didn't think she was going to die, either, but she did. Maybe she still meant to tell you about your dad."

"No, I don't think she ever meant to tell me. The times I asked about him made her so upset that she would get migraines. Once she recovered, we moved to another apartment, and I had to start all over again finding friends. I learned to stop asking her." She drove in silence through her mother's hills.

"Well, I just bet that if she hadn't died in that car accident, she would've told you."

She remembered her mother's last moments alive in the emergency room last February. Janie, called from work, had raced along the icy streets to be there at Fern's side as she died. "Mother," she'd whispered, even though the nurses had told Janie that Fern was beyond hearing. Nonetheless, she held her hand, stroked her arm and whispered again, "Mother, I'm here. It's me, Janie." In Fern's final moments, her lips quivered, her brow twitched, and her head moved ever so slightly. "No...Lee..." her mother said clearly, calling

Janie by her middle name. "Shhh," Janie had replied. "Rest now. Everything will be all right." The lie had come automatically, and it had only seemed to agitate Fern more. "So wrong...sapphires...yours..." And then she'd died.

"Maybe your dad was as big a jerk as you think my dad is," Jeff said, bringing her back to the present moment in the tunnel of woods.

The car swerved around a rut, throwing Jeff against his seat belt. She hoped he was wrong. All she had left of her father was the picture in her wallet, and the old anger stirred again. Mother had kept all of her memories to herself. When she took Taffy to town the day after tomorrow, she would find a suitable frame for that photo, she decided.

"Lookit, Mom, there's someone at our house."

The Bug rounded the last bend before Grandpa's cabin, and Janie saw the silver Cadillac sitting in the driveway. Waiting for them on the porch, Price Wanamaker lounged in the swing and propped his leather boots up on the porch railing. He sprang to his feet when she turned into the driveway and lifted a straw hat from his head. *Golden hair for a golden boy*, she thought, coasting to a stop and pulling the keys from the ignition.

He hurried down the porch steps and strode through the weeds of the driveway to open her car door. He grinned down at her, but she continued to sit still for a while.

"No, I'm not ready to sell yet," she said, finally climbing out of the car, ignoring the helping hand he offered. "Let me move in first."

He laughed and dug his hands into his pockets. "Oh, I'm not here about that. I was in town this morning, so I took the liberty of buying some new hardware for your doors."

She didn't know what to say. Speechless, she leaned an elbow across the top of the car door and stared at him.

"You *will* want your locks changed, won't you?" he asked.

"Yes, of course, but..." He'd been in town. Convenient.

No. If he'd slashed her tire, she reasoned, he wouldn't come here to change her locks.

Jeff climbed out of the car and scampered away.

"Just a minute," she called to him. "You've got to help unload the groceries and then watch Prissy while I put them away and fix lunch."

"Aw, Mom!"

"I'll just get my tool kit from my car and get to work," Price said.

"That's kind of you." Inwardly, she fumed at his presumptuousness, his high-handedness, his control. "But there's no need for you to go to the trouble. I can hire someone."

"Nonsense! I enjoy tinkering with my hands."

I'll bet.

She'd completely forgotten about this detail while in town, and Price was only trying to be considerate and save her from making a return trip. The lock would have to be changed if she was ever going to feel safe in this house. He was being generous with his time. "Well, all right."

"Are you going to unlock the door, or shall I pry it open?"

"I'll pay you, of course."

He laughed again. "I couldn't accept."

He was certainly being difficult, she thought. "How about if I give you lunch, then?"

His eyes twinkled and his grin spread a little wider. "I'll take a raincheck on that. You promised to let me show you around the place tomorrow, remember?"

She nodded and wondered why this tour was so urgent. "Before I can go anywhere else, I'll need to check on Elta Mae." She told him about her visit to the nursing home and the effect her presence had had on Oona's mother.

"You don't need to worry about her," Price said, too breezily. "I've already done that for you. She's fine. I stopped in to see her myself on my way out of town. Must've been shortly after your visit, as Mary Lou told me all about you. Anyway, Aunt Elta was fine. Resting comfortably."

"Aunt Elta?"

"She and Gran are sisters."

"I'd like to talk to your grandmother, too," she said, unstrapping the baby and lifting her onto one hip.

He grinned. "Then I'm your man. I can arrange it for you."

She watched him saunter toward his car and lift the trunk's hood. He was trying to manipulate her, she realized, jamming unsteady fingers into her purse where she groped among the scraps of paper for the skeleton key. *Stop it!* He's only trying to be helpful.

Sifting the heavy iron object from the clutter of her purse, she headed for the porch. *Coming home.* The thought was a powerful antidote, lifting the unease of only a moment ago. *Home.* Already it was feeling good.

Each footfall fell lighter the closer she approached *home*. The place was looking like home with small touches like the philodendron she'd placed on the
porch. She'd cared for that plant eight years since Jeff's birth, and she hadn't
managed to kill it yet. Now it sat on the railing, its tendrils drifting over the
edge, looking very happy to be there.

When she mounted the last of the porch steps, her feeling of lightness
sank as quickly as it had emerged. The philodendron's clay pot sat tilted at
a different angle from the way she'd left it. Black fingerprints smeared along
the sides of the pot. Someone had been here while she and Jeff were out.
Someone with dirty fingers had moved her plant.

"Something wrong?" Price said, returning to her side with a tool kit and a
paper bag stapled shut with a receipt.

She glanced at Price's immaculately manicured hands. "Someone has
been here while we were out," she whispered, as if that someone were still
within hearing distance.

Price looked around himself. "Everything appears okay to me."

She followed the direction of his glance. Jeff was struggling with a bag of
groceries from the car. The wicker chairs she'd found in the attic were still
positioned on the porch where she'd placed them. "There are fingerprints on
my plant."

He cocked his head at her and arched one of his blond eyebrows. He
didn't believe her.

She turned away from his scrutiny, jabbed the key at the keyhole and
missed.

"Allow me," he said, taking the key from Janie.

Jeff suddenly appeared, pressing close to them, as if he instinctively sniffed
trouble. He peered over the bag of groceries. "Is it all tore up again?"

"Relax, tiger," Price said, pushing him gently back, then leaning against
the door as he rattled the knob.

"I bet they're trying to scare us, Mom."

"No, honey. Why would anyone want to scare us?" Her heart skipped a
beat, she was absolutely positive.

"Don't you remember how Uncle Seymour and Griffin were so mad last
night about the people from the government? They didn't get enough land,
and now they want more, so they're trying to scare us away so they can get
the rest of Grandpa's land."

She burst out laughing in spite of her stretched nerves.

"Well, what if I'm right?" Jeff stuck out his lower lip.

"Let's be rational about this. Remember how we found fresh food in the kitchen? Someone has been living here. Maybe that someone came back today, only to find that we had moved in and locked the door. He would've known all along that this wasn't his house and the owners were bound to return..." It sounded reasonable enough. She wanted to believe it. But she couldn't.

TWELVE

*E*venfall was Oona's favorite time of her long day. It was when the men-folks rounded up the cows and bedded them down for the night in the barn. It was when the womenfolk, supper dishes done, rocked on their porches and swapped stories. It was when Oona could escape to her private place if the need arose.

She limped under the clothesline where her damp skirt flapped in the breeze. She crossed the chickens' yard. If anyone was watching her, they'd think she was headed to the outhouse. At the last minute, she veered off the path and ducked into the barn.

She always felt welcome here in this sweet-smelling place. A few con-tented chickens crooned at her from their perches. Bales of hay stacked up the sides of the walls and muffled the sound of her steps. The light was failing fast, and she moved to one of the open windows. Outside, she heard Griffy's distant calls and the tinkling response of the cowbells. They'd be here soon. Best get a move on.

Adjusting the spectacles to the very end of her nose, so that she could peer over their brim, she licked the end of her pencil and poised it over the notepad she'd found in Mae's bureau. She waited for the words to come. She leaned against the rough wood of the barn siding and tilted the notepad this way and that in the last rays of sunlight falling through the open window. She looked to the shadows of Bossie's stall for inspiration and sank down onto a bale of hay. Jagged ends tickled her through her cotton skirt as she thought.

That fureigner, the one who'd helped haul her out of the creek, sure had acted skittish at being discovered. He'd seemed relieved when she shook him off to make a hasty retreat. Now that she could stop and catch her breath for a moment, it occurred to her that his behavior was mighty peculiar. Had he known about the jug of white lightning she'd found in the creek? Lawd a'mercy! He was a likker agent, of course, and now he was going to think that evil brew was hers.

She licked the pencil again and started to write.

The shadows had deepened by the time she heard a soft low on the other side of the barn door. Good thing that she was almost done. She shoved the notepad, pencil and spectacles back into her pockets just as the door creaked open. The shadowy figure of a big man filled the fading light in the doorway.

"Mama! How's come you're in here where it's so dark? I thought you'd be up at the house bending everybody's ear about that cousin of yourn."

Cousin ain't all she is, Oona thought. She wanted to confide in her son, but it wasn't time yet to introduce him to his half-sister. She had her duty to do first. She let out a long sigh of exasperation.

"I plumb don't know, son. What are we going to do about that one? I was hoping one of you young'uns could have Uncle Tobias's place. I thought Janie was just coming for a visit, but now that she's fixing to stay... You mark my words, son. That girl ain't gonna stir up nothing but trouble."

"Don't you fret, Mama. I don't think she'll stick around long." He grinned like the cat that got the mouse.

But she couldn't stop worrying. If the girl dug too deep, like she promised she would, then she was bound to uncover the whole mess. Annalee, Seymour, Fern... And that was something Oona would *never* let anyone find out, not even if her life depended on it.

❧

JANIE'S TOE IDLY PUSHED at the floor of the porch, making the swing wobble. A warm glow of lamplight spilled out of the house, piercing the gathering darkness. A homey aura began to surround Grandpa's house once again, thanks to a lot of hard work, starting with the mystery person who'd cleaned up the vandalism yesterday afternoon while she and Jeff were at Oona's. After Price had installed the new locks today, Janie had mended rips, made the beds, and filled the cupboards with fresh food and an odd assortment of dishes salvaged from the destruction. Seymour had driven Oona over to inspect her work at suppertime and finally take the baby home.

Now, after a cold supper of turkey sandwiches, Janie slouched comfortably in the swing and watched Jeff prance along the driveway, chasing lightning bugs. It would feel good to crawl into a real bed tonight. Locusts rattled in the background. She almost didn't hear them anymore.

Then a new sound broke through the sleepy fog settling over her mind. Something was buzzing in the distance, growing louder and louder. Straightening in the swing, she planted her foot to stop its motion.

"It's a boat!" Jeff shouted, pointing south toward a distant shore. The lake and the sky were bright streaks compared to the black landscape of woods engulfing them.

She jumped up, bumping the swing into the side of the house, and watched Jeff dart away toward the edge of the cliff. He leapt over the obstacles of rocks and tree roots like an antelope, and her heart leapt, too. "Jeff, be careful!"

A motorboat sped up the old river channel, then suddenly veered out of it, following a straight line for the cliffs where Jeff stood. It didn't slow. Wide awake now, Janie raced after her son. She caught her breath as she caught his arm.

"It's that pirate again," he said, twisting out of his mother's protective grasp.

"Are you sure it's the same man?" Dexter, that's what they'd called him. Dexter, Oona's half-brother who'd lost his eye in a fight with Seymour.

"Sure I'm sure. Don't you see his hat?"

The lone occupant of the fishing boat sat at the rear of the aluminum dinghy and held onto the tiller. Even in twilight it was easy to see the red baseball cap pulled down over his face. She remembered the shack they'd passed yesterday and the man in the baseball cap. She remembered the same flash of red of someone spying on her in Oona's garden. Now, the man that Seymour didn't want on his property, steered his boat straight toward her position on the cliff.

He surely would've crashed onto the rocks lining the base of their cliff if he hadn't cut the motor and turned sharply at the last possible minute. The boat tossed to and fro in its own wake, and he stood up, defying its rocking motion. Having to tilt his chin up to see them, for the brim of his cap was pulled down low, he eyed them silently a full minute with his one good eye. Yellowed teeth gleamed from the shadows obscuring his face.

"Hey, y'all!" he shouted above the waves slapping against rocks. The master of his boat, he never lost his balance as he rode out its bucking. "I hear tell you're fixing to stay on."

"That's right, mister," Jeff shouted back.

News travels fast, Janie thought. Oona must've told him. He'd been lurking around the place, maybe waiting for a plate of supper after everyone else had left.

"Now didn't I tell you that's a fool thing to do?" He was a tall, lanky man, unlike his half-sister, Oona. His bib overalls hung loosely from hunched shoulders, exposing the knots of muscle on bare arms, shiny with a spray of spume.

She ignored his opinion. "You knew my grandfather."

He shrugged and made a grunting sound.

"I think you also knew what we were going to find yesterday when we arrived at my grandfather's house."

A toothy grin showed in the darkness. He remained silent.

"Since you're the closest neighbor," she continued, "perhaps you saw something?"

"Now I don't rightly recollect. What was I supposed to see?"

"Seymour thinks a gang of boys tore up the place. Maybe you saw them pass by your house?"

He snickered. "I reckon folks ain't likely to forget that old Tobias was purt near the only feller 'round here to get hisself a durn good deal out of them government boys."

"Excuse me?" What did that have to do with the vandalism, unless he was suggesting a nine-month-old plan for revenge? It didn't make sense.

"You tell me how's come my daddy plumb give away good bottomland to your granddaddy?" He stabbed a finger at Janie as if he were holding her personally responsible for an old grievance.

Trying to follow the connection he was making left her speechless. Dexter was talking about a time before he was even born, the time when Tobias Mullen moved here as a young man from West Virginia, looking for work in the iron mines and staying on to farm tobacco.

Dexter sat down on the bench at the rear of his boat and reached for the tiller. "Hey, boy, you ever fished up in that there city where you come from?" He laughed at Jeff's dance of excitement, then his voice turned husky. "You ever need a man 'round the place, you jest come and fetch me. But don't come by the crik. There's cottonmouths over yonder." Without waiting for a response, he throttled up his motor and roared away in a spray of spume.

They stood there silently watching his boat grow smaller as it headed straight out into the middle of the lake, fading into twilight. When it disappeared from sight, behind the island that bore a resemblance to a dragon, Janie let out her breath.

"Ow, Mom, you're squeezing me."

She relaxed her grip on his shoulder. "Sorry, hon. It's time for that bath now."

"But Mom, Dexter's going to take me fishing."

"Not tonight, he's not. Now, march." She turned him around and steered him back across the clearing and up the porch steps where she paused to glance over her shoulder at the empty lake.

"Mom, is he *really* a pirate?"

"No, honey. Why would a pirate come this far inland?"

He shrugged. "I dunno, but he looks like one, and he sure sounds like one. And he sounded sore at Grandpa. Like he's planning a pirate's revenge."

"You've got to check that imagination of yours," she said, pushing him through the squeaky front door and into the house. "I'll go find your pj's while you start the water."

She watched him stomp off toward the kitchen, where the bathroom had been added on. Could Jeff be right? A pirate's revenge might include vandalism and slashed tires. She pushed it from her mind and replaced it with a more pleasant thought. Anything. Grandpa's life dream of having a bathroom. The government had given it to him when they moved his house up here from the valley. Too bad that he hadn't lived long enough to enjoy it.

Janie headed into the front bedroom, which had been Auntie Mae's. For now, Jeff would use it until Janie could convert one of the attic rooms for him. She stood on the hooked rug next to the four-poster and waited for her racing heart to calm down after their encounter with *that man*. The top of the feather mattress reached her hip, and she wondered how Auntie Mae, a short, plump woman, had climbed into this bed all her life.

Angled against one corner of the room was an upright piano with yellowed keys. She could still see Taffy bent over it, her bare feet unable to reach the pedals. She remembered her off-key but enthusiastic voice accompanying the pounding notes. "Jesus loves the little children..." Auntie Mae coming in, clapping her hands to shoo them away so as not to disturb Grandpa who was napping in his recliner. Grandpa's conspiratorial wink as they marched outside. His whistle floated after them to continue their tune.

Distant sounds of water running in the tub brought her back to the present. The piano bench would make a good stool for Jeff to use, climbing into bed. She moved it into place, then dug through his suitcase to find his pajamas. Tomorrow they would empty the dresser drawers, line them with fresh paper, and unpack their clothes.

Now, the drawers were full of clutter, like the entire room. There were boxes of newspaper clippings, trinkets, photographs. Janie felt her pulse quicken again, this time with excitement. It would be an enormous task to go through every shred of paper, but she might find things belonging to her mother. Revealing things that could explain why she had run away or who it was that she'd married.

Janie stared at the framed photographs arranged carefully on the doily covering the dusty dresser. She recognized the family photograph of her grandparents with their prim, young daughter, Mae. Next to it was a baby picture of Fern. Grandma Esther had died giving birth to Fern, and so Fern had grown up motherless. An assortment of snapshots poked out of the rim of the dresser's mirror like pins sticking out of a pin cushion. One of them was a picture of Mae in a cap and gown. Even then, when her head must have been full of dreams, Mae frowned with worry.

Janie plucked out the picture to examine it closer, and two smaller photos fell out from behind it onto the doily. Black and white snapshots, frayed around the edges and limp with age, they had been hidden behind the larger photograph of Mae. Janie's attention immediately switched to them, and she turned on the lamp to study them better.

They were photos of a woman. Janie had never seen her before, but there was no doubt about a family resemblance. Jeff had the same high cheekbones and arched eyebrows; Janie had the same blonde hair and broad smile that showed off too much gum. This woman's hairstyle, though, was a smooth flip, the opposite of Janie's frizzy nest.

In one picture, the mystery woman was a bride, with a veil pinned to the back of her head and a necklace at her throat. She beamed with happiness. In the other, she stood outside in a wintry landscape holding a baby. Janie looked closer. She recognized the blanket that bundled the baby. Even though the picture was black and white, she knew the blanket was blue on one side and white on the other. Long fringe circled it all the way around. In the middle was a raised design of a rabbit. Yes, she knew that blanket. Her mother had given it to her long ago to use for her dolls. It had been *Janie's* baby blanket.

If the baby in this picture was *Janie*, then who was the woman cradling her with such effervescent joy?

She studied it again. The woman was standing in front of winter-dead remnants of plants bordering Grandpa's porch. A plastic Santa Claus was propped against the top step. A smooth hill sloped gently away from the house, down toward the river, looking like a distant ribbon flowing freely amidst frozen fields.

She flipped over the snapshot. The notation "six weeks" was scribbled across the back in a faded handwriting she didn't recognize.

She frowned, not understanding. Mother said she'd never brought her to Grandpa's house. Why would she lie about a thing like that?

Nonetheless, she liked the mystery woman and the way she tenderly held the baby. Perhaps she still lived here. Janie felt excitement soar through her.

"Mom?" Jeff appeared, dripping in the doorway, with a towel wrapped around him.

"Sorry, hon, I forgot to bring your pj's to you."

"What are you looking at?" Squeezing close to her, he radiated warmth from his recent bath. "Who is it?"

"I think the baby is me, but I don't know who the woman is."

"She looks like you."

"There *is* a resemblance, isn't there? She must be someone in the family."

"No, Mom, I mean she looks just like you."

"Do you really think so?" She wondered if she resembled the woman in the photo enough to confuse the mind of an old woman. Elta Mae had called her "Annalee." Was this a photo of Annalee?

"Cool." Jeff grabbed the picture of Grandpa's house and studied it. "I wish we had a Santa like that."

Janie laughed. "It was probably from the five-and-dime." And then she frowned again. This baby *couldn't* be her. Janie hadn't been born until the end of January. It would've been spring by the time she was six weeks old. Not Christmas. Yet, somehow Janie had ended up with this baby's blanket.

THIRTEEN

*S*leep should've come easily. Sinking into Grandpa's feather mattress in the back bedroom enveloped Janie with warmth, comfort and security, even if it was a false sense of security. Home... Janie had brought her son home.

An hour passed, but still she couldn't sleep. The grudge in Dexter's voice replayed in her mind. Spinning round this were the questions about the woman and baby in the photos. Then there was the memory of Oona's words: "Honey, you want whoever done this to come back in the dead of night?"

Another hour must have passed. In the dead of night...

Suddenly she bolted straight up in bed. She must've drifted off to sleep, but now she was wide awake. Something had awakened her. Pulling the sheet up to her chin, she stared at the black patch of her window and waited for whatever had awakened her to repeat itself. Another barge?

Something groaned, ever so slightly.

Jeff? She flung back the sheet and sprang from bed. Linoleum popped under her bare feet as she bounded across the floor. Grabbing the china doorknob, she rattled it, yanked it. Finally the door between the two bedrooms opened. Something was moving in Jeff's room.

Her eyes had adjusted enough to the night to be able to see. Curtains. That was all. A light breeze ruffled the gauzy curtains. Janie leaned against the doorframe and realized she was shaking. There was the curled outline of her son, asleep at the edge of the four poster. She resisted the impulse to scoot him into the center of the bed.

Then she heard the soft groan again, rising up through the floorboards.

Remembering the flashlight she always kept beside her bed, she shut the door and tiptoed back for it. She headed for the kitchen. The air smelled slightly sour, like spoiled food on unwashed dishes. But she'd cleaned the kitchen tonight before going to bed. The groan sounded again, this time accompanied by the slightest trace of a metallic ring. The sound seemed to be coming up through the kitchen floor, and she shone the flash on the iron pull ring of the trap door cut through the linoleum. Her heart thudded.

It was a narrow, dank, confining place, and the trap door provided the only way in and the only way out. Auntie Mae had kept her canned goods down there, at the bottom of a flight of unsteady, plank-like steps. It was a place that remained black as coal, even in broad daylight. Janie wasn't allowed to go down there.

She remembered Jeff's words. "You're always afraid," he'd said. True enough, when it came to closed-in spaces like that cellar. She would rather spend another night in a tent with a stranger trespassing on her cliffs, stopping barges, than go down there.

She took a deep breath. *That* cellar was at the bottom of the lake, she reminded herself, wanting to laugh at herself but unable to make her throat work properly. *That* cellar had been nothing more than a hole in the ground, and no one, not even the government, could move a hole along with a house. No, that cellar was gone.

Still, something seemed to be under the trap door. She approached it cautiously and wondered if this was another of Griffin's pranks. Maybe he'd left a wounded animal for her to find.

She grabbed the cool metal of the pull ring and grunted trying to lift the heavy door. Its weight threw her off balance, and she staggered at the edge of a dark pit. Steps led down into its darkness. So... A new cellar had been dug when Grandpa's house was moved up here to the cliffs.

And it smelled terrible. Must, mildew, and something acrid. Had the wounded animal died? No, it wasn't a dead animal smell. But it was more than a musty cellar smell.

She bit her lower lip and crept down the first step. With one hand, she groped for the edge of the kitchen floor. With her other hand, she played the flashlight's beam along the steps. Its circle of light shook from her unsteady hand. A faint buzzing rang persistently in her ears as she lowered herself, step by step, into the bowels of the earth. Halfway down the uneven steps, she paused to shine the light below. Damp, dank and dark beyond the reach of the beam. Jars of home-canned goods gleamed from rows of shelves. No dying animal on the stone floor.

She'd seen enough. She turned and retreated up two steps. Her heart thudded. Some invisible power above was about to close the trap door. The lid of her coffin. Hurrying, she stumbled. Groped for something above. Something, anything. A step, the edge of the floor. The flashlight slipped from her hands and clattered down the steps to the stone floor below. The light went out, and she was swallowed by darkness.

Jesus God.

Her fingers found the edge of the floor, and she squeezed so hard, they felt numb. If someone had slammed the trap door down on top of her fingers, she wouldn't know it.

Breathe, she told herself.

She crept up the rest of the steps, one by one, not letting go of the edge of the floor. It wasn't so dark anymore. Star light streamed in through the glass of the kitchen door, and she realized she was free, she was emerging from the cellar. She didn't care about the lost flashlight. Her heart pounded with an irregular beat. She'd been holding her breath, and now she let it out and took in a gulp of air. Stumbling into the kitchen, she let the trap door fall closed with a thud behind her.

She couldn't stop trembling.

It was her over-active imagination, that's all. It had tricked her into thinking a sound was coming up through the kitchen floorboards, but how could she tell, really? It was such a faint sound... It could've come from anywhere. Outside.

Sure. A wounded animal would be out in the woods, wouldn't it? Maybe Griffin had been stalking it, and when he shot, he'd missed the kill.

What was wrong with that man? Anger rose in her, displacing the fear from moments ago. What had caused that man to change from the nice kid she remembered from childhood? Well, he hadn't exactly been *nice*, but his mischief had been limited to frogs and garter snakes. Nothing cruel.

She pushed one of the kitchen tables over the trap door, securing it, then tested the back door. The new deadbolt Price had installed earlier that afternoon was still locked in place. Satisfied, she turned away from the kitchen and stepped into the shadowy front room. Twice as much furniture as was necessary for this small room had been placed here, in showroom fashion.

Later she would untangle the groupings, but now she bumped into them as she made her way through the shadows to the front door.

Its new lock also held securely. She peered through the door's window. The swing, the wicker chairs, and her philodendron sat motionless on the porch. Beyond, star light bathed the empty clearing surrounding Grandpa's house. The dark shape of Janie's car waited silently in the driveway. Opposite the driveway, she could see the outline of the tent protruding from the edge of the woods.

Everything seemed still. She unlocked the door and tiptoed out onto the porch. An owl hooted in the distance. Lake water slapped against the rocks of the cliff. An insect smacked her in the face. Creeping down the porch steps, she wondered what she was doing out here. Hadn't Oona said something about mountain lions?

The immense body of still lake water shimmered under a magnificent array of stars. Somehow, it didn't seem right that Grandpa's house sat atop a cliff overlooking a newborn lake. Or was it a dead river? Oona had called it a deadening. Whatever it was, the channel marker continued to blink out there. She watched its pattern and then realized the light was not as strong as it had been the night before when Jeff had pointed out its similarity to a dragon's eye. Something fuzzy was obscuring its brightness. Fog? No, couldn't be. Not with the stars blazing overhead.

She stepped closer to the cliff, and as she moved, she caught a whiff of something foul, like the sour odor from the basement. Something was dead nearby, she feared. She inspected the length of the lake, searching for the next channel marker. There it was, blinking brightly. Steadily. In the distance, the lake water reflected the light of a starry night. There was no fog tonight, but *something* fog-like obscured *this* channel marker, the one by *her* cliffs.

A rustling sounded from behind her, and she wheeled around to watch the sides of the tent shaking with fury. As suddenly as it had started, it stopped. Before she could react, the tent sides shook again.

No breeze could do that, even if there were one. No. Something was *inside* the tent. Slowly, she edged closer to the tent, until she had a good view of its flap. A low growl sounded from within, and then she saw the furry back quarters of a dog through the unzipped opening. The dog planted his feet firmly, and the sides of the tent rattled, as if he must be shaking his head furiously.

She laughed aloud with relief. The dog stopped his work. He backed out and twisted his body around to face her.

"Oh!" she gasped.

Hanging from the dog's jowls was the furry carcass of a rabbit. The small head lolled forward, and one eye remained wide open from its final moments of terror. Now the dog snarled at Janie. This dog that had been sleeping so peacefully today over at Oona's house, amongst the chickens, by night had turned into a killer. It curled back its lip far enough for her to see sharp teeth but not so far that it would drop its quarry. She swayed, feeling faint, and backed up against the peeling trunk of a cedar.

Still carrying its catch, the dog loped off into the woods, away from the lake. She stared at the empty opening of the still tent. Had the rabbit crept inside, seeking shelter, only to be cornered? She doubted it. For one thing, she was certain she'd left the flap zipped. Maybe Jeff had unzipped it this evening. She would speak to him about it tomorrow.

Starting back for the house, she kept thinking about the flap. And pranks... Someone could've unzipped the flap and left the dead rabbit inside for the dog — and her — to find. It sounded like one of Griffin's pranks.

FOURTEEN

"C'mere, Mama."

Lordy, not this again. The bedsprings would creak. Some of the young'uns had been up and prowling around all night, and if she could hear them, then they could surely hear her. Besides, that old cock was starting to yell at the world. Since the day she and Seymour were married, Oona had never been the last one out of bed. She was a woman who knew her duty.

The floorboards out front squeaked. Someone, trying to be all quiet-like, thought she could fool her mama. But nothing got past Oona. She knew it was Taffy out there, slinking outside. If that girl brought her another bastard baby, like Bonnibelle had done, she'd tan Taffy's hide real good.

Unless Griffy got to her first. Them two was always into it. But Griffy was only doing what a brother had to do. Look out for his sisters. Oona reckoned that's why Bonnibelle had never named a daddy for that baby of hers, 'cause she figured Griffy would kill the poor boy.

"Daddy, ain't you done yet? I got me chores to do. Same as you."

He groaned.

Oona tried to imagine Fern under Seymour's groping hands. Was that where he'd learned to do it? She bet not. Fern had been Oona's best friend. You couldn't keep something like that a secret between best friends.

No, it was more likely Seymour and Annalee had learned together. After all, they'd shared a bedroom growing up together, brother and sister, just like her own young'uns had to share the attic today. Was that why Annalee had run off all those years ago? Then how's come Annalee come back? Maybe

Seymour started up with her again, and that's why he and Dexter couldn't tolerate the sight of one another. Maybe that was why Annalee finally threw herself off them cliffs.

A shudder rippled through her at the memory of that day long ago. It had happened in the month of April, the day after Oona and Fern's senior prom. The same day that Annalee's neck got broken was the same day that Fern ran off. And Seymour was the connection. Hmmmm. Oona wondered.

"Oh Mama, oh Mama, oh Mama..."

Good. He kept coming back to her even though he had those flings every once in a goodly while. That meant she was doing her duty right. *She* knew how to keep her man. Unlike Annalee, Fern, or any of her daughters. Including the bastard one.

It steamed her when she thought of Janie. Wanted to have her cake and eat it too. She didn't want Price, but she didn't want Bonnibelle to have him neither. Oona saw the way Janie had fluttered her eyelashes at him. And they thought Oona wasn't so smart! Yessir, she'd show them all. Soon as she posted that letter to Mr. Roy Shoemaker, he'd come and take Janie off all of their hands.

One last grunt, and Seymour's business was done. Like a limp dishrag tossed aside after its job was finished, he rolled off her and curled up in a ball on his half of the bed.

Men! Women had been paying the price ever since Eve's first sin.

She climbed out of bed to start in on another day's chores. Oh, but her bones creaked this morning. That could mean only one thing. Must be a storm brewing, and she reckoned it would start soon as one Roy Shoemaker found out the whereabouts of his wayward wife.

THE MORNING DAWNED HEAVY and muggy. Janie slumped in one of the kitchen chairs and glared at the woodburning cookstove. More than anything, she wanted a cup of coffee. She'd watched Auntie Mae fuss around that stove as if it were nothing special, and now she wished she'd paid more attention to how her aunt had done it so easily. Split wood sat in a bucket beside the stove, but the thought of building a fire was more overwhelming than her need for a single cup of coffee.

Two nights in a row, she'd hardly slept. She could almost feel the baggy circles dragging at her eyes. The growing list of questions on her mind now entangled themselves like a foggy web, preventing her from thinking straight. Nor could she see straight. If she couldn't have a cup of coffee, then she knew what she had to do in order to clear her mind. Wearily, she pushed herself up out of the chair and went in search of her suitcase and her running shorts. She hated to exercise, but she couldn't argue with its merits for invigorating her. She dressed, left a note for Jeff, who slept through anything, and stepped outside into the damp air.

She turned her back on the haunting beauty of the lake where early morning shadows penciled long, thin lines across the still water. Grandpa was down there... The tent stood still this morning, overlooking his watery grave. Jeff must take it down later today.

The weeds in the driveway tickled her bare legs as she made her way out to the road. She set off at a gentle lope down the narrow lane of gravel, which was nothing more than a strip of sunlight piercing thick woods. The undergrowth in there was so tangled that it appeared primeval. How many places were left on earth, she wondered, with primeval forest? If this was one of them, then it would be a crime for anyone to intrude here. Griffin was right to be upset about the developers and tourists.

She hadn't gone very far on the gravel road before sweat started pouring down her sides, pooling around her midriff. A swarm of pesky little bugs pursued her. If she opened her mouth they'd fly inside. Half a mile farther, she could feel the sharp edges of the gravel pounding through her Keds and into her feet. She was melting away in the sun. A fork in the road took her away from the lake, up a gradual hill, and at the top, she stopped to catch her breath. Her head was ringing now, being forcefully awakened, and she turned around to look at the view behind her. The woods fell away down the hill, and over their treetops, she could see the lake spread out in its magnificence in either direction. Sitting in the middle of the lake was the hump of an island, the island Jeff had likened to a dragon. Griffin had denied it was there, but clearly, it was.

Gasping, she turned again and faced the gravel. Her feet were aching. It was her own fault for not having proper running shoes, but she couldn't afford them, not with Jeff's shoe size changing every three months.

She would've missed the path altogether if it hadn't been for the clump of purple wildflowers that caught her eye alongside the road. The path appeared at a convenient moment, offering her the shade of woods and a natural cushion for her feet. She wondered if it was a relic from the old days of loggers.

She turned onto the path and ran slowly through the tunnel of hardwood forest. Mature oaks and hickories towered above her, but their saplings slapped her in the face, along with some dogwood and blackgum sprinkled throughout. Sunlight filtered through their leaves, giving the air a lacy pattern of light and shadow. She was grateful for the refreshing shade. The air smelled of rotting leaves under this season's new growth. Her shoes thumped rhythmically along the smooth dirt. The path must be used frequently, for otherwise, it would be taken over by vines. She wondered who used it today with the loggers gone. Deer? Mountain lions? Something more deadly?

A patch of light ahead indicated that the woods were thinning into a clearing. In the middle of the clearing was a fenced pen, and in front of that were the outlines of two people. A woman shrank away from a lowering man.

Before she could make out who they were, something tripped her forward motion. Something cut into her ankles, snaring her feet. She plunged face down into the crumbly soil.

She lay stunned for a moment. The sudden stabs of pain surprised her. Blood and soil mingled in the scrapes on her knees and elbows, and she brushed at them. She scrambled backward, searching for what she'd stumbled into.

Someone was shouting. Something sounded like a pig squealing. The woods echoed with the sounds of running feet and swishing branches. A powerful stench drifted by.

Janie looked up and focused on the end of a shotgun aimed at her. She followed the length of its barrel with her eyes until she met Griffin's glare shining clearly through a riot of frizzy black hair and whiskers.

"You!" he said.

His single word resembled a growl and caused her heart to pound a little faster. New beads of sweat sprang up on the insides of her palms, and she brushed them against her shorts and stood up.

"Hi, Griffin."

The shotgun dipped slightly, as Griffin twisted his shaggy eyebrows and squinted at her. Finally, he lowered his weapon, and his unshaven face broke into a grin, exposing a row of gleaming teeth in the shadows. "Well, lookee here," he said, shifting the shotgun to his other hand. "If it ain't the city girl, out jo-o-o-ogging. How's come you do that? Show off them purty legs?"

"Griffin, it looks like a wire was hidden in the underbrush. It was strung across this path, and it tripped me. Do you know what it's doing there?"

"That there wahr is to keep the likes of you out of here."

"I...I..." Damn, but she didn't feel as brave as she was trying to sound. She took a deep breath to still her flutters and tried again. "I thought I was on Grandpa's property."

"He-e-ell no. This here neck of the woods belongs to Dexter. Now you turn on around an' git."

She stamped one foot where she stood and tilted her chin up to face him. "How was I to know? Where's the 'no trespassing' sign?"

"You're looking at it."

"All I see is a big bully," she said, breathing hard by now. "How much is Dexter paying you to impersonate a sign?"

"You don't hear too good, do you, girl?"

"All you're doing is imitating Dexter. How can you hold him up as a role model? Whatever happened to you, anyway, Griffin, to let someone else do your thinking for you?"

"You think you're so high and mighty," he said with a snarl. "Somebody oughta' take you down a notch or two, an' I might be jest the person to do it."

"Is that supposed to frighten me? Well, it won't work. You can't pick on me the way you were picking on your sister. Taffy was the one who was here with you before I interrupted you, wasn't she? What were you threatening her about this time?"

"That ain't none of your business. I wasn't finished with her, an' you made her let the hogs loose and then run off."

"Oh, *I* did all that?" she said, stepping closer to him, feeling bolder. She kept one eye on the nervous movement of his shotgun, but she didn't think he would actually shoot her. "If Taffy's hiding around here, then I'm going to go look for her. And I'll start with that hog pen."

She made a move to push past him, but he sucked in air and quickly raised the shotgun to poke against her ribs. "No you don't. You leave it be, or you're gonna be sorry."

She thought she saw fear flicker briefly across his face, and taking advantage of it, she twisted away from the barrel of the shotgun. "You better leave Taffy alone, or you'll be the one who's sorry."

Griffin sneered and resumed his nervous juggling. "Oh, yeah? Ain't no sassy broad gonna tell me what to do with my own sister. No one! You hear?"

She heard, but she was too stubborn to be scared anymore. "I respond to my name, and my name only. It's Janie Bainbridge. Got that?"

"Don't mean a hill o' beans to me. Ain't no Bainbridge folk 'round here. Never was, never will be, neither. Maybe you ain't even who you think you are."

"What are you talking about?" Her breath caught, making speech difficult.

"Ain't no room here for the likes of you. Iffen you knowed what's best, you'd git while the gittin's good."

"And suppose I don't?"

"Then I reckon someone's gonna have to teach you a lesson." He stopped juggling, and the wicked grin appeared again as he raised the sights of his shotgun to eye level. "Now go on an' git before you end up like your grandpa."

Maybe she'd pushed him too far. There was no point trying to argue or reason with a crazy man gone wild, she decided, and she turned and ran.

But why had he suddenly mentioned Grandpa? Was Griffin hiding him in his hog pen? Was that why he didn't want Janie to get any closer to it? That was ridiculous, too ridiculous even for Griffin.

But what *was* he hiding in his hog pen? She'd have to come back another time and see for herself.

And what did he know about how Grandpa had ended up? Dead, is that what he'd meant? Then he was threatening to kill her.

She ran, faster and faster, back along the trail the way she'd come, back along the gravel, down the hill, around the bend. She didn't stop running until she reached the safety of Grandpa's porch, where she collapsed, trembling and gasping for breath. Tears burned her eyes. She sank into the porch swing and took several gulps of air in an attempt to gain control.

Something was splintering this family apart, and she seemed to be its catalyst.

FIFTEEN

The morning sun was still low, but Oona was already sticky with sweat from her toil in the garden. *Nasty thistles just keep on coming. Never can get rid of them. Just like bad company.* She whacked at them with her hoe. Janie...whack...wasn't going to leave...whack whack...till she had some answers, was she? It would be over Oona's dead body before she let Janie bring the past into the present and drag it through the mud.

She paused to mop her brow. Danged heat was going to burn up her tomatoes before they got much of a chance to grow, and there wasn't anything she could do about it. It didn't set well in her bones that something, even the weather, was beyond her control. But she knew what to do about Janie that would take care of her duty to the girl and get her out of Oona and Bonnibelle's way at the same time. Yessir, she thought with a smug grin, old Oona had a few tricks of her own up her sleeve.

The laying hens squawked and scuttled out of the hen house. Bonnibelle must be in there with her bucket. *About time!* Griffy come out from the barn, carrying a tin pail of milk. He poured the cream off into another pail.

"Ain't you getting a late start on your chores, honey?" Oona asked, leaning on the end of her hoe.

He shrugged. "Reckon it was a late night."

"Chores don't wait, you hear? I don't care what you and Dexter are cooking up."

"Relax, Mama. Bossie's done. Daddy's letting her out to pasture now."

"Hmmph." Oona glared at him, but she couldn't stay mad long at this fine son of hers. "You going up town today?"

"Maybe. Whatcha need?"

She reached into the pocket lost among the folds of her paisley skirt and pulled out an envelope. "Got me a letter to post."

"Okay, Mama." He wiped his brow and tramped over to the garden. "I was fixing to get some motor oil for Dexter anyhows."

She smacked the envelope into his outstretched palm and glanced first over one shoulder then over the other. "Don't you show this to no one, you hear?"

Griffy scratched his ear and squinted at the letter in his hand. "Mr. Roy Shoemaker? Indianapolis, Indiana? What's this, Mama? You ain't fixing to ask no other cousin to come poke his nose where it don't belong, are ya?"

"Never you mind. You just mail it and hush your mouth about it, you hear?"

"Sure, Mama." Griffy shrugged and headed for the house.

This was something she'd rather do herself, but it couldn't wait till her next shopping day. Couldn't wait for Chumley, the mail carrier, to pick it up neither. If she asked Seymour to take her into town for a special trip, he'd want to know how's come, but she wasn't about to explain it to him. Men didn't understand these things.

Nossir, it was better this way, even if it did mean she had to trust a young'un. Things didn't always get done when you had to count on young'uns, but she reckoned she could count on Griffy. He was special.

She wondered how's come young'uns was like that. Lazy? She reckoned it was just that they'd never known a day of hard work in their lives. Never known hardships the way she'd known all her life. Well, not exactly her *entire* life. Only that part of her life since Fern got in her way.

She turned her hoe back to the thistles and whacked some more.

Fern... That woman done got what she deserved. Husband widowing her right off the bat. Only, Oona figured there never was no husband. She chuckled. Fern's mistake had been losing Seymour to Oona. Lord knows Oona would've taken Janie in long ago. Oona was a woman who knew her duty. Besides, Janie was the baggage that come along with Seymour.

That summer long ago when Mae brung Janie to stay with her and Uncle Tobias was when Oona should've taken Janie. But Oona was too busy chasing another baby, and Mae, who never had no babies of her own, fussed over

Janie like she was her own flesh and blood. 'Course, she wasn't, not really, not if Janie was Seymour's.

The hoe slipped from Oona's hands as new understanding dawned on her. The notion that was fixing itself on Oona's mind troubled her because something wasn't adding up rightly. So, she did what she always did. She pushed the troublesome logic from her mind. If Janie belonged to Seymour, then she didn't belong to Mae, which meant she wasn't Uncle Tobias's granddaughter, neither. And that gave her no rightful claim to his property, no matter what that deed said. Not Janie, not that husband of hers neither.

Oh, what had Oona gone and done? That letter to Janie's husband was only meant for him to come and take Janie off Oona's hands and out of Bonnibelle's way. But she'd mentioned the deed to help lure him down here, and now he'd come and the two of them would take the Mullen place right out from under Oona's nose when Janie didn't even have a rightful claim to it. Janie wasn't a Bainbridge. Not a Mullen, neither. She was a Potts, and an illegitimate one, at that.

Did that mean Oona was Uncle Tobias's last living relative? It was only fitting, then, that she and Seymour would get the Mullen place. After all the work they done on it.

The letter! Got to get that letter back! Can't let that husband of hers come down here and spoil everything.

Picking up her skirt to help her run faster, she waddled along the row of turnips to the end of the garden. She puffed up the slight hill to the mound where her house sat just in time to see Griffy back his junk car out onto the road.

"Griffy! Stop!" She waved her arms wildly, but the old green Ford roared away in a cloud of dust.

~

"SO WHAT ARE WE GOING to see on this grand tour?" Janie asked an hour later. Freshly showered, she'd put the memory of Griffin behind her when Price arrived to pick them up for the promised tour. Now she sat in the luxurious front of the Cadillac and stared expectantly out the window, but all she could see was a cloud of gravel dust.

Price's knuckles were white as he gripped the steering wheel, but at the mention of the long-awaited tour, he relaxed his hold, leaned back, and slowed the car. "First stop is Gran's house. Then I'll show you the site for the lodge and the fairways. And then I have a surprise."

"Oh, boy, a surprise!" Jeff said, leaning forward from the back seat. "What is it?"

"If I told you, it wouldn't be a surprise anymore," Price said, grinning.

Jeff frowned, impatient. "Can't we go any faster?"

Price winked at Janie. "Hang on, and let's find out."

Janie's foot pressed on her imaginary brake as the car floated over the wash-board lane. "This car certainly rides smoothly."

"Smooth, maybe," Price said, "but one day the tie rod is going to break loose, and then I'll have this 'perfect choice' of a car towed all the way back to Louisville to the old man's front door."

"Your dad, you mean?" Jeff asked. "Don't you like him?"

"Jeff!"

"No, it's all right." Price smiled at Janie, then turned to the rear-view mirror to address her son. "I guess I must like him because I've been trying all my life to live up to his expectations."

"And is this development of yours something that he expects from you?" Janie asked.

He laughed and shifted in his seat. "Hardly! He expects it'll flounder, but..." He lapsed into silence, and a dark look of determination crossed his face.

"But you'll make sure that doesn't happen," she said, finishing his sentence for him.

"You can bet on it."

From the look on his face, she wondered if he had a score to settle. There seemed to be more at stake than he was telling. He'd make quite sure, she suspected, that he wouldn't fail in this venture, especially if it meant proving his father wrong. And for some reason, he'd decided that he needed Grandpa's property to make his development the success that he was determined to have. Well, she thought, she could be just as determined and stubborn as he was.

The Cadillac glided around a bend, emerged from woods into a meadow and slowed as it approached a sun-drenched house overlooking the lake. Its cheeriness reminded Janie of how much work still lay ahead of her to finish achieving the same touches of hominess to Grandpa's house.

"Granny Rose will be expecting us," Price said, stopping the car in front of a gate covered with the open faces of blue morning glories. He switched off the engine and reached for his door handle.

Janie immediately felt drawn to the house. It stood two stories tall and freshly white amidst a riot of flowers. It crowned a peninsula jutting out into the lake at the entrance to a wide bay. There were no dangerous cliffs here. No sinister kudzu. A green carpet of neatly trimmed grass sloped in three directions from the house down the gentle hill to the water's edge. On the protected bay side of the peninsula was a small pier, holding fast a single boat with an empty mast reaching to the sky.

Price pointed at the road ahead, where woods resumed abruptly in the distance, as if an invisible wall kept them from encroaching into this cleared area surrounding the peninsula. "The fairway needs to go through there. Dad wants me to clear it with fire."

"Oona smelled a fire the afternoon we arrived."

He scratched his head. "Oona imagines things. She said something to me about it, too. She must've heard about Dad's idea and then decided I'd gone ahead and done it. She lives in her own twisted up version of reality." He shook his head. "Dad won't get his way on this. Come on. Gran wants to 'fortify' us." He climbed out of the car, pushed through the colorful vines taking over the gate, and led the way up the walk to the front porch.

"Where's that go?" Jeff asked, pointing to a flight of steps attached to the side of the house.

"My place is up there." Price tapped on the screen door and called, "Gran! They're here!"

Footsteps scurried from within.

"How come your stairs are outside?" Jeff asked.

"It gives Gran the privacy she needs." Price laughed. "I built a second-floor addition for myself to blend into Gran's original farmhouse."

"It reminds me of a beach cottage," Janie said, joining them on the porch where tubs of geraniums and hanging baskets of petunias lent an idyllic quality to the setting.

"Good. That's exactly the image I wanted for my development — a beach resort to service the landlocked midwest. And Gran's house, sitting here at the tip of the bay, will have to complement the lodge and outer buildings farther along the bay."

The screen door squeaked open, and Rose Bender bustled out onto the porch. She was dressed in the same black pants skirt and ruffled blouse that Janie had seen her wearing the previous morning. Only the gloves and hat were missing. "I do declare!" she said, giving Janie a big smile and squeezing her arm. "How good of you young folks to drop by and see an old woman like myself. My, but it's pleasant out here, isn't it? I believe we'll have our morning tea right here. Now, you sit yourselves down, and I'll be right back with it." She hurried inside.

"Slow down, Gran!" Price called after her. He shook his head, then explained. "Seventy-six years old, and she still can't act her age."

"I think it's marvelous that she's so active. I wonder how many people her age still go out digging in the woods for roots?"

He laughed. "Gran has always been independent. She makes everyone's ailments her business, too. Gives the doc up town a run for his money."

"If she enjoys nursing people, I wonder why Oona's mother doesn't live with her? They're sisters, after all."

"Elta Mae requires more care than Gran is physically capable of giving. Besides, they had some falling out years ago."

"Really? Rose is so kind and gentle, I can't believe she could even have a quarrel with anyone, let alone sustain it for years."

"Things aren't always the way they seem."

"Oh? What do you mean?"

A flush crept up his tanned face, and he jammed his fists in his pockets and rattled coins. "Nothing. I guess I'm on edge about this project. That's all." He grinned sheepishly, then motioned to the porch railing overlooking the bay. "Come on, let me show you where the lodge will be. You can see it from over here."

Skirting a hanging tendril of purple petunias, he pointed to a cleared area along the shore, about a half mile distant. He rested his hands on the railing and continued in a voice so low that Janie had to strain to hear him. "It will have four hundred units, a full health club, conference rooms, three restaurants, and a dock for fishermen and other water sports. But the main attraction will be the golf course. If it's not an eighteen-hole course, I might as well stop construction before it even gets started, take my losses and cut out."

"But that's not really an option for you, is it?" It sounded to Janie as if he had something to prove.

He chuckled. "No. That would mean Dad's right. I'd have to disappear somewhere. Out west, maybe."

"Why is it so difficult for you to consider the possibility that your father could be right about something?"

He turned around, leaned his elbows on the railing and stared up at the porch ceiling. "You don't understand."

"Help me to understand."

"Understand what, dear?" said Rose, reappearing at the screen door.

Price sprinted over to hold the door open for her. "Nothing, Gran. Janie doesn't understand...all the family relationships. That's all."

Rose peered at him curiously as she carried her tray outside and set it down on a wicker table. She directed everyone into cushioned chairs and poured tea into china cups decorated with flowers. "Then I must tell you about Elizabeth."

"Gran, no."

"Hush, now, Price. They're bound to hear talk, so they may as well hear it from me." She turned to Janie and handed her a cup. "Elizabeth was Price's mother, my daughter, you see, but I wasn't married at the time that she was born. I loved her no less for it, and we were quite content, the two of us, until I married Tom Bender around the time Elizabeth was old enough to go to school." She sighed and passed teacups to Price and Jeff. "I believe Elizabeth was teased quite severely in school for being illegitimate. Sometimes school-mates can be terribly cruel. Poor Elizabeth never got over the humiliation, not even when she married Price's father. J.P. Wanamaker."

"Uh, Gran, what's in the tea this time?" Price cautiously sniffed his cup.

"I declare, if you aren't the tease!" Rose clucked her tongue and passed a plate of biscuits and molasses cookies.

Affection shone from his face as he explained. "Gran prepares a tea for everything from stress headaches to successful business meetings."

"If you young people would only take better care of yourselves, instead of rushing off here and there like the whole world's afire and whatever your business is, it can't wait. I declare! You should have seen Price just yesterday. Tense as could be. Did that lavender ointment help you, dear?"

The tips of his ears flushed, and he grinned like a scolded schoolboy. "Yes, Gran, thank you."

"Price was in such a rush. Said he had some business up town that couldn't wait, not even for him to have a decent breakfast. I never — "

"Gran, do you have any more of that rosehip jam for these biscuits?"

"Well, of course, dear. You'll have to entertain our guests for me while I'm gone. I'll be right back."

The pink color drained from his ears when she left. "Don't pay too much attention to Gran. She can rattle on and on."

"She's an interesting lady." Janie wondered what it was about his trip to town the day before that he didn't want Rose to reveal.

"Maybe a little *too* interesting, if you ask me."

They drank their tea in silence as they waited for Rose's return. Soon, she hurried outside with a nearly empty jar of her homemade preserves. Offering it to Price, she sat down and took a deep breath.

"Now as I was saying about Elizabeth," Rose continued, drawing her teacup to her lips.

Price lifted one eyebrow. "Gran — "

"Tut, tut. This is my story, so you hush." Rose turned to Janie. "My Elizabeth thought that leaving the Chittenden Hills would make her happy. And maybe it did for a while. There was that time when J.P. became a colonel and was assigned to a post in Turkey, and Elizabeth had to entertain lavishly, being a colonel's wife. I believe those days abroad must have been her happiest."

The biscuit crumbled apart in Price's fingers, and he scowled. "Mother was never happy."

"It's because the Chittenden Hills was in her blood, you see." Rose's voice shook. "This was her home, and she couldn't get it out of her mind. But she was an outcast here." She paused and refilled everyone's teacups. "Now, I believe Price has it in his blood, too. He doesn't fit in with his father's world up there in Louisville. He's been jumpy and restless these last few days because he knows his father is coming here soon and will demand to see results."

Price flung the remains of his biscuit into his teacup and sprang out of his chair. "Are you ready for that surprise now? I thought you might like to go for a sail."

"Oh, yes! Yes, yes, yes!" Jeff stuffed the last of his cookie into his mouth and followed Price across the porch.

"What about the tour of Grandpa's property?" Janie asked. And finding out what Rose knows about Grandpa, she thought.

"We'll be able to see it best from the lake," Price said, clattering down the steps. "Come on."

Rose cleared her throat and spilled tea as she hastily set down her cup. She rested one hand on Janie's arm, detaining her. "Some folks believe this is God's country, and your grandfather was one of them. But things don't always stay the same. Times change. People and places got to change, too. Tobias didn't understand that."

She turned to Price, who had paused on the sidewalk. "Price, you've got to build your Resort because life must go on. But I'll tell you what. You've got to leave some things be. Tobias's land belongs to Janie now, and you got to leave it be. You'll find another way to have your Resort without that land. You leave her be."

The spark vanished from her face. Her frown made her look like an old, tired woman. It was a warning of some sort, and it set off an alarm in Janie.

SIXTEEN

*J*anie's spirits soared with the wind puffing out the sail. A fine mist sprayed their sun-bathed faces as they rocked through the gentle swells glinting like diamonds. They tacked first toward the channel, then back toward shore, then out to the channel again as they zigzagged downstream from Price's pier at the mouth of Chittenden Bay.

When they tacked toward shore, the boat caught less wind, and they fell into a lazy, drifting motion. Jeff dangled his fingers into the water, and Price relaxed over the tiller at the rear of the boat. "What did your grandmother mean?" Janie asked, taking advantage of the stillness.

Price stiffened from his relaxed slump. "About what?"

"She sounded as if she was in favor of times changing, and in favor of your building this Resort, but then she didn't want you to acquire my property."

"Does that mean you're willing to listen to my offer?" He perked up even more, looking a couple of inches taller.

"I didn't say that." Janie dipped her fingers into the water and watched the trailing ripples. "Didn't it sound like a contradiction to you?"

"Old people don't have to make sense, Mom," Jeff said.

Janie laughed. "Where did you come up with that?"

"There's a certain logic to that," Price answered hastily. "Besides, Gran has suffered enough. She wants to go forward. Her past is too painful."

"I expect she has, but she doesn't hide the fact that your mother was il-legitimate."

The wind tore at her words. Either Price didn't hear them or he was ignor-ing her. He angled the boat so that it caught more wind and raced toward shore. He pointed to a limestone promontory that extended out from the cliffs and appeared to rise and fall with their motion.

"That's where our property lines meet," he yelled above the whipping sail. "The fifth green will go up there."

Limestone rose from the lake in layers, forming a cliff similar to the one by Grandpa's house but more uneven. Kudzu burst out of the cracks and draped its vines down to the water's edge. Atop the cliff, crooked cedars and thick undergrowth crowded out to the edge of the promontory. A few colorful wildflowers bloomed under their shade on this rim.

Jeff shook her arm. "Mom! See those flowers? I bet those are the same ones your Auntie Mae brought to the cliffs."

Price cocked his head and gave them a puzzled look.

Janie laughed and explained. "I told Jeff the story of one of my memories from the summer I spent here as a child. Auntie Mae used to dig up some of her flowers and take them somewhere up on top of the cliffs." She felt her pulse quicken staring at that wild promontory.

"See, Mom?" Jeff said. "She planted her flowers up there. That's why there's flowers *there* and nowhere else. Do you see flowers anywhere else on the cliffs?"

"Well, no... But Jeff, you're making quite a leap. Why should her flowers still be alive after all these years? Maybe they weren't the kind that would come back year after year."

"They *could* be her flowers," Jeff said, sticking out his lower lip. "And I bet that's a grave up there." He turned to Price. "You're going to put a golf course on a grave."

Price didn't respond. "Coming about," he called instead, turning his attention to maneuvering the boat. The boom swung over their heads, and Janie and Jeff ducked to the other side. Picking up speed once again, they sailed away from the cliffs, out into the channel. Janie looked over her shoulder for barges. She would hate for the wind to die here.

Price seemed satisfied as they moved farther away from shore. Once he had them settled in their new direction, he spoke. "All the shoreline you see now, beyond that promontory, belongs to you."

"*All* that?" Jeff said.

"That's right. Tobias Mullen kept buying property others thought was worthless, and eventually he owned more land than anyone else around here."

"His tobacco must have been very profitable for him to buy so much," Janie said.

"I'm sure he got it for a steal."

Was that what Price planned to do, Janie wondered, if she agreed to sell to him? Steal it for less than its value? Well, it didn't matter, because she wouldn't sell at any price. "Grandpa lived for his land," she said, even though she'd known him such a short while.

"Bonnibelle thinks he killed himself," Jeff blurted out.

"Why would he do that when he had so much to live for?" Janie asked. "See how much land he still had left after the government confiscated what they needed?"

Price remained pensive as he gazed at the receding shoreline. Finally, he spoke in a low voice. "It's odd that he would go to the trouble of putting the deed in your name."

"You mean instead of simply naming me in his will?"

Price nodded. "There was no will."

"Well, I don't see what difference it makes. A will or a deed. The end result is the same. Maybe it was easier to change the deed rather than write a will."

Price shrugged.

"You don't think so, do you? What are you suggesting? Changing the deed proves he was thinking of suicide? That's crazy."

He sighed. "I don't know what to think. It just strikes me as odd. Anyway, you own the property now. That's clear enough. There is no will for anyone to contest."

So that's what he was getting at. "Grandpa must've wanted to make sure I own the property and someone couldn't contest any inheritance. I guess I have expectations to live up to, also. Only, I wonder what he expected from me?"

"Happiness," Price said, smiling.

Listening to the sounds of the wind catching the sail and the rhythmic swishes of the boat plowing through the rippled water, she thought about that. She would be content to stay out here all day, lulled by the wind and the sun and the water. Maybe that *was* happiness. She recognized the same feelings of contentment from that summer with Grandpa, listening to his tales, playing along the river, eating Auntie Mae's home-cooked meals, and she realized she hadn't felt such contentment since. Not until now. Maybe Price was right. She could almost feel the happiness radiate from her.

Radiating happiness, just like the bride in the photos.

"I found something interesting," she said, then told him how she'd found the photos hidden behind Auntie Mae's graduation picture. She described the woman she hadn't recognized and the happiness that had shone from her face. "I wish I'd thought to bring them along today to show Aunt Rose." *But I was too upset about Griffin.*

"You'll have other opportunities."

"There was a picture of Mom as a baby," Jeff said.

"It couldn't have been me. I wasn't born until the end of January, but in the photo, the house was decorated for Christmas. And the baby was already six weeks old."

Price shrugged. "Gran will clear it up for you." He focused his attention on the riggings. "Coming about."

The boom swept over their heads as Janie and Jeff scrambled to the other side. The boat circled in the water, then the sail caught the wind, popped, and they sped toward shore once again. The task of hiking out to balance the boat as it lifted up out of the water took all of her concentration. Price seemed determined to push the boat as fast as possible.

The hull of the boat reared up suddenly. Janie and Jeff leaned far out over water, but their weight didn't make the boat drop. Joining them, Price had to reach far to grasp the tiller and his riggings. His added weight finally brought the boat down. He pulled the sail in a little, allowing some of the wind to slip away, and the boat settled into its drifting pattern once again. They gasped and laughed and gasped some more.

"Can we do that again?" Jeff asked.

Price found his voice. "Depends on the wind, tiger. What's your rush?"

"It was fun, that's all." He turned away with a pout forming on his lower lip, spied something on the shore, then brightened. "Lookit, Mom! There's our house! You can see that neat place I was telling you about."

He pointed to a small cove, looking like a horseshoe sagging between two cliffs. A stream tumbled down from the woods, through underbrush, and emptied into the lake from the middle of the cove. Next to it was a path.

"See, Mom? Wouldn't that be a neat place for the tent? It's sort of flat. I bet we could swim there."

She shuddered, remembering Dexter's warnings of cottonmouths. "It looks pleasant from here, Jeff, but underneath the surface of the water, it's just rocks and mud. And probably lots of dead trees." Trees killed for a lake, or trees killed for a golf course — which was worse?

"Then maybe we could get some sand and turn it into a beach."

Price laughed. "You think like me, tiger. Only, I've already got plans for a sandy beach over in the bay. I thought a playhouse would do nicely here." He nodded at the cliff to the right, the one opposite the cove from Grandpa's house.

Speechless, she stared at him for several minutes that felt like an eternity. Finally, she said, "You want to have a *playhouse*? *Here?*"

"Why not? A playhouse on one of these cliffs overlooking the lake would be an interesting tourist attraction, don't you think? The lodge would ferry its guests over here in a pontoon boat. That cove would make a natural dock. Sure, why not?"

Up until this moment, she suspected, Price hadn't thought of a playhouse at all. He was lying.

"We could have a playhouse," he continued, "similar to the ones in Brown County. You worked at one, didn't you?"

How had he known? She cleared her throat, then spoke slowly. "I was a secretary for one of the acting groups, but I got laid off a couple months ago."

"Maybe you could consult me on this project. What do you think?"

She sputtered. "What do I know about opening up a theater?"

"Mom, you write movies. You could do it."

"Honey, that's not the same thing at all."

"But you could do it."

She studied her son and wondered. Hadn't he thought her afraid of everything only the day before yesterday? Now he was expressing confidence in her. Could she really do it? "I'll think about it."

"Good enough," Price said. "We'll get together over dinner and go over the plans. And my offer."

Janie raised her eyebrows at him.

Price laughed. "Don't look at me like that! I haven't made you an offer yet, but I will. Soon as I can put some figures together."

"Heck, Mom, I don't want to move again."

"Don't worry, honey. For the time being we're not going anywhere." She lifted her chin at Price. "Don't trouble yourself. My land is not for sale." She flinched a bit, referring to the land as hers, rather than Grandpa's. It didn't feel true. She was just the caretaker for Grandpa's land.

"Lookit, Mom, there's my fishing rock." As the boat drifted closer to shore, Jeff indicated the point where the cove met the main body of the lake. A large, flat rock stood out amidst the tumble of rocks and tangle of brush.

"That's where we had our picnic breakfast, isn't it?" she said. From the rock, the land sloped up through woods toward the cliff where Grandpa's house sat. "I didn't realize this cove was so close to our house."

"The land takes on a new perspective when seen from the lake," Price said.

A movement in the brush by the stream caught her eye. She thought she saw a shadow darting under the cover of a branch, and she remembered the person who could move through locked doors, vandalizing a place, then cleaning it up. She remembered the shadowy person who'd flagged down a barge, and the fingerprints left on her philodendron's pot. Whoever was hiding there in that brush could be the same person. "Did you see that? Someone's there — "

But Jeff interrupted her with a whistle. He pointed at the cliffs ahead, the cliffs directly below their house. "Wow! It looks like there's a cave under all that kudzu stuff below our house."

"Where?" Price said, leaning into the sail to see better.

The boat tilted precariously with his movement, and Janie and Jeff sprang back. The moving shadow in the brush was forgotten as Janie hiked out to compensate for the seemingly unconcerned Price. He adjusted the boom, and the boat finally settled back to its normal list.

"I don't see it," Price said. "Do you mean where all the kudzu vines cover the cliff?"

"Uh-huh. Mom, is it one of the caves you used to play in?"

"I didn't play in them. Are you sure you saw a cave?"

"There are lots of caves in the limestone around here," Price said.

"I know that. But a cave right under our house? Why wouldn't we have noticed it before?" Janie felt her stomach churn. The motorboat. The signaling flashlight. The moaning noises from the cellar. Could all of those mysteries be connected to this cave? Her spirits that had soared not so long ago now took a nose-dive into the cliff.

Price rested an elbow on the tiller as he shaded his eyes. "I think I see the opening now. You have to look in just the right spot." He pointed it out for

Janie. "Funny, but I've never noticed it before, and I've sailed past these cliffs a hundred times. That kudzu does a good job concealing it."

Janie leaned against him to follow the angle of his arm. "The kudzu also hides the cave from view if you're looking down from the top of the cliff or up from the rocks below, where Jeff likes to play."

"Out here on the lake is the only place where you can see it," Price said, "and even then, you have to get just the right angle. Sure is well hidden."

Janie felt something gnaw at her inside.

"I know, Mom! I'll bet those moaning sounds you heard were from a mountain lion that got trapped inside the cave."

"Oona has been putting ideas into your head," she said, even though she'd had the same thought.

"It's not so unreasonable," said Price. "There *are* mountain lions around here. That's why this land must be protected."

"You're doing just the opposite by building your Resort."

"On the contrary." His voice was low and controlled, as if he had gone over his reasons a hundred times. "No one can stop the development that will occur here on account of this lake. My development simply controls how it will happen in this neck of the woods."

"But the point is, Price, there won't be any woods left if you divide it up into little lots and sell them off for a huge profit."

He laughed. "Is that what you think I'm doing? You're wrong. Why do you think it takes so much land to do this project right? Because most of the land I buy will be preserved the way it is. I'll concentrate the residential areas together, you see, and attract buyers because of the natural beauty surrounding their homes. And because of the golf course and a few other amenities. But if Dexter sells to one person, and Crockett sells to someone else, and you sell to that developer up north, and so on, then it *could* very well end up divided into little parcels. We need one single organization to control what happens to all that land as a whole."

"Oh." He sounded so reasonable. So...honorable. Maybe she'd misunderstood him all along.

SEVENTEEN

"Coming about," Price announced, pulling the boom across to port and pointing the boat out toward the channel.

It was their signal to spring to the starboard side as the sail flapped in the wind then caught. As they switched, Janie saw the cove again and wondered about the shadow lurking there. A mountain lion? Or the person who'd vandalized Grandpa's house, signaled the barge, handled her potted plant?

Once they crossed the river channel, the wind died. They drifted idly in the boat. Each of them fell silent, lost in tranquillity. Janie didn't care if they ever returned.

Jeff stiffened suddenly, and his eyes grew to saucer shapes. "Is that the island?"

"Sure is, tiger. I thought we'd head there to eat this lunch Gran packed us."

The island rose as a rocky hilltop surrounded on all sides by shallows. They approached it from the east, where the safe and deep waters of the old river channel flowed. West of the island, the shallows extended all the way to the opposite shore. Random clumps of treetops poked their leafy heads above water in the shallows. Price warned them that under water the place was a virtual jungle of hidden branches. Janie imagined how they could ensnare an unknowing person in their watery grave. Like Grandpa.

On the island itself, however, only a few scrubby bushes and one stubborn kudzu vine clung to the long and narrow hump of rock. It *did* resemble a sleeping dragon, a cliff, pockmarked with years of erosion and stranded out here by the rising water level of the lake.

"Okay, you two navigators!" Price called, passing an oar to Janie. "You need to help me look for obstacles. Floating logs, treetops just below the water's surface, that sort of thing."

"And dead bodies?" Jeff asked.

"Jeff! What a thing to... Get back! Don't lean so far over the edge!"

"But I see one, Mom. A tree, that is. Dead ahead."

"Let's use the oar to push us away from it."

Together they maneuvered the boat around to the far side of the island where it couldn't be seen from the river channel. The crow's feet at the corners of Price's eyes deepened as he scanned the area in search of the best place to make fast the boat. His frown seemed to reflect her thoughts — there was no point in inviting trouble by advertising their presence.

"That looks like a good place," said Jeff, pointing. "It looks kind of brushy, and we could hide most of the boat. You never know what kind of pirates might come along."

"I expect you're right." Price nodded solemnly. "Well, matey, I'm putting you in charge of that detail."

He raised the centerboard and steered the boat into the brush still growing out of the water. Hopping onto shore, they pulled together, dragging the boat halfway out of the water. Several scraggly trunks grew out of rocky crevices in the dragon's back, and Price tied up the boat to one of them. He unloaded their picnic basket, then lowered the sail while Jeff set about finding debris and branches to strew across the boat.

Janie sat down on the crest of the island. She closed her eyes and lifted her face to the baking rays of the sun. Jeff's sneakers made little scrabbling sounds against loose pebbles. An occasional ripple broke the surface of the water. Price rustled the wrappings of the lunch his grandmother had prepared.

Rose. Janie must talk to her privately and get Rose to tell her about Grandpa and his two daughters. Maybe Rose even knew Janie's father.

The scrabbling and the rustling stopped. She knew Price was watching her, and she wondered what he was thinking. If he was comparing her to the dozens of women he must've known. It seemed like forever since she'd known a man. A tingling spread through her, but it was the heat of the sun, she told herself.

"Lunch is served, Madame."

She opened her eyes to narrow slits and saw him grinning at her as if he'd been able to read her thoughts. Instantly, a flush crept up her cheeks. Damn him.

After a lunch of chicken salad and homemade bread, Price helped Jeff rig a fishing pole. From her perch on the crest of the island, Janie watched them scrounge for the perfect branch, some twine from the boat, and bread as bait. It didn't seem to matter to them that they had no hook. Their fun came from rigging the pole. Eventually, though, Jeff gave up.

"It's no use," he said. "I'm gonna go hunt turtles."

"Don't take too long, tiger. We're losing the wind, so we'll need to head back soon, or else row." Price came over to Janie's side and sat down next to her. Folding his knees up to his chin, he draped his arms across them.

She followed his gaze across the expanse of water to the limestone cliff, tracing a sunny boundary between woods and water. The pattern of intervening ripples threatened to hypnotize her, and the sun's heat held her sluggish. He sat there rigidly staring at the distant cliffs, giving himself an air of remoteness.

She knew all about that, didn't she? No one understood better than Janie what loneliness meant. She'd felt it every waking moment since Roy had left. Not that she regretted his absence. No, quite the contrary. Roy had consumed so much of her adult life — she'd married him too young — and once he left, she hadn't made any connections to another adult. She'd been adrift at sea, and she had only just begun to realize that it would be nice to find an anchor somewhere.

How could Price Wanamaker, a man accustomed to fawning women and an adoring grandmother, understand loneliness as she understood it?

"Why are you doing this?" she said, blurting out the irritation he made her feel.

He turned to give her a puzzled frown. "I like to sail. It's a challenge between nature and my skills as a sailor. When I win, I feel recharged."

"And when you lose?"

He scowled. "I don't lose."

"So here you are, developing a resort in the wilderness because you like to sail?"

He chuckled. "Not because of sailing. This is my home. Oh, I've thought about packing my gear and hitting the road. Backpacking in the Rockies. Rafting the Colorado. Scavenging the west coast."

"Why don't you?"

"I might have to if I can't make a go of The Resort."

"It's very important to you, isn't it?"

He offered no comment but turned away to brood once again at the cliffs across the lake. The moment stretched between them in quiet camaraderie. Finally, he broke the spell. "I meant it, you know. About the playhouse. I need your help."

First it was her land. Now it was her help. She shrugged. "What do I know about opening up a playhouse? I was just a secretary for one, that's all."

"They say it's the secretary who runs a business."

She laughed.

"Look, all I'm asking is that you take a look at my plans," he said. "Dinner, tomorrow night? I make a mean Caesar salad."

The last place she wanted to go was to his lair. "I still owe you for changing my locks. *I'll* cook. *My* place, tomorrow at six."

His face broke into a broad grin and his eyes twinkled. "Maybe we can go over some figures, too." He let go of his knees tucked under his chin and swept his arm in a wide arc indicating the cliffs opposite them.

So he was back at that again, was he? She sprang to her feet. "I'll find Jeff and tell him it's time to go."

He opened his mouth as if to say something more, then clamped it shut. Watching the lake, he said, "I'll get the boat ready."

She turned away and glanced along the length of the island until she spied Jeff on his hands and knees, inspecting the rocky slope at the opposite end. "Any luck, hon?" she called to him.

"Naw. No turtles, but I found something else, and it's even better."

"Oh?"

"It's a cave, and I bet there's something in it."

Janie allowed a tone of conspiracy to creep into her voice as she picked her way along the spine of the island. "Goblins?"

"Maybe. Come see, Mom!"

"Well, I don't know, if there are really goblins..." Exaggerating a shudder, she tiptoed through the weeds. Scraggly shrubs clinging to the rocky backbone of the dragon scratched her bare legs.

"It's okay. They only come out at night."

She squatted next to him, and he looked up from his inspection. His eyes shone from his make-believe world. Motherly pride glowed inside her. She had to admit feeling grateful to Price for providing them with this outing today.

Memories of herself as a girl on a summer day long ago flashed through her mind. She'd trudged after Grandpa through the woods that now lay at the bottom of the lake. They'd crossed the river in his boat that day and headed through the woods, up a hill, which had seemed interminable for a little girl, to its rocky summit where the woods thinned and afforded them a spectacular view of the river winding through the green blanket of woods. He'd shown her a cave, too, that day.

Could this be the same cave? Excitement mounted. This might very well be the rocky crest of that same hill where Grandpa had brought her that day. The cave he'd shown her had a yawning opening, like the jaws of a dragon, Grandpa had said. The entrance was well down the hill and would be under water today, she thought with a wave of sorrow.

The old days were gone, along with Grandpa and his river. If he'd lived long enough, the loss of his way of life would have killed him. Better for him to have died with the river. It was ironic that the lake, which brought her son such pleasure today, had cost Grandpa his beloved river. Seeing the lake would have broken Grandpa's heart.

What would it be like for Jeff's children? This "island" would be gone, as the lake still had not risen to its expected level, and Jeff would probably remember this day with as much a sense of loss as she remembered the rare times she'd spent with Grandpa on his lost river.

"Look here, Mom," he said, bringing her back to the present. He moved aside from the hole he'd been inspecting. It was a round opening in the side of the dragon's back, and it was no more than a couple of feet across.

"Are you sure this is a cave, Jeff? It just looks like a hole to me."

"Sure, Mom. I've already been inside. Poke your head in."

"Oh, Jeff, I don't know that I can." She felt her heart pound with panic and her palms grow clammy remembering the reaction of claustrophobia when Grandpa had led her into his cave. "Let me have your pocket flash, and I'll just look in from out here." He handed it over, and she shone the beam inside a cavern larger than Grandpa's front room.

"See, Mom?"

"Yes. You're right. It looks like the cave runs right under this hill, down toward the water." Excited, she swept the beam across the damp walls and down the sloping floor a hundred feet or so to where the cave ended abruptly in a pool of lake water. Could it be the same cave? The jaws of the dragon would be somewhere down in that pool of water, then. She straightened up and handed the flash back to her son. "I think this is the same cave I visited years ago with Grandpa."

"Wow!" His face lit with excitement. "Do you think the dragon still lives here? Can we go inside, please Mom?"

"Not this time. Price is waiting for us."

"Aw, heck, why do we have to leave so soon?"

"I expect Price has work to do," Janie said, smiling. "And so do we."

Jeff scuffed his toe at a loose rock. "At least we have our own cave I can explore, instead. You know, the one we saw in the cliff below our house."

Janie frowned. "I don't want you climbing around on that cliff by yourself. Understand?"

"Aw, Mom."

"Besides, I want you to take the tent down when we get back."

He looked away. Janie caught his hand and tugged gently. "Come on."

He gave up, and they started back toward the other end of the island where Price awaited them in his sailboat.

But when they crested the spiny hump of the island, Jeff dropped to his feet.

"Get down!" he said, pressing his binoculars to his face. "Pirates!"

Janie obeyed, caught up in his game. She peered over the top of the island and saw the motorboat approaching them. It was still far enough away that its soft hum was barely heard, but it tore across the lake in a straight line for the island.

"It's really Dexter," Jeff whispered.

"Are you sure?" She felt her heart thud.

"Sure I'm sure."

"We can't stay here like this. He can't see us this far off. Let's get back to the boat and Price." They clambered back over the hump of the island, tripping over rocks, and arrived breathless to the brushy point where they'd left the boat hidden.

Price had uncovered it. Piles of Jeff's carefully gathered brush sat to either side of the grounded boat. The picnic basket was nestled back into its spot amidst coils of rope, and the unfurled sail flapped idly.

"If it isn't Peter Pan and Wendy!" Price said, winking. "All set to leave Never Never Land and sail home?"

But Janie couldn't even smile at his light-heartedness. All she could do was point out the motorboat bearing down on them.

Price turned and watched it for a moment, then shook his head. "Poor Dexter. This island used to be a hill on his property. He thinks it's still his, even though the lake is now public. Don't worry about Dexter. He's harmless enough."

"What's he want with us?"

"Probably thinks he can tell us to leave," Price said with a sigh. "He doesn't like it when people come to this island. He thinks he has to protect it."

Janie stepped closer to Jeff and circled her arms around him. How had Dexter known they were here?

Just then, the angry whine of his outboard motor suddenly dropped in pitch as Dexter cut the engine and swerved around a buoy, away from the island. Jeff wriggled out of her grip and held his binoculars up to his face to watch Dexter pull a fishing pole out from underneath the bench seats of his aluminum dinghy. A few minutes later, the wake from his boat washed to their feet in a procession of little waves.

Price climbed into his sailboat and checked the riggings. "Okay, mateys, are you ready to cast off?" There was no longer a lilt of gaiety to his words.

Dexter's boat bumped rhythmically against the buoy. The end of his fishing line plopped into the water, then the reel whirred softly as he probed the waters. From this distance, Janie could only see shadows obscuring his face, shadows from the bill of his cap and the patch over one eye. She shuddered, wondering if Dexter had been the shadow she'd seen earlier that day when they'd sailed past the cove by Grandpa's house. That's how he would've known where to find them.

He cast his line out again, and as she listened to the spinning of his reel, she couldn't help but feel that this show was for her benefit. She was the real object of his search.

EIGHTEEN

*O*ona sat beside Seymour in the cab of the truck and held her double chin high as if she occupied a throne. A beer flat full of tiny strawberries angled precariously where the mountain of her tummy nearly met her stubby knees. Let Janie fool with the danged things. Oona was tired of the mess of preserves. Besides, none of the mouths at her house watered for them anymore. It was into the heat of June, and no one was much interested in eating at all.

When they turned into old Tobias's driveway, Oona saw Janie and her boy sitting on the porch. She was reading some sort of book to him. Figgers. She's bound and determined to make a sissy out of him.

The boy popped up when he saw them. He ran over to the truck, curious like any boy ought to be. Soon as he was satisfied that it was just the two of them, he scampered off, looking for mischief over yonder on the rocks.

"Don't you wander off so close to that there cliff, you hear?" Oona yelled as she struggled out of the cab with her flat of strawberries. "You like to make my heart stop just watching you."

"Jeff, don't go near that cave," Janie yelled. She was so worked up about something that she took her sweet time coming to Oona's rescue. "Need a hand?" she asked, holding the door of the truck.

"How's come you didn't come to supper?"

The girl looked like she didn't know what to say. Her face turned pink, and she grabbed her throat. "I...I didn't know we were invited. I'm sorry."

"Lands, child! Do I have to invite y'all every time we eat? You oughta know better'n that. Bad enough y'all're staying way over here."

"Oona, you're very kind, but we can't eat with you every day. Besides, I've been working this afternoon, ever since Price brought us home, so Jeff and I just grabbed a quick bite to eat."

Oona lifted her nose, but she didn't spy any evidence of work around the place. There was no warsh pegged to the line. No garden freshly dug. Work, hah? It was another excuse, that's all. Young'uns all wanted to avoid her, and she was getting sick and tired of it. She sniffed and thrust the beer flat of berries into Janie's hands. "Well, here, I brung you these. It's the tail end of 'em."

Janie looked down at the little runts she held as if they was gold nuggets. "How...neighborly! I don't remember anyone ever doing anything like this before."

Oona clucked her tongue. "I reckon that's the city for ya." She huffed and puffed and set off down the driveway toward the porch. "Bless me, but I need to sit a spell."

"Seymour — "

"Oh, leave him be, honey. He's happier sitting there in his truck." Oona pulled her weight up the steps and eased herself into the porch swing. The boards of the roof groaned overhead where the rusted chains were anchored.

Janie moved easily along behind her, and Oona hated her for it. Well, she reckoned, her day will come. Once her man gets down here and she has herself seven more babies like Oona done had, we'll see how quick she is on her feet.

Janie came as far as the porch steps where she set down the flat of strawberries and wrapped her arms around the column holding up the roof. She looked off in the direction of the boy, like she'd rather be over yonder with him instead of here with Oona. She could tell. Though, Lord knew why. He clumb up on one of them big rocks overlooking what used to be the valley. Not no more, thanks to them gov'ment boys that come in here and turned the valley into a deadening. Now that river swole up like a dead catfish with a bloated belly. Oona shivered and looked away. She would have to get away from this place soon.

Creak...creak... Janie frowned up at the roof, and Oona laughed. "Bless me, child. I done sit here many a time and it ain't never fell in yet. And Mae, bless her soul, in her last years, she done made me look like a skinny thing, though Lord knows why since she never had herself no babies."

"I wonder why Auntie Mae never married?"

"Oh, I reckon there warn't a man alive that would take her."

"Take her? Don't you mean it the other way around?"

"Now don't you go twisting my meaning around like everyone else does," Oona said, folding her arms across her bosom. Janie had no sense at all. Oona speculated that the girl must have some of Mae's high falutin' notions in her head. Lord knew, she had Fern's pigheadedness.

"Sorry."

She didn't look sorry, Oona thought. "Humph. I reckon Mae kept herself so busy fussing over your grandpappy, she didn't have no more to give no other man. What man is gonna play second fiddle to that?"

"If Auntie Mae devoted her entire life to taking care of Grandpa, then she must've been devastated by his disappearance."

"Yep. It killed her, I reckon." Oona closed her eyes. *Janie don't need to know about the white lightning.*

"She must have been frantic," Janie continued. "How long did they search for Grandpa?"

"They give up after a day and a night. Everyone knowed it was his time, and he wanted the river to take him. It was fitting."

"They gave *up*?"

The pitch to Janie's voice made Oona open her eyes. She sighed. "Honey, he was a old man. Mae got one of them there feelings in her bones that he'd passed on." *What was wrong with this girl? She looked like Oona had taken a butcher knife to the old man herself. Sure, Oona missed him. But dang it, passing on is part of life, just like growing old is. Janie sure had a lot to learn.*

"And Auntie Mae lived just a few months after Grandpa died?"

There it was again. That word. Every time Janie said that word, it sent a chill down Oona's spine. Don't she know it's proper-like to talk around *that word instead of saying it outright? Like "passing on." Or "the Lord called him." Or "it's his time." But young'uns, they ain't got no respect.*

"Yep," was all Oona said instead of scolding her like she ought to. "Three or four months was all."

"How did she die?"

The chill rippled through Oona's layers of fat. She crossed her arms under her bosom and glared at the girl. "The Lord took her in her sleep" was the final word she gave on the matter before clamping her jaws shut.

That gave Janie something to think about for a while, fussing over some potted plant like it was a blue-ribbon quilt. Lord, Oona suddenly recalled. Annalee used to have more potted plants than you could shake a stick at. Janie was doing what Oona had feared. She was dredging up that whole story from the past, and it should ought to be done and over with.

"How did she pass her time," Janie said. "Auntie Mae, that is? Once she was alone? After Grandpa — "

"Well, Mae, she'd always been a house afire up until the deadening come. Then she wouldn't do much 'cept shut herself up inside the house and sit in her recliner with her...uh...cup o' coffee. Don't know why folks waste their hard-earned money on that stuff. And she'd listen to the radio. Like Seymour over yonder." Like Seymour all right. Warn't no coffee in her cup. "Bless me, but I don't know what's so all-fired important about that radio."

"It's a link to the outside world."

"Hah? They ain't got nothing on us. Nossir. Well, I reckon it's time we best be getting —"

"Wait. I almost forgot. I have something to show you first. Let me put these berries inside. I'll be right back."

Janie picked up the flat and disappeared inside before Oona could say Jack Sprat. Humph. Now she was stuck here, watching the boy pitch rocks into the deadening while she waited. She was shifting her weight, aiming to pull herself out of the porch swing and leave anyhow, when Janie returned. The girl held onto a couple of photographs like they was treasure.

"What's this?" Oona said, feeling the beginnings of a rattle in her bones.

"A picture of someone. I thought you might know who she is."

"Lands, honey, I cain't see nothing close-up without my specs no more. My eyes ain't what they used to be. My boy Owen brung me some right fine specs from Nashv'lle, but I reckon I left 'em up home." Oona pulled heavily on the chain to heave herself out of the porch swing.

"Could that be what's in your pocket?" Janie pointed to the wire rims poking out from the pocket in Oona's skirt.

"Well slap my bones, here they be!" Steadying herself, Oona pulled the wire rims from her pocket and carefully unfolded them. When she'd adjusted them on the end of her stubby nose, Janie handed her one of the pictures. What was this all about, anyhow? Some sort of trick?

The lenses tugged at her eyes, distorting the face on the picture. Still, it was clear from the veil hanging down over that blonde hair that this was a bride.

"Lands, child, the light ain't too good here. Who's this here?" Oona moved the photo from close range to arm's length, but still the image did not focus. She bent over and twisted her neck as she strained to study it.

"I was hoping you could tell me who she is."

Oona frowned and stuck out her lower lip. "Humph! Anyone can see plain as day that's your mama."

"Mother? No, it can't be. Besides, I found these pictures tucked behind a larger one of Auntie Mae's graduation. They were all sticking out of the frame of the mirror hanging over her dresser. Like she was hiding it. Why would Mae hide a picture of my mother, her own sister?"

"Well, your grandpappy didn't take too kindly to the way Fern up and left. Next thing he knew she was married, to boot." Oona tossed the photo back to Janie, pulled off her spectacles and returned them to her pocket.

Janie stood there gawking first at Oona then at the pictures in her hand. "This isn't my mother. Look again."

"I seen enough. It's your mama, all right. You never knowed her when she was young like I did. I oughta know, 'cause we was best friends." Dang it! She hadn't meant to let the cat out of the bag.

"Did you go to Mother's wedding?" Janie asked, ignoring, or maybe not clever enough to notice Oona's slip of the tongue.

"Child, no one 'round here went to her wedding," Oona said, relieved to change the subject. "Fern got married up yonder somewhere in Indiana. Evansville? Mae must'a got a'hold of this picture and hid it away from Uncle Tobias."

Janie frowned like a doubting Thomas. "But Mother said she didn't move to Evansville till after she was married. I was born there. Then, when my father died in the service overseas, Mother moved to Indianapolis to make a fresh start. I was only a few months old." She scratched her head and studied the other snapshot. "Did she ever bring me here for a visit when I was a baby?"

Oona snorted. "Your mama never stepped foot back here after she run off."

"Somehow, I was here as a baby. This other picture shows the same woman holding me as a baby, and we're standing by Grandpa's house along the river."

"Oh, honey, all babies look alike," said Oona, bursting into a cackle. "Besides, don't you have a river up there called the O-hi-o?"

Janie started to say something, then frowned instead. Oona didn't like it. Something fishy was going through that girl's mind, Oona knew it. Maybe she'd best have another look at that picture. This time without her specs. Only, she couldn't give away the truth that she could actually see anything without them. Specs was a sure sign of respect. Like her gold teeth. And she wasn't about to lose her hard-earned respect.

Oona edged away from the swing and managed a look over Janie's shoulder. The girl turned the photos away from her.

"Did my mother meet my father in Chittenden? Did you ever know him?"

Oona looked up from her task and snorted. "Of all the haywire ideas! Lands, no. Your mama always thought she was too fine for the boys 'round here. I believe she wrote that your daddy was from Evansville."

"No, I'm sure he wasn't."

Oona shrugged and leaned forward to get a better angle on the picture. "That's what happens when folks think they're so big for their britches they cain't never come home again. I reckon Fern got what she deserved."

Janie clutched the photo to her bosom. "What do you mean?"

"She thought she was running away from this place, but she was really only running away from herself, is all."

"Why would she run away? What was there to run from?"

"Oh, I reckon she took some notion into her head. And she paid for it. She passed on a lonely woman."

"She had me. And Jeff." Janie laid the pictures down on a chair, crossed her arms and turned away. Sulking, Oona reckoned.

When Oona glanced down at the bride in the picture and finally recognized that moody face staring up at her, she had to grasp the swing's chain for support. Lawd a'mercy! Annalee! Heaven help us all! Oona would have to get those pictures away from Janie before anyone else saw them.

NINETEEN

"But Mom, I don't want to go to Aunt Oona's," Jeff had said to his mother as she dropped him off the next morning. "I want to explore the cave under our house. You said you'd come with me."

Janie hated disappointing her son, but she hated even more the small lie she'd had to tell Oona regarding an appointment with a lawyer. It was true that she needed to consult a lawyer about finalizing her divorce, but today she had other things on her mind. Taffy.

The roads around here wandered with no particular purpose, and Janie wondered if she could remember the right way to town. There must be more than one route. Could Taffy be waiting for her on another road? The woods appeared as empty and forlorn as the day she and Jeff drove down here from Indiana. That had only been three days ago, but it felt like a lifetime.

Suddenly Taffy stepped out from behind a bush into the road, and Janie had to swerve to avoid hitting her. She wore the same faded brown skirt and white blouse, but they still looked clean and fresh on her. Deep circles underscored her dark, sulking eyes. She quietly settled herself into the passenger seat.

"I was afraid you wasn't coming," Taffy said, her voice barely above a whisper.

"I said I would, didn't I?" Janie noted that her cousin carried no suitcase, which left her with a combination of disappointment and relief.

Taffy nodded slightly then turned her attention to a stretch of kudzu blanketing the woods outside. She must've seen that view every day of her life, yet it captured her devoted attention now. Or was she just avoiding Janie's questioning looks? Taffy clung to the handhold till her knuckles whitened, and she pushed her knees rigidly together.

"You look awfully pale," Janie said. "You feel all right?"

"Fine."

"I thought you might have a suitcase with you," Janie said with a weak laugh.

Taffy's mask dropped for a fleeting moment as she turned to stare at Janie. Her eyes widened, and panic shone from the whites. Her thin lips quivered, then she composed herself as quickly as she'd exposed herself and turned back to her study of the passing scenery.

"I expected you might be running away." Janie tried to laugh it away, but her laugh came out sounding very feeble.

When they reached the fork in the road where Janie and Bonnibelle had met Rose digging for goldenseal root, Janie tried again. "Tell me, Taffy, what's this herb Aunt Rose is giving you? She said it could be a poison if you took too much."

Taffy moaned a little, then cupped her palms to her face. She slumped over and heaved with soft sobs.

Giving up, Janie decided to let her friend cry and pretend she didn't notice. She turned her attention back to driving.

Ten miles later, they reached the stop sign halting them at the edge of the deteriorating but paved road that entered town. Taffy had controlled her sobbing to an occasional sniffle.

"Where to?" Janie asked.

"You can just let me out at the courthouse. I'll meet you back there later."

"When? I've got a few things to do."

"Don't rightly know. Hour, hour and a half."

"Look, Taffy." Janie laid a hand on her shoulder. "You can trust me. Let me help you. What are friends for? Just tell me where you're going, and I'll take you there. My errands can wait — "

Taffy's eyes widened, as if with horror. "I don't want no help. And don't you try to follow me, neither." Ready tears spilled onto her cheeks again as she fumbled with the door handle.

"Okay. Sit still, and I'll drive you to the courthouse."

When she pulled into a parallel parking space, one of many such red-metered spaces on Main Street, Taffy jumped out without a word or even a glance in her direction. Janie sat still behind the wheel and watched her friend flee around a corner and disappear from view. She resisted the impulse to follow her and concentrated on the courthouse instead.

She locked the doors and climbed out of the Bug. In spite of the heat, a clammy shiver tickled her, as if someone were breathing down the back of her neck. She glanced around herself. Rumbling slowly past was a lone farm truck. A woman in the passenger seat gaped out her window at Janie. Across the street a few old timers squatted on the courthouse steps and watched her every move. The people of this community were curious about her, nothing more, she thought with a sigh of relief.

The courthouse, built from that same dazzling white limestone in Grandpa's cliffs, wore a cupola on top. Somewhere inside were records. Maybe there was a record of her mother's marriage that would give her a clue to the identity of her father. She crossed the street, then paused to say "Good morning" to the old timers.

"Hey, Miss Mullen, you ain't gonna find Bonnibelle in there." One of the old timers wheezed with laughter then turned to spit into the bushes.

She shaded her eyes. It was Gus, the lanky man from the Lazy Dew Motel who'd wanted to talk more than his smoking partner would allow. Hope soared through her at the prospect of catching Gus away from the stifling influence of his friend from the motel.

Sinking down onto the step next to him, she smiled and waited as he continued to chuckle over his joke. "My name isn't Mullen. It's Bainbridge, after my father. Wilson Bainbridge. Did you ever know him or his family?"

Gus looked around at his friends. As if on cue, they all scratched their heads and stroked their chins in unison. "Reckon you won't find no Bainbridge in there neither," Gus finally said, erupting into more chuckles.

"So he wasn't from around here?" Janie sighed. "How am I going to find his family?"

"Maybe he ain't got none," one of Gus's friends suggested.

"Some folks cain't shake their families anymore'n a hound can shake its ticks," said another. A ripple effect of wheezes passed through them.

"Well then," Janie said, "maybe he used a false name." She dug into her purse and pulled out her old wallet. The coin purse sprang open, and coins spilled out, bouncing down the steps. Janie pulled out the worn photo of her father and handed it to the men for their inspection. "Any of you ever seen this man?" While they passed it around, she chased down each penny.

They stroked their whiskers and shook their heads.

"Dadgum," Gus said, "but don't he look familiar."

Janie peered over his shoulder at the stranger who was her father. "I always suspected my father was someone from around here," she said, "because why else would Mother run away? Grandpa must not have approved of him, and so they ran away together and eloped."

"Twarn't a soul old Tobias didn't like," Gus said.

"Now that ain't rightly a fact," said one of his friends. "You forgot about old Emlyn Dexter."

"Another Dexter?" Janie stared at them with wonder.

"Little lady, these here parts are chock full of Dexters."

"Not no more they ain't. Not since the gov'ment boys come and cleaned them out."

"Purt near cleaned us out, too."

Janie's mind felt as if it was swimming through the murky, obstacle-infested waters of the lake. She shivered at the thought. "Tell me about this Emlyn Dexter. Who's *he*?"

"Ain't no more. He's dead and gone."

"Went to the penitentiary for makin-likker."

"What?"

"Mo-o-o-onshine, some folks call it. White mule. White lightning."

"That's what you meant by white mule? *Moonshine*?" Janie frowned. Over at the Lazy Dew Motel Gus had said something about buying Grandpa's white mule. But Gus was wrong. Grandpa hadn't made moonshine.

Gus and his friends laughed so hard they held their sides. Janie felt herself steam inside.

"Don't fret, girlie," Gus said, choking off his laughter. "Folks got to make a livin'. How else they gonna do it?"

"It's...it's illegal. You just said that Emlyn Dexter went to prison for it. Did he die there?"

"He-yell, no! But his old lady died whilst he was in the penitentiary. Left their boy all alone. Little Dexter."

"How horrible," Janie said with a shudder. What kind of living was it to leave a child all alone?

"Oh, he done all right." Gus chuckled. "Always was a loner. Liked it better that way. Still do. Well, Little Dexter was doin' right nicely for hisself up until old Emlyn come back from the penitentiary thinkin' his boy needed a new mama. So he up and married Elta Mae. Got hisself a passle full of young'uns from that one. Oona's one of 'em."

One of Gus's friends wagged his head and took up the story. "It didn't set well with Little Dexter to all of a sudden have all them brothers and sisters. Then when old Emlyn up and kicked the bucket, all the land he done got from the earnings of his moonshine got divvied up. Little Dexter only got a sliver of the pie. Then the gov'ment boys come and gobbled up everything. All them brothers and sisters sold out and moved away. 'Cept for him and Oona. After all his daddy done worked for, Little Dexter was left with only a tiny piece of land nobody else wanted. Up there right close to old Tobias's place."

Gus pointed his finger by his ear and traced circles. "Some folks think Dexter's a little tetched."

"Who wouldn't be?" his friend countered. "The man lost everything but the shirt off his back."

"But not Tobias — "

"Hush your mouth, Gus!" His friend wagged his eyebrows in Janie's direction.

"Old Tobias was too crafty ever to get hisself kotched."

Janie stared back and forth at the pair. "Are you implying that my grandfather was mixed up in *moonshine*?"

"Naw, he don't mean that," said the friend.

"I think you do," Janie replied, her voice rising steadily. "I think you're not only implying that my grandfather was making moonshine but that he actually *benefited* from it, while Dexter's father paid the consequence."

"Now lookit Gus, see what your big mouth gone and done this time? That's only hearsay."

Gus, speechless, scratched his head and frowned. One of his friends piped up, as if offering an explanation during the lull in conversation. "This here's a dry county, little lady."

"T'was a likker agent snooping 'round Earl's just tother day asking a pot full of questions about old Tobias's place," Gus said.

Janie was sure her heart had skipped a beat. Earl was the name mentioned by the men on the barge that had stopped in front of Grandpa's house that night she and Jeff had spent in the tent. Earl was the one who would know what that activity had been about. Earl might know who the shadow was who had signaled the barge to stop in the first place. Earl was connected to the mysteries suddenly shrouding Janie's life. "Who's Earl?" she said.

One of Gus's friends spat into the bushes then wiped the back of his hand across his chin, prickled with the stubbles of a haphazardly shaven beard. Then he turned to Janie and stared intently at her. "Gus don't mean nothing. Half the time he don't know what he's talking about. Ain't that right, Gus?"

Gus scratched behind his ear. "I reckon I get a little mixed up ever' once in a while."

"But who's Earl? You *said* Earl."

Gus poked the front of his red flannel shirt and lifted his eyebrows into two tall arcs. "Boys, did I say that?"

They wheezed in return and slapped their knees. One of them said, "Gus, I reckon them false teeth are gettin' in the way of your mouth."

Another of them said, "Naw, it ain't his mouth, it's your ears. Ain't you cleaned out the wax this year?"

Janie gave a loud huff and snatched back the picture of her father. Obviously Gus and his friends were covering up what they knew. Well never mind. She'd find Earl without their help. And her father. She'd dig up the past before going forward with her life. Turning her back on them, she hurried on up the steps into the dark and cool interior of the courthouse.

And they were wrong about Grandpa and moonshine. They had to be wrong.

TWENTY

Oona tucked her skirts up around her chin and eased her bare bottom down onto the wooden bench seat. She had to wiggle just a bit to position herself directly over the hole, and she always got a splinter or two in the process. Thin bands of light slipped through the cracks around the wooden door, which hung askew on rusted hinges. Dang that Seymour. She'd been after him to fix the outhouse door since she didn't remember when.

"Haaa-haack-choooo!" Dust motes scattered in the strips of light. She wiped her finger across her nose, then reached into her bunched-up pocket and pulled out the pictures. Nossir, it wouldn't do to have that girl go showing *these* around. She didn't want Taffy to see these and get any ideas.

She studied Annalee's face in the dim light that seeped in through the cracks. Sure had been a pretty thing. Bore a likeness to Seymour. They had the same smile. But then they was brother and sister. Oona always thought Seymour could've been handsome.

Too bad about the baby, though. It would've been nigh onto thirty by now, had it lived. Oona reckoned Annalee was burning in hell for killing that baby. If she was bound and determined to jump, then fine. But she had no right to take that innocent baby with her. And now Janie was trying to dredge it all up. Oona lifted her eyes from the photos and glared at the dust motes, settled once again, into their beams of light.

"Mama?"

Someone was calling her in the distance.

"I ain't gonna watch that brat all day for ya." It was Bonnibelle, and her voice was getting closer. "Mama, where are you? I'm gonna leave, you hear?"

Clutching the photos in one hand, Oona glanced around herself. The old Montgomery Ward catalogue sat under a pile of newspapers on the bench next to her.

"Mama, I know you're in there. I heard ya."

Lawd a'mercy, but that girl was directly outside now, and she was beating on the door like she was going to pull it open and come on in. Oona grabbed up the catalogue and stuffed the photos inside. She'd find a better place, later.

"I declare, cain't you give a body a moment of peace?" Her voice snapped at the girl, but her heart was pounding in her chest like it was fixing to explode.

~

THE OLD TIMERS HAD DISPERSED by the time Janie emerged from the courthouse nearly an hour later. She stopped to blink from the blinding reflection of sunlight off the white stone steps, fortifying herself from her disappointment. There had been no record of her mother's marriage, no record of Wilson Bainbridge ever being born in this county. None of that should be too surprising, she insisted. All it meant was that her parents had married elsewhere.

From up here, she could see along the length of the two main blocks of this lazy town. Taffy was nowhere in sight, and Janie wondered where she should turn next. How long would it take to seek the Earls out of their hiding places in this town? How many places could they hide? She scanned the old brick buildings squeezing close together and their assorted shops: a feed store, garden supplies, two hardware stores, two five and dimes, and one modest clothing outlet whose specialty seemed to be double knits. The only movement was an occasional farm truck and a few shoppers and several aimless lookers, ambling down the sidewalks. The women clutched the collars of their cotton shirt-waist dresses. The men following along behind in denim overalls lifted their straw hats in greeting like lids of jacks-in-the-box. Janie felt as though she'd stepped twenty years back into time.

The time distortion clouded her objectives. There was more to do than look for Earl or dig for family records. There was the tire to pick up from Melvin. She wanted to check on Oona's mother. And buy a frame for her father's picture.

As she started down the steps, Taffy appeared rounding a corner onto Main Street. Her gait was staggered, aimless, and she bumped into a farmer who popped the lid of his hat. Janie hurried across the street to meet Taffy at the car, but Taffy didn't seem to see her. She passed the Volkswagen and took tiny, frantic steps down the street.

Janie ran after her and shouted, "The car is back there." Finally catching up to her, she caught the sleeve of her white blouse. It was limp and wet, from sweat.

Taffy paused and turned to give her a vacant look. Janie was reminded of the rabbit Griffin's hunting dog had trapped in her tent the other night. Taffy was reduced to a wild animal, knowing it was cornered, sapped of the will to resist.

Gently, Janie tugged at her, pulling her back toward the car. Taffy didn't resist. She allowed herself to be steered into the passenger's seat. Janie closed the door and hurried around to the other side of the car before Taffy could come to life and escape. She looked as if she wanted to.

"Mind if I do a couple of errands before we head out?" Janie asked tentatively.

Taffy didn't react, as if she hadn't heard Janie.

"Good," Janie continued, pulling the car out into the street. "It won't take long." She sped up, as if that would make the errands go faster. The distance wasn't far, and before Taffy could lift her face from her palms to protest, Janie was turning the Bug into the parking lot of a drive-in hamburger stand. Only one other car was there, an old turquoise one, and Janie steered the VW into a space at the opposite end of the covered row of stalls.

Taffy looked up from her clasped hands. Her skin took on the waxy pallor of a statue's. "What are we doin' here?"

"I thought you might be hungry," Janie said with an unconvincing laugh. "I certainly am." Something gnawed at her stomach, but it wasn't hunger pains.

Taffy moaned softly. Her gaze dropped back to her hands again.

"I wonder if the carhops still wear roller skates," Janie said, killing the sputtering engine and peering at the menu on the side of the wall.

"Don't," Taffy whispered. "We got to go. *Now.*"

Janie took her eyes off the menu. She glanced over at Taffy, who was finally looking at *her*, Janie, and not at her own hands. It was a beseeching look, and her eyes glowed with fervor. Her chin quivered, and her brow wrinkled. Taffy's chest heaved with the after effects of sobbing.

"Don't you want anything? You look like you haven't eaten for a month."

"Don't make fun of me," Taffy said.

The tone of Taffy's voice made Janie heartsick, and she wanted to swear immediately that she would *never* consider doing that. How had she come up with such an idea?

"I want to get out of here."

A girl in a short skirt emerged from the small, square hut attached to the end of the row of stalls. Balancing a tray, she headed for the turquoise car. Taffy gave all her attention to the carhop, who was fixing the tray to the driver's window. If there was any color left in Taffy's face to drain, it drained now.

"Well, if you don't want to eat," Janie said, "then I'll forget about my errands and get you back home."

The carhop started down the walkway toward the VW. Daintily picking a notepad from the pocket of her apron, as if her fingernails were freshly painted, she was an understudy of Bonnibelle the way she chewed gum and wiggled her hips.

"I cain't go home neither," Taffy said, sinking lower in her seat. She covered her face with her hands.

Janie sighed. The carhop had stopped beside her.

"May I help you?" she said in a high-pitched voice.

"No, I guess we've changed our minds, but thanks anyway," Janie said, reaching for the ignition.

The carhop ducked down to peer inside the window. "Taffy? That you?"

Janie glanced over at Taffy, but her cousin only curled herself into a tighter ball. "She's not feeling well," she said to the carhop.

"Where you been keeping yourself, girl?" the carhop asked.

Taffy didn't respond.

Feeling compelled to fill in the awkward moment of silence, Janie said the first inane thing that came into her head. "You know her?"

"Uh-huh," the carhop said between pops of her gum. Apparently she hadn't picked up on Janie's idiocy. "Used to work here, but couldn't keep the orders straight."

"Oh." A wave of sympathy washed over Janie as she watched the trembling shoulders of her cousin, her best friend. So she'd had a job and had been fired. Just like Janie. "Well, thanks very much," she said to the carhop and switched on the engine. She backed the car out of the space and steered out onto the road.

"I lost my job, too," Janie said, guiding the car on an aimless, slow crawl through the two blocks of town. "That's why I came here. I had no pay-check, but I still had rent to pay. I couldn't face looking for another dead-end job."

Taffy sniffled.

"Do you want to come to my house and talk about it?" Janie continued, pulling the car off to the side of the road. She wasn't ready to go back yet, not until she'd accomplished something, anything, in town.

Taffy looked up from her hands. Horror crossed her face.

"Well, it's not a pirate's lair, for goodness sake. We used to have some pretty good times there when we were kids. Swinging together out on the porch and watching the river flow by. Remember?"

"Got my fill of good times in that house," Taffy mumbled. The curtain of her limp hair dropped along with her chin.

"Sometimes it helps to talk about problems. I'm your friend, remember? What are friends for, but sharing things?"

Taffy sniffled, and Janie held her breath, hoping her friend might speak. But she turned away and hid her face in her hands.

She'd have to rebuild their friendship before she could ever regain Taffy's trust. Starting off by talking about herself, reminiscing, not demanding any-thing, might be a safe approach.

"I never understood," she began, "why Mother refused to allow me to re-turn here after that summer. It was like she was afraid of something happen-ing to me, or afraid of something I might learn. I don't know. Now I'll never know. It must be terrible..." Was Janie pushing her luck too far? "...Terrible to keep a secret all to yourself and think that you can't share it with anyone."

"You could'a come back."

She startled, not only from the shaking of Taffy's voice but also from the unspoken accusation. Maybe her best friend had felt abandoned. Maybe she'd been mad at her all this time. Guilt fired her cheeks.

"I should've come back, I know, but there were too many obstacles. Moth-er, school, then I got married and had Jeff right away. I used to write to Grandpa, but he never wrote back. Eventually, I stopped trying."

"He couldn't write neither."

"What do you mean?" Janie's fingers felt clammy, hesitating over the steering wheel.

"I mean he couldn't write, just like me. How's come you think I got fired back at that there drive-in? Because I see words all mixed up and letters that ain't there. I cain't read, and Uncle Tobias couldn't, neither."

"But..." Janie started to protest. She searched her memory. Hadn't Grandpa read bedtime stories to her? Of all the stories he'd told that summer, surely some of them had been from books. But now that she thought about it, she couldn't remember any of them coming from books. Grandpa couldn't read, that's why he hadn't responded to her letters. And now Taffy was telling her she had the same problem.

"It's all right," Janie said, dropping her voice to a soothing level. It's just a condition — dyslexia. Lots of people have it. There are specialists who can help you read despite this problem. You'll be able to get a job, if you want one, Taffy."

"Why wouldn't I want a job?" Taffy's voice rose to a shout. "I could get out of Mama's house. Get her off my back. Get *you* off my back."

"I'm sorry — "

"Not everyone can get jobs easy as you."

"Who said it was easy? Taffy, didn't you hear what I just told you? I was *fired*."

"At least you got a high school diploma."

"Don't you?"

"They didn't want me. No one wants me. All I want is a life like everyone else. A job. Money of my own. But no one wants someone like me to work for 'em. Sure, I had me a couple of jobs in Chittenden, and back yonder at the drive-in, too, but they fired me real quick-like when they found out I can't read. Called me too stupid. Just like my teachers back in high school."

"Taffy, dyslexia has nothing to do with intelligence. Let me find a specialist who can help you."

"No, no, no! I just want everyone to leave me alone."

"Reading will give you that normal life you want."

"Maybe that ain't so normal around here. Maybe Mama's right, and I should find me a man."

Impatience crept into Janie's voice. "Reading will open up a whole new world for you. If there's a chance to overcome this problem, then *take* it, for goodness sake."

"Maybe I don't want to open up a new world. Maybe that ain't so safe. Besides, it's too late for me." Taffy buried her face in her hands and sobbed.

"I don't believe that," Janie whispered. "It's *never* too late." Something more than dyslexia was the cause of this much grief, she thought, pulling the car back out into the street.

They drove in silence to Melvin's garage. Taffy didn't look up from her hands as the car turned into the parking area next door to the garage and puttered to a stop.

"Stay here," Janie said. She started to hit the doorlocks but stopped in time. Her cousin didn't deserve to be treated like a child.

She hurried out of the car and rounded the corner of the garage. A few broken-down cars sat on the other side of the lot, but no one stirred. Through the glass windows, she saw no one inside, either. Melvin must be "busy" in the back, she thought, with his stack of tires for company. She was just about to cross the threshold of the front door when a sound stopped her.

"Hack-in-chooooooey!"

She'd heard that sound before. From the barge. That night in the tent. The barge that had stopped in front of her cliffs. Someone on the barge had sneezed like that. Could the person she was hearing now be the same person who'd hauled something out of the water by her house?

It was only an instant that she stood there, frozen. Then she glanced over her shoulder to see if anyone was watching her. No one. She darted inside, hoping that no automatic bell would announce her. She heard none. An electric fan circulated a rubbery smell around the dim interior of the shop area. At the back of the room was a doorway into the garage, and she heard voices and laughter coming from there. She ducked, keeping a display of window washer fluid between her and the garage in back. She crept along, closer to the door separating the shop area from the repair area, until the sound of laughter and voices was clear enough to understand.

"I'm out," said one voice.

"Okay, let's see what you got, Little Brother," said another. After a pause he added, "A flush. Well, I'll be danged. You got my week's pay. I'm done."

A snicker answered.

"Owen," the first voice said again. "Where in he-yell you learn to play like that? Down in Nashv'lle?"

"Naw. The old man learned me."

"Well," said the first voice, "You Potts been beating us Crocketts for years. Stealing us blind."

"Oh yeah?"

"Yeah. Now that little sister of yourn is working on my daddy to buy our land. Where's she gonna get the money, lessen you boys give it to her after stealing it from me?"

Another snicker. "Bonnibelle? We ain't got nothing doing with her."

"Sure. And I'm the queen of England."

Sounds of scuffling movement sent Janie leaping for the front door. The whir of the fan covered the tripping sounds she made stumbling over the threshold. Outside, in the heat of the day, she gasped for air, still tasting rubber. Her sandals clattered across the cracked cement as she hurried back to her car. Slipping inside, she slammed the tinny door behind her and sat there for a moment, panting. Taffy looked up.

"Tire's not ready," Janie said, starting the car. She shot out of the parking lot and glanced over her shoulder. Faces crowded the doorway, watching her peel away. A chill coursed through her. Melvin was a Crockett, a friend to Griffin's brothers, and somehow he was mixed up in Bonnibelle's deals. Melvin could keep her tire for all she cared. Then a new thought crossed her mind.

Whoever had slashed her tire had deliberately led her to Melvin.

TWENTY-ONE

"Mom, how come you set the table out *side*?"

"I thought it would be more pleasant to eat on the porch."

"I bet *he* won't like eating with the bugs."

"The breeze off the lake blows most of them away, and the citronella candle will take care of the rest."

"With all that wind, I don't see how we can eat out there."

"We'll manage, hon. Would you set the dressing on the table for me?"

"He won't like that egg pie stuff, neither."

"Jeff, if you're going to have a problem with this meal, you can fix yourself a peanut butter sandwich and eat in the kitchen."

"No, it's okay." He grabbed the bottle of dressing and hurried out of the kitchen.

Janie knew her son wouldn't miss the evening for anything. He was convinced, after all, that his mother was having a "date" with Price. Ridiculous! Dinner was nothing more than payment for Price's changing her locks.

She smiled. It was a nice idea, though.

Jeff returned in a flash. "Mom, that tablecloth is gonna blow the dishes clean off the table."

"Maybe you could find something to weigh down the corners?"

She put the quiche in the oven and crossed her fingers that she'd fired it up to the right temperature. She looked at her watch. He should be here any moment. That would give them enough time to enjoy a drink before the quiche was ready. If it baked at all.

Maybe she should start on one early to help steady her nerves. *Was* this a date? Maybe she was so out of touch that she couldn't even recognize a date. It had been, after all, nine or ten years since she'd had her last date. When Roy had entered her life.

Carefully, Janie picked up two cut lead crystal wine glasses she'd found after her trip to town. They'd been wrapped in tissue paper in Grandmother Esther's hutch, heirlooms, apparently, and they were probably the most valuable possessions in this house. Their intruder hadn't been after anything of value. He'd left the contents inside the hutch untouched.

She carried them outside to the front porch and added them to the table. The breeze whipped the crisp, white tablecloth against the kitchen table's legs. Jeff had helped her drag it out here, then he'd anchored the corners with rocks, dribbling dirt along the edges. She tucked the ends of the cloth under his piles to keep them from doing any more damage to the mismatched assortment of dishes.

She'd brought the Zinfandel with her from Indiana. It had been a farewell gift, of sorts, when the company had let her go. She preferred to think of it as payment for a guilty conscience. Chuckling, she inserted the corkscrew and proceeded to shred the cork, another skill she'd had to learn since Roy's departure.

Jeff sat on the porch steps with a pile of rocks next to him. One by one, he plunked the pieces into the weedy driveway where Price would park his car. Pouring herself a glass of wine, Janie wondered if her son would "accidentally" let a rock slip in Price's direction when he arrived.

A roar on the road just then announced the silver Cadillac's arrival at the forefront of a dust cloud. The car skidded to a near stop, then turned in and nosed slowly into the line of fire of Jeff's rocks. Price sprang out and flashed a big grin.

"Mom, I don't believe it," Jeff shouted with dismay. "He brought flowers."

"How lovely!" She met him at the top of the porch steps and buried her face in the yellow and pink roses. "And they smell heavenly."

Flushing, he thrust his fists into his pockets. "They're from Gran's garden." Dressed in a royal blue golf shirt and khaki trousers, he didn't look as if he belonged here in the backwoods.

"Excuse me while I put these in water," she said. She'd found a crystal vase in Grandma's hutch, too.

When she returned a few minutes later, carrying the vase of flowers, Price was in the driveway, talking to Jeff. Her son stirred a design in the gravel with his foot and said, "I guess it's swell."

"Best place for a boy to grow up is right here in the Great Outdoors," Price said.

"Sure."

"Kind of lonely without many kids in the neighborhood, though. How'd you like to have some friends?" Price looked up at Janie and winked.

She wondered what he was getting at. "Would you like a glass of wine?" Her voice sounded a bit too cheery, she thought, setting the vase on the table next to the bottle of Zinfandel.

Price whistled and joined her on the porch. "Where'd you find that? This county is dry."

"So I discovered on my shopping trip to town," she said, pouring him a glass.

"Bonnibelle's gonna be sore at you, Mom," Jeff said, pitching a rock over the roof of the Cadillac.

"Why don't you go throw those rocks into the lake? I'll call you when dinner is ready."

He stuffed rocks into his pockets and glared at Price. "You ain't gonna like dinner, either."

"*Aren't*, Jeff," Janie called after him as he stalked away toward the cliff. "I'm sorry," she said to Price, handing him a glass of wine. "I don't know what's gotten into him." She knew exactly.

"He doesn't like me, does he?"

"Actually, he's angry at his dad," Janie said, avoiding the subject of liking or disliking this man. She wasn't sure herself. "So he blames anyone who gets in the way."

Price nodded solemnly and swirled his wine. The sinking sun flashed sparks through the diamond-shaped cuts of crystal. "I was the same way," he said finally in a subdued voice. "My dad sent me away to boarding school. Summers off, Mother and I came down here to Chittenden. She said it was to visit Granny Rose, but I knew better. It was to get out of Dad's way." He raised the glass to his lips and swallowed half the wine in one gulp.

"At least you knew your father," she said, sitting down on the swing.

Price sat down next to her and propped his arm along the back of the swing. "I hated going away to school," he said, "but I hated even more what it did to my mother."

"It must've been difficult for her." She remembered what Rose had said earlier about her illegitimate daughter. She couldn't picture Rose in that plight. "Was it because of your mother that Rose had a falling out with her sister?"

Price stared at her silently.

"I'm sorry," Janie said, jumping up from the swing and moving to the other side of the porch. "I didn't mean to sound so insensitive."

Price chuckled softly. "It always surprises me to see honesty. But you guessed right. Actually, it was Elta Mae who wouldn't have anything more to do with her sister once my grandmother found herself in the family way — without a husband."

"I wonder what Elta Mae thinks about Bonnibelle?"

"She doesn't even *know* Bonnibelle anymore. Each day is a new day for her."

"How sad."

"Not really," Price said. "Times change. Lives change. We can't continue to cling forever to what must eventually be let go."

"Tell that to Dexter," she said with a laugh. "Do you suppose it was an accident that he happened to go fishing at that exact spot when we were on the island yesterday?"

"Maybe it's his favorite fishing spot."

"I don't believe that. He's trying desperately to keep his world from changing."

"His world already has changed," Price said. "There's nothing he can do about it."

"What does he do that allows him so much free time to take off and go fishing?"

"He's a hog farmer, like so many folks around here."

"And that's lucrative enough to allow him to hire Griffin?" Janie asked.

"I believe it's more like a partnership. Griffin does the work while Dexter goes fishing."

"What's in it for Griffin? Why doesn't he help his own parents, instead?"

"The land Seymour farms doesn't belong to him. It belonged to Tobias — you, now. Griffin had some sort of quarrel with Tobias."

"Did he? What about?" Janie wondered if Griffin had an interest in seeing Grandpa disappear.

"I believe it was regarding the deal Tobias made with the government when they were buying up land. Your grandfather came out of that deal with a lot of money in his pocket and all the prime land besides."

"And that must be why Griffin resents me so much — being given something he thought Grandpa should've lost like everyone else."

"No, I don't think he wanted that. Griffin's quarrel was merely sour grapes. He was sorry Tobias hadn't given him the land, instead."

"What if Grandpa's disappearance wasn't purely accidental? What if someone helped him disappear? That same person would want to get rid of Jeff and me." She shivered.

"Are you suggesting *Griffin*? You shouldn't worry about him, you know. He's mostly a lot of hot air."

"Maybe it's not hot air. Maybe he's mourning the passing of those old ways and lives you were talking about a moment ago."

"What's the point of that? It's a waste of time."

"Why are you always in a rush?" Janie countered.

Price stared off at the lake. Somewhere in the distance a fishing boat droned. "There's too much life to enjoy, and too little time."

"And too little money," she said. "I'll have to find my pleasures in the simpler things. Anything else requires more money than I'll ever see."

"Suppose you had enough money to go west, or wherever your dreams send you, and still have a vacation home here to come back to?"

So he was still on that subject of selling, was he? "Even if I had the money, maybe I'd choose the simpler pleasures in life."

"Have you planned for Jeff's future?"

"I need to check on dinner," she said, setting her glass down so abruptly that wine spilled onto the cloth.

Oona had been right about him, Janie thought, slamming the screen door in his face as he jumped up to help her. Oona had warned her that she didn't trust this man, and now Janie saw that Oona was right. It was only Grandpa's property Price was after, and that's why he'd shown interest in her. Concern over her locks. Sailing. Flowers. And now Jeff.

She marched into the kitchen and pulled open the heavy oven door. Moving the pan, she watched with dismay as the filling jiggled. How would they pass the time while they waited for the pie to bake in this interminable oven?

Then she remembered the photos she'd found hidden in the mirror of Auntie Mae's dresser. Maybe Price could identify the mystery woman and the baby. She threw down the hotpad and left the room, crossing through her bedroom to Jeff's room. The dresser now held souvenirs of Jeff's outdoor adventures — rocks, twigs, jars of bugs — but the mirror was still the way Auntie Mae had left it, with pictures poking out of the edges of the frame. Janie scanned them quickly, but the photos that had been hidden before were no longer there. Had she misplaced them?

She was trying to think where else she might have put them when she heard Price's yell outside. She rushed out to the porch in time to see Price sprinting for the cliff. Jeff was nowhere in sight.

TWENTY-TWO

"Omigod!" Janie screamed, leaping off the porch.

By the time she reached the cliff, Price had disappeared over its edge. He scrambled down the vine-covered wall. A spray of smaller rocks knocked loose as he reached for hand holds and foot holds. It was twenty or thirty feet to the boulders below.

Where Jeff lay. Motionless. Her baby sprawled across the rocky shoreline. One leg and an arm rocked gently in the lapping edge of the lake.

"Call an ambulance!" She cried and remembered that no one was near enough to hear her. No one had a phone.

Janie covered her face with her hands and felt the life force drain out of her body. Down into the lake. The lake...had claimed too many lives. Grandpa... The lake was evil. It sucked the life force from its helpless victims.

"Get him out of the lake!" she screamed.

It must have been her hysteria that made Price turn to look up at Janie. He said in a calm voice, "He's going to be all right."

"How the hell do you know? Get him out of there!"

Price ignored her. Bending over Jeff, he used his calm voice again, even though her child appeared unconscious. "I have to move you now, tiger. Easy does it. Almost there..." Little arms dangled lifelessly as Price cradled him in strong arms.

"Over there!" Janie shouted, pointing in the direction of Jeff's fishing rock. "You can climb up easier over there." She ran along the top of the cliff where it sloped gradually down to meet the rocky border of the lake. It was maybe fifty feet away, but it felt like a mile or two.

"I don't think anything's broken," Price said, slowly, too slowly, making his way along the rocks. "But we'd better let Doc decide that. Get an ice pack for his head, and we'll take him there now."

"No!" She could feel panic welling up within her. "We have to take him to the hospital."

Time slowed to a maddening crawl as Price climbed the slope toward her. "The nearest doctor is in Stony Lonesome, and the nearest hospital is ten miles beyond that. Let Doc decide if he needs the hospital. Now get that ice pack."

~

IT WAS THE CAVE Jeff had wanted to explore.

In the days that followed, Janie kept blaming herself. *She* was the one who'd told Jeff to go throw his rocks in the lake. Why hadn't she guessed that he would finally fall over the cliff?

And if that weren't enough, she'd completely lost control of herself, screaming at Price, who was only trying to help, crying all the way to town, begging him to go faster. Price didn't respond to Janie's hysterics but spoke soothingly to Jeff, instead.

Fortunately, Jeff didn't remember much about that ride.

Coherence returned long enough for Janie to notice one interesting thing: the doctor's office was located on the same street Taffy had visited.

The quiche never did bake.

She moved her camp stove onto the black surface of Grandpa's woodburning cookstove.

Visitors came and went, but Price was the only one who came regularly every afternoon. He brought new comic books with him each time. Too embarrassed to see him during these visits, Janie fled upstairs to the attic, where she'd set up the typewriter she'd bought for a dollar in a garage sale. The ream of paper had cost more. She could fill all five hundred pages and still not be done with her screenplay. She hammered away at the keys, filling the pages with gibberish, anything to avoid facing her lack of control, her failure as a mother. As a single parent.

~

FEATHERS FLUTTERED INTO the air, stirring up a powerful smell of dust. The chicken Oona had her eye on side-stepped her as she closed in on it. She clucked her tongue and scowled.

Dang it all, iffen that boy hadn't've gone and like to broke his neck, Oona wouldn't have to be out here chasing chickens mid-week. There wasn't nothing more powerful than her chicken soup, though, and she figgered it was her duty to boil him up a pot of it. It'd fix him up real good now that the worst had passed. Lord knew, his mama didn't know nothing about taking care of him. After all, she's the one that done took the boy to that place where he could fall into the deadening.

She stood there in the middle of her chicken yard and waited for the stupid one to sashay within her reach. Then, with lightning-quick speed reserved only for certain occasions, she snatched the little bantam by the neck and popped it good. *Humph! Skin and bones, that's all it was. Not much good for nothing besides broth.*

A car door slammed over the squawking ruckus, and she whipped around to unleash her fury on the distraction. A man stood there, watching her. A dang fureigner. She should ought to've heard that there white Chevy rattle up, what with the shiny boat it pulled along behind. Not just any fureigner, but a *tourist*! She knowed they was a'coming.

Only, this one here didn't look like no one special. Wasn't much of a man, scrawny as he was. Red stubbles buried a dimple on his chin, and dark, stringy hair only made him look like some mismatched thing the cat would drag in. Why, she'd bet her last dollar he didn't have no woman to look after him. So this was the kind of tourist Junior Wanamaker was planning on bringing here.

Gathering her wits, she lowered her arm that held the broken bird. "You looking for someone, mister?"

"Yes, ma'am. You know where I can find Oona Potts?"

She saw the letter in his hands. Flustered, she dropped the chicken and wiped her hands on her apron. Here was trouble already, and it was only midday. She'd plumb knowed it was a'coming. As hasty as she'd been posting a letter to Roy Shoemaker, he'd moved even faster. Greed was the only thing she knew could make a man jump like that, and she didn't like the notion one bit. Well, she reckoned, she'd just have to think on it a little harder and a little quicker. She was plumb out of ideas, now that her plan had gone to heck fire.

~

IN THE MIDDLE OF THE WEEK, Price didn't come for his usual afternoon visit. A strong breeze riffled Janie's papers and made her look up from the old Royal. That's when she realized he hadn't come that day. Storm clouds billowed up across the lake, blotting out the late afternoon sun. Maybe Price had slipped in while she was banging away at this pointless exercise. Her fingers hovered over the keys as she paused to listen. All was quiet downstairs.

Too quiet. Silently, she rose from her work table and tiptoed across the floor and down the steps. She paused at the foot of the steps, in Grandpa's bedroom, which she'd taken over. Her bottle of rosewater cologne sat on the dresser. Her gooseneck lamp and houseplant guide sat on the nightstand. Her television sat useless even with rabbit ears.

Something creaked, banged, then creaked again.

She moved across the room to the door separating her bedroom from Jeff's, turned the china doorknob and peeked in at her son. He'd fallen asleep with a comic book open across his chest and Beads tucked under one arm. *Poor, sweet baby! What have I done to you?* She tiptoed to his side and started to tuck the sheet around him.

Creak, bang.

The screen door stirred in the wind. Jeff kicked at the sheet in his sleep and rolled over onto his side, away from her.

Lace curtains ruffled at the window. A storm was brewing, and it lured Janie away from her son's bedside and out onto the porch, where the swing slanted sideways, coming within inches of the house. The long tendrils of her philodendron blew away from the railing like a mane of hair.

She moved the pot down to the floor, in a protected corner, then sat in the swing, anchoring it. Unable to resist the storm, she watched it gather its forces across the lake. Gray clouds hypnotized her as they swirled and shifted patterns like a kaleidoscope. They mushroomed till they'd completely captured the afternoon sun, then they continued their march toward Janie's cliff. Wind pushed the clouds along and rattled leaves in its path.

A sudden chill in the wind made her shiver, even though June was normally sticky with relentless heat. Perhaps it wasn't the wind that made her shiver, but rather the realization that she'd lost track of the time.

She got up to check on Jeff again and latched the screen door behind her. Already it was much darker in the house. How long had she sat out there, listening to the wind? Her face felt damp from the muggy air. Her sticky curls stood out in a mass. She must look like Frankenstein's bride, she thought.

Jeff was still asleep, this time hovering close to the edge of the bed shoved against the wall. The sheet tangled itself around his feet. As Janie moved around the foot of the bed to straighten his sheet, she noticed that his comic book was gone. It must have fallen over the side of the bed during his thrashing. She got down on her hands and knees to look under the bed for it.

All she could see were boxes. She nudged them aside until she cleared a narrow path to the wall, but still she couldn't see the missing comic book. The bed was high enough off the floor that she could easily crawl under it if she wanted to, but the thought alone sent a chill down her spine and the familiar tightening sensation in her chest. This is ridiculous, she thought, reaching with her arm, groping around the boxes for the feel of the magazine. Her head and shoulders followed her reaching arm into the dark, dusty, narrow space. She'd probed far enough, and was about to withdraw in defeat when her fingers found, instead, a leathery solid something. Pulling on it, she dragged it out from under the bed.

It was a Bible, and she stared at it dumbly. The gold lettering on the cover had faded, but it had that unmistakable look with its black leather cover and gold-edged pages. She opened it and flipped through the onion-skin, listening to it crinkle.

An envelope fell out.

Jeff thrashed on the bed. She pulled herself up to look at him. His brow knit, and his eyes moved under closed lids.

"Jeff," she said, gently shaking him.

He sat up, opened his eyes just enough to frown at her, reached for Beads and fell back to his pillow. His face relaxed, and he was asleep again.

He'll never sleep tonight. Another time she would've forced him to get up, but now all she could think about was the Bible she'd found. She gathered it up, along with the envelope, and tiptoed out of the room.

Was this the Bible her grandmother, Esther, would've read from every night? Janie hugged the book to her chest. She'd never known her grandmother, and she tried to remember any stories Auntie Mae might have told her. But Mae hadn't known her own mother long enough to fill a reservoir of home-spun stories. Grandpa hadn't talked about his wife. He'd only wagged his head at her mention. Janie remembered how his eyes had misted over as he declared Esther "a good woman."

Although Janie hadn't known her grandmother, she understood the significance of this treasure. In the family Bible, Grandma Esther would've recorded the history of the family. There should be records of marriages, births and deaths.

But why had she hidden it away under the bed?

Janie listened to the drum roll in the background of her imagination. Reading the family history needed a special place, an unchanged place where she could almost step into the past and bring back to life the memory of snuggling against Grandpa's flannel shirt with the top of her head resting under his whiskery chin. He used to tell her stories up in the attic on rainy afternoons, and that's where she'd go now.

No sooner had she reached the top of the steps than the storm hit. At first there were only a few raindrops, splattering one by one against the house. Then they gathered a wild fury and drummed in waves of intensity, a percussion of rain pelting the tin roof directly overhead. She caught her breath, wondering if Grandpa's flimsy cabin could withstand the battering.

She squeezed past her work table and peered out the small window under the gabled roof. It overlooked the lake, where sheets of rain thundered across the water toward her. Jeff's island had disappeared under a gray torrent, and whitecaps frothed where they'd sailed with Price less than a week ago. She wondered if he was out there now, if that's why he hadn't come today, armed with new comic books. Absently, she chewed her fingernails.

She backed up against the cot, where she'd slept as a child. It tucked under one side of the sloping ceiling. She sank down onto it, making it squeak. Dust billowed around her. She coughed and glanced down at the thick volume on her lap and the envelope sliding off the leather cover. The plain white envelope was flattened with time. Wrinkles were pressed into it.

She grabbed it up and lifted the flap. Inside was a dried cluster of flowers, and she carefully pulled out the delicate stalk. Even so, one of the florets broke off. About the size of a pencil head, it retained its blue color. Forget-me-nots, she thought, sliding the cluster back into the envelope. Then she turned to the Bible.

Her fingers trembled as she flipped it open. One of the onion-skin pages ripped. Chiding herself, she turned more slowly to the center of the book, where she found the section containing family records.

There it was... The births were entered, the first generation in a painstakingly tidy hand, which must have belonged to her grandmother. On the Mullen side, there were Tobias and four brothers. On the Ramsey side, there were three sisters: Grandma Esther, Elta Mae Dexter, and Rose Bender. Janie must remember to ask Rose about her grandmother. It seemed hopeless right now even to think about her other grandmother — her father's mother, whoever she'd been.

At least Janie now had the record of her mother's family, thanks to this Bible. She looked again at Esther's list of the births of her children. First was Mae, then two stillborn sons three and five years later. There was another entry for Fern twelve years after Mae's, but it was in a different handwriting — a hasty, backwards sloping scrawl. Grandpa's? No, not if Taffy's claim was true. Grandpa hadn't been able to write. Nor was it Auntie Mae's careful handwriting, which Janie could recognize from Christmas cards.

Janie winced and scanned the column of deaths. She found Esther's listed with the same date as Fern's birth and written in the same backwards handwriting.

Oh, Grandpa! She lifted her eyes from the pages before her to the small square of the attic windowpane, streaked with raindrops. Grandpa and his twelve-year-old daughter, Mae, were left alone with an infant. Why hadn't he ever remarried?

Then she remembered. Gus had mentioned a "lady friend."

She looked again at the open pages on her lap and found herself. A strange sense of pride overcame her. Below Fern's entry, in the same backwards handwriting, was Janie's own name — Jane Lee Bainbridge. Here was the family where Janie and her son belonged. She didn't know the details, but her search was over.

She turned the page and found two more branches of births, a branch for Rose, and a branch for Elta Mae. Rose had only one child, a daughter, Elizabeth, who was Price's mother. Elta Mae, however, had a string of babies, starting with Oona.

Then she found what she was looking for — the column of marriages. Her index finger traced the list: Esther Ramsey and Tobias Mullen, Rose Ramsey and Tom Bender, Elta Mae Ramsey and Emlyn Dexter II, Elizabeth Ramsey and John Price Wanamaker, Annalee Potts and Emlyn Dexter III — *Annalee?* — Oona Dexter and Seymour Potts, Janie Bainbridge and Roy Shoemaker. This last entry was in Auntie Mae's smooth handwriting.

Wait a minute. Where was Fern's marriage? Janie traced the names again but still did not find a single mention of Wilson Bainbridge. As if he'd never existed. Maybe that was it. Maybe he *never* had existed. Maybe Janie had been born out of wedlock and Fern had invented the story about Wilson Bainbridge to cover up her embarrassment. Then who *was* her father? She looked again.

Annalee? The name Oona's mother had called her. Annalee had married Dexter the third. Her neighbor? *That* Dexter? What kind of woman could've married a man like him? Then she remembered the hard-luck story Gus had told her about Dexter. The man had certainly suffered more than his share of tragedy. Losing his wife must've sent his mind over the edge.

She turned back to the column of deaths and found Annalee's listed along with an infant daughter, Lee. *Janie's middle name!* She looked again. The coincidence didn't end with the shared name. Annalee and baby Lee had both died on January nineteenth, the very day that *Janie* was born. She'd have to ask Oona about that.

Her fingers moved quickly to Elta Mae's branch of births, and she found Lee's birth recorded only two months before her death.

She closed the book with a thump and sprang to her feet to stare outside at the sheet of rain. She heard it ping overhead with increasing fury, reflecting the anxious drumming of her heart.

What could account for the deaths of a young mother and her baby? It had to have been an accident. Add this tragedy to the loss of his parents and later his land, and it was no wonder that Dexter acted so strange. He was especially strange to Janie, and she wondered if it was the coincidence of her birth on the same day as his daughter's death. Did he associate Janie with his personal tragedy? All these years, he must have subconsciously blamed Janie for his own loss. No wonder.

Maybe Annalee had been Mother's friend. Maybe news of her sudden death had sent Mother into shock and premature labor. That would explain the coincidence of Janie's birth and Annalee's and baby Lee's deaths. Maybe that was even the reason behind Mother's refusal ever to return to the Chittenden Hills. A return here would've reminded her of the tragedy.

Lee would've been a distant cousin, Janie's age, and she felt the ache of loss now for someone she'd never known. The snapshots of the unidentified mother and infant suddenly came to mind. Of course. They were Annalee and her baby, Lee. Janie must've been given Lee's baby blanket after the tragic accident. She shuddered.

It would be up to Janie now to assume the role of family historian and update the records.

A door slammed downstairs.

"Mom!"

At the sound of her son's voice, she forgot about the family line and clattered down the narrow stairs. Miraculously, she didn't trip. At the foot of the steps, the door between the bedrooms was securely shut. She grabbed the china doorknob, but the hardware rattled, too loose under her fingers to open the door. Wind whistled through the crack under the door, tickling her bare toes. Something crashed to the floor and tinkled into broken pieces.

She leaned against the knob as she tried it again, and this time the door opened. She pushed against the strength of the whistling wind. Sheer curtains puffed out from the window, open to lakeside. With pages flapping, songbooks lay scattered across the floor, amidst the broken glass of a picture frame that had blown off the dresser. Stepping carefully, she hurried to the window.

Hail chinked onto the porch outside. The wind whistled with a shrill urgency through the cracks of the house, and the house responded with groans and creaks. She slid the window shut and turned to face her son.

"Is Dexter gone?" he asked, sitting up in bed.

"Dexter?" The sound of Janie's heart hammered in her ears. "He was never here. What made you think he was?"

"He told me about the goblins in the mine — "

"Jeff, you've been dreaming."

"But it seemed so real. He was right here, Mom, standing by the bench."

"No, honey. You must've mistaken him for Price." It didn't ring true to her. How could anyone mistake those two?

"Mo-o-om!" Jeff's voice suddenly raised in pitch as he frantically searched under the sheets. "Where's Beads?"

Before she could answer, a knock sounded on the front door.

Second Family Tree

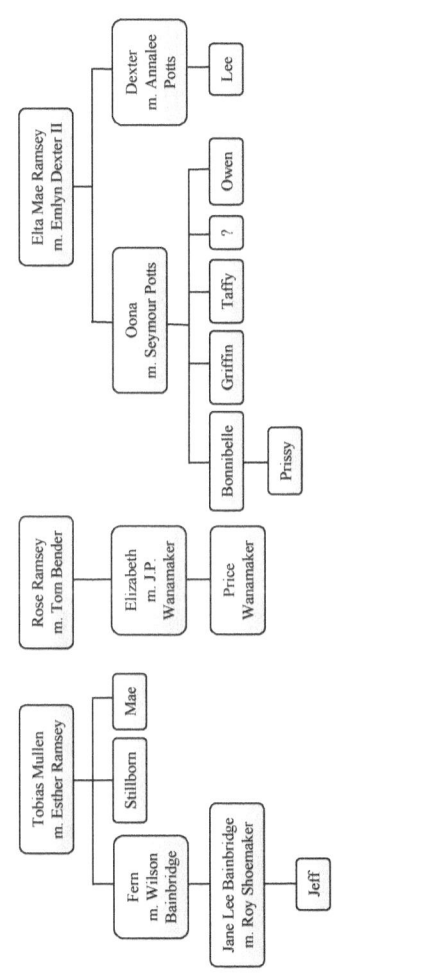

Tobias Mullen
m. Esther Ramsey

- Stillborn
- Mae
- Fern
  m. Wilson Bainbridge
  - Jane Lee Bainbridge
    m. Roy Shoemaker
    - Jeff

Rose Ramsey
m. Tom Bender

- Elizabeth
  m. J.P. Wanamaker
  - Price Wanamaker

Elta Mae Ramsey
m. Emlyn Dexter II

- Oona
  m. Seymour Potts
  - Bonnibelle
    - Prissy
  - Griffin
  - Taffy
  - ?
  - Owen
- Dexter
  m. Annalee Potts
  - Lee

m. = married

TWENTY-THREE

*O*ona squatted on her stool and yanked on Bossie's teats while muttering obscenities in rhythm to the streams of milk that pinged into the tin pail at her feet. Bossie shifted her weight, switched her tail, and turned to gaze at Oona with her doleful, brown eyes.

"I know, I know. I ain't a man. But I reckon I can do in a pinch. Else you'll be mighty sorry come morning."

Bossie answered with a testy moo.

The idea! Everyone leaving Oona with all the chores! It wasn't like Seymour and Griffy to skip milking time *and* supper. But boys got to sow their wild oats every once in a good while. She reckoned that after they was done sown, they'd come home with their tails between their legs.

But Taffy was a different story. It was downright disgraceful for a girl to stay out all last night and today, too. That girl never would learn her lesson, no matter how long she stayed away. She may as well not bother to come home now, 'cause she'd have to face Oona's bodacious fury. Oona didn't like being wrong, even over a little matter like this morning when she thought she heard Taffy slinking back home. Well, it hadn't been her, and now that girl for sure had ruined any chance she ever had to get herself a man.

Oona paused for a minute to stretch her fingers. She wasn't accustomed to this. Bossie flicked her tail into Oona's face.

A powerful storm had blown in tonight. At least by now it had let up some. They needed a rain, but this much this fast was just as bad as no rain at all. Probably washed all the top soil out of her garden. And that hail would've beat up the rest of it real good. She shook her head and got back to work.

The barn was damp from the rain that seeped through cracks and from the wet animals nestled here. Their musky odor gave the air a touch of warmth that Oona always found comforting. Her complaints tapered off along with Bossie's milk.

When she finally rose from her stool, she heard a rustle in the hay and turned to see a shadow filling the gray doorway. "Well, mercy be, look what the cat done drug in."

Chewing on a stem of hay and wearing a cocky grin, Dexter watched Oona bustle about the barn.

"You holding up the wall, or something? Long as you're here, git yourself busy. There's the Guernsey yet to milk."

"I come looking fer your boy."

Oona stopped long enough to plant her hands on her broad hips. Fool man. "Well, when he shows up, I'm gonna get me a piece of his hide first. Why in blazes you think I'm doing his chores? He ain't here. I thought he was with you."

"Nope. I ain't seen him fer a couple days." He lowered his voice. "Seymour here?"

Oona snorted. "You oughta' know better'n that."

Dexter relaxed and sauntered closer to Oona. "What'cha got fer supper?"

Oona sighed. "Does it look to you like I'm cooking? When you gonna git yourself a new wife to do yer cooking fer ya?"

"You know I cain't never marry again."

"Ain't nothing gonna bring Annalee back. Not even that there Janie Bainbridge, and she's hell-bent on trying." *Nigh onto thirty years Annalee's been gone, and Dexter still looks like he's fit to be tied just from hearing her name. Reckon I should'na said nothing. When's that man gonna stop mourning?*

Dexter mumbled something, but Oona knew better than to ask him to repeat it. Might as well change the subject now.

"You hear 'bout her boy's accident? Yep. Bonnibelle told me. The boy got to horsing around and fell off that there cliff just like I always knowed he would. Plumb broke his neck, but that there city hospital wasn't 'bout to take him. He's lucky to be alive, but I reckon we won't be seeing him for a whiles. Seymour come home this afternoon long enough to carry over some of my chicken soup, and he ain't come back yet."

Oona stretched her back and listened to her bones pop. Dexter was still looking at her all funny-like out of that one eye of his. Like he wasn't hearing her. She reckoned she'd try again.

"I jest hope that Janie Bainbridge don't sell off our land to Junior before her man puts a stop to it." She caught her breath, giving Dexter a chance to add his two cents worth, but as usual, he didn't. All he did was slide loose hay around with his dirty sneakers. "Emlyn Joseph Dexter! You ain't heard a word I said."

"Oh, yes I have." His voice was all quiet-like. Something was brewing in his mind, she could tell.

"What you need to do is git yourself a woman," she said.

"I don't got no room for no woman at my place."

"Hah! You don't know nothing, do you? A woman can make do with what the Lord gives her. My girls — "

"Your girl's got herself knocked up."

That took the words out of her mouth as if Bossie had swished her tail into it.

Dexter continued, grinning, like he done got the upper hand from her silence. "She come to me yesterday and told me herself."

The mounting fury made her feel like an over-stoked furnace. Her voice sounded strange, even to her, coming through gritted teeth. "I thought Bonnibelle done learned her lesson."

"Not that one."

He might as well have pushed her over with a feather. Then, he meant Taffy. Why, that girl thought she was so high an' mighty, but she warn't no better'n Bonnibelle. Oona felt as if a black thundercloud hovered over her head. "How's come she told *you* and not me?"

Dexter laughed and spat out the hay. "Wanted me to marry her, I reckon."

The furnace of her fury fixed to explode. "I'll give her a thrashing the likes of which she ain't never seen. Why, you're her uncle. I declare. What's wrong with that girl? Ain't she got no respect? The idea! I always knowed she was Daffy Taffy, but where's her head?"

A rustle and a sob from the hayloft made them look up.

"Well, speak of the devil. Git your bee-hind on down here, girl. That where you done spent last night and all of today while I work my fingers to the bone?"

Taffy crawled down the ladder and turned to face them. Oona had never seen her such a wreck. Tufts of hay stuck out of her hair and clung to her clothes. Tears streamed down her cheeks. Two black shiners encircled her puffy eyes.

"He's lying, Mama."

Oona scowled first at her daughter, then at Dexter, then back at Taffy. "Why, you filthy little slut."

"He's the one that done it, Mama. He forced his way on me."

Thoughts of murder crossed Oona's mind. She could feel tiny blood vessels swelling in her eyes until she thought they would burst. "Don't you say no sech thing about your own uncle. Go on an' git outa my sight."

Taffy stared at them for about half a second, then grabbed her mouth.

"I'm tired of you," Oona continued. "I don't wanna see you no more. You hear?"

An explosion of thunder boomed, and the girl high-tailed it out the back door of the barn. The door was left standing open behind her. It wasn't Oona's fault.

～

THE GLOOM OF PREMATURE twilight permeated the house. Moving through the darkness, guided by the urgent staccato of tapping on her front door, Janie wondered who could've braved the storm to call on her. Rain drummed on the roof, and the wind howled, as if crying for a way inside.

Through the lace curtains she could see the outlines of two women huddled together on the front porch. The one who knocked pulled a black cape tightly about her and rocked back and forth on muddied shoes.

"Mom, who is it?" Jeff whispered from the bedroom behind her.

"Great-Aunt Rose," Janie answered, hurrying across the front room. "I wonder what brings her out on a night like this?"

Jeff's pattering footsteps trailed behind her as she undid the new bolt Price had installed. Visions of his small, fragile sailboat capsizing in the roiling waters of the lake filled her mind. He must have gone out on the lake today and hadn't returned. That's why he hadn't come to visit Jeff today. And now Rose was out looking for him. Rose, and yet another woman in Price's life.

Janie flung open the door. "Please, come in."

"Oh, my dear." Rose laid a gloved hand on Janie's arm and looked past her shoulder. "And there's the dear, young lad."

"What's wrong, Rose?" Janie slipped the wet cape off her aunt's thin shoulders.

"Nothing wrong, my dear," Rose said, catching Jeff and enfolding him in her arms. "I came to check on our young patient is all. Price would've brought me, but he's been in such a dither about this venture of his. Said this time he had to get to the city before the bridges wash out — "

"You mean he's gone to town?" Relief swept through Janie.

Rose nodded. "There was some business that his father insisted on. So I got dear Susan here to drive me over in her truck as soon as she closed up the office."

The woman standing silently behind Rose was holding a basket. She lingered in the doorway until Rose released Jeff and bent down to untie her shoes. Then Susan rushed to Rose's side to offer an arm of support.

"Susan works over at the office, you see," Rose said, smiling up at the woman who'd brought her. "It's not a long walk from my house over to the A-frame where Price has his office, but dear, oh dear, I'm afraid it was muddy."

"Please come sit down, at least, while you untie your shoes," Janie said.

Rose shook her head, and she flushed from her upside-down position. "No, dear, you don't want muddy footprints tracked everywhere. Now, Susan, you run along. I know you're anxious to get home to your little ones."

Susan waited until Rose was done with her shoes, then she took a backwards step to the door. "Will you be all right?"

Rose's laughter was like the tinkle of a wind chime. "Of course, my dear. Now do as I say and run along. Price will come fetch me later on."

"But he had a dinner meeting in the city," Susan said. "It'll be late before he's back."

"Good! That will give me more of a chance to visit with Janie and Jeff."

Susan shrugged and set down the basket at Rose's feet. "Then I'll be off." She retreated into the gloom of the storm, closing the door behind her.

Above the steady downpour drumming on the roof, Janie listened as the other woman's footsteps faded away, a car door slammed, and the vehicle started up. Rose, in stockinged feet, was already leading Jeff into the kitchen. The way her aunt took charge made Janie feel that *she* was the guest, not

Rose. She followed them into the kitchen and hung up the wet cape on a peg by the back door.

"Now, about that young patient of ours," Rose said, rummaging through her basket. "Dear, I believe we're going to need some more light. It gets dark early when one of these storms hits. And I'll need some boiling water." She held up a jar of twigs in the faint light.

"Are you making another poultice?" Janie asked, flooding the room with electric light. "The first one seemed to work well. What's in that stuff, anyway?"

"Oh, just a little witch hazel — "

"Does that mean you're a witch?" Jeff said.

"Goodness me!" Rose burst into laughter. "I always keep a little dab of this on hand. It makes a dandy poultice for a nasty bump like yours. You never know when it may come in handy."

Thank goodness for Rose, Janie thought. She moved slowly to the stove and searched through the cast-iron skillets for a pot in which to boil the water on her camp stove. She should either devote her energies to firing up this woodburning cookstove of Auntie Mae's or else drain more of her savings into an electric stove. But that sounded too permanent.

When Jeff apparently lost interest and retreated to his comic books, Janie lowered her voice. "Rose, shortly before you came, I found the family Bible."

Rose set down her jar of twigs and stared off into space. Her eyes misted. "That would be Esther's. She was devoted to the community church, you know."

"There were records in it," Janie said.

Rose bustled to Janie's side. With her index finger, she tipped up Janie's chin and peered deeply into her eyes. The cornflower blue of her penetrating gaze was soothing. Healing. "You learned about Annalee."

She nodded. "But I don't know *who* she was, or *how* she died."

"And you will, my dear, all in good time. First we'll tend to your son, and then you and I will sit down with a cup of tea and have ourselves a nice chat. Earlier this evening, when the storm hit, I experienced a sudden feeling of unease, and I realized there are things you must understand. I fear our chat is long overdue."

TWENTY-FOUR

"M o-o-om, Beads wouldn't just *vanish*." Jeff pushed aside the bowl of warm soup, crossed his arms on the kitchen table, and pouted.

"Of course not, honey. He must be in the house somewhere, and we'll find him. First, eat some more soup. It'll give you strength."

"Not hungry." His elbows shoved the bowl farther away, this time sloshing broth across the table.

Her patience slipped away on a sigh, and Janie planted her knuckles on her hips.

"Dear, let me try," Rose whispered, laying a conspiratorial hand on her arm. She pulled a vial of clear liquid out of her basket and winked.

Jeff watched her with as much suspicion written on his face as Janie felt. "What's that?" he said.

"Price used to call this 'bedtime nectar' when he was little. It's a special treat, but you can only have it in bed."

"Oh boy, can I have some?" Jeff asked.

"Of course, dear. Run along to bed, and I'll be right there."

When he was gone, Janie intercepted Rose. "What's in that?" she asked, nodding at the vial.

"Dear me, nothing to worry about," Rose said with a little laugh. "It's sugar water, is all, with a tiny pinch of something else to help take away the pain."

Janie's eyebrows arched. "It's not that stuff you warned Taffy about because too much was poisonous?"

"Goldenseal?" Rose clutched her chest and laughed with the sound of windchimes. "Of course not. This is powdered root of lady's slipper. Perfectly harmless. It'll help him relax." She caught her breath and eyed Janie thoughtfully. "Maybe you'd like some, too?" She winked, and then she was gone.

Janie stood there, staring at the empty doorway where Rose had stood a moment ago. It was a tempting idea to take something that would help her relax, but she needed to remain alert. With prowlers on her cliffs and moaning sounds from the cellar, it was imperative to remain alert.

She followed them into the front bedroom where Jeff had already climbed into Auntie Mae's four poster. Janie felt a mixture of jealousy and gratitude as she watched Rose expertly fluff the pillows and tuck the sheet around her son. When he was comfortable, Rose offered him the vial of bedtime nectar, and he licked it clean. It was a home remedy, that was all, Janie told herself. It wasn't going to hurt him. Maybe it would help.

Healing energy, flowing from the yarb doctor's fingers, charged the air with its power. Rose slowly massaged Jeff's head in little circles, working her way closer and closer to the wound, then she gently applied the poultice of witch hazel twigs. Her expert touch convinced Janie that Rose knew what she was doing. Jeff relaxed, and after a while, Janie felt herself relaxing also.

The percussion of rain on the tin roof had softened to a soothing drizzle by the time she and Rose finally settled into the front room with cups of tea. Janie suddenly realized how exhausted she felt. Her mind swam, as a wave of dizziness overcame her, and she wondered if Rose had added a bit of the lady's slipper to her own tea. Or something else.

The motion of the rocker brought the smiling, wise woman in and out of focus. Then the room shifted slowly up and down. Back and forth. Around and around. Too much adrenaline had been flowing too long, and Janie felt drained. She sipped her tea and forced herself to concentrate on Rose's tale.

"Annalee," Rose began, her voice barely above a whisper. "Oh dear, but I haven't thought of her in years. It takes me back."

Rose's tidy bun cushioned her gray head against the high back of the rocker. Her face misted over with memory, and she dabbed a lace hanky at the corner of one eye.

"Annalee and Seymour was brother and sister, you see, and they grew up right here on your grandpa's farm. Of course, that was back in the days when his farm was mostly down by the river. Annalee and Seymour's daddy was the hired hand down there. I expect Tobias had to hire a man on account of his not having any sons. It was his greatest dream, you know, that his two daughters, Mae and Fern, would marry and settle down on the farm with him. Dreams don't always work out the way a person plans, do they?"

Rose's hand trembled as she reached for her cup and took a long swallow of tea, and it occurred to Janie that Rose must've had a dream that hadn't worked out the way she'd planned.

"Annalee and Mae were close in age," Rose continued, setting down her cup with a clatter. "They grew up together as sisters would. More than that, they were best friends. And as sisters often are, they were as different as night and day."

Janie wanted to point out that Oona's mother had mistaken Janie for Annalee, as if there was a resemblance, but her mouth felt numb, and she couldn't find the words.

Rose chatted on. "Annalee meant to go to far-off places and experience the world, you see. But Mae hardly ever left her own back yard. Oh, she spoke of leaving many a time, but she never could quite come to do it. That time Mae went to Indianapolis to persuade your mama to allow you to come for a visit was the farthest away from home that Mae ever traveled. Poor Mae must've been terrified to make that trip. She started planning it back when you was still a baby, and she kept on talking about it right up until her end, bless her soul." She shook her head, and a few wisps of gray hair slipped from her bun to straggle about her neck.

"Her sense of duty drove her," Rose said. "Mae thought it wasn't right that you didn't know your own grandpa. Oh, Mae would've been so pleased to see you come down here on your own. A pity she couldn't have lived long enough to see it."

Duty. There was a lot of that down here, Janie thought. Her mother had escaped it by fleeing north.

"Now Annalee was a different kettle of fish," Rose said. "Annalee may have been born on a farm, but in her heart she was a city girl, through and through. Annalee stayed home long enough to get her high school diploma, and then she left. I do believe it broke both their hearts that Mae wouldn't go with her. But as determined as Annalee was to leave, Mae was just as determined to stay and care for her daddy and little sister. Stubborn, the both of them."

Rose paused to shake her head, and then continued. "Annalee found herself a job checking groceries over yonder in the city. She worked over there for years, saving every penny she could, saving in order to take fancy trips every once in a while. My, the places that girl went! New York, Florida, St. Louis... Oh, she tried to get Mae to move to the city with her, but she never would. Had to look after her daddy and little Fern, who was growing into a pretty, young lady. I believe Annalee must've thought she was going to become a spinster, when along came her old high school sweetheart. They rekindled the flame real quick."

"Dexter?" Janie finally said. She remembered the list of marriages in the family Bible.

Her voice somehow broke the spell, however. The fountain of information spilling from Rose dried up at the mention of his name. A scowl clouded her face, making her appear like an old, tired woman. She sipped silently at her tea. "Dexter" had finished her story for her.

With trembling hands, Janie reached for her own tea, spilling it. She felt dizzy, disoriented. The shadows from the corners of the room shifted, playing tricks on her eyes that already felt like sandpaper. On the wall next to her grandmother's hutch, as if it were a movie screen, she imagined she saw the bride from the photo that had disappeared.

Annalee.

The shadows were playing tricks, and she shivered and looked away, back to the comforting pool of golden lamplight that flooded Rose. The sudden motion made her head swim and her focus spin. Rose and all the mismatched pieces of her grandfather's life seemed to float before her. Only Janie was the stable one. Or was she?

Janie cleared her throat. "And then what happened?"

But the old lady seemed reluctant to speak now. Her face sagged with lines of fatigue. "He brought Annalee back to the Chittenden Hills where her spirit of adventure died." Her head bowed and her voice fell to a murmur. "Oh dear, after all these years, this is still difficult. But this is what you must know." She looked up at Janie now and pegged her with a piercing blue gaze. "It wasn't long before they had a baby, you see. A girl, which disappointed *him*. Annalee's life was as good as over, and so she took it."

Janie waited, but Rose leaned her head back and closed her eyes. She didn't mean to continue. "Annalee took her own life?" she finally asked.

Rose sighed. "Such a waste. She jumped from the cliffs. They thought it was fitting to bury her up there, since suicides aren't allowed in the cemetery. And there she rests, as alone in death as she was in life."

"She was *that* depressed?"

"Annalee wouldn't eat on account of her depression, and she was losing her milk. So, I was treating her with goldenseal root..." She opened her eyes and searched for her tea cup. "Oh dear, I've said too much."

Janie shivered.

Rose rushed on. "Annalee suffered from a severe case of the depression that new mothers sometimes feel. In its milder form, it's not so uncommon, but *he* made it worse for her."

"And...the baby?" January nineteenth the baby had died, along with Annalee, according to the records in the Bible. It seemed so senseless. She didn't want to know, but she had to know.

Rose winced, as if the memory of thirty years ago was still too painful. "Annalee took the baby with her."

Janie gasped.

Rose dabbed at tears forming in the corners of her eyes. "It wasn't her fault she was born a girl. Annalee knew if she was gone, her baby didn't stand a chance. She was wrong, of course, but that must've been her thinking. The two of them were buried together up there on that cliff. There. Now you know everything. Maybe now you'll understand why Annalee's story is one best forgotten. No one around here wishes to remember it."

The horror of Annalee's story washed slowly over Janie, clearing her head somewhat. Annalee hadn't wanted to live, had murdered her own baby, because Dexter wanted a *son*. It didn't make sense.

Rose stifled a yawn. "Oh dear, where is Price? I left him a note. He should've been here by now."

Janie glanced at her watch. How could it be after ten? They hadn't talked that long.

The cold tea cup confirmed the passage of time.

The more Janie uncovered her own past, the less she seemed to know herself. The less she *knew*. Rose was wrong. Janie didn't know everything. Not yet.

TWENTY-FIVE

*J*anie startled awake. The book she'd been reading before falling asleep in the recliner slid from her lap to the floor. Beyond the perimeter of golden light from her reading lamp, shadows danced in the corners. Something was out of place, but sleep fogged her mind too much to understand.

A steady rain drummed on the roof. Thunder rumbled and shook the room. It died away, and a soft rattle floated out from the shadowy kitchen. She tensed and swung her legs around to spring from the chair, but the motion made her head spin. What had Rose put in her tea?

A grunt followed the rattle, and she realized it was Rose, snoring from Grandpa's bed, where she hadn't minded spending the night. After ten, when her story about Annalee was done, it became apparent that Price wasn't coming to fetch her. Janie would take her home in the morning when Jeff was awake.

Now, she rose slowly, steadying herself, and started for the door to Jeff's room. Lightning pulsed through the room, exposing shadows like a negative. She froze. The sound that must've awakened her, repeated itself: a tapping so gentle it was barely heard above Rose's snores.

It came from the front door, and she wheeled around to face it. Price? "Who's there?" she whispered.

The tapping faded away, and she wondered if it had been her imagination. She tiptoed to the door and put her ear against it. Rain and wind swished through leaves and sounded like sobbing. No, it was *real* sobbing.

She unlocked the door and pulled it open to a spray of wind-driven rain sieved through the screen. Someone huddled on the porch, slumped against the wall of the house. A wet curtain of limp hair hid her face.

"Taffy? For goodness sake, what are you doing out here in the rain at this hour of the night?"

Taffy lifted her chin to stare at her through the straggles of wet hair hanging in front of her face. "I would'na bothered you, but I saw your light."

Her teeth chattered, impairing her speech. Almost instantly, she seemed to regret having come here, and she backed away, clutching at the rips where her white blouse hung askew. Little tufts of straw clung to her drenched body.

Janie felt her heart thud with alarm. "Come in, will you? You're soaked and you'll catch pneumonia."

Taffy trembled. "Are you...alone?"

"Well, there's Jeff, of course, but he's asleep. It must be after midnight." She didn't intend to tell her about Rose.

"I'm a bother." Taffy's jaw quivered, and she hesitated in the puddles at the edge of the porch.

"Of course you're not a bother. I often stay up late, reading. How about a cup of hot cocoa?" Janie had to come out onto the porch to grab Taffy by a slippery arm and steer her inside to the snug comfort of the lamplight. Only then did she see the black eyes. She gasped. "What's happened?"

"Nothing."

"For goodness sake, Taffy! You've been in a fight. You've come two miles in a downpour by yourself in the middle of the night. You've — "

"It ain't so far by the crik."

Janie locked the door behind Taffy. "Is everyone okay at your house?"

"No worse'n usual, I reckon."

"Well, let's get you dry, first," Janie said, pulling Taffy into the kitchen, toward the bathroom. "There's a clean towel on the shelf, and you can use my robe."

Once the door was closed behind Taffy, Janie tiptoed across the kitchen and softly closed the door to the bedroom where Rose was snoring. Then she turned on the light and went about the task of warming milk.

Taffy looked like a faded daisy when she emerged later in the hot pink robe. It covered her from her chin to her toes, but her teeth kept chattering. The hot cocoa couldn't warm her, nor could the coziness of the front room, which kept at bay the dampness and gloom and earthy smells of a drenched night.

Janie ached for her cousin, sitting all alone on the couch and looking as if she were completely alone in the world. She joined her and put her arm around Taffy's shoulders. The touch startled her, and the robe slipped open, revealing the wet skirt underneath.

"Why, Taffy, no wonder you're still so cold. You didn't change out of your wet clothes. Now, come along." Janie stood and started tugging at Taffy's arm, but Taffy pulled away. "No, I ain't fixing to stay long."

"But of course you are. You're not going back out in that storm."

"Don't tell me what I got to do! You're just like the rest of them." Her raised voice surprised both of them, and Taffy slumped down into the fake velvet cushions and buried her face in her hands.

"The rest of *who*?"

But Taffy wouldn't respond.

"Look," Janie said, "you're the only one I've ever been able to talk to in my entire life. Don't abandon me now, when I need a friend the most. I came here to the Chittenden Hills hoping I'd find a place where Jeff and I were welcome. A place that felt like home. But ever since we arrived, we've been far from welcome. From the very first day, when we found Grandpa's house ransacked — "

"He done it."

"Excuse me?"

Taffy lifted her face. Tears streamed down it. "I come here tonight to tell you about it. I don't know what else to do. It ain't your fault none. It was Dexter's doing. You hear? He pitched a fit when I told him I wasn't coming back no more. Mama could find someone else to do the job. Well, he didn't like that none, and he grabbed the first thing he laid his hands on and threw it across the room and didn't stop till he got through every last room."

"But...why?" Janie focused on the puffy, black rings around Taffy's eyes. "Is he the one who hit you?"

"Not then," Taffy said a bit too hastily. "I reckon he thought if he made such a mess it'd make me come back just to clean it up. Which I did that night you was at dinner, and I run off. I was scared he'd come back, but he didn't."

Then it dawned on Janie. Taffy had been here, looking after the place. Taffy had let Dexter in. Dexter and Taffy, alone together in an abandoned house. Dexter, angry because Taffy wasn't coming back. To him. Janie's voice was hoarse when she finally found it. "How could you do it?"

"Don't get so high and mighty with me. I love him."

Janie swallowed hard. "Go on. Tell me about it."

"There ain't no more."

"I think there is." She reached for Taffy's hands and stared into the velvety depths of her friend's tear-filled eyes. "That's why you came here tonight. To talk to someone about your feelings. I'm listening. Come on, honey. Tell me."

Taffy gulped. "I know he...he ain't perfect."

She could say that again. Janie had to bite her tongue to keep quiet.

"I heard tell your husband wasn't perfect neither."

"That's right. I left him."

"So I left Dexter, too. But that don't mean I stopped loving him."

"I'm sorry." As soon as Janie said it, she realized that she wasn't really sorry. In fact, she was elated to hear Taffy's senses were returning.

Taffy pulled away from Janie and stood, then wandered aimlessly about the room. She fingered the doilies on the end tables, she picked up framed pictures of family and friends, she ran her fingers along the backs of chairs and stroked the fronds of Auntie Mae's ferns that had somehow escaped Dexter's destruction. She was imprinting, Janie realized. Imprinting all of these mundane objects so she'd never forget them. Did that mean she was planning to run away, like Janie's mother, and never return?

Taffy stopped, finally, at the front window. Sporadic flashes of lightning illuminated the broad expanse of lake before them. Nothing penetrated the darkness of the woods.

Then she started to speak softly, as if to herself. "It's Uncle Tobias's fault. He shouldn't ought've died. But he did. And I had to come over here to check up on things. Water plants. You know. Mama knew she could give me a job simple as that. Only it wasn't that simple, 'cause Mama didn't know that Dexter was here, waiting for me." Taffy trembled and picked pieces of straw from her hair. She took a deep breath and continued.

"He...he said I'd like it. I fought him at first. He's my uncle, you know. But you see, the fact of the matter is...he was right. I never thought I'd wind up loving him that way — he's old enough to be my daddy. But I did. I loved him. He treated me like...like a woman, you know. Not like a little dumb girl, the way everyone else was treating me. He made me promise to come back. At first I swore to myself that I wouldn't. But then I thought about it. You see, it was already too late. I was ruined. So I figgered I might as well come back. We been meeting here ever since. That is, up until I found out you was coming. Then I reckon I knew I couldn't face him no more."

Janie thought of the fresh food she and Jeff had found when they arrived. Taffy and Dexter had set up housekeeping here.

"This place stood empty all winter," Taffy continued. "Who would ever know?"

"So my arrival ended your affair?" Saying it aloud, Janie thought, sounded very strange.

"It was going to end anyway," Taffy said with a snuffle. "I'd been feeling poorly, so I went to the yarb doctor, and she done give me some powder stuff. Said it would settle my stomach. I guess I knowed then, but I had to...had to see a real doctor to be sure."

"That's why you wanted me to take you to town?" Taffy had trusted her, Janie thought.

"Then a couple days ago I told him about the...baby coming...and he give me these." She pointed at her black eyes. Tears streamed down her face, and she turned away. "Said it was my fault."

"No, he's wrong," Janie said, rushing to her side.

Taffy shook herself loose from Janie's arms. "It don't matter. Nothing matters no more. Dexter don't want this baby. Mama won't have it in her house. Not me, neither. She kicked me out! I cain't support it if I cain't keep a job, now can I? There just ain't no other way." She ran from Janie to the bathroom and slammed the door behind her.

Janie followed her and knocked softly on the door. "Taffy?"

"Go away and leave me alone."

There was nothing Janie could do. Feeling helpless, she wandered restlessly through the house. She listened to the rain drum on the roof, she carried the mugs to the kitchen, she checked on Jeff. From his room, she could hear Rose's steady snore continue. How could anyone sleep through the events of this wild evening?

It had started with Rose's tale about Annalee.

Understanding crashed over Janie. Now she saw the parallel between Taffy and Annalee. Both of them hurt, rejected by Dexter on account of their babies. Had Taffy come here tonight to repeat Annalee's fate and throw herself over the same cliffs?

Janie hurried back through the front room and into the kitchen. Both the bathroom door and the back door stood open. The pink robe lay in a heap on the floor. Rose's black cape hung on a peg, beside the empty peg where Janie's yellow slicker had hung moments ago.

Taffy was gone.

Rain spattered inside through the screen of the back door. Beyond the screen, the back door stood open to empty blackness.

Janie ran there, pushed open the screen and stood on the back stoop long enough to allow her eyes to adjust to the dark. Rain spit at her. Lightning pulsed, illuminating the wet landscape in the flash of a heartbeat. It was just long enough to see a raincoated figure standing poised at the edge of the cliff's highest point.

TWENTY-SIX

*N*ossir, Oona wasn't about to go to bed with half of it empty. Her fury had passed, along with the day, and now she sat alone under the kitchen light. Alone, she bent over her sewing needle. Alone, she listened to the pounding of the rain on the roof and waited to hear the sound of the truck outside. It was coming down in buckets tonight, holding her a prisoner in her own house. Alone.

Except for the baby, of course, but it was asleep in the crib. Besides, it didn't count. Kids never counted till they was at least fifteen. Round about the time they start getting themselves into trouble. Then, it seemed that the trouble never ended.

For instance, she plumb knew that boy would fall. Only thing she didn't figure was how soon it would happen. Of course, Oona had the good sense not to allow her young'uns down by the deadening. Unlike that Janie What's-Her-Face. She reckoned the city girl done learned her lesson real good by now, and she'd high-tail it out of here once the boy was fit. That would finally get her out of Oona's hair, and that would solve her first problem. Maybe things would even settle back down. Bonnibelle would catch herself her man and Seymour would sooner or later forget about Fern. Well, maybe not *forget*, exactly, but at least he wouldn't be reminded of her day in and day out.

Janie could leave, and it still wouldn't solve the second problem, the bigger problem of who was to claim Uncle Tobias's land. If Janie wasn't Tobias's granddaughter, then it was Oona who deserved the whole kit and caboodle. Until she rightfully got it, Griffy would keep on fussing.

Most important job for a woman was to keep her menfolk fat and sassy. She *had* to get that land for Griffy's sake, and she *had* to get Janie long gone for Seymour's peace of mind.

Then maybe the men would come home where they belonged instead of gallivanting from this end of Dew Crik to the other end, where Earl's Pool Hall sat.

Yessir, it seemed that some days the trouble never would end, and this time it was all that there boy's fault. If he hadn't fell, then Oona wouldn't've missed the revival meeting last Friday night. And if Janie had known how to tend to her boy, Oona wouldn't've had to take matters into her own hands and cook up a pot of her chicken soup. And if Seymour hadn't've carried her pot of soup over yonder this afternoon, he wouldn't've seen Janie's face and remembered Fern all over again. And if he hadn't've remembered Fern all over again, then he'd've come home where he belonged.

But no, he'd probably gone off to Earl's, and it was all Janie's fault for bringing that boy down here where he could fall over that cliff and make Oona send him chicken soup. Seymour had just better not miss carrying her to the revival meeting day after next or there'd be heck fire to pay.

'Course, Bonnibelle would find a way to get up town come hell or high water. She was bound and determined to get what she wanted, and what she wanted was Price. Although it seemed strange to Oona how she was going about it. Said she was fixing herself up with a new fellow up town, someone who'd help her hook her man. Nothing never stopped her from getting what she wanted.

Not Janie, neither. Janie wouldn't stop her.

Funny about Janie's mother, though. Fern. Fern could've had herself Seymour all them years ago if only...

Lawd a'mercy! Sudden understanding made her prick her finger with her needle. She'd plumb forgot that Janie was Fern's daughter, too, and so that made her Tobias's granddaughter after all.

Like Oona always said, it took a big woman to fess up to her shortcomings. But she didn't have to like it none. She never was one for book learning, and so she had to rely on her uncanny ability to figure things out. Sometimes, though, it didn't always add up. Like this one. How on earth could she've ever forgotten sech a thing?

No matter. That's why the good Lord give her that brother of hers to feed all these years. Dexter would take care of Mr. Roy What's-His-Face, Oona figured, and then she still had a chance to make everything turn out just the way she wanted it to.

～

STIFLING A CRY OF ALARM, Janie leapt off the back stoop. Mud splattered in her face, but it didn't matter. She cringed from the icy touch of pelting rain, but that didn't matter, either. Nothing mattered besides reaching Taffy in time. She had to prevent any more accidents.

It would be an accident if she fell. Not suicide. Despite the parallel between Taffy's and Annalee's circumstances, Janie wouldn't believe that Taffy was contemplating suicide. Why bother with a coat?

Silence was imperative. The slightest noise might startle her. Any sudden movement would surely send her plunging to death. Jeff had fallen over by the kudzu, but where Taffy stood, there was no kudzu to break her fall. The cliff dropped in the sheerest face under her feet, and one slip would surely result in death.

Silence was impossible. Janie splashed through puddles and mud, tripped on vines, crunched twigs. Wet leaves slapped her.

The next pulse of lightning flickered and paralyzed the scene on the cliff like a strobe light. A second figure bent over Taffy. Arms outstretched. Taffy leaned backwards at an alarming angle. Thunder rumbled, muffling Taffy's scream. Rocks tumbled and scraped against rocks as she disappeared over the edge and her scream faded away. Something smacked into water. The splashes died away into ripples, and the rain swallowed all human sounds. Darkness smothered the cliff and silence descended with the rain. A deadening terror froze Janie to her spot behind a wet bush.

～

NOSSIR, OONA DIDN'T TAKE kindly to missing last week's revival meeting. And the way she reckoned, it was all Janie's fault. She stabbed the needle into the dress she was sewing and frowned at it. The only time of day she could sew was when the day was over and her chores were done, and she couldn't make her fingers go fast enough to suit her. Maybe one day Griffy would buy her one of them fancy sewing machines.

Lord knew, she couldn't count on anyone else for nothing. Last week, however, even Griffy had let her down. He should ought've been here to drive her to the revival meeting. He knowed his daddy couldn't be counted on. She reckoned she needed Griffy more'n Dexter did.

Dang it, but her mind was slipping again. Dexter, being a deacon in the church, would've gone to the revival meeting, of course. He could've carried her over there. But he and her boy was up to something.

It still rankled when she thought of Dexter and the news he done carried to her in the barn right after supper all them hours and hours ago.

The very idea! She always knowed Taffy was dim-witted, but how on earth could she accuse her very own uncle of leaving her in the motherly way? Why, she didn't believe for one minute that Taffy was even in the motherly way, let alone that Dexter had gone and done it.

Lord knew why the girl was really sulking in the barn, for that, of course, was where she was. She'd never run off, not in a million years.

Then a new thought struck her, and it made her miss a stitch. Maybe she really was in the motherly way, and Griffy was out at this very minute looking for the boy that really done it. It'd be just like her to be dumb enough to tell her brother, unlike Bonnibelle. Griffy was a good boy, and he'd know he'd have to demand satisfaction for a wrong done to a Potts. That's what being a man was all about. Taffy couldn't understand that any more than she could understand that Griffy would get himself into a passle of trouble iffen he took his shotgun to something bigger'n squirrel.

Oona wagged her head and dropped her sewing to massage the sides of her nose where her spectacles pinched. Nossir, there was nothing but trouble these days, and she reckoned she knew who had dredged it all up.

≈

THUNDER AND LIGHTNING exploded together, lighting up the emptiness where Taffy had stood moments ago. Janie stifled a cry and lurched forward. The memory of Jeff lying on the rocks at the base of the cliff flashed through her mind. This time it was Taffy, but nothing would have broken her fall, as it had for Jeff.

Was she dead?

Janie had failed to help her cousin. She was too late. Someone else had beaten her. The dark figure stood outlined against the gray background of the lake. The way he hunched over the edge of the cliff, peering down at where Taffy must lie, reminded Janie of a spider poised over its prey.

Had he pushed her? Was he the same shadowy figure who'd signaled the barge last week?

Janie froze in her tracks and remembered the words she'd heard drifting from the barge: "get rid of her, or come next week..." Those instructions had come from the man with the dramatic sneeze. Taffy's own brother. Owen, the name of the person Melvin had been talking to.

And now Owen's instructions were being carried out by the spider-killer.

A branch slipped from Janie's fingers and thwacked her from behind. At the same instant, the hooded figure on the cliff straightened and turned to look in her direction. He'd heard the noise. Statue still, she prayed that the shadows here were deep enough to conceal her.

Someone had witnessed his crime, Owen's accomplice must be thinking.

Tears stung her eyes. She bit her lower lip to silence the sobs that wanted to rack her body. Taffy couldn't have survived. If Janie didn't escape with Jeff and Rose, the three of them wouldn't survive, either. They'd likely become the next targets.

Then another light joined the electrical display, a light that swept across the expanse of the lake. A barge was coming. It seemed to jolt the spider into action, and he skulked along the edge of the cliff, heading away from her, toward the easy access to the rocky shoreline. Was he going down there to where Taffy lay? To check his handiwork? To finish the job if it needed finishing?

Janie had to stop him.

TWENTY-SEVEN

*N*ow was her chance. While the spider-killer moved away from her, Janie sprang from her hiding place and bounded across the open space toward the cliffs where Taffy had stood moments ago. As she approached that sheer drop, though, she felt as if her blood were freezing. Her knees knocked, and she was numb all over. She dropped to a crawl and groped with shaking fingers for the rocks that lined the edge of this cliff to pull herself the last few inches.

The sounds of lapping water far below lured her attention downward. Lightning strobed through the murk of night and rain, and for an instant, a single instant frozen in eternity, she saw a body sprawled down there amidst the rocks. A body in Janie's yellow slicker.

"Taffy!" she whispered, choking on a sob.

Taffy's head lolled back. Her spine twisted at an unnatural angle atop the rocks. She appeared to be dead.

Then the sound of thrashing drew Janie's attention to the kudzu spilling into the lake a few feet beyond Taffy's body. It was the shadowy figure who'd pushed Taffy. He was edging out onto the precipice, probably to confirm his deadly work.

Janie shrank back. Her movement disturbed a small rock and sent it skittering over the edge of the cliff. She held her breath. The figure down there stopped, then peered up in her direction.

Had he seen her?

The pounding of her heart echoed in her ears. She shimmied backwards, as Jeff had shown her, until she could no longer see the shoreline far below. The barge bore down on them, sweeping its search light from cliff to cliff.

How long would it take him to climb back up the slope and overtake her?

She stood up and ran. All that mattered was speed. She darted straight through the clearing for the patch of light spilling out from the kitchen door.

The spider-killer couldn't have climbed the cliff this fast. Could he?

She dashed inside. The door squeaked behind her, and she leaned heavily against it, bolting it.

It was a false sense of security.

She reached for the light switch, then stopped. The sudden disappearance of light would be the confirmation he would need that *she*, and not someone else, had witnessed his crime. She ran to the darkness of Grandpa's bedroom.

"Rose." She whispered, even though he couldn't hear her now. He was outside. At least she knew that much.

Rose grunted, rolled over, and resumed snoring.

"Rose, wake up." Janie shook her.

The old lady looked frail as she lifted her head from the pillow. "No, Tobias..."

Janie's hand pulled back. Reflections of the barge light sliced through the darkness, putting an end to her hesitation, and she shook the old lady harder. "It's me, Janie. Wake up."

Rose stiffened beneath Janie's touch, and she struggled to sit up, pulling the sheet with her. "What is it, dear?"

"Terrible accident. Got to get help. *Now!*"

Rose smoothed her braid. "It's all right, dear. You go, and I'll stay here with Jeff."

"No, you don't understand."

"Understand what?"

"No time to explain," Janie said, glancing over her shoulder at the barge's light, slipping through the darkened room as if it were searching for witnesses. "He's coming for us. We have to get away while we can."

"Who, dear? Who's coming for us?"

"The killer! I don't know. Maybe the barge. Oh, *please* come." Leaving Rose sitting up in bed, Janie darted away to rouse her son.

In the doorway between the two bedrooms, she froze. The search light seemed closer now, as if the barge had stopped outside to shine its light directly into this room. Looking for her. She dropped to the floor and crawled to his bed.

"Jeff. Jeff."

She reached up and shook him and prayed that he would be easier to awaken. She should pick him up and carry him to the car. But he was too big for her to carry anymore. He wrapped his arms around his pillow, resisting her attempts to awaken him.

"Dear?"

Janie turned and saw Rose standing in the doorway in the hot pink robe and slippers, standing there in full view of anyone who might be watching through the windows. "Rose, get down."

Light swept the room, but Rose remained boldly upright.

"Mom? What's going on?"

"Jeff, get up," she said, throwing his robe at him. "We're going to Oona's house."

"*Now?* I'm sleepy..."

Rose scurried to Janie's side and helped her drag Jeff out of bed. Clutching him between them, they stumbled to the door into the front room. The crystal knob rattled under Janie's shaking fingers, and the door creaked open to a slit. Light pooled from her reading lamp by the recliner, leaving the rest of the room in shadows. The front door, and the car beyond that, seemed impossibly far away. The spider-killer would've had ample time by now to climb back up the cliffs and wait for them as they emerged from the house.

Jeff tensed at her side, as if he'd caught her anxiety. Rose moaned softly.

The car keys were back in the bedroom. Oblivious to the sweeping light, Janie ran back to Grandpa's dark bedroom. The keys were in her purse, which sat on the dresser, by the window. She paused there and peeked outside. Answering flashes of light reflected from the rocks beneath the cliff where Taffy lay. Flashes of light, signaling the barge, just as they'd signaled that first night Janie and Jeff had spent in the tent. And, just like that first night, the barge came to a complete stop next to the channel marker.

This was their chance. Janie grabbed her purse, dug for the keys, and ran back to Rose and Jeff. Now was the time to make their dash, now that the spider-killer was occupied with the barge.

She led the way across the lit front room and flung open the door to the porch. Taffy's puddle was still there where she'd huddled such a short time ago. She jumped over it, and they bolted out onto the porch and down the steps into the weeds at the end of the driveway.

Thunder burst overhead. At any moment she expected an arm to reach for her from the darkness.

Her face touched something filmy. She shrank back, wiping at the cobweb, then pressed on. The moon was buried behind storm clouds, and the darkness felt like a shroud. She could barely make out the humped shape of her car ahead.

Almost there.

Then her feet slipped on a few pieces of gravel. Her ankle gave way. A hand caught her before she fell. She gasped and stared at the shadowy figure clutching her.

Rose! Rose steadied her.

A tremble started in her knees and tickled through her, threatening to take control. *No.* She stood there in the darkness, gathering her inner strength, staring at the darkened figure of Rose beside her. Ethereal sounds floated through the drippy air — voices from the barge, clangs of metal, the splashing of waves.

"Come, dear," Rose whispered, nudging her toward the car.

Jeff was already there, standing by the door, and it suddenly occurred to Janie that the spider-killer could be hiding inside the car. No, she'd locked it, hadn't she? But a locked door wouldn't stop a killer, would it? Maybe he'd tampered with the engine. Or slashed the tires again.

Her mind refused to review the possibilities. She only had one choice, as she saw it, and that was to escape. With a child and an old woman, they wouldn't get far without the car.

Keys in hand, willing her fingers to stop shaking, she opened the door and pushed Jeff into the back seat. So far so good. She helped Rose into the front, then ran around to the driver's side.

In the darkness, she stabbed at the ignition several times before her shaky fingers connected. The key slid in half-way, then her moist thumb slipped. She took a deep breath and pushed the key the rest of the way. Her foot fumbled for the clutch. The engine coughed. It choked with too much gas. She eased her heavy foot off the accelerator. Then the clutch popped out from under her other foot, and the car lurched forward. The engine died.

Something thumped onto the roof of the car.

"What was that?" Jeff cried.

She gritted her teeth and tried again. This time the car roared to life. She threw it into reverse and spun the tires on wet weeds. A branch slid off the top of the Bug. She breathed a sigh of relief and backed out of the driveway.

Once on the road, Janie flicked on the headlights and stomped on the accelerator. If he hadn't seen them, he'd certainly heard the car by now. How long did they have before he took chase? He could've hidden a car nearby for his getaway.

Damn ruts! She couldn't drive fast enough.

Trees jerked past their windows as the car dipped through the ruts. Each trunk might have been the spidery figure of the killer. None of them, however, broke loose from the woods to charge at them.

"Dear, perhaps you'd best tell us now what's happened." Rose's gentle voice startled her.

Janie took a deep breath, relaxed her grip on the steering wheel, and told them about Taffy's visit. "She was depressed," she said, then described Taffy's subsequent flight to the cliffs, the appearance of the shadowy figure, and her fall. She related everything except Taffy's confession, the reason for her depression.

"We ought to go to my house instead of Oona's," Rose said in a stiff voice, ignoring the tale of Taffy, as if tonight's events hadn't occurred. "We'll be safer there."

"But Taffy's family will want to know about her," Janie said. "Someone has to bring her up. I'll leave you two there while I go for the sheriff."

Rose turned away from her and sniffed. *Something about Oona disturbed this otherwise generous old lady.*

They bounced in their seats as Janie urged the Bug faster than it should go over these ruts. If the spider-killer didn't get them, then whiplash might.

"Sometimes, dear, our eyes play tricks on us after a catnap, especially after an ordeal such as you have recently suffered."

"You think I imagined Taffy's fall?"

"Look out, Mom!"

Rounding a bend, the car's headlights caught the outline of a shadowy figure in the middle of the road.

TWENTY-EIGHT

*J*anie swerved, then fought to keep the car on the road. Her headlights caught the crazy dance of tree trunks that lined the road, and she had to swerve again to dodge their mad assault.

The car came to a sudden stop, and her head lurched against the windshield. She pressed on the accelerator again, but the car only rocked as one tire spun itself a hole in the soft ground alongside the road. Tears sprang to the corners of her eyes, and she allowed her forehead to fall against the steering wheel.

A dark figure appeared at the window, and she immediately jerked upright. She slammed her palms against the steering wheel and turned to face him.

"Bonnibelle!"

Taffy's sister gave Janie a look of wide-eyed surprise. She was dressed in something dark.

Janie rolled down her window a few inches. "We need help."

"I can see that."

"We're stuck. Help push us out, and I'll give you a lift." No matter how much Janie disliked this girl, she wouldn't leave her out here in the rain, alone on the road with a killer lurking nearby.

They all jumped out to help. At least the Bug was small enough that they could push it out of its hole. But this delay was giving Taffy's killer a chance to catch up to them.

Perhaps the killer already *had* caught them.

No, she didn't believe that. Bonnibelle talked a mean talk, but she couldn't kill her own sister. Could she?

When the car had finally been freed, Bonnibelle climbed into the back seat with Jeff. The smell of her wet body permeated the small air space in the car. For once, the popping of her gum was silenced. Rose fell into the front, and Janie stepped on the accelerator once again.

"What on earth are you doing way over here on a night like this?" Janie asked.

"I was just gonna ask you what in tarnation you're doing out, driving like a bat out of hell."

"It's Taffy... There's been a terrible accident."

"Oh, yeah? How's come you run away, then? You're just like your mama after all, ain't you?"

Janie felt steam rise off her, but she wouldn't take the bait. "Don't you want to know what happened?"

"Don't matter. When Taffy went missing, she made her own bed."

"What are you saying?"

"I'll tell you what I'm saying, girl, so you listen, and you listen good. I done told you to stay away from Price. You hear?"

It took a long minute for the change of subject to get through. Price was the last thing on Janie's mind. "You're kidding," she finally said.

"I kid you not. You invite him over to your house *every* day, just because this little brat — "

"Bonnibelle, shut up."

A cry of indignation escaped from the back seat, but Janie didn't care. *Serves her right if she's offended. What about her sister, for God's sake?*

The monotonous rhythm of the windshield wipers swishing back and forth filled the uncomfortable silence. She felt Rose's tension beside her and knew that she was stealing sideways glances at her in the darkness. They continued the rest of the way through the rain-spattered night in silence.

Lights blazed at Oona's house despite the hour, and Janie trembled, feeling relieved of pent-up anxiety. Her teeth clattered, and she shivered from a wet chill as well. Oona's house had never looked so good.

The car lurched to a stop on the road in front of the house on stilts. Janie wouldn't pull up into the quagmire where the junk cars sat at odd angles. The front door opened, and Oona's boxy outline filled it. She wanted to cry, but there was no time for that. They all climbed out and started through the mud and rain toward safety.

She didn't care about the rain anymore. They were already soaked. Taffy had taken Janie's raincoat, and even if she hadn't, Janie wouldn't have spent the time required to put it on. She shivered in her wet clothes, but foremost on her mind was retrieving Taffy's body and finding protection from her killer.

It wasn't suicide. Taffy had cared enough to protect herself. She'd taken the time to put on a raincoat.

The yellow slicker.

Omigod. That shove was meant for *Janie.* Not Taffy. It had been too dark for the spider killer — Owen's accomplice? — to see his victim's face. Not too dark to see the yellow coat.

Janie had worn it at Oona's house.

Everyone knew. Everyone had seen her in it. Anyone would naturally assume that a person in a yellow slicker poised on the cliffs outside Grandpa's house would be Janie.

∽

DANG IT ALL, OONA knowed it wasn't the truck. The way Janie come running to her, maybe she had news of the menfolk. She was sobbing her heart out, and Oona caught her and clasped her to her generous bosom. The world couldn't get along a day without Oona.

"Land o' Goshen, child. You look like the devil hisself is after you." Oona pushed her away to look at the bedraggled girl.

"Need help — "

"Now, jest keep your britches on, child. What the devil happened to you?" What was the widder-woman doing trailing along behind her in the dead of night? Aunt Rose. Oona never did trust her, not since that ruckus with Mama.

Oona had to shake some sense into the girl. Her fingers clutched those toothpick arms and squeezed. Janie winced. What's wrong with girls nowadays? Then she remembered Fern. And Annalee. Why, she reckoned, the same thing that's always been wrong with them. They ain't got the sense of a jackrabbit.

"Get the men! They've got to come — "

"Now, slow down, honey, and catch yer breath."

Bonnibelle slinked past them, like she didn't want no one to see her. Thank the good Lord that at least one of her girls was finally getting a dose of good sense.

By this time the widder-woman and the boy done caught up to Janie. "Good evening, Oona. It seems there is a problem."

A problem. And they was a'coming to Oona like they should ought to. The yarb doctor wasn't the only one in these here parts who could fix things. "What problem?"

"No time to explain," Janie said, out of breath. "Taffy's... She fell from the cliff."

Oh, Lord, Oona thought. She always knowed that dim-witted girl was a'heading for trouble. That's why she'd had to get rid of those pictures of Annalee. No telling what ideas Taffy would get if she was reminded of her Aunt Annalee.

But Oona had made sure Taffy would'n'a seen 'em. Which meant Janie was playing some sort of cruel trick. "No, honey, you're dead wrong," she insisted, determined to nip this yarn in the bud. "Taffy's out yonder in the hayloft, making out like she run off. You cain't fool me."

"No! Seymour and Griffin...where are they?"

Oona let go of the girl and folded her arms under her bosom. Why was she asking for *Seymour*? Had Janie finally found out he was her daddy? "Ain't here."

The girl done looked like she was horse whupped. But only for a split second. Then she stuck out that chin of hers and said, "I'll go alone." She grabbed her boy and pushed him and the widder-woman inside. "They have to stay here with you."

"Now hang on a gawl-durned minute. You ain't going nowhere by yerself, missy, and leaving everyone else here for me to tend all alone. Bonnibelle, you go on with your cousin, now." Someone would have to spoonfeed this girl.

Bonnibelle stamped her feet, and the whole house shook. "Uh, uh, Mama. I'm wet as a catfish. I ain't going back out there in *that*. It ain't fit fer a dog. 'Sides, I got me a baby to take care of. You go on, and I'll look after all of 'em."

"Hah! You never was any good at looking after anyone in all your borned days. You're best at climbing around on rocks at night. *You* go."

"I'll be most happy to stay with the little ones," said the widder-woman.

Janie screamed. "Don't you realize it's too late? Taffy is dead. I'm going for the sheriff." She turned her back on all of them and ran out into the rain.

Taffy, dead? Lord. Oona got a move on. She didn't like leaving the yarb doctor in her house to poke through her things, but what choice did she have? Something, sure as the devil, was wrong. As Janie was starting the car, Oona heaved herself into the passenger seat. Janie stared at her and killed the engine.

Oona glared back. "Well? Watcha waiting fer?"

"Will Jeff be all right?"

"I reckon so fer a while, leastwise." It was the widder-woman that worried her. Couldn't tell what kind of witchery she'd leave behind to upset her household.

The girl started up the car again, and it jerked, turning in a complete circle.

"Now tell me what happened."

"Taffy came to my house. She was upset...I'm not sure why. She went outside in the storm — "

"Keep your eyes on the road, child. This hill gets dang slippery in a good rain."

Did the fool girl listen? The little car plummeted down the hill while she jabbered about someone struggling with Taffy, pushing her over the cliff into the deadening. At the bottom of the hill, the car skidded left, and Oona had to reach over to grab the steering wheel.

"What are you doing?" Janie yelled, fighting the spin of the car.

"You turned wrong," Oona said quietly.

"I'm going for the sheriff."

"No you ain't. Not till after you show her to me."

"But we can't go back there. The killer..." Her voice trailed off, even though it had risen to a right fine pitch for calling the hogs.

"Tut, tut, child. You expect me to believe that for a minute? 'Sides, what if it ain't like you figger?"

Oona stared, deep in thought, at the dark of night this little toy car done plunged itself into. The way she figgered it, Taffy had probably met up with the real daddy of her baby and was trying to get herself a husband, only she plumb didn't know how to do that, neither. All Taffy had to do was come to Oona with the name of the real daddy, and Oona would see to it that the boy married her all proper-like. What are mothers for? But Taffy didn't know that, neither. Taffy always had to take the bull by its horns. If she had an accident, then it was her own danged fault.

"Maybe you're right," Janie whispered, yanking on the steering wheel and whipping the little car around in the road. "Maybe she's not dead and she needs our help." The little car spurted forward, on its way to the Mullen place.

"Well," Oona said, "I wish that girl would'a picked a better night than this."

Janie made a little choking sound. "I don't believe you said that."

What else could Oona say? She stared at the raindrops on the window. "Bonnibelle was right about one thing — it ain't fit fer a dog out there."

She wondered what "job" Dexter could possibly have had for Griffy on a night like this. Lucky for her son that Dexter hadn't found him. But where in the name of the Lord was he?

Janie stopped the car all of a sudden.

"What's wrong now, honey? You run out of gas?"

"No. We'll walk the rest of the way in case he's waiting for us."

"Who?"

"The man who pushed Taffy, of course. We can't let him see us."

"Well, I'll be gawl-danged! You think I'm gonna *walk* in this downpour?"

But the girl ignored her and slipped out of the car anyhows. She disappeared into the shadows.

Oona could see that if she was going to keep an eye on Janie, she'd have to hurry up. Like it or not. She sheltered her head with one hand and struggled out into the rain.

"Shhh. This way," said Janie's voice from somewhere in the dark.

Oona plodded along, thinking of her cozy kitchen and the dress that awaited her on the table. She could picture a new sewing machine sitting next to it. If Griffy only knew, he'd see to it that she got one. Such a good boy.

Bonnibelle was probably warming herself up some leftovers. Lands, but that girl best remember to scrub her stove when she was done, or there was going to be heck fire to pay.

The boy was probably wide awake up there in the attic, listening to the baby squall.

Lord only knew what the widder-woman was up to. Had she found Oona's special box yet? The one she kept hidden beneath her bed. It was where them pictures would've gone if they hadn't've up and disappeared from the Ward's catalogue. Taffy'd found them after all. Lord knew that girl was always poking around where her nose didn't belong. And *that's* what all the fuss was about. Oona's bones shook.

She still couldn't believe that Taffy got herself in the family way. But Dexter wouldn't lie to her. Would he? It only figgers it'd happen sooner or later, dim-witted as that girl was. What Oona couldn't figger, though, was traipsing around on them cliffs on a rainy night. She ought to know her own flesh and blood, and she was plumb sure that her oldest girl was leastwise smart enough to come in out of the rain, Annalee or no.

Which meant that Janie was lying to her. She wasn't going to let on that she'd found out about that mess with Annalee, Seymour and Fern. But Oona knew. Fury simmered inside her like a kettle of rabbit stew.

Only reason Oona was traipsing around in the rain was on account of Fern bedeviling Seymour all them years ago. Iffen it hadn't been for that, Janie wouldn't be here today leading Oona around by the nose, but at least Oona knew her duty when she saw it. Which was more'n she could say for the rest of the world.

"There's the place," Janie whispered, pointing.

Ahead, Oona could see the open space of the deadening. She remembered the valley, and how it was before the deadening come, back in the good old days. Lake, some people call it now, but not her. They ain't got no respect. But one thing never changed. The cliffs. They was just as treacherous today as they was back in Annalee's day.

Lawd a'mercy! Taffy didn't really *jump*, did she? Like Annalee did all them years ago? All because Janie found that gawl-durned picture, she brought Annalee's ghost back. Taffy found it, and that's what gave her the notion. That picture should've been burned long ago, but no. Mae had to keep everything. Like a squirrel hiding nuts away for the winter. Because Janie found it, dredging up the past that should've stayed buried, she as good as pushed Taffy herself. Iffen Taffy was down there, which she still didn't believe.

Oona stood at the edge of the cliff and made herself peer over the edge. The water looked all angry-like the way it slapped against the cliff. Janie was crawling over rocks. She showed up black against the white limestone. Even in a storm the limestone looked white. It took Oona's breath away to watch.

She scanned the rocks but didn't see Taffy lying nowheres. She'd show up black, too, wouldn't she?

Janie done dragged her all the way over here for nothing. Got her soaked to the bone. Probably come down with pee-neumonia. All because of some hysterical city girl. Thought she saw Taffy fall off a cliff, when Oona knew good and well that her daughter was hiding in the hayloft. Taffy would finally learn her lesson real good, and then she'd come out. *Ain't never gonna get that girl outa my house for good.*

Janie climbed back to Oona's side. She was shaking all over. Hair sticking up every which way. Spitting as she tried to speak. "Taffy's...not there."

Oona felt dizzy. The rabbit stew was about to boil over.

TWENTY-NINE

*J*anie was only dimly aware that Oona was planning her life for her. She insisted that Janie come back to her house, that she and Jeff stay there the night, as she'd wanted them to do the first day they'd arrived here. Last week sometime, wasn't it? Now, Janie's mind kept turning back to one astounding realization: neither Oona nor Rose believed her story about Taffy.

Taffy was dead. Someone had pushed her, but where was the body? Maybe it had floated downstream, or maybe the barge had picked it up, or maybe there was no body because Taffy had walked away unhurt, or maybe... Maybe they were right, and she'd imagined the whole thing. Rose could've slipped something into her tea, some herb to make her hallucinate.

"She's in the hayloft," Oona kept insisting, but when Janie went out to the barn herself to check, she couldn't find her cousin. "Don't worry yourself none, honey," Oona insisted. "She'll be back in a day or two with her tail between her legs."

But Janie dreaded the forthcoming days because she knew Taffy wouldn't return.

Toward dawn, Griffin staggered in under the weight of his father. He appeared not at all surprised to find Janie slumped on one couch. Through a pretense of sleep, she watched him raise his eyebrows at Rose, stretched out and snoring on the other couch. He clumped into the other room where Oona still sewed at the kitchen table. Bed springs squeaked, and Janie guessed he was lowering the burden of Seymour onto the bed partitioned from the rest of the kitchen by a curtain. More footsteps clumped as he returned to Oona's side.

"What are *they* doing here, Mama?" he asked in a voice loud enough to be heard from the other room.

"Janie and her boy are a'staying with us from now on, son. Says there's been trouble over yonder. Taffy."

During the pause of silence, Janie strained to hear the suddenly lowered voices. She imagined the looks of disbelief passing between them. The sofa springs squeaked as she leaned forward. That would cut off their conversation for sure, she thought, holding her breath.

The sound of Griffin's chortle, however, must've covered up any noise she'd made. "Like I always said, Mama, the trouble ain't with Taffy. It's with that city girl cousin of yourn."

"Hush your mouth, son. She'll hear you."

"I don't care if they hear me up in Stony Lonesome. That Janie Bainbridge knows if it wasn't for her, no trouble would'a been stirred up in the first place. She knows she ain't welcome here. She knows she may as well go on up north where she belongs — "

"Son, she says she saw someone push Taffy off the cliff. Says she's gone to the Lord. I could tell she was thinking you might'a done it. So you better come up with a danged good reason where you been all night."

"Hell's bells, Mama. I don't got to tell her nothing. Anyone ought to know I wouldn't never touch a flee on either of my sisters' heads."

"I know it, son, but you best be ready for more trouble. She's fixing to go to the sheriff come morning. No telling what they might ask you."

"Don't you worry, Mama. The bridge between town and here is warshed out. She ain't going nowhere. And long as she's under *my* roof, she ain't gonna get a chance to stir up no more trouble. I'll see to that, even if I got to tie her to her bed."

"Now, son — "

"Taffy, huh? Mama, where is she, anyhows? You don't think there's any truth to it, do you?"

"Tsk, tsk, son. There ain't no telling what kind of devil's work the widder-woman done to make Janie think she was seeing Taffy. Probably, it was a pair of mountain lion, spatting. Yessir, that's what Janie done saw and heard. That's all, I reckon."

"All the same, Mama, you reckon I ought to go over yonder and check it out?"

"You ain't going no place till after you've had a decent amount of sleep, son."

~

THE RAIN TAPERED OFF toward the middle of morning, as Janie's patience drained away. Seven people were confined inside the tiny house. Seymour, the eighth, preferred puttering in the damp outdoors, and Janie couldn't blame him. She would've joined him if Oona were to relax her guard for only a minute.

Rose fretted about Price, her garden and her house. Jeff kept insisting in a louder-than-necessary voice that his head no longer hurt. Probably, Janie thought, because hers now hurt in a massive way. Oona slammed pots around the kitchen and snipped at Bonnibelle about not disturbing her brother, asleep in the attic. The baby's cries grew more anxious. Janie had to get away before the Potts family smothered her.

Oona protested, but by late morning, Janie pulled Rose and Jeff away. They piled into the car, leaving Oona planted amidst squawking chickens. Her knuckles dug into the sides of her hips, but Janie didn't care how angry she was. The woman didn't even seem concerned about her missing daughter.

She drove Rose home in silence as she wondered what she was going to do. She couldn't go back to Grandpa's house where she would be an easy target for Taffy's killer. But she couldn't run away, either. She'd come too far to turn back now.

Taffy's body had disappeared, and the parallel to Grandpa's disappearance produced a slow ache in her gut. Had Grandpa been pushed over the cliff, too? Like Taffy? Like Annalee? She wondered what Grandpa had owned that would've made someone want to kill him for it. For that matter, what did *Janie* have that would cause anyone to come after her?

Then she understood. It was the property. No one wanted it as badly as Price.

She had to clutch the steering wheel tightly to hide the shaking in her fingers. The car jerked too sharply around the last bend, and Rose gave her a sideways glance.

The farmhouse Price had converted into an image of a beachfront cottage sat on its peninsula and dared to appear sunny despite the dreary day. In the aftermath of the storm, clouds were slowly tearing themselves apart over-head. A single ray of muted sunlight slipped through the rent in the heavens, as if spotlighting the cottage with a welcome beacon.

Janie pulled into the empty driveway and turned off the engine. Apparently Price had not yet returned.

"Dear, you can't stay alone in that house at night," Rose said, laying her hand on Janie's arm. The woman always seemed to read other people's distress.

So it was settled. She and her son would stay with Rose for a day or two. Until the bridge was rebuilt and she could go find the sheriff.

$\sim$

SHE SHOULD'VE LISTENED to Rose. But Janie had insisted on returning to Grandpa's house to pack up a few things. And lock the door. It would be safe in the middle of the day, she thought. Jeff would be her look-out. It wouldn't take long. If they didn't return to Rose's house within the hour, then Rose had Janie's permission to go fetch Susan.

Why hadn't she listened to Rose, Janie thought as her car puttered around a curve, bringing Grandpa's driveway into full view. Sitting there in front of the house was a beat-up white Chevy hitched to a shiny, new motorboat, altogether about as long as the length of Grandpa's house.

When she saw him sitting on the porch swing, *her* swing, she let out a gasp. "Roy!" The word escaped from Janie before she realized its impact on Jeff.

"Dad? Is that really my dad?"

He didn't remember his own father clearly, she thought. He'd been hardly more than a baby when Roy started staying away nights.

"What's he got that boat for?" Jeff asked.

"I don't know, hon." Janie felt a knot in her stomach. In a flash of memory, she saw all the odd jobs she'd held, struggling alone to pay the bills while Roy, who'd never paid any child support, was off somewhere spending money, apparently on fancy boats.

It was too late to escape. The instant she slowed before turning into the driveway, he saw them and cautiously stood. Jeff bobbed up and down in his seat, straining to get a better look at his father. She had no choice but to turn in and stop the car. Jeff bolted from the car, and she shut off the engine.

Seeing him now, smoothing his hand over his slicked-back hair, causing the dragon tattoo on his biceps to weave sensuously with his motion, she wondered when he had changed from the handsome man she'd married into this roughneck. Or had she been so blind she'd never noticed? Shuddering, she tried to understand why she hadn't spent her last penny on a divorce, but she failed.

Let's get this over with fast.

She climbed out of the car as if she wore lead weights on her ankles. The best thing Roy had ever done for her, she thought, was leaving them. He was a finished chapter in the book of her life, and she was growing stronger by the day on her own.

The question now was her son. He'd fantasized for two years about his dad returning, but now that the moment was here, he shied away from the man.

Good.

Jeff went straight for the boat and ran his hands around its gleaming, white hull. Without a mark on it, it looked as if it had just left the showroom floor. Where had Roy come up with enough money to buy such a boat? Had he stolen it?

Janie lingered by her car. Roy brushed carelessly past her philodendron and sauntered down the porch steps toward their son. It would've taken only a hint of encouragement for Jeff to spring into his father's arms, but Roy didn't open them. Instead of a hug, he tousled the mop of his son's black hair.

Jeff's face beamed with admiration. Over the top of the boy's head, Roy grinned with that lop-sided ogle of his that made Janie wonder if he had a screw loose.

Some of the old anger bubbled up to the surface. A froth of obscenities and accusations forced their way into her mind. "Hello, Roy," she said instead in a calm but shaky voice. He'd never physically abused either of them, and all she could feel was disgust. The accusations didn't matter anymore because the anger was dead. All that mattered was for this man to stay out of her life.

Roy hiccuped and grinned. The dimple on his chin showed through the ragged beard. "Where've you been? I've been waiting here for you for hours. I was about to think no one was living here, and since I'm part owner, why, I was just going to move on in and make myself at home."

Janie gulped, steeling herself with resolve, searching for words that escaped her. Never in a million years would she let him have this place. Never would she leave it empty long enough for him to claim it in her absence.

Roy whistled and surveyed the land around them. "Say, this is a nice place. Always wanted me a place on a lake. Well, Puddin' aren't you glad to see me?"

"Give me your address so my lawyer will know where to reach you."

"What's this about a lawyer?" He wrinkled up his face with a look of pain, but she could see the smirk that lingered. "My address is right here. I'm home."

"Where've you been Roy? Out for a beer with the boys for two *years*?"

"Well, Puddin', I realize you're probably a little sore, but I'll make it up to you, I swear."

"You lost that chance a long time ago. I don't even want to talk about it. Come on, Jeff." She whisked past him, pulling her son with her as she marched toward the porch.

"Please, Puddin', listen to me," he said, grabbing her by the wrist and wrenching pain into her arm. "I was up in the steel mills all this time making a bundle of money just for you."

"I really don't care where you were. Our marriage ended long before you left."

The sound of a car on the road made them all look up with momentary surprise. She'd be glad for another guest, *any* guest, to avoid being alone with Roy. The car that rolled into view, however, was not Seymour's truck nor Griffin's green Ford nor Price's silver Cadillac. It was a Jeep. It slowed by her driveway, then sped away in a cloud of dust. Janie and her son were alone again with Roy.

THIRTY

*O*ona knew where to find Seymour. He thought he still had a few secrets, but she knew better.

Worthless old man. Why didn't she let Fern have him all them years ago? Then he'd have been Fern's problem, not Oona's. Then Janie never would've come along and poked her nose into that business of thirty years ago. She'd found out about it, sure as the cock crows, forcing Oona to put an end to the root of the evil, once and for all.

Oona sloshed through Bossie's pasture and ticked off Janie's faults on her fingers. First, Janie had sent Seymour into a drinking binge the likes of which Oona had never seen. All because Fern's daughter reminded him of them days long ago.

Then, Janie put them high-falutin' notions into Taffy's head and made her run off for real. Oh, she was a clever one, that Janie. She'd concocted that story about Taffy falling off the cliff, but Oona knew better. She knew it was just Janie's way of telling Oona she knew all about that business between Seymour and Fern.

Oona shuddered as she left behind the sweltering mugginess of the open pasture and squeezed between the barbed wires into the drippy coolness of the woods. Pushing her way through brambles toward the crik path, she continued her finger count of grievances.

Janie was trying to steal Bonnibelle's future husband right out from under her nose.

Janie was also stealing the Potts' God-given land.

Janie was stirring up all that trouble about Annalee, which was making Dexter crazy.

Oona thundered along, feeling her jowls jiggle with each stomp of her foot. Up yonder was the big, flat rock sticking out into the crik. Seymour sprawled on the springy soft moss covering that rock and looked like a turtle searching for a patch of sunlight breaking through the storm clouds. He clutched that milk jug the way an old snapper wasn't about to let go of its little furry varmint. She'd figured it out, all right, when she'd come across that milk jug last week. Crik water would keep that white lightning just the right temperature. She didn't like it none that Seymour's rock had to be so close to the old treehouse, but at least her babies was all growed up and wouldn't be playing in the treehouse no more where they could spy on their daddy.

"Ain't you supposed to be doing your chores, Daddy?" she screeched at him. "There's a screen's been needing mending all spring."

Lazily, he turned his head to look at her.

"Iffen you warn't so worthless," she continued, "I'd wager you have yourself a still hid somewheres."

He chuckled. "You think you know ever'thin', don't you, woman?"

She planted her knuckles on her hips. "I know plenty, old man!"

"Oh, yeah? Whaddya know, Mama?" His face was splotchy red. He ought to know better than to challenge her, especially when he'd been a'drinking.

"Why, you fool old man. I know where you was last night. I even know her name. That's what I know." There. That made him stop and think.

His eyes was out of focus. He squinted, then spat in the crik. "Well I'll be danged," he finally said softly. "You know more'n me, then. Who in blazes you talking about?"

"Don't you sass me, old man. I know all about it. And I know if you hadn't've let the devil get the best of you and stayed home where you should ought've been, Taffy wouldn't've up and run off. You as good as chased her off, I reckon." She watched him struggle to his feet.

The hand that held his jug jabbed itself in her direction, as if he was trying to make peace with her. Well, it was too late for that. She grabbed the jug from him, spilling some of its brew on her own hand, before he could say Jack Sprat.

"Mama," he started to say.

But he never finished because Oona waddled to the edge of the crik and upturned that there milk jug. She watched it pore like pee into the crik.

"Mama!" His voice cracked.

"You best mend your ways, old man," she continued. "I cain't do my duty proper-like when you go off a'drinking like this."

"Goddammit, woman, you don't know nothin'."

"Don't you tell me no sech. Why, I even know who Janie is." She hadn't meant to say that. Sometimes things slipped from Oona's mouth before she could stop them.

He blinked, and his eyes suddenly came into focus. "Huh? What're you sayin'?"

It was too late now to back down. Oona huffed up like a laying hen. "Janie Bainbridge is your own flesh and blood, that's who she is. You thought I didn't know, did ya? But I knowed all about you and Fern." She left the rest of it unsaid. She didn't have to spell it out.

The last drops dripped from the jug, and she looked around for more of his stash. When he made a choking sound, she looked back at him. Even the splotches was gone, leaving his face looking chalky.

"We're about to come into our rightful money," she said. "And since you're so worthless, I plumb had to get me some outside help. But not no more. I reckon it's past time you straightened up."

∾

THE LOCUSTS' BUZZ ECHOED in Janie's head as she stood face-to-face with Roy. What on earth had motivated her to leave Auntie Mae's address with Roy's mother so that he could find her?

"Look, Puddin', here's something that'll make you feel better. I brought you a little present." Roy reached into his shirt pocket and pulled out a small bottle of perfume, which he extended to Janie.

"Gee, Dad," said Jeff, "did ya bring me a present, too?"

"Isn't that boat enough, sport?" Roy waved to the sleek craft behind the abused Chevy.

Jeff's face fell and his shoulders sagged. Janie took a step backwards, but Roy was on her in two strides. He took her hand in his and placed the bottle in it. Looking away from the red straggles of beard contrasting with the black ring of greasy hair, she stared at the small bottle in her hand. It had been opened. Used.

Roy released her and sauntered over to the boat. "It's a humdinger for a place like this," he said, running his fingers along its smooth length as if he were caressing someone's thigh. "I wonder if that lake is big enough for the two of us? You can thank your Aunt Oona for letting me know where to find you."

"Oona?" Janie's voice fell to a whisper. That woman had meddled far beyond her limits.

"Yep. There's one decent woman who wants to set things straight. I came as soon as I got her letter, 'cause she said a man was needed around the place, and I'm that man." He whistled and turned slowly in a complete circle. "How much you figure this land is worth, anyhow?"

"It doesn't matter," Janie said, biting her words, much the same as Oona, "because I'm not selling. This is Jeff's and my home now."

"Now don't be so hasty. Think about it. I bet we could make a bundle of money off this place, then find ourselves a *real* place down in Florida and never have to shovel a lick of snow again."

Janie opened the bottle of perfume and poured its golden liquid contents into the weeds lining the tire tracks of the driveway. "Go away! And take that boat with you."

"Dammit, Puddin', what'd you go and do that for? That cost me good money."

"So you can't give it to tomorrow's girlfriend. Please leave *now*."

"I'm not going anyplace without my son."

He caught her by surprise. He'd never cared about their son before. Why would he want him now? A numbness iced over her. This had been her darkest fear.

"You've never had time for Jeff before. Why the sudden change of heart?"

"He's getting older. He needs a man around. I don't want him tied to your apron strings—"

"Do you see me wearing a goddamned apron?"

"Don't cry, Mom."

"I want him for a couple of days at least — "

"Until he gets in the way of your lifestyle?"

"What about my rights?"

"What rights? What about all those nights you stayed away from home when Jeff was a baby? Even if you still had any rights then, you certainly gave them up two years ago when you vanished." Now she regretted having saved the lawyer's fees instead of spending it on a divorce that would've been easy to get. She hadn't expected him ever to return.

"I had to get myself on my own two feet."

"You should've discussed it with us first — "

"Puddin', you know I'm a man of action rather than words."

"You could've had the decency to tell us why you wanted to leave, or you could've sent us a postcard to let us know where you went. Or, you could've sent us child support if you were concerned about your rights as a father. Oh, why am I wasting my time talking to you? I asked you to leave."

"Not without what's coming to me." He folded his arms and leaned against the fender of his car as if daring her to remove him. She could almost see the gears spinning in his brain as he summed up the worth of the property around him. "That your tent, sport? How about I take you camping for real?"

"Oh, boy! Could I, Mom?"

Roy's voice lowered to a growl. "You don't need to ask her. I'm your dad, and us men have to stick together. I'll have to teach you about women."

"You mean *girls*?" He turned back to his mother as if looking for help.

She started to put her arms around Jeff, then dropped them. Was it true what he'd said about the apron strings?

Roy followed Jeff's look, but his eyes focused on Janie's legs. "You can kick me out of your bed, and I'll honor that until you're ready. But remember, Puddin', I'm still your husband, whether you like it or not. And when you're ready to ask me back, I'll be out here waiting."

Sweat tickled her sides. He didn't want her. He only wanted the money from Grandpa's land. If she didn't walk into Grandpa's house, as if she'd never left it for a minute, then he'd claim it. She could tell from the eagerness shining on his unshaven face. Her eyes darted to the spot on the cliff where she'd last seen Taffy, and her heart thudded. She reached into her purse for her new key and steered Jeff toward the front porch.

"Mom, it's not forever." He tugged at her arm and made her look down into his anxious face. Could it be that he actually wanted to go with Roy? He didn't know how uncaring his father was.

However, if Jeff *did* spend a couple of days with Roy, then her son would see firsthand what kind of father Roy was. He'd see the truth, and he wouldn't be able to blame Janie for telling him what he didn't want to hear. Then fear caught in her throat. What if Roy took Jeff and disappeared again? She couldn't bear the thought of losing her son. She squeezed his shoulder and pushed him on toward the house.

"Dammit, Puddin', what is it you want? Money? Here, I'll give you money."

Jeff twisted under her grip to look back. "He's throwing dollar bills on the ground!"

Tears slipped down her cheeks, and she stopped, rod straight. She refused even to turn around. "I don't want your money. It's too late for that effort. I don't need anything from you, Roy. In fact, I don't need anybody's help in raising my child. Jeff and I are doing fine alone together."

She'd said it, and she believed it. She really was the sole, responsible parent. Not only was it okay to be a single mother, it was what she preferred. If she took his money now, it'd be the same as giving Roy the right he'd only reject a few days from now. She squared her shoulders with pride and marched up the front porch with Jeff. A breeze fanned her flushed cheeks.

"There it goes, Puddin'. You're throwing away good money again."

Jeff flinched, ready to run after the money blowing away with the breeze, but Janie squeezed his shoulder again.

"Let it go, honey. We don't need it that badly." She stuck the key in the lock, but the door was already open. Last night in their haste, she'd forgotten to lock it.

Jeff glanced one more time over his shoulder, then gave his mother a look of wonder before bolting off toward his bedroom. Janie closed the door behind her, locked it, and leaned heavily against it. It was good to be home again. Home! Taffy's killer wouldn't get past Roy-the-guard outside. She breathed a sigh of relief, feeling tension drain from her.

"Mom!" Jeff cried from his bedroom. "You found Beads!"

THIRTY-ONE

He'd meant what he said about waiting. Two hours passed, and Roy was still out there, leaning against the fender of the white Chevy. Smoking, and watching, and waiting.

I didn't find Beads.

Too bad there weren't any telephones. Too bad Susan had made a trip here for nothing, only to be subjected to Roy's appraising looks. Janie had convinced Susan that she was okay, that her ex had come, coveting Grandpa's property. Susan should tell Rose not to worry. Janie would have to stake out her claim to Grandpa's house, or lose it.

Then he took up his station once again, and at least she felt safe for the moment. It was funny, she thought, how patient he could be at first when he was after something he really wanted. The problem with Roy was that he'd never wanted any one thing for very long.

Someone had put Beads there, on Jeff's bed, for him to find.

She felt strangely calm as the hours ticked by. She could outwait Roy, but in the meanwhile, his presence outside should deter the spider-killer from returning for Janie. She suffered a moment of weakness when she saw Roy move a sleeping bag into *her* tent then set up a cookstove nearby. Had she been too harsh?

No. He'd brought on his own fate all by himself.

Too many thoughts nagged at her, robbing her of sleep. *May as well stare at a blank piece of paper in the typewriter. Got to work on that play...*

Why had she *had* to appear so strong? So stubborn. So *stupid*.

Where was Price?

She hauled the typewriter downstairs from the attic, where the air wasn't moving at all, and set it up on the kitchen table where there was some cross-ventilation. Her foot caught at the pull ring of the trapdoor, and she realized the table had been pushed aside.

Beads had reappeared.

The table had been moved.

The day faded into night, and the night crept by. Each time she peeked out the window, the glow from Roy's lantern calmed her a little more. It was like having a guard dog on duty outside. Maybe she could relax enough to stretch out on Grandpa's bed for a little while.

She awoke to sunlight streaming through the window. After the storm, daylight had an added sparkle. Her spirits lifted. They'd survived a night alone in Grandpa's house. The spider-killer hadn't returned. Everything would be all right.

Of course, they weren't entirely alone. They had Roy to thank for that. The least she could do was offer him a cup of coffee. When she sent Jeff out to rouse his father with an invitation to breakfast, however, he quickly ran back inside.

"He's gone! Him and his car and the boat, and his sleeping bag and everything." Jeff's face screwed up as if he was about to burst into tears. "And it's all your fault."

"Jeff, honey. He'll be back, if he really meant what he said."

But he didn't stay to listen. He ran outside to the comfort of his rocks. She saw him, huddled over far away from everyone on his flat fishing rock. He was a little boy feeling all alone in the world. She knew that pitching pebbles into the lake was a release for him, and so she left him alone, but it didn't ease the ache in her heart.

~

OONA, BENT OVER in her garden, cradled a mess of mustard in her skirt. When Bonnibelle snuck up on her, she liked to drop the whole mess. "I declare, child! You ain't got no call sneaking up on a body like that. Get your bee-hind in here and help me pick supper."

"Uh-uh, Mama. Look how muddy it is after the rain. And I just got out of the wash tub."

Oona straightened up and put a hand on her back where she felt bones pop. She looked her youngest one up and down. Where'd that girl get a skirt like that, anyhows? It was so tight over her rear end, she couldn't hardly walk in it. "What're you doing all gussied up this early in the afternoon?"

"Ain't too early, Mama. We got the revival meeting, don't forget."

Oona frowned. "Bonnibelle Potts, I ain't never seen you in sech a all-fired rush to get to no revival meeting in all your borned days."

"You don't want to miss it again this week, now do you?"

"Honey, we ain't going nowhere till your brother gets home."

Lordy, what the dickens had happened to Griffy? She hadn't seen hide nor hair of him all afternoon. He'd slept till noon, then tore out of here like the place was on fahr. If he didn't get back soon, why she didn't know how she was going to manage between supper and the milking once again. It didn't look like there'd be no revival meeting again tonight. Lordy, but she had a bad feeling in her bones.

It's all Janie's fault. Neither Griffy neither Seymour was the same since that girl blowed into our lives. Why couldn't she've stayed gone, like Fern?

"Mama, there ain't no point waiting for Griffin, 'cause he ain't coming with us tonight."

"How's come you know that?" Biting off her words made the sagging skin tighten beneath Oona's chin. She didn't like it when someone else knew something she didn't know.

"'Cause he told me when he left he wasn't coming back."

"What do you mean he wasn't coming back? Of course he's coming back. You don't know nothing, that's all."

"Griffin, Griffin, Griffin!" Bonnibelle shouted, sashaying back to the house. "I'm sick to death of him. I got me other things to think on that's more important than Griffin."

"Like Junior Wanamaker?" Oona called after her, not quite ready to give up her duties.

Bonnibelle stopped dead in her tracks and turned around to throw her mama a coy smile. "Price ain't no fun no more. Not since your cousin come around here."

"Well, slap my bones! Bonnibelle Potts, I never thought I'd live to see the day you'd give up on that man."

"I ain't said nothing about giving up on Price." The smile slid off Bonnibelle's face faster than a greased hog. "But for your information, Mama, Price ain't the only catfish in the river."

"That so? Just look at you, girl. You ain't dressed for church. You cain't fool me none. You got your cap set for someone."

"I can dress how I please. I'm a growed woman now. And maybe I know what I'm doing." Bonnibelle huffed and stomped away.

Oona started to call after her, then thought better of it. She wouldn't have no child of hers sass her like that. But then she remembered the last time she'd put her foot down.

It troubled her bones that Taffy was still gone, and she wondered if she'd been too hard on the girl.

～

THE SOUND OF A MOTORBOAT made Janie look up later that afternoon from the pages of manuscript that were beginning to stack up. The predicted tourists must finally be finding this lake. She ripped a page from her typewriter as the boat coughed and sputtered, slowing in front of her place. Of all the miles of shoreline, she wondered why boaters were attracted to *her* cliffs.

She rolled a fresh piece of paper into her typewriter and stared at its intimidating blankness. The first boat she'd heard here had signaled the barge to stop in the middle of the night in front of her house. The next time it had been Dexter, coming to call on them in his version of a neighborly fashion. His was the only motorboat she'd confirmed on the lake. Was it him now that she heard, roaring away from her cliffs? Or perhaps Roy had launched his show boat.

She stood up to peer out the kitchen window. Trees obscured the immediate shoreline, but she heard the disembodied drone of an outboard motor in the distance.

Where was Jeff? His fishing rock was empty.

She moved to the door and stepped outside. "Jeff!"

All that answered her was the receding hum of the boat. Her son wouldn't have gone for a ride with a stranger. Would he?

Stop it! Her son knew better than that. Visions of apron strings dangled through her mind.

She hurried to the cliff's edge for an unobstructed view of the lake, but by the time she got there, the boat was only a speck in the distance. She watched it disappear around a jutting peninsula far away. The boat was heading up Dew Bay, and it occurred to Janie that Price might have been her visitor.

"Jeff!" she called again.

He didn't answer, and something gnawed at her stomach. She traced the rim of the cliff and peered down over its edge to the rocks below where she knew he liked to play. A wave of dizziness hit her as she kept remembering the sight of Taffy's body down there, bent into unnatural angles. And not so long before that, the sight of her own son. When she reached the wall of kudzu tumbling down the limestone, she stopped. She didn't think after his accident Jeff would persist in searching for a way into the kudzu-hidden cave, but she called his name again, anyway.

Rustling leaves, stirred by the breeze, responded. Nothing more. Even the hum of the motorboat had faded. She might as well be completely alone in the world.

She turned away and hurried in the opposite direction, toward the cove where Price had said he wanted to build his playhouse. It must have been Price in the boat. Jeff would've thought it was okay to go with him, but still it annoyed her that he hadn't asked permission first. She found a boulder and sat down to wait for the boat to reappear from around that peninsula guarding the entrance to Dew Bay.

Twenty minutes later, the gnawing sensation had worsened. She stood and paced. Maybe Jeff *hadn't* gotten into that boat.

She climbed down the slope to the crescent-shaped cove. Undergrowth spilled from the woods like fringe decorating the muddy curve of the shore. It made a perfect hiding place, and she remembered the movement she'd seen here from Price's sailboat.

Someone *had* been here recently. A trail of small footprints, fresh since the storm the night before last, dug into the soft mud. Jeff hadn't gotten into any boat, she thought with a sigh of relief. He'd come along this way. But where had he been going? And why would he wander away without seeking permission first?

The footprints led to the point where the creek tumbled into the cove. There was a path alongside it, the same path Bonnibelle had followed from her house that day she came in search of a ride to town. The small footprints joined a trail of larger footprints, and together they turned onto the path. A chill coursed down her spine. Both sets of prints faded up the incline where the ground was more solid, more sheltered from the rain by the forest canopy.

"Jeff?" A note of anxiety crept into her voice.

She didn't wait for an answer but plunged onto the wooded path. Dexter's warning of cottonmouths flashed through her mind, but she didn't care.

Someone had lured Jeff away.

Roy, no doubt. Rage boiled, threatening her attempt at calm. The next time she saw her husband, she'd strangle him with her apron strings.

THIRTY-TWO

*J*anie didn't realize how swollen the creek had become from the recent storm until she reached a point on the path where it emerged onto the road. The tumbling waters had spilled over, washing away gullies of gravel along with the planks serving as the bridge. If this was where Roy had parked his Chevy to whisk Jeff away, he wouldn't have gotten very far without a bridge. Following the road, she chose the direction that led past her house, in case Jeff had returned during her absence.

He hadn't.

She continued up the road. This was the same course she'd taken that morning on her run. She picked up her pace.

By the time she reached the path she'd followed before, where the wire had tripped her, she still hadn't come across the white Chevy. The creek intersected the road again, and like the first bridge, this one was washed away, too. Roy couldn't have come this way in his car. Had he gone the other direction from the first washed-out bridge she'd encountered?

She stood there, wondering what to do next, when she noticed the flowers that had first caught her attention on her run. They were trampled. Someone had come this way. Jeff? Had he deliberately trampled the flowers to leave a sign for her?

If her son and his abductor had followed this path, and Griffin had caught them...

Not finishing the thought, she dashed into the woods, running faster than safety dictated. Griffin would think in his demented way that Jeff was "snooping." Anger and dread propelled her along the creek path. Her pounding heart matched the thump of her sneakers.

The smell hit her first, and she remembered the hog pens, not far from where the wire had been strung across the path, only a few inches above ground. It had tripped her before and sent her sprawling at Griffin's feet. She wouldn't make that same mistake again, she thought, slowing her step. The wire must be some sort of trap, alerting Dexter to unwanted visitors. What would they do to a small boy, being dragged into their domain by his unknowing father?

The way Griffin had acted so menacing, so protective, made her suspicious of him. He was hiding something. She wouldn't do Jeff any good if she was caught now, but she *had* to have a look inside that hog pen to see what Griffin was hiding there. She hoped his guilt didn't have anything to do with...Grandpa.

The path widened ahead into a clearing that housed the outbuildings of the farm. There was an assortment of sheds and barns and rusted machinery. Janie stepped off the path and into the protective undergrowth at the edge of the woods. In this fashion, she crept closer to the hog pen. Finally, she had to hold her nose. She looked around.

Nothing moved anywhere. No human sounds. She stepped out of the shadows of the woods and peered over the weathered boards. Hogs. Hogs snuffled in the pen.

She hadn't really expected Grandpa to be in there, she thought, stepping quickly back into the wooded shelter. She was letting her imagination run away with her. Maybe Griffin was a little hostile, but he wouldn't have done away with Grandpa.

Then she reminded herself that someone had killed Taffy, thinking she was Janie. It didn't take an over-active imagination to think of Griffin as a killer.

She shivered and continued along the strip of woods bordering Dexter's farm. Up ahead, a corn field lay between the woods and the run-down house she and Jeff had seen that first day from the road. Corn stalks looked out of place. The only fields she'd seen breaking apart the woods had been tobacco fields. She wished the corn were taller, though. It was too early in the season to be tall enough to hide her approach to the house.

She waited for someone to appear, someone to find her looking suspicious in the edge of the woods. No one appeared. Hogs continued to grunt and snort, chickens crooned from the barn, cows let loose with an occasional moo, locusts trilled, and crows called. But the sounds she listened for — the sounds of men's voices or clinking pails, or humming machinery — were absent. It appeared to be a farm, but no farming seemed to be occurring. Where was everyone?

Boldly, she stepped out of her hiding place and strode up to the front door of the house. No one intercepted her. The clunking sounds of her own footsteps on the splintering wood of the front porch startled her. The door stood open behind the screen, and she peered in before knocking. It was a Spartan room, dark from boarded-up windows and layers of dust.

"Hello?" she called.

No one answered. She glanced over her shoulder, but no one emerged from one of the outbuildings, either. She waited, then impulsively opened the screen door and stepped inside. Her heart hammered from her boldness, but she took a deep breath and looked around.

She sneezed. How many years of dust and neglect were layered in here? Clay pots sat everywhere — some on their sides, some broken or chipped, some empty and some with dried-up soil and twigs. Shreds of lace curtains drooped over the windows that didn't admit anymore light.

"Jeff?" she whispered, tiptoeing through the room that someone had apparently cared about once upon a time.

In the kitchen, a black woodburning stove sat idle in one corner under a pile of junk. A bucket of scum held a few dishes, and a foul odor emanated from it. A jumble of junk food and dirty dishes balanced on the table, and beneath it were crumbs and empty wrappers.

She hurried through a door into a back room and stopped suddenly with surprise. The bedroom. It didn't look as if anyone had slept here for many years. In one sweeping glance she took in the dresser, with its lace doily, comb and brush, still filled with blonde hairs, the neat row of dried-up perfume bottles, bits and pieces of crumbled flowers. A rocking chair. An empty baby's cradle, its wicker snapped in several places. White paint had peeled away into a dingy gray. A brass bed, once beautiful, now mottled with neglect and buried under a rumpled pile of smelly bedding. Flowered wallpaper bubbled away from water stains on the walls.

Then the focal point of this room drew Janie to it. Dominating the wall above the bed was a full-length portrait, crowned by an oval, gilt frame. Joy radiated from the bride's smile, which showed too much gum. Despite this magnificent centerpiece, a chill tickled Janie's spine. This was a larger version of the same photo she'd found hidden on Mae's dresser. It was a picture of Annalee, Dexter's young wife who'd died so tragically in the accident similar to Taffy's.

This had been Annalee's room.

Janie stepped closer to the portrait. It was large enough that she could make out the pendant round Annalee's throat. Sapphires clustered into the shape of a forget-me-not. Janie sucked in her breath. It was the same pendant her mother had worn. The same pendant with the broken chain, which now lay hidden in a pouch at the bottom of Janie's lingerie drawer.

She backed away from the portrait and bumped into the dresser. Putting her hand out for balance, she felt the dried flowers crinkle beneath her fingers. She picked up the fragments and stared at them. Forget-me-nots.

That's what this room was, Janie realized. A shrine to Annalee, who'd loved the delicate flower. It was a room where her memory would never be forgotten. Janie could almost feel Annalee's ghostly presence. The faint waft of her perfume. The filmy brush of her ghostly touch on Janie's cheek. Dancing dust motes on a ray of light slipping through a crack in the boarded-up window. The creak of a floorboard under her light step.

The hairs stood up on Janie's arms. That wasn't a ghost! Silently, she crept to the doorway and peeked around the corner. She didn't see anyone, and she sprinted forward.

Suddenly her motion jerked to a stop. A smelly hand clamped over her mouth. The acrid taste of oil on his fingers smothered her lips and stifled her scream. His other hand reached clumsily around her waist and pressed her spine into his heaving chest. A scratchy feel of denim and a fetid smell of manure mixed with sweat encircled her, holding her helpless against his strength. She wanted to faint.

"Well, well. Lookee what the cat drug in." Griffin's breath tickled her ear and the back of her neck.

She thought he was going to wrench her arm from its socket as he dragged her through the house, outside into the light of day. There, in the driveway, sat a rusted truck, which hadn't been there when Janie had slipped into the house. Dexter stood at the tailgate shoveling dried ears of corn from the bed of the truck into a waiting wheelbarrow. He looked up from his work when Griffin and Janie struggled outside. Even though his eye patch covered a good portion of his face, Janie could still see his scowl.

"You're hurting me," Janie said, her voice muffled by his smothering hand.

"That ain't the half of it, girl."

Dexter leaned on his shovel and peered at her. His single black nugget eye roved up and down her body, taking in the sweat-stained T-shirt and the cut-off shorts. He nodded at the cab of the truck, then turned to Griffin. "Get her in there."

Obedient, Griffin released his hand from her mouth in order to yank her with both arms toward the truck. Dexter was moving the wheelbarrow toward a shed when Janie let out an ear-piercing scream.

"Now what'd you go and do that for, girl?" Griffin put one hand to his ear and tightened his other arm round her waist. "Ain't no one for miles gonna hear you."

"I'm not going anywhere with you." She gasped, digging in her heels, pushing with two hands against his one arm that held her like a vise. Her struggle did nothing to loosen Griffin's hold. Not even the kick she landed on the top of his foot. Her sneakers couldn't inflict enough pain to get through Griffin's thick skin.

"Oh, yes you are," he said, making a sound that was a cross between a snort and a laugh. "You was trespassing. Didn't I warn you once already? Now you're gonna have to pay. It's up to the boss to decide what to do with trespassers."

"Okay, I'm sorry I trespassed, but Dexter's not God, Griffin. Why don't you think for yourself for a change? Is this any way for you to treat your own family?"

A purple flush crept up Griffin's thick neck. She could almost see the steam rolling out of his disheveled, black curls. Steam, slipping out from under his woolly beard. The steam of anger, pushing its release through the patches in his overalls.

Maybe she'd gone too far.

With one massive hand, Griffin yanked open the passenger door of the truck. Squeezing her with his other arm, he shoved her inside, then climbed in after her and grabbed her before she could scramble out the driver's door.

Then the driver's door opened, and Dexter appeared. He stood there, eyeing her for what seemed an eternity. Slowly, a grin spread across the stubbles of his chin. His grin matched a mind that was mad enough to maintain a shrine to a dead wife for thirty years.

"What we gonna do with this little lady, Griffin?" he said, springing lightly behind the steering wheel.

"Gotta teach her a lesson."

"A lesson, eh? Yep. That's what she needs, I reckon. Keep her nose out of other folks' business. How we gonna do that, Griffin?"

"How 'bout iffen we take her over yonder to the next county? Let her walk back."

"Naw, stupid. She likes to walk. And we ain't got the rest of the day."

"You're right," Griffin said. "Earl got shorted and he's about fit to be tied — "

"Earl?" Janie gasped.

Dexter reached across Janie to shove Griffin in the shoulder. "Shut up, stupid." Then he leaned back, allowing his bare arm to slide across her breasts. He reached for the ignition and cranked the engine with a wicked grin on the uncovered half of his face.

THIRTY-THREE

*S*hrinking from Dexter's touch and body odor, Janie plastered herself against the back of the seat. This wasn't happening, she thought. What about his devotion to Annalee?

"See here," she said, mustering only a shaky voice. "The door was open. I called out. I'm sorry..."

Griffin snickered. "I got a idea. Let's take her to the cave."

"Shut up, stupid." Dexter reached across Janie and her breasts again to give Griffin another poke.

"Look, maybe I made a mistake," she said, "but you have no right to treat me like this. I'll press charges."

"She's gonna press charges." Griffin mimicked her voice, and he and Dexter burst out laughing.

"All right, I won't press charges if you just let me go." Over her dead body she wouldn't, but they didn't have to know that.

"It's too late for that, girl," said Dexter. "You know too much."

"I don't know anything."

"You seen too much."

"I've seen nothing..." Her voice trailed off with her lie.

"We'll take her to the shack," Dexter said.

Griffin scowled. "What d'ya need to do that for? I don't like it none."

If Griffin didn't like it, then Janie definitely didn't like it. A trembling spread from the tips of her toes through the ends of her hair, standing out in a wild mass, not entirely from the humidity.

"Well, let's git a move on," Griffin said, "afore Crockett finds his corn gone."

"Who gives the orders 'round here, boy?"

The two men glared at each other in silence for a full minute, then Griffin backed down. He turned away to stare out his window. A purple flush crept up the back of his neck, giving Janie an idea. All she had to do was wait for her opportunity.

Dexter steered the truck onto a dirt road skirting the perimeter of the corn field. He turned off it suddenly and plowed into a fjord in the creek, which joined up with another field road on the other side.

Once the truck lurched onto the main road, Dexter turned his attention to Janie's legs. He took his blackened index finger and traced the scratches on her legs. "A pretty gal like you ain't got no call getting yourself all cut up like that."

She brushed his hand aside. "Don't touch me. Isn't it enough what you did to Taffy?"

The veins in Griffin's neck stood out as he jerked his head around to glare at Janie. "Taffy? What do you mean?"

Dexter snorted. "Feisty, ain't she?"

Yes, it might work, she thought. "You must've known," she said to Griffin, ignoring Dexter. "That day I found you and Taffy arguing in the woods — "

"She had some cock'n bull story about wanting to see Dexter, but I wouldn't let her. She never saw him, and you're lying."

"She found a way to see him," Janie said, waiting for the silencing slap from Dexter. But he was strangely quiet.

"I didn't make her run off," Griffin said.

"She didn't run away. She..." Janie was backing herself into a corner if she admitted what she'd seen.

"Mama said she run off."

"Your mother is wrong. Taffy committed suicide — "

"You lie!"

" — because she was depressed about the baby she and Dexter were expecting."

"BABY?" Griffin's voice rose to a roar.

"That's right," Janie said.

"Bul-l-l-l-lshit." Dexter snarled, coming to life.

Janie looked back and forth at the two enraged men and watched her plan unfold.

Griffin leaned across her to confront Dexter. She could see his veins throbbing at his temples and his eyes bulging. "I always swore I'd kill the bastard who laid a finger on one of my sisters."

"You threatening me, boy?" Dexter said with a gentle laugh. Apparently he realized he had to treat Griffin with caution now. "You listening to a broad? She don't know what in he-yell she's talking about. 'Sides, I cain't make no babies. I never had me one."

Griffin's face softened as he thought this over.

"That's a lie," Janie said. "Griffin, haven't you seen the baby bed back there in Annalee's room?"

Dexter stirred from his thundercloud with a low rumble of laughter, then suddenly slapped her. "You lying bitch."

"Hey, you leave her alone, you hear?"

"You trying to give me orders again, boy? I reckon I gotta learn you a lesson, too."

The side of Janie's head stung. She felt dizzy. "Griffin, did I ever lie to you when we were kids? When you and Taffy and I played together?"

Slowly, he shook his head.

"Hah!" Dexter snorted as he yanked at the steering wheel and jerked the truck off the road and onto an overgrown driveway. They were thrown forward as Dexter stopped the truck suddenly in front of a gate fashioned from barbed wire. It hung between two trees flanking the lane. Weeds growing waist-high brushed against the underside of the truck and channeled into a strip centered between two ruts of tire tracks.

Griffin took a key from the glove compartment, then swung his heavy frame out of the truck. Janie started to follow him, but Dexter grabbed her arm and gave it a sharp twist. She cried out, and he hissed into her ear while Griffin unlocked the gate.

"You shut your mouth about that baby crap, you hear me? I know where your old man took your boy. You git my drift?"

"You can't threaten me. Jeff is perfectly safe." She tensed with doubt.

Dexter said nothing but merely grinned as he crunched the gears and urged the truck through the gate. On the other side, he didn't stop but picked up speed.

"Hey, aren't you going to wait for Griffin?"

The truck bumped along the rutted lane. Weeds brushed past. Dexter guffawed for a full minute before finding his voice. "We don't need him."

Janie cringed. The man was just trying to frighten her, she reminded herself. And he was certainly doing a good job of it, too. Roy had taken Jeff... Hadn't she thought so? At least her son would be safe. Roy wouldn't hurt him.

That didn't make her feel any better.

She glanced over her shoulder and saw Griffin chasing behind them in the distance, waving his arms. Dexter chuckled softly next to her.

She scanned the terrain ahead. There was a ridge, and on the other side of it, just out of Griffin's sight, that's where she could make her escape. She would suddenly wrench herself from Dexter's unsuspecting grip and spring from the truck. She would have to move fast enough to take Dexter by surprise. She'd leap from the moving truck, roll into the tobacco field, and crouch under the thick leaves before Dexter could stop the truck. She'd only have a small head start. Tobacco fields grew on either side of the rutted lane, so she wouldn't have much cover until she reached the woods. If she could outrun Dexter till then...

He must have read her thoughts, for he twisted her arm, making her wince. At the same time, the truck sped up as it hit the ridge, jostling her off the seat with its unkind bounces. They roared past her planned escape.

"We're almost there," he said.

Ahead, the fields ended abruptly against a wall of woods. A weather-beaten shed, looking as if it were barely hanging together with a handful of rusty nails, slouched under a sycamore tree.

"I reckon you'll come around," he continued. "Same as Taffy. She didn't want to at first neither, then she found out she liked it, and she kept coming back for more."

Tears welled in the corners of Janie's eyes. She fought to keep her sobs under control.

"Now, Bonnibelle, she's a whole different kettle of fish. Ain't no man alive can give her enough." He shook his head slowly. "Lord knows I ain't no spring chicken no more, but I still got it in me."

He stopped the truck and pulled Janie toward his side. She grabbed the steering wheel, to prevent him from dragging her out of the truck's cab, but he soon pried her fingers loose. She tumbled down onto the red soil, beginning to crack already from a day and a half without rain.

"No!" She screamed and tried to twist her arms so that she could claw him, dig her fingernails into his flesh, twist herself out of his grip — whatever it would take to free herself or postpone his torture.

"Ain't you the feisty one?"

She wrestled away from his hands, groping and clawing at her clothes. She sank her teeth into his stinking arm, but he didn't flinch. Instead, a low chuckle rumbled from his throat.

"You want it," he whispered. "Just like your ma."

"My..." The struggle drained out of her, leaving her a limp heap on the ground. "My mother? You filthy, no-good, vile..."

He straddled her on the ground and ran his grease-stained hands over her body. "Go on and want it." His voice was husky.

No...please, Mother, why didn't you tell me?

Janie was only slightly aware of ripping sounds and feverish fingers roving across her. She mentally distanced herself, as if she were only watching a bad movie instead of living the nightmare. Lashing out at him, she gasped, "What about Annalee?"

His fingers suddenly stopped. He pulled back into his madness, and she feared she'd only made it worse for her. "That whore wasn't no use to me," he said, "not once she got herself knocked up. It wasn't even mine."

Griffin's fist exploded from nowhere and landed on the side of Dexter's head. He rolled off Janie and spun to the ground. Griffin leapt atop Dexter and pummeled his face.

"You bastard! Cain't you ever keep your cock in your pants?"

Dexter howled, "You owe me, boy."

"I don't owe you nothing. I quit. My daddy took your first eye, and I'll take the other one."

Dexter screamed. "Your daddy would'a took his turn on her, too."

Flesh smacked against flesh.

"You the one that done it to Bonnibelle?" Griffin cried.

It took Janie a full minute to realize she was free. Slowly, her senses returned to her as the numbness melted away. She scrambled to her feet and stumbled in a disoriented circle. Where was she?

"Go on," Griffin yelled at her. "Git outa' here."

Backing away step by step, she watched the two men rolling on the ground. They were going to kill each other, she thought, spinning on her heels and running.

THIRTY-FOUR

*P*lunging into the tobacco field, Janie expected the sounds of their struggle to give way to a cry of alarm once Dexter realized she was escaping. She expected to hear the truck start up and cut her off down the road. However, the punches and grunts continued, and she risked a glance over her shoulder. Locked in arm grips, the two of them wrestled on the ground. Griffin had saved her from the man he idolized.

She stumbled through the neat rows of spindly plants with over-sized, glossy leaves. They brushed against her skin as Dexter's fingers had grasped at her. Shivering and sweating at the same time, she ran faster.

Dexter had attacked Mother.

Ahead, a sheath of kudzu finally spilled from the edge of the woods. The vine that had seemed so sinister before now offered her protection. Diving into the network of vines, she gasped for breath and doubled over from pain stabbing her ribs.

Mother had run away because Dexter had attacked her.

She couldn't stop shaking. She sank down into the cool leaves. The snarl of vines rose up around her, sheltering her while she let the pain in her ribs subside.

Mother couldn't face anyone. She'd run away, and then Janie had been born.

Oh God.

There was no Wilson Bainbridge, and Dexter was Janie's father.

She didn't know how long she'd sat there, crumpled over in a stupor in the kudzu, listening to the muffled curses of the raging fight, when she heard a twig snap somewhere nearby. She dropped lower into the kudzu, onto her stomach, tasting the damp smell of the earth. She slid leaves aside and spied the newcomer.

A man, dressed in camouflage, skirted the patch of kudzu where Janie lay hidden. He had a thick mustache, and he frowned in the general direction of the fighting men. He crunched through underbrush, toward the shed in the tobacco field. He didn't look in Janie's direction, where she hid only a few feet away. She watched him approach the men. One of them should've been dead by now, Janie thought.

"Here now, boys," the stranger shouted. "Break it up."

They stopped throwing punches, and they fell away from each other. Surprise shone on their faces. "Who're you?" Griffin said with a grunt.

The stranger ignored the question. "That your corn?" he asked instead, pointing to the bed of the truck.

"What's it to you?"

The stranger pushed his splotched hat back from a bald forehead. "Got a report from a man, name of Crockett. Says a truckload of his corn was stole right out from his silo."

Dexter and Griffin slowly pulled themselves up from the ground and looked cautiously at each other. "Don't know nothing about that. You sure Crockett got his story straight?"

"Sure I'm sure. Ain't too many folks raising corn 'round these here parts. Ain't too many folks that *want* corn, neither. This here's tobacco country."

"Maybe I'm working out a deal with Crockett," Dexter said slowly, tentatively. "Maybe old man Crockett wants to sell his place to me. Maybe he *give* me a little corn to help me make up my mind."

The man in camouflage scratched his bare forehead. "Well, now, that does pose us a problem, don't it? I hear tell Mr. Crockett is selling out to the Wanamakers, and that Potts gal is the one that closed the deal for him."

Griffin's face flushed. His fists clenched and unclenched, as if they were itching to connect to someone's head.

"What're you boys fixing to do with all that there corn?" the stranger continued.

Silence.

"You wouldn't be fixing to make no mash with it, now would you?" he asked, persisting with his investigation.

"What would we be doing such a tom fool thing like that for?" Dexter's voice was so low that Janie could barely hear him.

"There's a still 'round here," the stranger said. "Don't you go saying there ain't, 'cause I know that smell when I smell it. And I know you boys know all about it. Only thing I don't know is where it's at. It's time you folks down here in Chittenden learned you cain't take the law into your own hands."

Griffin's fingers dangled limply at his side. "Mister, you've got yourself the wrong boys. Crockett's the one with the corn."

"Shut up, stupid," Dexter said, landing his elbow in Griffin's ribs. "That don't mean nothing. 'Sides, your old man's got it, too."

The stranger pointed his index finger at them. "All right, boys, you listen to me good. I know that still's hid real good around here, but I'm gonna find it, you hear? And when I do, there ain't gonna be no more moonshine in this here county. And then you boys ain't got no more reason to fight, 'cept to survive, once you get inside the penitentiary. Got that?" Leaving them standing there, scowling at each other, the stranger in camouflage — a revenuer — turned his back on them and headed through the rows of tobacco in the direction of Janie's kudzu patch.

Without waiting another moment, she sprang to her feet and ran. Vines caught at her ankles. Locusts trilled at her with their monotonous clamor. She pushed past scratching branches. Tree trunks seemed to dance crazily past her. Circling around and around. There had to be a way out of this nightmare somewhere.

Dried twigs and leaves crackled beneath her feet as she fled through the woods. No matter how much distance she covered, she could never outrun the buzz of the locusts. Ahead, the curve of the land fell away into the shape of a bowl.

She tripped down the slope without knowing where she was going. Suddenly she lost her footing on the soft, slippery ground. Frantically, she reached for the skinny trunk of a sapling to steady herself, but it was just beyond her reach. Losing her balance, she fell sideways, and the motion sent her tumbling down a sharp bank. She landed against the trunk of another tree and lay there gasping, trying to recapture the wind that had been knocked from her. Clutching the smooth bark of the tree that had stopped her, she pulled herself up, staggering from a wave of dizziness.

She'd landed at the bottom of the bowl. The rise down which she had fallen now surrounded her on three sides. The trees crowded together closer and closer, closing in on her, tighter and tighter. Or was it her breathing? The beat of her pulse drummed in her ears.

Janie took a couple of deep breaths and picked herself up. She rubbed her palms together, brushing off the dirt, then wiped in vain at the smudges grinding into the torn pieces of her T-shirt, clinging like rags to her sweat-drenched body. *Got to get out of here!*

She kept going, running blindly in what she hoped was the opposite direction from the men. She couldn't be sure.

All she could see were trees.

She crashed onward through the woods. Her heart pounded faster, and her breath came in shallow gasps. The locusts' buzz roared, a drill through her head. The rise where she ran was the crest of another wave, and at the bottom of its hill was a creek.

Swallowing a lump in her throat, she sank down onto a fallen log and considered her plight. How long would it take for one of the men to find her? For Price to come looking for her? He'd never know where to search. Her car was back at her house. By the time he even mounted a search, it could be night, and then she'd have to spend a night alone in these woods. Alone, except for Dexter, Griffin, and a stranger stalking nearby. Goosebumps sprang up on her skin. She couldn't be far from a road.

No, she had to avoid roads. Roads were where Dexter would be lying in wait for her to emerge from the woods.

If only she could see the sun and get a bearing on her direction. But all she had was a meandering creek.

Not *her* creek. This one had to be miles away from the creek that led through Oona's pasture and eventually past Grandpa's house. Still...this creek had to lead somewhere. Either into the river or into the lake. All she had to do was follow the creek, and it would take her someplace where she could find her way.

Pushing the thought of cottonmouths from her mind, she stood up and plunged along the contours of the land, following the twists and turns of the creek. She tried not to let the stream out of her sight, but sometimes it disappeared behind impassable mounds of brush. She wished she'd grabbed some lunch. Was it her imagination, or was the afternoon growing dimmer, the air colder? She shivered.

Hours passed. The crystal on her wristwatch had cracked during her fall, stopping time at nearly two. It had to be way later than that by now.

Then she came to a sudden stop. The woods opened up, and in the distance, she could see a vast expanse of water glinting under a late-afternoon sun. The lake had never before looked so beautiful.

From the outline of the opposite shore, Janie recognized the point where she stood, overlooking the lake, somewhere south of her house. She remembered the landmarks Price had pointed out to her that day from his sailboat. Rose's house couldn't be far. She turned south, keeping to the cover of woods.

She hadn't gone far when she came to the promontory, the one with the touch of wildflowers. Jeff had guessed it was the grave Auntie Mae had visited in Janie's childhood. She approached it now cautiously, knowing before she saw them that the flowers would be forget-me-nots. With her hands, she scooped away the accumulation of decaying leaves and twigs, until the cluster of flowers stood erect next to a stone marker lying flat in the earth. Crude letters had been carved into it, reading: "Here lies the sapphire of my life. Honey, I will forget you not."

Tears sprang to Janie's eyes. This show of tenderness didn't match the Dexter Janie knew today. What had happened to change him into the monster with groping hands?

Janie pushed herself up and stumbled on. Her mother had ended up with Annalee's necklace. Had she stolen it? Perhaps caused Annalee's tragic fall? Impossible! Janie would never believe that. But if Dexter believed it, that could explain his behavior. He'd take out his revenge on Janie.

When Rose's house finally appeared, it looked like a drop of sunshine, reflecting sparkles from the lake. Janie hurried on.

She tripped up the front steps to the porch and fell against the screen, smelling of dust and rust. She pounded on the door and pressed her sweaty cheek against the screen's coolness. Where was the familiar tapping of Rose's nervous footsteps?

She pulled her cheek away from the screen and turned slowly to look over her shoulder, fully expecting to see Dexter's truck sitting in the driveway. It wasn't. Beyond the graveled semi-circle was the sunny strip of dirt road, and pressing against it was the dark wall of woods from which she'd emerged.

She shivered and knocked again. "Rose!" she called.

From inside, a clock chimed. She forgot to count. Its memory echoed in her mind five or six times. She tried the door handle, but it was latched.

The heady scent of petunias in their hanging baskets made her dizzy, and she had to cling to the doorframe for stability as she turned to look at the woods again. Somewhere, there was a short path leading to a nearby A-frame where Price had his office and a secretary with a truck. Susan. Janie could run there, but the thought of entering those woods again sent irrational waves of panic through her.

Something rumbled in the distance. A car, maybe, although she couldn't see it yet. No, it had to be a truck. Dexter's truck.

She ran.

Her feet clattered across the porch and down the steps to the concrete sidewalk disappearing around the corner of the house. At least back here she was out of sight from the road.

She could see Rose's garden sitting atop a sunny knoll in the middle of the peninsula jutting out into the bay. Maybe Rose was out there. Janie looked for her sunhat bobbing up and down amidst the teepees of pole beans, but all she saw instead was a blackbird fluttering nearby, eyeing the untended garden.

Farther down the sloping hill, Price's sailboat bumped against the dock.

Tall spikes of unknown flowers guarded the flagstones leading to the back porch. A dish, containing a few dried-up crumbs, sat on the porch next to a bowl of water.

From around front, she could hear the sound of the vehicle bearing down on Rose's house, then thunder past.

She shuddered and felt the surrounding aloneness chill the marrow of her bones. Everything was hauntingly empty.

Jeff. Rose. Price. They were all gone.

The back door creaked open just then. She heard a gasp and looked up.

Rose stood at the door. Her fingers covered the circle of her mouth. "Oh, my dear." She bustled out onto the back porch, down the steps, and caught Janie in an embrace smelling of lavender. "Oh, my dear," she repeated.

Janie pulled away, not wanting to be touched by anyone.

Rose seemed to understand, and she motioned Janie inside. "I was in the cellar," she said, "looking for an extra jar of rosehip jam, which I was *sure* I'd put up, but I declare, I can't find anything down there."

"Rose..." Janie started to gasp.

"Hush now," Rose said, pushing Janie into the welcome kitchen. "What you need is a cup of tea."

"No... Sheriff..." It was almost blinding the way the kitchen dazzled Janie with its white cupboards and white tile. The red-checkered tablecloth and red geraniums at the window added a touch of pungent cheer. Rose patted a needlepoint cushion tied to a white chair, but Janie huddled by the doorway. Everything sparkled with cleanliness, so unlike herself.

Rose nodded, as if understanding. Her glance took in Janie's bedraggled appearance. "Perhaps you'd like to freshen up a bit first?"

Janie allowed herself to be led down the hall to the bathroom. She watched Rose turn on the faucets and sprinkle something from a bottle. Steam rose from the porcelain tub sitting on clawed feet, and its lavender scent drifted across the room. Rose closed the door behind her, and Janie stripped off her clothes, dumping them in the wastebasket.

She stepped into the healing warmth of the water and thought this was wrong. Wrong to feel this good while *he* was out there, maybe searching already for Jeff. It was wrong to waste this time before filing a report with the sheriff, but she couldn't help herself.

No matter how much she scrubbed, she'd never feel clean again.

She understood now why her mother had run away. It was the easiest solution. Never to come within reach of Dexter again.

But Janie was tired of running. She wasn't like her mother. She wouldn't rest until she had Jeff back and Dexter safely locked away.

Finishing her bath, she dried off and slipped into the pressed underwear and shirt-waist dress Rose had left for her. Its mothball scent made her wonder how many years out of fashion it had been hanging in the wardrobe. Had it been Elizabeth's dress?

"Do you feel better now?" Rose asked when Janie returned to the kitchen. She motioned to the needlepoint cushion, and this time Janie sank down and watched Rose carefully pour out the tea.

On the table sat a ceramic kitten holding a ball of yarn, and Janie picked it up. On its bottom was a label with a backwards-sloping handwriting explaining that the yarn changed color according to the weather. It should be snowing now. The kitten slipped from her fingers and thudded on the table.

You couldn't trust anything. Not anyone.

"Careful, dear, that was a gift — "

"Hello?" A man's voice floated down the hall. "Gran, let us in."

"Price?" Rose chuckled. "I do declare, but men have no sense of timing at all. I'll be right back, my dear." Rose patted her arm and hurried from the room.

Janie's head jerked up. She listened to the exchange of low whispers, the rush of footsteps, the hand slamming against the doorframe. Then Price appeared, frowning, towering over her. His face was drained of color.

"What happened?" he whispered.

Looking up at him, she wondered how much to tell him. How to begin. She was still searching for the right words when someone else appeared in the doorway beside him. A man. An older man.

She turned to look at the newcomer, to study the familiar face. His glance was no longer averted. Although he'd aged since the wallet snapshot had been taken, she would recognize Wilson Bainbridge anywhere.

THIRTY-FIVE

The screen door creaked, and Oona looked up from her bucket of sudsy water. She heard Seymour's heavy boots stomping across the back porch toward the kitchen.

"You 'bout ready, Mama?" he called.

"Well, bless my soul, Daddy. Where you been?"

"Out milking the cows, where do you think?"

That man was nothing but one surprise after another, she thought. A plate slipped from her fingers into the suds.

"Shake a leg, woman. Wouldn't do to be late." He strode to the bedroom corner and whipped the curtains back. "You know where my church-meetin' tie is?"

For once in Oona's life, she couldn't think of a thing to say. Seymour hadn't stepped foot inside a church since his sister Annalee's wedding. And she didn't believe, not for one minute, that he was about to start now.

Nossir, something was a'brewing. That was for plumb sure. But anyhow, it looked like she and Bonnibelle was going to get to go up town after all. And Oona wasn't about to be the cow's tail. She wiped her reddened hands on her apron and waddled after him. "I declare!" she finally sputtered. "Everyone's in a all-fired rush tonight. I never seen no sech."

⁓

"GRAN, I'LL TAKE CARE of this," Price said, pulling Janie gently from the chair. Then he turned to Wilson Bainbridge, still leaning against the door-frame. "Dad, would you excuse us, please?"

Price led her from Rose's kitchen, down the hall to the front porch, past the hanging baskets of petunias and around to the side of the house. Twilight hung suspended in the air. It was a time that matched Janie's state of numb-ness, a time when color had drained away from the day. She shivered as he pulled her up the steps to his deck, spanning the width of his grandmother's house. Their footsteps sounded hollow, echoing the emptiness she felt.

Price slid open one of the glass doors, reached in to flick on a light, and stood aside for her to enter his living room. "Sit down," he said, indicating a white sofa with overstuffed cushions.

She remained standing by the sliding glass door as he disappeared around a potted palm to the inside arm of a bar. It looked inviting in this large room of white and chrome, but all the whites reminded her of how unclean she still felt from *his* fingers.

Price emerged finally with a shot glass filled with a clear liquid. He strode across the room and handed it to her. "Be a good girl and drink this down."

She pushed away his offering. "What is your father's name?" Her voice cracked.

"Huh?"

"That man downstairs. He's your father, isn't he?"

"Uh..." Price's cheeks flushed. His gaze darted around the room. He was stalling.

"His name!" she snapped.

"John Price Wanamaker." He thrust the shot glass under her nose. "This will work better than Gran's tea."

She reeled backwards from the potent smell. "What is it?"

"Moonshine."

Her eyes widened.

"Go on. Drink it."

She took a sip and choked immediately, but the burning inside warmed her. "Where did you get it?"

"A place called Earl's up in Stony Lonesome."

"Jesus," she whispered, handing him back the glass. "So that's why Gus wouldn't talk about Earl." Then she remembered the barge at night. Its crew had something for Earl, and they'd hauled something dripping out of the lake.

A container of moonshine.

Grandpa's house must be a drop sight for moonshine to change hands. No wonder she and Jeff were in the way. No wonder someone wanted to get rid of her. But who? She inched away from Price. Had he really gotten his supply of moonshine from Earl?

"Why don't you tell me what happened today?" Price asked in a soft voice, setting the glass down on the nearest table.

His face was creased with apparent concern, and she felt tears welling up in her eyes. Damned tears. She wasn't going to disintegrate. A display of weakness was probably what he wanted. She squared her shoulders, sniffed, and told him about it, using spare descriptions. She told him about Taffy's apparent murder, the disappearance of her body, Roy's arrival and Jeff's subsequent disappearance, her discovery of Annalee's bedroom, which led to being caught. Dexter had tried to attack her, she said, but Griffin had stopped him in time. She couldn't find the words, however, to tell him that Dexter was her father.

Then who was the man downstairs?

"Come on," he said, grabbing her by the elbow and sliding open the door. "We're going to the sheriff."

"But the bridges — "

"Never mind about that." He pulled her outside onto the deck.

It was about time, she thought. A tear slipped onto her cheek, despite her resistance, and she wiped it away quickly as they clattered downstairs. Twilight had slipped into a dull gray, a mere shade lighter than the surrounding darkness of the woods.

He called to Rose through the lamplight spilling out of her open front door, then hurried Janie into the driveway. A Jeep sat there, and he opened its door and fairly pushed her inside. Then he sprang into the driver's seat, and they roared away.

"We don't need bridges," he said, grinning at her from the darkness. "I got caught in town during the storm. The tie rod broke on that Cadillac, as I predicted it would on these roads, so I figured it was time for a new car."

They drove on in silence, bouncing through the darkness, plowing through streams whose waters were beginning to recede. The headlights pierced the descending night. All Janie could think of was her son. Had Roy reminded Jeff to take a bath before bedtime? Had Roy remembered to read him a story? What had he given him for dinner?

It surprised her when Price spoke again. "There's the sheriff's office," he said.

She realized then that they were in Stony Lonesome, and she had no idea how much time had elapsed. It was Friday night, the storm was past, and the town was alive with people. He pulled up behind a familiar truck. She spied a corn cob in the truck's bed and sucked in her breath. "Dexter!"

Price reached over and clasped her hand. "It's all right. He can't hurt you now."

"Let's go."

"And forget about Jeff?" He scratched his head.

"Jeff is with his father." She couldn't bear to see *him* again. Price didn't understand.

"Then what about Taffy? And the charges you need to file?"

"Don't tell me what to do!" she shouted. Maybe Taffy wasn't dead. Maybe Janie had imagined the whole thing.

"Relax," Price said, reaching for his door handle. "I'll be with you."

"Look!" She grabbed his arm and pointed, then sank down lower in her seat.

Coming out of the office were two men in earnest conversation. One of them was *him*.

It all came back to her in a flood of pain. The way *he'd* pawed her. The way *he'd* attacked Mother, too.

"Dexter," Price whispered, as if his jaw were cemented together. "Someone ought to lock him up once and for all."

The man *he* was laughing with was the old-timer Janie had met at the Lazy Dew, then again at the courthouse. Gus, she thought his name was. Now she watched them laugh together and slap each other on the back. What stories were they swapping, she wondered. Was Dexter bragging about his exploits?

She sank lower in her seat and trembled with rage. Her mother would've felt this way, too. That she could never show her face around here again, for fear of that man. No wonder she hadn't wanted Janie to return here, even if it meant giving up a relationship with Grandpa. "What's he doing with Gus?"

"They're buddies," Price answered.

"Obviously, but what are they doing *here*?" Had Dexter no fear of getting caught?

"Gus is the sheriff's father. That old man used to be sheriff himself some time ago." Price sighed and started up the Jeep.

~

NO SOONER DID THE TRUCK make it to the top of the hill where the country church sat high and mighty, than everyone wanted to up and leave Oona. The truck hadn't even come to a stop before Bonnibelle dumped her baby in Oona's lap and climbed out.

"Hey, what the Sam Hill?"

"Sorry, Mama, but I got myself something else to do. Something real important. For Price. He give me a job, remember." Bonnibelle turned her back on the church and tottered off in her high heels toward town.

Humph, thought Oona. She knew where that girl was fixing to go, and it wasn't all the way into town, neither. Only thing she knew of between here and town was the Lazy Dew. What was she going to do about that girl? Maybe this time she'd come home with a husband first, before she got herself into trouble. She hoped it was Junior. Bonnibelle could do a whole lot worse. Lord knew who the new boyfriend was.

"Go on, Mama," said Seymour. "You and the baby go on in without me, and I'll give Bonnibelle a lift."

She plumb knowed it. Seymour, she reckoned, couldn't wait to get to the pool hall, and the revival meeting was just an excuse for him to get there. She glared at her no-good husband.

"You don't want Bonnibelle to twist an ankle, do you?" he continued.

"Twist her ankle, my eye, Daddy. I know — "

"Go on, now, so's you ain't late."

She stared him down for a full minute. She hated to be the last one, whether she was the last one to know what was going on, or whether she was the last one to church meeting. She wagged her finger at him. "You come right on back, you hear me?" She snatched up her pocketbook and Bible and hauled herself and the baby down out of the truck.

He gave her that half of a smile of his, like the cat that got the mouse. But he couldn't fool her. What he didn't know was the way she steamed inside, the way that smile of his reminded her once again of Janie. Yes, it was her cross to bear, all right.

Seymour roared away in a cloud of dust, then screeched to a halt next to Bonnibelle. Oona watched the two of them drive off together. *Humph. In cahoots, they was.* Shaking her head, she straddled the baby on her hip and headed inside the church. The day her rage would boil over was coming ever nearer, and then, she feared, she wouldn't be no upright woman no more.

THIRTY-SIX

he double globes of the lamp were painted with pink roses. Vining leaves shaped the gilded base. Janie couldn't take her eyes off the cheery lamp that sat on a lace-covered table between her and Rose. She was glad now that Price had insisted she stay the night here.

Hunched over in her platform rocker, Rose seemed particularly interested in watching Janie sip the herbal tea she'd brewed. It was as if the old woman waited for her special potion to take effect. Janie rattled the cup on the saucer and set it down hastily on the lace cloth.

Creak. Creak. In the background, a grandfather clock kept score of the passing evening. Tick. Tick.

What had Rose put in this tea that made Janie feel so numb?

Maybe it was the rapid succession of events that she couldn't understand. Nothing mattered but one of them — Jeff was gone. "Why?"

She must've voiced it aloud, because Rose cleared her throat and began to answer. "I believe it's the quest for belonging, dear. Everyone wants to belong somewhere."

"Jeff and I belong to each other," Janie said, feeling cold inside and sick to her stomach.

"Maybe that's not enough." Rose planted her hands on the arms of the rocker and pushed herself up. She shuffled over to a bookshelf, opened its glass door and removed a leather-bound volume. Then she returned to the table and moved aside the lamp, making room for the book, a photo album. The pages crackled as she turned them, pointing out photos that followed

Elizabeth's growth. Identifying each picture was a caption written in a careful, backwards-sloping handwriting.

Janie could swear it was the same handwriting she'd found in her grandmother's Bible.

"You were Grandpa's 'lady friend," Janie said, blurting it out when she remembered Gus's near revelation. She put it together with the handwriting samples. Someone had had to fill in the Bible for Grandpa if he was unable to write.

Rose snapped the book shut and fell into her rocker. Closing her eyes, she leaned her bun against the wooden headrest. Pain etched its way across her face.

"I'm sorry," Janie said. "It's none of my business."

"No, dear. It's all right. It was dreadfully wrong in some ways. Esther was my sister. Although it wasn't until after she passed away that Tobias and I... We were discreet, or so we thought. Elta Mae found out, and she tried to convince me of my folly. I wouldn't see it, though. I was blinded by love. Then Elizabeth was born — "

"Elizabeth!" Janie gasped. Elizabeth was Janie's aunt, not the cousin she'd thought she was.

And what about Price, her half-brother? They shared a father, otherwise known as Wilson Bainbridge.

No. Dexter was her father.

She felt confused. Unable to think straight. Maybe Rose had done something to her tea again.

"I understood how painful it had all become," Rose said. A faint smile wisped at her lips. "It was of the utmost importance to protect that secret and honor Esther's memory. It pained Tobias never to be able to recognize Elizabeth, and later, Price. He thought he was protecting me by so doing."

Price was Grandpa's grandson.

"I don't see why you and Grandpa couldn't have married if my grandmother was already gone."

Rose let out a long breath of air, and Janie thought at first that she hadn't heard her. Then she spoke softly. "The timing was wrong, my dear. I accepted Tom Bender's marriage proposal. Perhaps too quickly. Perhaps not. Tom was a good man, and I loved him for that. He accepted my Elizabeth with no questions. Once he died, Tobias and I had grown too old to rekindle the flame of our youth. We were comfortable enough, being together quietly. He was to come here for supper that night he disappeared."

"Then he wouldn't have committed suicide."

"Of course not, dear."

They sat in silence, savoring lost memories, lost hopes. The sound of a soft baying floated through the open window.

"That will be the dog," Rose said, straightening. "Excuse me for a moment while I go throw him some table scraps."

"I didn't know you had a dog."

"I don't, dear. He belonged to Tobias. Another lost soul now, without Tobias. He comes around here regularly, and I give him food."

"Let me help — "

"No, no. I won't be but a minute." Rose laid her hand firmly on Janie's shoulder, then dragged herself out of the room, moving like an old, tired woman.

Rose was shrugging off the weight of bearing her secret alone. It must have been dreadful, Janie thought, to have kept such a secret all these years. She wondered if it would've come out on its own without Janie's personal quest for answers to the secrets Fern had kept from her. Her hand trembled as she lifted the album onto her lap and flipped casually through the pages. She felt close to the answers she'd been seeking. Maybe she'd come far enough, and it was time to let the past rest.

But she pressed on, turning pages, looking for something, no longer knowing what it was. Then her fingers slipped, and she stopped at one page. The caption described the studio portrait as Elizabeth's engagement picture. The other half of the page was empty, but a caption identified the blank space as being a portrait of J.P. Wanamaker at the time of their engagement.

Janie realized that the snapshot she carried in her wallet of "Wilson Bainbridge" would fit perfectly in this blank space.

Someone had removed it, and eventually it had ended up in Janie's wallet. She could imagine how it must've happened. Fern, distraught over her pregnancy, had stolen it in order to create a fictitious father for her baby.

There was no Wilson Bainbridge. Price *wasn't* her half-brother.

"I remember the first time J.P. Wanamaker breezed into the neighborhood," Rose said, slipping up behind her, pulling Janie out of her thoughts as if she'd been able to read them. "He was just the same then as he is now. The world revolved around his needs. You know?"

Janie nodded, shutting the album. She knew.

"But he captured my Elizabeth's heart. She thought the sun rose and set over that J.P. Wanamaker."

"You didn't agree."

Rose pursed her lips, then sighed. "He gave her what she wanted more than anything — a place where she could belong. He gave her a name. Respectability. She'd never had that here, you see, where people knew too much about her."

"Do you think it's possible to know too much about someone?"

"Well, now sometimes if you *do* know too much, you can't belong any more."

Suddenly Janie started to cry, feeling as if a burden had been lifted from her heart. Rose reached down and enfolded Janie in her arms.

It was a cry of relief, and a cry of dread. Janie knew the truth now, and she didn't know which was more horrible — that Dexter was her father, or that she was the product of rape.

~

OONA SAT ON THE CHURCH STEPS watching the last of the congregation get into their cars and drive away. She bounced the baby up and down to keep her from squalling too much. Between squalls and car door slams, Oona could barely hear the river babbling over yonder down the hill and behind the church.

Reminded her of the old days. If she closed her eyes, she could almost imagine the sounds were from the old Chittenden River, before the deadening come along. Compared to that one, this one wasn't hardly a river at all. This one was no more'n an oversized crik emptying into the bay.

From somewhere in the darkness over yonder on the other side of the river came the rumble of a train, bringing with its echo the promise of even more rain to warsh away her topsoil.

Where was the fool man? Probably so besotted in that there back room at Earl's Pool Hall that he wouldn't reckon five minutes had passed.

I ain't gonna stick around here all night.

It wasn't so bad walking. If only she didn't have to lug around this baby. Not that Oona didn't have the muscle for it in her arm. What she was lacking was enough air in her lungs.

In the pitch of evenfall, she walked down the hill and up the next one, following the winding course of the river toward town. The closer she came to town, the more houses she passed, where junk cars and trucks sat every which way along the grassy banks next to the oiled-down road.

"Evenin."

"How do."

Oona spoke to the folks that sat in their aluminum lawn chairs waiting for someone to pass by. She shook her head with pity. How folks could choose to live up town was beyond her understanding. Poor Mama, living out her last years like that.

The Lazy Dew was dead ahead, and Oona jerked herself to a stop. One of the cars parked askew came to life all quick-like. It revved up its engine and laid rubber getting away. It wasn't so dark that she couldn't tell it was green, and she knew it wasn't just any old green car. It was that old green Ford that had been sitting in front of her house for months. The one Griffy finally got to running a week or so ago.

So that's why he hadn't come home in time for the church meeting. But what in tarnation was a good boy like her Griffy doing in a place like the Lazy Dew? And where was he off to in such a all-fired rush? He could'a given her a ride.

She stood there with one hand planted on her hip, trying to contain her anger, when the bushes ahead yonder started to move and a'rustle. Like something was hiding in them. Lawd a'mercy. She never did like this place. All them fishermen give her the willies. A woman all alone out here.

"Aunt Oona?" said a small voice from the rustling bushes.

She liked to jump out of her skin. Surely, the devil was afoot tonight. "Jeff? That you, honey child?"

A sob answered her, and Janie's boy bolted out of the shadows and landed against her skirt where he threw his skinny arms around her hips.

"What in tarnation you doing out here at this hour?" she said, biting her words off and feeling her jowls shake.

"There's...it's...come quick!"

"Now, hush, child. Auntie Oona's here. You look like you stepped on someone's grave. Where's your mama, anyhows?"

He choked a bit. Oona reckoned he'd been crying but didn't want anyone to know. "It's Dad! I think he's shot. Oh, please, Aunt Oona, get some help."

She grabbed him by the shoulder and gave him a little shake. "Here now, boy. Settle yourself down and tell me from the beginning what's happened." She hoped Griffy's green Ford didn't have nothing to do with this.

"Dad...took me fishing..." He stopped to snuffle, and Oona had to give him another shake to get his story moving on out of him. "Then...Bonnibelle..." He wiped his nose on his sleeve and screwed up his face. "They were...*kissing* when Griffin came..." His eyes got big as saucers, and he hiccuped. Oona had to shake him again. She didn't have all night. "He told Dad to get away from his sister, but Dad just laughed at him. They started fighting, and that's when I ran out, to go find help, but I heard the gun go off, and after that, I saw Griffin come running out. Oh, Aunt Oona! Griffin's shot my dad!"

She hauled off and slapped him across his snotty little face. "Don't you lie to me, boy. I won't hear no sech."

His jaw hung open, and his eyes got even bigger. It was clear as day to Oona that he didn't know how to lie. Well, he'd have to pay for his lie, just like his mama was gonna pay for Fern's lie. All of a sudden, the boy twisted away and run off toward one of the cottages of the Lazy Dew. "Here, now, boy!" she yelled.

Then she thought better of it. Let him go. Of all the tom-fool ideas. Her boy shoot someone?

Once Janie come 'round here, there'd been nothing but trouble. Her snotty boy may be lying now, but one thing was for sure. Oona herself had seen Griffy up and run off, and that gave her a bad feeling in her bones.

THIRTY-SEVEN

The first thing Janie saw, as the Jeep slowed to turn into Grandpa's driveway the next morning, was the sheriff's car parked out front. Before Price could shut off the engine, Janie was out of the Jeep.

"What's happened?" she asked, feeling her voice crack. Surely the sheriff hadn't sensed that she'd wanted to talk to him last night.

Price caught up to Janie and put a protective arm around her shoulders. "What's the trouble, sheriff?"

He nodded at Janie then spoke to Price as if Janie were incapable of answering for herself. "Is this Mrs. Bainbridge?"

"Yes, I'm Janie Bainbridge," she said, moving between the two men. "Now please tell me what's wrong."

The sheriff took off his hat and fingered its brim. "I'm afraid I may have some bad news, ma'am," he said to the hat. "It's about Roy, uh, Shoemaker? I'm told he's your husband?" He shook his head. "Well, anyway, he had an accident last night, and I'm afraid he, uh, didn't pull through."

"What? You mean, Roy is dead?"

"I know it's a shock, Mrs. Bainbridge. Uh, I mean Mrs. Shoemaker. We've been trying to reach you all night." The sheriff looked back and forth between Price and Janie.

"And Jeff? What's happened to Jeff?" She could feel hysteria rising in her voice, despite her attempts at control.

The sheriff scratched his head. "Who's Jeff?"

"My son! He was with his father. Where's my son?"

"Now take it easy, ma'am. When we got there last night, there wasn't no one there 'cept for your husband. He'd been shot. Looked like he'd been dead for a while." The sheriff stopped to rub his chin and narrow his eyes in thought. "So you say your son was there?"

"For chrissakes," said Price. "The boy wouldn't have shot his dad. He's only eight years old. The poor kid probably witnessed the shooting and ran off in a fright."

Janie didn't realize she was swaying until she felt Price's arms steady her. "Dear God," she whispered.

"Don't worry, ma'am. We'll find him." The sheriff narrowed his eyes at Janie. "Now I have to ask you, ma'am, where *you* were last night?"

"This is really too much," Price said. "She was with me."

"Ma'am, I'll have to ask you to come along with me. We'll need a statement from you." His eyes roved across the out-of-date dress she was still wearing.

∽

THE SWEET-SMELLING HAY soothed Oona's raw nerves, as always. Except for that danged cock outside calling to all the world to get up, it was quiet in here. There was an occasional stomp of a hoof or a shifting of chicken feathers. None of 'em wanted to answer the cock's call, including her own family.

Except for Griffy, who'd never come home last night.

She'd lain awake all night listening for him, but he never crept in. Bonnibelle did, not all that long ago, but not her boy.

Oh, Lord, what had that little lying snot gone and done to her Griffy? He'd pay for it, and so would his mama.

Then there was Seymour. Letting on as if he'd mended his ways. All anxious to carry her off to revival meeting when it was the moonshine he was really after. It all came back to that. She reckoned it left her no choice.

A shadow fell across the open door. "Mama?" her boy whispered, hushed like the morning.

She liked to fall off the bale of hay where she'd been sitting and brooding. "Griffy, is that you?" She plumb knowed it. Of course he needed her. They all needed her.

"Mama, I told you not to call me that. Griffin's my name." He stood before her, and she could see the droop in his bear-like shoulders, the sag of his chin. Alarm signals jangled through her raw nerves, for what she saw before her was a beaten man.

"Griffy!" she cried.

"Hush, Mama, they may've followed me."

"'They'? Who's 'they'?"

"Now, simmer down, Mama. I think you know. I ain't got long. I just wanted to say good-bye is all."

"Why, I won't hear no sech — "

"Now, Mama, you ain't got no choice in the matter."

"Don't you sass me like that, boy. I'm your — "

"You ain't bigger than the law, Mama. I ain't gonna let you into the Mullen place no more."

"Spit it out, son. What are you trying to say?" She wanted to shake him, to shake out the feeling of sickness spreading through her.

He crumpled before her onto the straw floor. His hulk heaved with sobs. "I shot him, Mama. I shot and killed a man last night, but I didn't mean to. It's just...after yesterday afternoon...and what I found out about Dexter...I couldn't control myself no more."

"It's a lie!" She fell next to him and tried to cradle her baby. No one was going to take him away from her. "Think on it again. T'warn't you."

"No, Mama. It was me, all right, but I only meant to scare him. Get him to leave Bonnibelle alone. I didn't think he'd jump me. I didn't think the gun would go off."

"You cain't be sure he's dead." She remembered Griffy's green Ford taking off like banshees was after it. He hadn't stuck around long enough to see who got shot where.

Griffy shook his head in her lap. "It was pernt blank, Mama. Ain't no man alive could walk away from that."

She'd have to think this through carefully. Together, they'd figure out what to do. But, oh, it was a sorely vexing morning. Her bosom heaved as she struggled to draw in a deep enough breath to still the hammering of her heart. She had to be able to think.

Griffy rolled off her lap and sat up. He wiped the back of his arm across his nose, then drew a folded-up knife from his pocket. "Give this to Dexter, Mama, and don't ask no questions."

"But — "

"I said no questions. It's his, that's all, and I'm done with it. I'm done with him."

"You're throwing away your life, son. She don't deserve it. She ain't as good as you."

"Bonnibelle? Nothing wrong with her that a good whupping wouldn't fix."

"I ain't talking about your sister. She ain't no count. I'm talking about your cousin. That there Janie Bainbridge. She as good as shot her own husband herself."

"But, Mama, she wasn't even there."

"That don't matter. Iffen she hadn't've up and run off from her husband, then he'd've never followed her down here only to get hisself shot and stir up a hornet's nest of trouble. It's all her fault, and she's gonna be the one to pay, not you."

"No, Mama, that ain't right. 'Sides, it was you that sent that letter asking him here."

"Are you trying to tell me it's *my* fault?"

"Ain't no one's fault, Mama. Sometimes things just happen. Folks you thought you always knowed, you come to find out you don't know them at all. And sometimes bullheadedness gets in your way and you can't see for yourself what's right and what's wrong. And then you just gotta forget about all that and look deep inside yourself where you know for yourself what's right and what's wrong. Ain't no one else can know it but yourself. And...and if you want to be a man, then..."

He choked and snuffled, and Oona didn't want to listen to this foolishness no more. She feared what he might say. "Listen to me, son. One of my brothers got hisself a place up in the mountains where you can hide till this all blows over — "

"No, Mama." He squared his shoulders and stood up. "I almost come here last night to tell you good-bye and that I was fixing to hightail it into the woods. Maybe head for your brother's place. But I guess I thought about it overnight, and I guess I figgered I can't listen to no one no more. Not even to you, Mama. I'm a man, and I gotta do what I know in my heart is right. And so I — "

"No, Griffy... Griffin, my son..." From her knees, she reached up to clasp his hands and beg him to forget all about this.

"And so I got to turn myself in. I got to start righting the wrongs. Don't worry, Mama. They'll go easy on me. It was a accident. I ain't got nothing to hide."

"You just don't know nothing."

"I know all I got to know, Mama. And I know I can't fight them no more."

"Fight who?"

"The times. The changing times." He sighed and squeezed her hand, and then he slipped out into the new day, leaving Oona alone with nothing but her emptiness.

THIRTY-EIGHT

*S*omeone had taken Jeff. This was the only thought playing through Janie's mind as she pounded on Oona's screen door shortly after the sheriff had allowed her to leave.

"Well, bust my britches, child," said Oona, huffing across the linoleum floor. "I done thought we ain't never gonna see the likes of you no more." Her hands dripped from scrubbing something, and she wiped them on her apron before holding open the screen. Streaks of red shot through Oona's eyes, and the tip of her nose was red, too.

She'd been crying, Janie thought. It was about time she mourned her daughter.

Oona clucked her tongue and continued. "What's the point of having family if you don't see 'em every day? Now you come on in and sit a spell."

"I didn't come to visit. I came to talk to you about Jeff."

Oona peered over Janie's shoulder. "Where is he, anyhows?"

She'd hoped Oona knew. Her heart sank.

"Well, child, you gonna make me hold the door open all day? Why'n't you come on out to the back porch where it's cool, and we can talk a spell while I finish my laundry."

Janie wasn't sure how her mind could give her body the command to walk, but somehow she followed Oona through the house. *Someone had taken Jeff. Maybe it was the person who'd shot Roy.*

Oona pushed Janie into a folding chair on the back porch. "Now you sit here so's you'll stay outa' my way." Then she turned to the washtub and began feeding dripping wet clothes through the wringer while cranking it and catching the clean clothes simultaneously with a basket. It appeared to be an operation that would require at least three hands from an ordinary person.

But Oona was no ordinary person. Had *she* been the one behind all the madness of the last ten days?

"The sheriff said *you're* the one who reported the shooting. How'd you know about it?"

Oona stopped her work long enough to glare at Janie. "Well, honey, the Lazy Dew ain't all that far from the church."

"Then you heard the shots from the church? Did others hear it, too?"

Oona shook her head and turned back to her tub of wet clothes. "No, honey, I didn't even hear it."

"Then who did?"

"Your boy, I reckon."

"Then you *did* see Jeff?"

"Oh, I saw him all right. He was scared as a jackrabbit, blubbering about something funny going on. I wish now I hadn't've fetched the sheriff and got myself involved at all."

"But what happened to Jeff?"

Oona shrugged. "Don't you worry none about him. I reckon he's off in the woods somewhere crying his heart out. He'll come back when he's good and ready."

Janie buried her face in her hands. Sobs racked her body. Oona was wrong. Someone had taken Jeff, and Oona was hiding something.

"Dagnabbit, there's that baby squalling again." Oona flung her arms from the washtub, and drops of water sprayed the porch.

Janie sniffled and wiped her eyes. "I'll get her." It would give her something to do while the sheriff was mounting a search for her missing son.

"Bless you, child."

Janie felt sorry for Oona all of a sudden, in spite of the way she interfered in people's lives. It wasn't fair for her to be left behind with all the work to do, keeping her large family clothed and fed. Oona didn't appear to resent it, though. On the contrary, she seemed to flourish with the importance of her position.

Thankful to escape Oona's exclamations, Janie fled inside to comfort the baby. She was standing in her crib, chewing on something, dribbling drool down the front of her T-shirt and diaper. Janie pulled the wadded-up thing from the baby's mouth. It looked like part of a black-and-white photograph.

Then she saw the rest of it sticking out from under the crib's mattress. It was the photograph of Annalee in her bridal dress, wearing the sapphire necklace, the same photo that had disappeared from Janie's house. She felt the hammer of her heart, and she didn't know if it was from the possible danger of chemicals in the baby's system, or from the fact that the stolen photo had ended up *here* in Oona's house. Had Bonnibelle stolen it?

When she was done changing Prissy, Janie carried her, along with the torn photograph, to the back porch. Oona was gone. Through the screen, she could see a basket of wet clothes sitting outside under the line. A few of the clothes had been pegged up and flapped in the breeze, scenting the air with soap.

A trail of wet drops led across the stepping stones in the chicken yard, and Janie followed them with the baby on her hip. It was time for Oona to answer a few questions. She stopped at the outhouse, feeling embarrassed, realizing that Oona must be inside.

As she stood there hesitating, staring out past the empty garden, past the empty pasture, a movement at the edge of the woods caught her attention. She looked up in time to see Oona disappear into the woods on the other side of the pasture. The creek was over there, the same creek that eventually led to Janie's house. She shifted Prissy to her other hip and started across the pasture after Oona.

When she entered the woods, Oona was gone. Remembering her last flight through woods, she felt her knees weaken. But she pressed on, anyway, until she heard the sound of voices ahead. She offered her finger to the baby to chew on. Oona's voice floated out from behind leaves ahead.

"Dang it, old man," she was saying. "I thought I got rid of your last jug. Tell me where you're a'makin' it, or else I'm gonna turn you in to that there revenuer so fast it'll make your head spin."

"I ain't makin' likker, old woman."

"Hah! Don't you sass me. I know what's what. How else you done make such a fine mess? Griffin always has to do your chores for you. It should've been you last night that went to fetch Bonnibelle outa' there instead of Griffin. Then no one would've got shot, and my boy wouldn't've had to run off. My boy's gone, and it's all because of that there moonshine you brew for the devil, you hear?"

"I know, Mama," Seymour said quietly. "I know it ain't caused nothing but trouble. You got to help me."

An awkward silence followed, then Oona spoke carefully, in a style unlike hers. "We'll start by carrying ourselves uptown to that there revenuer's office.

"No, Mama, Dexter's the one — "

"You shash your mouth," she said, raging again. "He's a man of the Lord."

"Maybe so, but he brews the best dang white mule this side of the Chittenden. I give him corn, and he gives it back to me in his jugs. Iffen not for that, I'd'a killed that bastard long ago.

"It's all Fern's fault — "

Prissy spit out Janie's fingers and started babbling. Oona's accusations died in midstream. *May as well show our faces now while we can still pretend not to have heard anything.*

Pointing out plants, Janie talked baby talk to Prissy and brushed noisily through the woods. Prissy jabbered back as Janie broke into sight of the feuding couple.

Oona scowled, then changed quickly to her mother-hen face of disapproval.

Seymour looked as if he was beyond any comprehension as he lifted a milk jug to his lips. Was it true that he drank to forget Fern? She and Oona had been best friends. No wonder Oona didn't talk about it anymore.

"Oona, look what I found in the baby's crib." Janie held out the torn photograph.

Oona clutched at her bodice, and color drained from her face. "Where'd you get that?" Her extra chin shook as she snapped off her words.

"I told you. In the baby's — "

"Gimme that. I been looking all over for that." She snatched it from Janie's hand. "Bonnibelle took it, I reckon."

Janie had never seen Oona move so fast. "Why didn't you tell me about Annalee?"

Oona's lower lip stuck out. "Lands, child, you come out here just to tell me I'm a old woman and I cain't see things right no more?"

"You're not an old woman, and you know it. Annalee and Mae were best friends. You and Mother were best friends. What's the connection between Annalee and my mother?"

Oona's face turned pink, and she looked to Seymour for support.

But Janie wouldn't let up. "I think Annalee threw herself off that cliff because of what her husband did to my mother."

"Well, you think wrong, child. Dexter didn't do nothing to Fern. It was Seymour, that's who."

A choking sound erupted from the rock where Seymour sprawled. The jug slipped from his fingers with a thud onto the rock, then tumbled into the creek. He watched it wash away, then he spoke softly. "Is that what you thought all these years? Well Mama, you wasn't there. I was. Dexter was all over Fern, but I stopped him in time. It didn't happen. Nothing happened. 'Cept what I done to Dexter. Dang it, I should'a took both his eyes."

"But, Daddy, I thought... All these years... It was you and Fern. And then there's Janie with no daddy of her own, 'cept for you. Why, she's the spittin' image of you."

"Well, you thought wrong, Mama. I don't know where Janie come from, but it warn't from me. You're the only woman for me." He sniffled and squared his shoulders and slowly pushed himself up to a staggering position. "Woman, I can't sit around here jawin' all day. I got a screen to fix. I got chores to do."

"Come on, old man," said Oona, taking his arm. "I reckon I best fix you some coffee."

Tears glistened in their eyes as they leaned on each other and started off toward the house. Neither one of them appeared to notice Janie trailing along behind.

∾

SHE LEFT THE BABY SAFE in her crib, then sped home. She wasn't sure she could believe anything anyone confessed to her, but it didn't matter. The foremost thought on her mind was Jeff. Who had taken him? Dexter?

The instant she pulled into the driveway, she knew something was wrong. The front door stood wide open. Something littered the porch. She sat in her idling car for a moment, wondering what to do, when she recognized the litter. They were brown, furry pieces, pieces of Beads.

Her heart thudded. She jumped out of her car and ran to the porch. Stooping to pick up a piece of worn fur, she called out, "Jeff?"

Something lay just inside the screen door. Another furry piece. Maybe this was a trap. Griffin would be accustomed to setting traps, she thought.

But her son gave her no other choice to go except forward. Cautiously, she opened the door. Creak. The house was still. A trail of stuffing led to the kitchen, and she followed it. She had to know if Jeff was at the other end.

The table had been moved aside, along with a box of cast-iron pots and pans. The trap door was open, exposing the black pit below. Janie's stomach twisted. One of Beads's furry legs rested on the top step. A trail of fur and stuffing vanished down into the blackness.

Someone wanted her to go down there.

Janie stood still. The sound of her heart hammered in her ears. Her breath was already coming in gasps, and she hadn't even entered the pit yet. Surely, that's where she had to go. If Jeff was down there...

One foot hovered over the first step. Her other foot lowered itself onto the second step. She thought she heard the bees buzzing again. The same buzzing that had awakened her in the middle of the night last week. Another step. And another. A faint light flickered down there in the shadows. She clutched the edge of the kitchen floor that was rising up to chest level, chin level, eye level...

There was definitely a light at the far end of the cellar. What would a light be doing on the shelves of mason jars? She'd dropped her flashlight down here and hadn't cared to return for it, but she remembered that it had extinguished itself when she dropped it. The light she was seeing now had to be something different. She opened her eyes wider, but it didn't help her to see any better.

The daylight streaming down the steps from the kitchen above guided her along, and finally her foot felt the cool stone of the cellar's floor. "Jeff?" she whispered.

There was only the answering hum of the bees coming from the end of the cellar, where the faint light flickered in the distance. Then a floorboard creaked overhead. A shadow crossed the shaft of light from the kitchen above, and the trap door to freedom slammed shut.

She felt as if she were spinning blindly, smothered by a blanket of darkness. Her feet planted firmly on the floor of the cellar, and she focused on the faint light that flickered at the far end of the cellar. With hands groping in front of her, she moved toward the light and brushed against something metal. Her fingers slid across the cool glass of a jar, and then it fell with a crash to the stone floor. A potent smell filled the air, a smell like the shotglass Price had placed under her nose last night in his apartment.

Moonshine in Grandpa's cellar?

Of course. She remembered the suggestion Gus had made that Grandpa had been involved in moonshine. She remembered the barge and her theory about Grandpa's house being a drop site. Of course they'd store it here.

Crunching past broken glass, she followed the dim light until her head hit against a low ceiling. She ducked and entered a tunnel.

As she tripped along the stone passageway, the dim light at the end of the tunnel grew brighter. The sour smell, stronger. The buzzing, louder.

A lantern sat on the dirt floor ahead and hissed. Irregular shapes jutted out from limestone walls and cast jagged shadows into deep recesses.

One of the recesses opened into a cavern. A bright hole in one of the cavern's walls indicated passage to the outside world, and she ran to it. Already her chest felt lighter. Until the stink in the air made her gag.

In the middle of the cavern, a huge pot sat over a fire. Its smoke drew upward, through a shaft in the cave's ceiling, a vent to the outdoors. A coiled network of pipes and wires attached to the contraption over the fire, and the whole thing rumbled as if it were alive with bees.

A still. To make moonshine. And someone had hidden it here, right under her house.

THIRTY-NINE

*B*arrels lined the cavern's walls.

The moonshiners must have a careful system, Janie thought. Brew a batch, and hide it under water for pick up. The barge. Griffin's brothers on the barge must pick up the goods and carry them away to Earl. The system ran smoothly until Janie and her son moved into the house on the cliff above.

The moonshiners had tried to frighten her away. It hadn't worked.

All of a sudden, the sound of a motorboat outside pulled her attention away from the still and toward the bright hole in the wall leading outside. She squeezed through the hole into a curtain of kudzu, the same kudzu that spilled over Grandpa's cliff. Boats had come and gone in the night from this vantage point.

This cavern had given them free access to her house. Through the tunnel. And the trap door in the kitchen. New locks on the outside doors hadn't mattered.

She shivered and looked up. The motorboat she'd heard was heading across the channel. Toward the island. She recognized the baseball cap of the man sitting at the tiller. Propped on the bench in front of his knees was a small sneaker, as if a child lay motionless on the floor of the boat before him.

Janie plunged through the kudzu. "Jeff!" she shouted. But Dexter's boat was too far away for her son to hear her.

She ran, tripping over the tumble of rocks that spilled along the base of the cliff. She climbed up to the top and ran across the clearing. "Jeff!" She scrambled back to where she'd dropped her purse and grabbed her car keys.

That madman had her son. She was a good swimmer, but not good enough to swim after a motorboat. Not that far. She needed a boat to go after her son. The nearest boat she knew of was Price's sailboat. Slow, but at least it would get her there.

She forced the Bug faster. The minutes dragged by as the car careened along, over the ruts. Finally, the cheery farmhouse-turned-beach-cottage appeared ahead. She didn't feel cheered, though, as she spewed gravel turning into Rose's empty driveway. A wave of disappointment crushed her. The front door was closed, too. No one appeared to be home.

The car lurched to a stop, and she sprang from it, running, heading for the grassy peninsula where Price moored the sailboat. When she saw it there with its sail lowered, bumping softly against the dock, she felt another stinging blow of disappointment. She'd never sailed a boat before.

No matter. She'd watched Price. Her fingers moved rapidly across the knots holding the sail together in its rolled-up bundle. She pulled on different ropes as time ticked slowly by, experimenting, until finally the sail started to rise. Murmuring a prayer, she fastened it, then untied the moorings.

The boat started to drift away, and she remembered to lower that board in the center. This was too easy, she thought, turning the tiller, pulling on the boom, feeling the boat's response to the wind catching in the sail.

It wasn't until she was out in the middle of the lake, plowing through choppy waters toward the island, that she wondered how she would overpower the man who had nearly overpowered her only yesterday. Without Griffin's intervention, he would've succeeded.

Never mind, she thought, tacking across the old river channel. She'd figure that out later. Now all she could think about was getting to her son.

She must've pulled too hard on the boom, for suddenly, one side of the boat reared up out of the water. She leapt to the lifted side and leaned out, but the boat didn't settle. She leaned farther, and after agonizing minutes, she felt it drop a few inches.

The island loomed ahead, and clouds boiled up on the horizon behind it. Dexter and Jeff should be easy to spot on the spine of that rocky island, but where were they? There were only two places to hide — on the other side of the rocky hump, or inside the cave.

Just then the wind shifted, and before she knew what had happened, she was flung into the water. Clinging to the rope controlling the boom, she struggled up for air. She was still wearing Elizabeth's dress, and its skirt billowed up around her. The boat was on its side. The sail floated atop the water.

Had Grandpa been taken as quickly, surprised when his boat capsized?

Without a backwards glance, she kicked off her shoes and started swimming for the island. It wasn't too far, and she was thankful now for all the summer weekends she'd spent at the reservoir. The heavy skirt dragged at her, draining her strength, but she plowed on. Her approach to the island had been silent. She had a good chance of surprising that man.

Something brushed against her under water, something that felt snake-like. She shot forward, then her feet touched muck. Looking over her shoulder, she didn't see the snake. She slogged on through the muck into the reeds surrounding the island. By the time she reached solid rock, she was shivering. She dripped out of the water and hastily checked herself for leeches or whatever other lake slime might have attached itself to her. All clear. She crept around to the back side of the island where Dexter must've hidden his boat.

There was no boat.

Had she made a mistake? She'd seen him heading here. Too much time had elapsed, though, while she'd gone for Price's boat and sailed it here. They could be anywhere by now. And now she was stuck on this island with no way to rescue her son. No way to get off this rock. She'd sunk Price's boat, besides.

No, it was still floating out there, on its side. A lot of good that was.

Out of ideas and feeling sorry for herself, she sank down into a ball to contemplate her situation. That's when she heard a soft sound rising above the steady wind. It was the hum of a motorboat, growing in intensity as it wound around treetops still sticking out of the water. Hope stirred within her, and she lifted her face from where it had dropped onto her wet knees. Maybe if she could flag down that fisherman, he'd give her a ride to shore, and she could start over. What she *should've* done was go to the sheriff. That's what she'd do now.

Then again...

The boat was bearing down on her position on this island. As it came closer, she recognized the red baseball cap. Her heart sank. Dexter had tricked her. He'd made her *think* he was heading here, knowing that she'd find a way to follow him. He'd been waiting for her, hidden over there behind those leaves still bushing out of the water.

How could she have been so stupid?

Banging across waves, the aluminum boat bore down on her. At the last minute Dexter swerved sharply, cut his motor and rocked violently in his wake. Just before broadsiding a branch protruding from the shallow water, he leapt out of his boat and wrestled it to shore.

"Don't this beat all?" he said, grinning through yellowed teeth. "Couldn't do like you was told and stay away from here, could you? Ain't that just like a woman?"

"Where's Jeff?" She stood up, clenching her fists. All she could see at the bottom of Dexter's boat was a bundle of rags.

He spat into the lake. "How much you wanna know?"

With his single eye fixed on the front of her wet dress, plastering to her chest, he took a step toward her. With his attack yesterday still fresh in her mind, she turned and ran. Another idea took shape in her mind. Keeping to the eastern shore, in case a boat passed by in the channel and spotted her need for help, she scrambled over loose rocks and ignored the stabs of pain they produced in her bare feet. Dexter was at her heels. She could smell his foul breath. He'd been drinking, and that would give her the edge she required.

Not daring to look behind her, she muttered a silent prayer for the hours she'd spent running, conditioning her for this moment. Up ahead was the end of the island. Dexter's scraping sounds fell farther behind.

"You cain't get away from me."

At the northern tip of the island, she risked a glance over her shoulder. Dexter was scrabbling up the humpy spine of the island, apparently thinking he could intercept her on the western shore. She waited until he rolled over the top, then she sprinted back the way she'd come.

Back to the southern end of the island where Dexter's boat waited with a bundle of rags in its bottom. Dexter yelped with surprise behind her as she splashed into the water, dragging the boat with her, shoving it out into the water and hauling herself inside. The boat rocked as she lunged toward the motor at the stern.

How did the thing turn on? She contemplated it for an instant before spying the keyhole. Where was the key?

Panic welled inside, and she looked frantically around herself for some means to start the boat. Dexter leaped into the water, plunging closer. She

grabbed an oar and dipped it into slippery muck, bumping it against a floating branch. She pushed hard, and this time the boat moved a few inches. Its
hull scraped against branches under water, and then caught. Dexter reached
with one hand for the edge of the boat. She lifted the oar from the water and
slammed it down on his hand.

"Why, you bitch!" He wouldn't let go.

She banged again.

Muffled murmuring came from under the rags, pulling her attention away
from Dexter. In that instant, he threw himself over the side of the boat and
wrestled the oar away from her. Then he pounced on the wad of rags and
plucked Jeff out from underneath. He tossed Jeff, bound and gagged, into
the lake.

Janie plunged after her son into the waist-deep murk. Before he could
sink into the clutches of the bush under water, she lifted him out. Jeff trembled against her.

She carried him to the island's shore and started to work at his bindings.
She'd loosened them when Dexter sprang on her once again. He wrested Jeff
from Janie's grip.

"Put him down!" Janie screamed. She would gladly kill this man.

He paid no attention to her as he dragged Jeff over the hump of the island.

"Leave him alone! It's me you want, not him."

At least that made him stop. He dropped Jeff like a sack of potatoes. Jeff
cried out, and Dexter turned and looked Janie up and down.

"You're just like Taffy," he said, his lips curling into a sneer.

But I haven't given up yet, like she did.

Janie saw her son slither away behind this madman. Still tied, he scooted
for the hole in the side of this rocky hump. The hole that led to the cavern
Jeff had shown her.

Dexter sauntered down the slope to her. Slid his fingers across the stubbles of his chin. Adjusted the eye patch a little lower over his cheek. "So you
come 'round, huh?"

His body odor invaded her space first, and she cringed backwards.
"Haven't you figured out yet who I am?" she said through gritted teeth.

"Tell me, darlin'." He reached for her wrist and pulled her closer to him.
His single eye focused on her wet bodice.

"You raped my mother." She whispered so Jeff couldn't hear. "You made her pregnant, and I'm that child."

With his other hand he touched her, sending a chill through her.

She tried again. "You filthy bastard. How can you do this to..." She struggled for the word. "To your own *daughter*?"

His hand drew back, and he frowned at her. "Is that who you think you are? Well, I ain't got no daughter." He thought some more, and then understanding spread across his face. "I reckon I know what you're after. It's the still, ain't it? But you ain't my blood, and you ain't got no claim on me."

"Claim?" She sputtered. "What about my mother? What you did to her?"

He snorted and tightened his grip on her wrist. "I don't know where you come from, girl."

"My mother! Fern! You raped her!"

"I didn't do nothing, and Fern warn't your ma, neither. She warn't anybody's ma. She was sealed up tighter'n a drum. Didn't have all the parts she needed to be a woman. Even I couldn't break through. I was gonna fix her up real good with my knife — save herself a trip to the doctor — she'd'a thanked me for a'makin' her into a woman — when along come Seymour."

Janie shook. "*Was gonna*," he'd said. He'd come at Fern with a knife, but Seymour had saved her. Had saved her from the horror of Dexter's knife.

Janie's teeth clattered. If what Dexter had said was true, then whose child was she?

He yanked her against his chest. "How many babies you want to make, darlin'? I ain't never made none yet, none that anyone's ever been able to prove, that is."

Janie felt dizzy with fear and loathing. "You and Annalee had a baby."

"It warn't mine, neither. She tried to pawn if off on me after she got herself knocked up, but no way. Not after she went gallivantin' off to the city the way she done. Tobias's little brother. That's who done it. Not me."

"Grandpa's...brother?"

"You don't listen too good, do you girl? He ain't your grandpa if Fern warn't your mama."

"That's not true!"

"He give to *you* what should ought've been mine by rights. Old Tobias was partners with my daddy, and he should've gone to the penitentiary too, but no, he tricked my daddy. Made him go, instead, then stole the whole thing all for hisself. That still is mine. He had no right to give it to *you*. You ain't even his kin. He cain't do that. I reckon I learned him good."

Alarm pumped through her, and she squirmed against him. "What have you done to Grandpa?"

"Now I'm gonna learn you, too."

In a flash, Janie lifted one leg and sent her bare heel crashing down on top of his foot. His grip loosened on her, and she wrenched herself away. She aimed her next kick into his groin, and he howled, doubling over. She wasted no time running to the cave's entrance.

"In here, Mom," Jeff whispered.

Without hesitating even for a second, she plunged through the hole into the darkness of the cavern. Her fingers scraped slime. She breathed in wet, pungent air. Blinded from the light outside, she saw nothing.

"This way, Mom."

"Where?"

"*Here*." His small hand touched hers — he'd slipped out of his loosened bindings — and she clung to his hand. "Come on. We can hide at the back of the cave." He tugged on her until she followed, slipping and sliding.

Suddenly, the light from outside disappeared from behind them. Dexter's shadow blocked the small, round entrance to the cave. "Ha, ha, stupid woman!" he shrieked. "It was my plan all along to get you in there. I reckon there's room enough for two more. Y'all're gonna get along right fine."

Janie felt her head spin from the man's crazy rants.

He went on. "You couldn't resist the bait I set out for you, neither, them pieces of stuffed toy. Ain't it just like a woman to get too curious for her own good?"

In the darkness, Janie felt her heart hammer. She gripped Jeff to her.

"You think old Dexter is stupid, do you? I'll let you out when you're ready to sign over the deed to me."

"Never!" Janie shouted.

"Mo-o-om, shhhh! He'll find us."

Dexter roared with laughter. "Need some time to think it over? Go on, ask the old man. You ain't goin' nowhere till I'm ready to let you out. Ain't no other way out of there." Dexter's shadow moved about the entrance, then total blackness descended.

"What's he doing?" Jeff said, leaning closer to her.

"He must've rolled a boulder in front of the cave's entrance. Don't worry. It means he's leaving."

The sound of Dexter's guffaws sent icicles tickling her spine. He hiccuped, then he fell silent. After a long few minutes, a growling sound broke the silence. "I ain't so dumb as you think, bitch. I'll be back later to see if you're ready to do as I say."

Jeff wailed. "How long is he going to leave us here?"

"Long enough for us to be gone before he returns."

"Mom, I don't think you understand." Jeff's voice wavered.

"Hush, now. I know another way out of here."

She didn't have to see her son to guess that his eyes were as wide as saucers. If they survived this day, he'd never again be able to accuse her of being afraid of anything.

FORTY

*J*anie listened in darkness for the sounds of Dexter's motorboat fading away. It seemed like hours that passed instead of minutes as she tried to appear brave, trapped inside a tomb, facing the dragons of her claustrophobia.

"Jeff, do you still have your pocket flash?"

She heard him digging into his pockets. The switch clicked, and a faint light flicked on. "I guess it needs new batteries, huh, Mom?"

"I guess so. Turn it off for now. We may need to save it for later. Let me just try this rock first and see if I can push it out of the way." She groped in darkness for the cave's small entrance and leaned her shoulder into the boulder Dexter had positioned to block their exit.

It didn't budge.

"Jeff, help me."

They squeezed together in the narrow space and pushed harder this time. The boulder still didn't move.

"What about the other way out, Mom?"

"I was hoping we wouldn't have to use it." The gaping entrance to this cave, which Grandpa had called the jaws of the dragon, would be under water today.

"Want me to try one of those other holes in the ceiling?" He flicked on his flashlight and shone it across the ceiling until he found a narrow crack. "Maybe you could lift me up and I could squeeze through that."

"Maybe. Let's look some more, first."

The light from Jeff's flash didn't reach far enough to see much of the cave in one sweep, so they carefully followed one wall of the cavern. The floor sloped downward, and the underground room narrowed, pulling them deeper into the bowels of the earth.

"Mom, this place smells worse than where he took me last night. To the cave below our house."

"Hmmm. Maybe there's a pot of mash in here, too."

"Dexter cut up Beads."

"I'm sorry, honey."

"Mom, are we going to die?"

"No, honey."

"But Griffin shot Dad. I saw him. And then Dexter grabbed me when I ran away from Oona, and I'll bet he's gone now to get Griffin to shoot us, too."

Janie heard his sobs and found him in the dark. She cuddled him close to her. "I'm sorry you had to see all that, Jeff, but Griffin won't hurt us."

"But he works for Dexter in the cave, Mom. He was there for a while. They argued."

"That's over. Come on, let's keep looking."

"Is that water down there?"

They'd found the other entrance to the cave. They would have to dive into this pool of water, swim underwater through the jaws of the dragon, and surface on the other side, out in the lake somewhere. But could Jeff do it?

"What's that, Mom? It looks like a log." Jeff shone his light on something lying against the opposite wall of the cave.

"What would a log be doing in here, silly? It must be a rock." Her knees started to shake as she approached the object. It wasn't shaped like any rock she'd ever seen.

The first thing Janie saw under the faint light of Jeff's flash was movement, as some insect scuttled away from the rectangular thing. Then she saw the glint of some slimy substance coating the flesh.

She grabbed Jeff and turned him away from the sight of Grandpa. Something clattered to the stone floor, and suffocating blackness descended on them once again.

"Mom! You made me drop my flashlight."

She pulled him away in the darkness, and now she was thankful for the absence of light. Her stomach roiled. In another second, she might've vomited. She only hoped Jeff hadn't seen him.

"That wasn't a rock, was it?" he whispered, as if Grandpa were still capable of hearing.

She opened her mouth to answer, but the words couldn't come. Blindly, she pulled him back the way they'd come, back toward the entrance Dexter had blocked.

"Was that Grandpa?" he said.

She nodded, even though he couldn't see her.

"Please don't cry, Mom."

The sudden maturity in his voice made her stop. Remembering her need for strength, she sniffed and wiped her eyes with the back side of her hand. "I'm okay, Jeff. For almost a year we've thought Grandpa was...gone. Now this doesn't change anything, does it?"

"Look, Mom," Jeff said in his soothing, newly adult voice, "we've got to get out of here. I'm going to try that crack in the ceiling."

She nodded. He was right. They had to try something. Better to try the crack than that pool of water back there by Grandpa's body.

"I think it was over here, Mom." He pulled on her hand. "Look, you can see light coming in through the crack."

She bent down for Jeff to climb onto her back. Staggering under his weight, she tried to stand up the rest of the way. The ceiling was low enough that Jeff could reach it. He must've grabbed hold of the crevice above his head, for suddenly he pulled himself up onto her shoulders. She reached frantically for his ankles to help steady him, and she felt him teetering.

"No, Mom, you're making me lose my balance. Let go."

It took enormous trust on her part to tear her hands away from Jeff's ankles. Then one wet sneaker disappeared from one of her bruised shoulders, and the other followed. She waited for him to fall on her head, but only pebbles sprayed down on her.

"It's just wide enough," he said. "I've got my head through."

"What do you see?"

"Nothing much. Wait a minute." Jeff's sneakers thrashed overhead. "I'm almost there — " He stopped and screamed. Janie's heart skipped a beat.

"Jeff, what happened? Answer me!"

A full minute of silence followed his scream, while she imagined the worst. Silence frightened her the most. She almost felt relief when he broke into wild bursts of sobs.

"Listen to me." Janie must remain calm. "Tell me what happened."

Gradually Jeff's screams subsided to moans, and he spoke amidst sniffles. "I'm stuck. Some big rock fell on my arm. Owieeeee, Mom, it hurts."

"All right, Jeff. I'm here, and everything will be okay."

"But Mom, it's bleeding bad, and you're down there and I'm up here."

"Can you push the rock away?"

"It's too big."

"Try, Jeff, you must try."

He grunted several times then began to wail again. "I moved it, but it rolled back on my arm. Ow-w-w-w-w!"

"Jeff, can you pull your legs up to relieve some of the pressure on your arm?"

A few more pebbles rattled down on her head, and she heard Jeff's sneakers slide and scrape, pushing against the crack. His hard work was broken periodically by moans, and finally a wild scream of pain followed.

"I can't."

"Okay, honey. Sit tight and wait for me. I'll be right there."

The jaws of the dragon were her only hope now. She'd make sure to give Grandpa's corpse a wide berth. It was slow going in darkness, holding her arms out in front of her, probing the space in front of her with a toe before shifting her weight from one foot to the next. It couldn't be more than a hundred feet, but it felt like a million miles. She could hear the echoes of Jeff's sobs around her.

Finally, her probing foot sank into water. She threw herself headlong into the water, and Elizabeth's skirts billowed up around her again. She thrust her arms in front to cushion any blow from the opposite wall, curving down into the pool.

When she reached that wall, she grabbed it and clung. Her eyes were wide open, but she saw nothing, as if she were swimming with her eyes shut. She sucked in a big gulp of musty air, then pulled herself under, groping downward along the cave's curving wall. It startled her to feel so warm, as if the water were a blanket coating her, protecting her from the drafty dampness of the cave. Down, down... She pulled herself downward through the silky blackness. Her nostrils burned, and her lungs felt as if they would explode at any moment. But she pushed herself a little farther, groping along the rocky wall, searching for the curve in it that would indicate the roof of the jaw-like opening to this cave.

It wasn't there.

She shot upward and gulped in a breath of musty air. Clinging to the slimy wall, she waited for her panting to subside. The puffing skirts of Elizabeth's dress restricted her swimming, and she considered removing it.

But that would take too much time. She dove down again, quicker now. She pulled herself along with renewed strength, hearing nothing in her head besides Jeff's moans. An undercurrent of water rushed against her, trying to push her back into the cave. She angled her foot down to press onward, and it touched something that felt like plastic. But not plastic.

Vinyl!

Something soft squished under the familiar feel of vinyl. It was her raincoat, she realized, and Taffy was still in it.

She opened her mouth to scream. Took in water. Choking. She shot upward and broke into the musty air of the cave once again. Where she coughed and gagged and sputtered to clear her lungs.

"Mom?" Jeff cried.

Her lungs were clear enough. She inhaled deeply and pulled herself under yet again. Back to where she'd touched vinyl and the soft *thing* inside it.

She shot forward to where she'd felt the undercurrent trying to push her back into the cave. This time she scraped rock. Rock against her foot. Rock *behind* her foot. She'd made it through the jaws of the dragon, but now she didn't have enough air left to make it to the surface.

Got to go back...breathe again...

The undercurrent rippled against her, and she hesitated, remembering Taffy back there. She pressed on, kicking her feet, pushing off against the rock wall of the cave. It was too late to go back.

Her skin tingled. Even the ends of her hair, streaming behind her, tingled. Yellow dots of light danced around her head. The inky water that she slipped through took on a tint of sepia.

No! She wasn't going to pass out.

Suddenly, before her, she saw Grandpa rocking in his porch chair, puffing on his pipe. She heard his throaty chuckle and his soft, low voice calling to her, telling her stories about dragons. Never any stories about the family. He'd been as isolated from them as Janie had been.

No. She shot past her vision. The burning spread from her lungs to the tips of her toes.

When she broke the surface of the lake, she gasped more from surprise than a lack of oxygen. A wave immediately splashed over her, choking her, in this welcome daylight. Gulping air, she cried and struggled to tread water while she got her bearings. The island lay dead ahead.

"Jeff!" she called out, waving one arm. "I made it!"

An engine roared behind her.

"Mom! Look out!"

Circling in the water, she saw the aluminum dinghy bearing down on her. It moved so fast that its prow tilted up from the water's surface. All she could see protruding from the top of the boat was a red baseball cap.

Jesus God.

Fueled by a burst of adrenaline, she pumped her already over-exerted arms through water, crashing blindly toward the island's shore. She'd seen the way Dexter liked to push his boat, as if on a collision course, then veer away from shore at the last possible moment. If only she could swim fast enough, she could reach that pocket of shallows surrounding the island. The shallows, with its deadly underwater debris.

"Hurry, Mom!"

Faster, faster, she swam. Her arms raced through the water. Her legs thrashed against the puffy skirt. The boat's engine roared in her head.

Frothy spume splashed over her. She could smell his breath bearing down on her. Something wrapped itself around her ankles. Too late! She kicked harder, disentangling herself from the underwater vine of kudzu. The boat was almost upon her.

At the last moment, she thrust with her legs to lift herself partially from the water and crash to one side, plunging suddenly out of the path of the oncoming boat.

"Ha, *ha!*" She could hear the wicked sound of Dexter's laugh. "I got you now!"

The whining engine dropped to a growl, and the boat crashed down across its own wake as Dexter changed his direction to follow Janie.

He was gaining on her. Even if she beat him to shore, he'd overtake her there. It was hopeless. She might as well give up. Like Taffy.

Her chest ached and her arms trembled. The water called to her.

"Mom!" Jeff sobbed.

She couldn't give up.

She risked a glance over her shoulder. Her side-swimmming maneuvers had gained her a little distance from Dexter. She turned carefully into the flooded field of kudzu. Vines brushed against her. One wrong move and they'd snare her.

She looked again. Dexter steered his boat through the flooded kudzu and steadily closed the gap between them.

The boat sputtered and coughed and died.

Dexter leaned over the edge of his boat and peered down at the dead engine dipping into the water. A stream of obscenities flowed from his mouth to describe everyone's mother, including the origins of kudzu. Then he swept his cap from his head and hurled it at his feet. The eye patch slipped with his motion and revealed the shriveled socket, which was all that remained from Seymour's defense of Fern.

Before Janie could blink, Dexter had thrown himself into the water. He clung to the engine and started pulling vines from around it. As he worked, one of the vines looped around his chest. Then another vine wound itself around his arm.

His arms and legs flailed, and he went under. One hand waved frantically above the surface, then his head emerged. His single good eye opened wide with terror, along with his mouth. He coughed and choked. "Help!" he sputtered, then disappeared again.

Janie moved toward the ring of turbulence encircling the spot where Dexter had been a moment ago.

"No, Mom, don't!"

She hesitated at the sound of her son's cry, then continued. But before she could reach Dexter, a kudzu vine floated freely on top. The thrashing grew still.

EPILOGUE

*I*t was overcast the day they formed a ring of six spectators on the promontory. First to be unearthed was the clump of forget-me-nots. They sat in one of Rose's buckets, off to the side. Resting against the bucket was the stone marker with its message of sapphire love.

Jeff's eyes gleamed with interest as he watched the gravediggers haul the last bit of soil from the lid of the pine coffin. He shouldn't be here, Janie thought. She swayed a bit, and Price tightened his arm around her shoulder.

Janie was here today with her family and a privately hired crew to see if the baby Lee had died with her mother in that tragic fall thirty years ago.

"You're doing the right thing, child," said Oona, slapping her on the back. "You got to take matters into your own hands."

The tops of the gravediggers' heads were visible as they stood in the hole and worked their roping around the coffin.

Janie wished she could feel so certain. In one hand she clutched the sapphire necklace. Annalee's necklace. Fern had received it, Janie guessed, as payment for hiding Annalee's baby from Dexter's wrath. There was always the chance, though, that Fern had stolen the necklace and Janie was some other orphan. There was always the chance that Janie was violating the sanctity of this forlorn cliff, overlooking Grandpa's flooded river.

She would always think of him as Grandpa, even though he was really her uncle. He must've known.

Now she had no choice. *She* had to know. About Lee. This violation would confirm or deny her suspicions once and for all.

Seymour, his moist eyes on the necklace dangling from Janie's fingers, cleared his throat and spoke up. "I recollect when Dexter give that there necklace to my sister for a wedding present." He shook his head slowly. "We none of us ever thought back then that he'd've turned into such a bastard."

"Daddy! You watch your tongue." Oona bit off her words. "He may've fooled you, but he was still my brother."

"*Half*-brother, Mama." Color flushed Seymour's cheeks, and he fiddled with his thumbs, apparently lost without a radio to tune or a jug to hold. "Maybe he fooled all of us." Seymour nodded at the hole in the ground. The gravediggers stood on the rim and readied their ropes. "Annalee would'na gone nowhere without that baby, so when Dexter said it was in there with her, and he nailed the coffin shut, no one had a reason to believe it warn't."

"Dexter never let no one get a look at 'em." Oona nodded and explained to Janie. "Said it was too painful to look at his little family in death. But now you got to know the truth, child. Don't we all?"

Seymour grunted. "This here ain't gonna be none too pretty for no woman's eyes. Whyn't y'all go on home, an — "

"And let you out of my sight?" Oona said. "Never again!"

"Ain't it enough that your revenuer hauled off every last bit of Tobias's still?" Seymour asked. "Ain't it enough that me an' Bonnibelle found ourselves honest jobs at the Lazy Dew?"

Oona folded her arms across her chest and sighed. A smile played about her double chin. The furrows creasing her brow smoothed themselves out. "I reckon it's gotta do, Daddy." Then she turned to Janie. "Sometimes you gotta count on someone else."

The pine box creaked against the roping as the hired men lifted it from the hole. Janie leaned closer to Price. He deserved the land. He was Grandpa's only real descendant.

Janie still wasn't so sure about herself. Even so, Grandpa had wanted her to decide what to do with the land as if she *were* his granddaughter. A name on a deed must have been the easier way for him to give her his property while protecting Rose. In death, he hadn't wanted to risk Rose's embarrassment by revealing the family secrets in a contestable will.

Was she doing the right thing by keeping Grandpa's house and taking Price's money for the rest? By turning this cliff into a small, private cemetery and disturbing Annalee's eternal slumber?

The hired gravediggers wrestled the coffin from the hole and heaved it onto level ground next to the pile of freshly dug earth. Oona turned away from the sight and trudged over to Rose. She nodded down at the bucket. "Ain't no more mule killin' weather. I reckon this is as good a time as any to take a start off of that there plant for Taffy's and Uncle Tobias's graves."

Rose smiled gently. "I'll help you, dear." She lifted the bucket and took Oona by the arm. The fresh mounds of their graves lay only a few feet away.

If Taffy had actually taken her own life, Janie would never know now. Or if the shadow on the cliff with Taffy — Dexter? — had pushed her. Or if they'd argued, and she slipped... Janie would never know. At least these graves put to rest the terrible tragedy.

But it wasn't over yet. The hired men were busy with the coffin, streaked with earth. They worked at the lid with a crowbar. When it creaked open, they shrank back. Janie's family pressed forward, Jeff at the forefront.

Her son gasped.

Before she could glance away, she glimpsed a pile of blonde hair stuck to the fragments of dried flesh peeling away from bones. The remains lay shriveled within a blue satin gown. The jaw had fallen open, as if grinning up at them. Annalee owned the last laugh. Her arms lay empty.

A shiver of understanding numbed Janie's spine. Her mother, Annalee, had died in order to protect the baby from Dexter and build a new identity for her as Janie Bainbridge.

"Put her back," Janie said to the gravediggers. "Let her rest." Having defined herself, she turned her back on her past. "Let it be," she said, taking Price's arm. "I'm ready to talk about that playhouse."

Final Family Tree

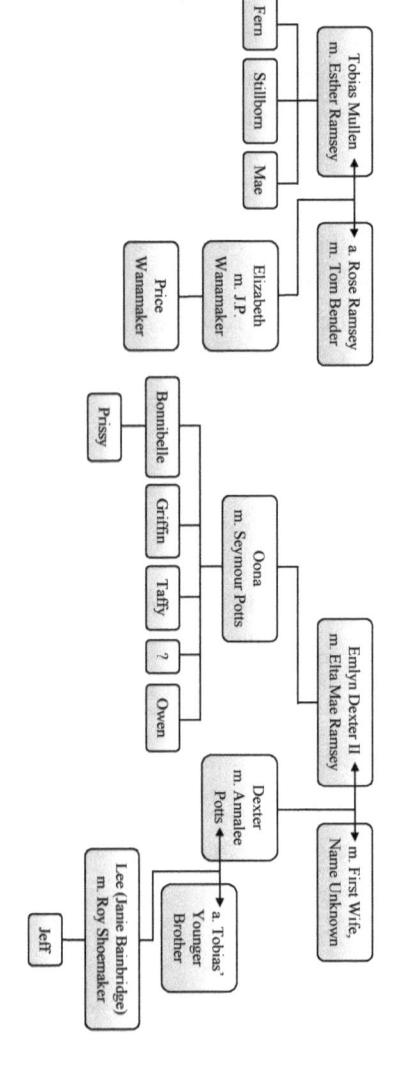

m. = married
a. = affair

Tobias Mullen
m. Esther Ramsey

Fern

Stillborn

Mae

a. Rose Ramsey
m. Tom Bender

Elizabeth
m. J.P.
Wanamaker

Price
Wanamaker

Emlyn Dexter II
m. Elta Mae Ramsey

m. First Wife,
Name Unknown

Oona
m. Seymour Potts

Bonnibelle

Prissy

Griffin

Taffy

?

Owen

Dexter
m. Annalee
Potts

a. Tobias'
Younger
Brother

Lee (Jamie Bainbridge)
m. Roy Shoemaker

Jeff

ABOUT THE AUTHOR

*R*ebecca Williamson writes suspense with romantic elements in exotic settings.

She lives in Colorado and enjoys traveling. Her next novel, *Tenth Mountain*, will come out early next year from D.M. Kreg Publishing.